Praise for
THE UNDETECTABLES SERIES

"A compulsively readable race against the clock to stop a supernatural killer – downright delightful and unapologetically queer."

Polygon.com

"Unputdownable. Grim and caring, twisted and witty, *The Undetectables* is gripping and charming in equal measure. You won't want to leave Wrackton, while also being really glad you don't live there."

Deirdre Sullivan

"If you aren't already deep into spooky season then here is the perfect book to get you in the mood."

Irish Examiner

"A fun and breezy urban fantasy novel that has an interesting take on using magical forensics."

SFBook Reviews

"If you're looking for a mystery that makes you think, mixed with a healthy dose of supernatural, diverse representation and some of the best dialogue I've seen in a long time then [...] *The Undetectables* is the book for you."

Geeking By

"I got so invested in these characters and by the last page I simply did not want to leave them behind. I'll take a hundred more cases that need to be solved by the Wrackton gang, even if I need to commit them myself."

Reads By Ross

Also by Courtney Smyth
and available from Titan Books

The Undetectables

The Undead Complex

The Unfathomable Curse

An UNDETECTABLES Mystery

The UNSOLVABLE CASE

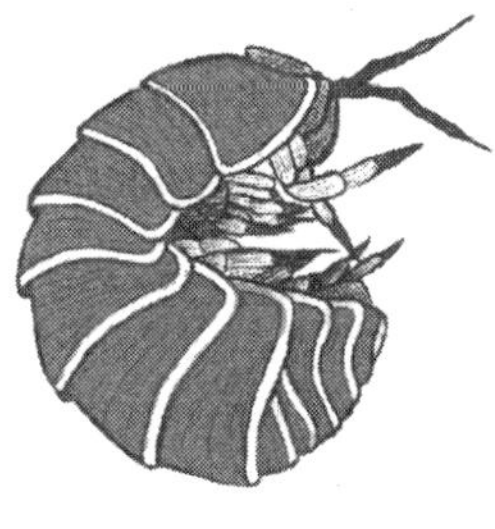

COURTNEY SMYTH

TITAN BOOKS

The Unsolvable Case
Print edition ISBN: 9781835412237
E-book edition ISBN: 9781835412244

Published by Titan Books
A division of Titan Publishing Group Ltd
144 Southwark Street, London SE1 0UP
www.titanbooks.com

First edition: September 2026
10 9 8 7 6 5 4 3 2 1

A CIP catalogue record for this title is available from the British Library.

EU RP (for authorities only)
eucomply OÜ, Pärnu mnt. 139b-14, 11317 Tallinn, Estonia
hello@eucompliancepartner.com, +3375690241

Printed and bound by CPI Group (UK) Ltd, Croydon, CR0 4YY.

For Michael
Right again, I see

ONE

*THEN (Many years ago.
More than a hundred, fewer than eternity)*

Once upon a time, three young witches vowed to cheat death and have since been dying to tell the tale. This is an old story, with many parts, but it is important to know this. Some of those parts have been papered over with half-truths, and some with outright lies. It is a story with no discernible beginning – it perhaps began when they were born, or when they realised the world had not been made for them. Perhaps it began with Rose – known hereafter by a different name – wanting something for herself, outside the safety of her little trio of witches. But it likely began when Ruth – who will also be known otherwise hereafter – found the graves of their mothers-to-be and set the three of them on a forsaken path.

It may also have its roots in love.

Whatever the truth, it lies in the margins where it transforms from 'story' to 'legend', though it usually slips away whenever anyone tries to grasp it. (This is by design.)

But now it is time to know it in its entirety.

'You aren't *ready*,' Ruth said, storming into the room and startling Ana from her reverie.

For hours she had been at her workspace, surrounded by vials, crystals, wax candles, pouches of sulphur and a plate of glass, her elbows holding down stacks of paper covered with her spidery scrawl denoting rounds of experimentation well into the hundreds.

Tonight was the feast of Samhain – a massive celebration of both the dearly departed (largely those who had died at the hands of Apparents who did not trust what they did not understand) and of Morrigan and Hecate, the goddesses honoured by all of Occulture (when they deigned to remember them).

But tonight, Wrackton would celebrate something different. Something new. Ana, Ruth and Rose would make sure of it.

While Ana was terrified of the possibility of failure – one miscalculation, one single variable out of place that would cause them to lose everything – it didn't mean she wasn't *ready*.

'I resent that assertion.'

Ruth's dark eyes glinted, her lashes sweeping the tops of her high cheekbones. The hair she often threatened to cut off was carelessly, effortlessly piled atop her head. Carelessly, effortlessly beautiful as always. Ana had loved her her whole life and still, somehow, found it in herself to love her a little more every day.

'Rose is ready too. Has been for weeks. Edwin is afraid she will labour soon, so she's been preparing the shroud in every spare moment. I believe he thinks it a blanket.' The ghost of a smile played across Ana's lips, but Ruth didn't react and Ana frowned. 'You are usually quick to pass derisive comment on Edwin Dorren.'

Ruth's eyelashes fluttered as she leaned over Ana's shoulder to check her calculations. 'I am somewhat distracted by the necessity of our success. My love,' she added, as though the words were suddenly unfamiliar to her. 'We are low on time, and even lower on time for mirth.'

'We *always* have time.' Ana took Ruth's hand, turning it to kiss her wrist.

'Not as much time as you'd like us to have.'

'Not even five minutes?' She moved her lips up to the inside of her elbow, her fingers gently trailing up the fabric of Ruth's skirt, the edges ragged and blackened. There was no making Ruth behave the way Apparent society thought she should, and she didn't give a damn for Occulture rules. Her appearance was a costume to her; a way to move through the world that meant no one asked questions that should not be asked.

Ruth exhaled.

'I understand,' Ana said, electing to not feel rejected. 'I plan for us to have *endless* time, soon. Hence being hard at work in every spare moment. But you have to let me finish this, or it shall never happen. I have been following Morrigan's instructions to the letter, and I believe I am right.' She tipped the side of a crystal and it lit up, a strange, salt-white glow that illuminated her entire chamber.

The culmination of months and months of endless work. Something that would change Occulture for ever.

Ruth's lips curved into a smile, her eyes dancing, but again she said nothing.

Ana felt something curdle in her stomach – a sense of no return. This was not the Ruth she knew, and she did not know how to get her back.

'And you yourself are prepared?' Ana asked, returning to her calculations. Her hands were shaking, and she could not make them stop.

Ruth paced back and forth instead of answering, humming a song she, Ana and Rose had made up for each other, though Ana would never be sure it was their own invention, as it had appeared in their heads after a lengthy conversation with Morrigan (one of many) and felt, on occasion, too clever to truly be their own.

'Elder and oak, willow and red. Larch the fifth and buried again. Lost in our garden, witches to mourn, forever the ghost of my heart and yours.'

Ana felt her hands steady as Ruth hummed – until, that is, Ruth reached into her skirts to pull out a knife.

Glossy and oily, the knife was made of fragile obsidian.

'Oh.' It did not feel right to have it in her chambers. Something so dark, and so necessary, felt out of place among Ana's dresses and trinkets and papers and wires.

'I did wonder if it was not a little… phallic.' Ruth grinned. 'But I could say such a thing to a goddess like Morrigan. A foolish notion, when we are just people. Us, I mean. Me, you and Rose.'

Again, that smile. Ana's Ruth smiled with abandon; *this* Ruth was all coyness and something buried. Ana felt her hands shaking again.

A bell tolled outside in the village and Ana grasped the crystal. It did not have a name; she did not know how to name such magic.

'Samhain waits for no one, nor does the apocalypse.' Ruth lifted her arms in a gesture that Ana recognised, and she felt something settle within her, even as they shared a look of apprehension.

Certainty.

Ana reached beneath her papers and pulled out a sheet carefully listing out the steps Morrigan had given them that first night.

The night they had found the origins of their world. Of Occulture as they knew it, not far from Wrackton. The night Morrigan had spoken to them, sung to them, listened as Ana's little trio explained the world as it was to them. A world the goddesses of Occulture had not seen in hundreds of years. A world that had changed since the trials that had stopped Morrigan and Hecate from walking among them, the Apparent terror that still threatened Occulture today. The three witches listened to the voice of a goddess trapped within the catacombs beneath the vampire stronghold, and made a vow to each other. A solemn promise they would follow through on, whatever the cost: Morrigan would be free again soon. There would be peace at last.

'Is it all done?' Ana asked, pointing to an item on the list. The apocalypse list, Rose had called it, as if it were ingredients for a pie.

'The glaziers were easy to convince. Your letters helped.' Ruth's hand emerged from her skirts, paper clutched in her fingers. The letter had been folded and refolded, Ana's words of conviction. She was used to convincing those around her of the truth; three days ago, Ruth had realised it might also work on paper. 'I feel sorry for the artist they originally hired, but alas. Needs must. The glass will be made to our specifications. Easy to switch two poor likenesses to three, and they were most amenable to changing the background pattern to your… geometric suggestions. When I spoke to Morrigan this afternoon—'

Ana whirled around to face her. 'You were at Oakpass?'

Ruth paused. 'Paying yet another visit to Sir Kingston, before he left for Mount Hallow.' Again, that twitch of her lips. 'Your letters, again, worked better than I could imagine.'

'The power of persuasion,' Ana said weakly. 'What did Morrigan say?'

There were no words for the burning emotion ripping through her, a maelstrom of anger and betrayal and something akin to jealousy. She had been slavishly writing calculations while Ruth was—

'That as much as I would like to be the one who frees us from the shackles of society, better still if it is you. Rose will meet us in the Observatory; it rests on your shoulders. The glass will prevent anyone remembering the less savoury moves we make tonight. The longer it's in place, the stronger the magic.'

'She is certain it will work?' Ruth laughed then, and Ana blushed. 'It is just that you were not always capable of such magic. That that is why we're doing this, tonight. To return to what Morrigan used to have. The old ways of magic shared between us all.'

'You need not explain, nor have concern. Morrigan has never

been more certain of anything. By tomorrow's light, everything will be different.' Ruth's expression was unknowable again, like a stranger had replaced her, had continued to replace her on and off.

'I want to see her myself,' Ana said, a sense of jealousy overtaking her, a desire to pitch all her work into the fire. She had been here, hunched over her desk and petrified of failure while Ruth had flitted around with ease, everything effortless and simple, drawing obvious favour from a goddess.

'See who?'

'Morrigan. I do not like that you saw her without me.'

Ruth dropped to her knees, taking Ana's hands. 'My love, it was necessary. You were at work here; she needed someone unencumbered.'

'She said we couldn't see her again,' Ana said sullenly, feeling like a child. There would be much time to consult with goddesses when this was done.

'She called to me. She knew you were busy and that I had fulfilled my duties,' Ruth said smoothly.

Ruth always knew the right thing to say.

Ana should've been more afraid, at this point in the story. She should've felt panic that things were moving too fast, that they were not all on the same page, that there were wheels in motion that could not be stopped.

Instead, she was focused on the future. A little bloodshed now, endless lifetimes later. (If a goddess promises you the world, you listen. You have to.)

Ana looked at herself in the glass, her hands on her long hair for what was likely the last time.

'Must we choose them tonight? The... sacrifices.' Her voice dropped to a whisper, afraid of being overheard.

'I have everything in hand. Seven souls is all we need. The memory of Hecate will guide me. As will Morrigan,' Ruth added quickly.

Ana faltered, her hands stilling in her hair.

'I know it is a sacrifice to ask this of you, but Morrigan believes you are the one.'

Ana let her arms drop. 'Hair first, then my hands.'

Ruth smiled, twisting the knife in her fingers. 'You will be the most beautiful harbinger of doom Wrackton has ever seen.'

Little did she know this was the last time Ana would smile back at her.

'You are a terrible liar, Ruth Montrose,' Ana said, and Ruth's eyes softened.

Little did either of them know just how true this would turn out to be.

'Don't call me that anymore,' Ruth said, lifting Ana's chin, pressing her lips to Ana's pulse, teeth grazing the skin, removing all trace of doubt.

'I will call you Elisabella,' Ana whispered.

The Samhain celebrations had started. Music soared into the damp night sky and Ana had her invitation tucked in one bloodstained pocket as she made her way to the epicentre of Wrackton. The newly-proposed council for Occulture would be in attendance tonight; most witches, trolls and faeries were loudly on the side of ushering in a new world (though not the one Ana would bring). If the demons were against it, Ana was afraid to ask. Her witch mother would not speak on something so divisive, and her father would not concern himself with what he called the 'trivialities' of the rest of Occulture. She had passed twenty summers, and so her interests were part and parcel of what he did not concern himself with.

The Observatory was in sight and Ana staggered, both from the loss of blood and the pain of it. It soared above the town, the circular glass windows in the roof among brick and stone, some panes as oily as the blade Elisabella wrought, some clear and shining like a beacon, all asking the people of Wrackton to come in and worship, come in and remember, while simultaneously forgetting who Morrigan and Hecate were. What they could be. How it could all happen again.

There was a reason the vampires were on Mount Hallow, re-enacting the deaths of Morrigan and Hecate while they wore the faces of other witches, and why the demons were holding a vigil at the crypts, and why everyone else was best placed to allow what was to happen, happen.

Someday the villagers would walk into the Observatory and they would think of her.

The music swelled, and so too did Ana's resolve. She took a deep breath and burst in the door of the Observatory. Her hair was shorn, her hands cut and her body draped in a dress coat Rose had stolen from Edwin.

Elder and oak, willow and red, larch the fifth and buried again.

'Child!' Observer Ericsson, who had been admiring the new stained glass to the rear of the Observatory wall, hurried to her as she collapsed in the doorway. Her body shook, unable to take it in. This part was not an act.

'Your hands! Your... Your hair!' Observer Ericsson said, reaching for her, as though they could repair the damage done.

She almost felt bad for tricking them. For abusing their kindness in such a way.

But it was a means to an end. It was what they had planned.

'It's the vampires,' she wept. 'They're planning... They're planning a war. They have terrible weapons – monsters! Oh, they're *monsters*.'

Observer Ericsson took her cut hands and held them up to the light. Gashes deep enough to be believable, but not enough to hurt as adrenaline coursed through her like a hex.

It had hurt Elisabella to hurt her, she knew.

'The re-enactments are real. They took me to Mount Hallow and planned to sacrifice me, and then march on the Redwoods. They thought they could use Samhain as cover. They nearly killed me,' she sobbed.

The invocation of the faerie Redwoods did the trick – instant wariness. Instant fear.

'Are you sure it was the vampires?' Observer Ericsson asked, but their tone suggested they had already decided, already believed what should have been unbelievable.

'They want to break Occulture. They want to tear down the fabric of our society. They want to lead. They want to *rule*.'

'Do you have names?' They glanced back to the main chambers where the townspeople were gathered.

'I tried to escape,' Ana went on. 'I tried! I crouched among the trees, hid myself as best as I could – he said that if I told anyone, he would burn me in the fires of m-mother Morrigan. I got away. It was a kindness, but I can't… I can't pretend I didn't *hear* them.'

'Who?'

'I can't. I can't—'

'Stay here. Stay here, my child. I will… I will be back.'

But before Observer Ericsson could move, Sir Kingston burst in the door, his face contorted with rage.

'SHE WAS MINE TO KILL!' he shouted, summoning the townspeople who put two and two together, distrust blooming as quickly as it was seeded.

Had anyone thought to look closely, they would see Sir Kingston had accessorised with an emerald ring, that he was moving with the slowness of someone with weeks, rather than months, of a pregnancy left. (This is what denial of truth does to time.)

(This is also how you start a war.)

If things had gone to plan, Ana would have forevermore been a star.

But as it stands, she became a goddess. She would be remembered for ever.

That is all that went well. The rest, as they say, is history.

Though history has a habit of repeating itself.

VIVISECTION I
OR: PERIMORTEM A PRIORI

Samhain, eight years ago

Theodore Wyatt's greatest regret in life was dying while wearing a cat costume. You've heard this story before, but it's important to remember it.

After all, it's always been about him. To say otherwise would be a lie.

The night he died, key players moved across Broadwick Mansion like dolls in a miniature, each guided by an unseen hand.

I invite you to look at that miniature now. Broadwick Mansion, three townhouses pressed together, understated opulence oozing unforgivable wealth. Three stories high with a ballroom full of Wrackton's elite and a basement that had yet to become Undetectables HQ – though we know the seeds that were sown this fateful night – and that had yet to be graced by a cat-eared ghost standing next to his cat-eared corpse.

The clues, I will admit, are minimal. (That was by design.)

But they're there, if we walk back through the scene. We'll take thc kcy players:

Theodore Wyatt, our disgruntled victim, busying himself at the buffet table, self-conscious among the ethereal beauty of Occulture.

Vincent Van Doren, our similarly disgruntled (now-deceased, at the hands of the serial killer known to some as the Whistler) Night Mayor of Wrackton, who was as blissfully ignorant as everyone else to the fact he had just a half-dozen years left of his reign.

Grey Quinn, our drunken menace.

Ezra and Imogen Broadwick, our gracious hosts.

And we'll take what we should know by now:

First, that Theodore was killed by a witch. (Mallory Hawthorne was right about that, at least.)

Second, that the killer is someone named here.

Third, that all of our players would say they were not responsible, if they were asked. (The Undetectables *did* ask, many times, over the years.)

But let me ask you in turn: who *can* be responsible, if there's someone else pulling the strings? Who is the real killer in all of this?

Answers, answers. There, if you puzzle over them enough.

Let's pivot the miniature mansion – a diorama preserving a moment more crucial than memory serves – and peer into the ballroom. See our key players mid-action on that night, surrounded by folk in costume, abuzz with joviality. Know the scene is full of food, of drink, of murder.

At first glance, it's nigh impossible to understand how we

end up with a dead man and no explanation. The case that the Undetectables have believed so unsolvable has been waiting for them all along.

Solving it in time just might save them.

(Or not. Time will tell.)

TWO

NOW – Evening of Tuesday, 29th October

Eight years after his first untimely death, and almost two years after his second, Theodore Wyatt was a wanted man.

Five months ago, Theodore revealed he was, in fact, the Wrackton Digger. Although this particular case had been secondary to the Undetectables' eminently more pressing issue of the Wickermere Reaper, he'd given the rest of the team the runaround while he was digging up the corpses of, in no particular order: a centenarian, a terminally ill person, his own body, and the Whistler – the serial killer known as Jacob Gabbott – all while pretending to help solve it. This had gone down about as well as one might expect, which was to say, very badly.

Four months and twenty-nine days ago, the Honourable Dr Night Mayor Priyanka Ray issued an executive order – at the behest of Interim Helm of the Ghoul Council, Nova Khan – that Theodore Wyatt, Samhain ghost at large, must be captured by any means necessary.

Seven years, three hundred and sixty-three days ago,

Theodore died for the first time. (He tried very hard not to contemplate the second death.) This Samhain would mark the eighth anniversary of meeting his (ex-)friends Mallory Hawthorne, Diana Cheung-Merriweather and Cornelia Broadwick, and becoming the Undetectables' first official case. It had been many years and counting since he'd ostensibly begun betraying them, but only five months, eleven hours and fifty-eight minutes since his former friends became aware of it.

It had been *zero* days since Theodore had experienced feelings about not being *asked* his feelings about his present situation. Alas, as he was no longer among friends, the likelihood of his feelings being considered ever again was slim to none.

He was the Notorious Theodore Wyatt now. Aloof and at large.

He raised an invisible finger and tapped at the permanent tear tracks on his cheek, the ones that had appeared after his second death (the one he didn't like to think about). He was, in a way, a clown in clown makeup that accurately conveyed his tumultuous emotional state about 50 per cent of the time. He'd looked into the history of clowns once, and learned that no two clowns had the same makeup. It was an artistry that was not recognised by—

'I know you're there,' someone said dryly, cutting through his internal narration.

Defeated, Theodore allowed himself to materialise fully. A little – annoying, unwanted – voice in his head had recently reminded him that he had avoided testing the true extent of his ghostly powers, and he'd been enjoying dabbling in the art of invisibility ever since. Unable to go to work – on account of the whole Aloof and At Large thing, and also because he had likely been fired in absentia – it was something of a relief to use his scientist's mind on such a pleasing form of unfettered self-experimentation.

Some might say it was a good distraction.

The only downside was the fact he hadn't *quite* been able to prevent himself heating up a room, or from causing static arcs to jump from his semi-corporeal body the second his mind wandered. The resulting damage he caused to various electronic items meant that the living were generally displeased by his presence, even when they couldn't see him.

They just had no idea how lucky they were, that they could use electronics at all. He was of the firm belief that he would be a much calmer, much *better* person overall if he was able to rewatch *Bones* just *once*. The juddering vision alone made it impossible – electromagnetic emissions had a habit of making him feel as though he were stuck in a blender (another, separate impossibility). The hardest part of being a ghost was giving up one's hobbies and interests. And also, bread. Never again would he consume fresh baked bread. A travesty. An intolerable notion!

Of course, Theodore did not *say* any of this as he finished materialising into the room, his faux cat ears a-quiver, his purple cardigan billowing around his body. Instead, he sighed dramatically.

'What announced my presence this time? The comforting sense of warmth? The destruction of your beloved… digital organiser?' He waved a dismissive hand. It annoyed the living to have their emotional support electronics treated as antiquated variants.

'My walls were talking.' Theodore had also not *quite* mastered the art of being quiet, as it were. 'It couldn't be anyone else. At least you're home.'

Theodore looked around himself, still trying to think of this new, unfamiliar place as *home.*

His real home was in the basement of Broadwick Mansion. His real home was with the Undetectables, who didn't want anything to do with him. His real home was broken, with his friends – his family – believing the worst of him.

He'd run away from all of it, knowing what they believed was true.

But as with all truths, there was more than meets the eye.

This room – Home 2.0's main set piece – was a sitting room. More of a salon, really. Damask wallpaper and elegant panelling completely at odds with the rest of the ramshackle shithole in which Theodore was forced to dwell. A gothic nightmare where the resident ghost actually made it feel *less* haunted.

Diana would've loved constructing a diorama of this building, poetically weathered as it was. Mallory would've enjoyed sitting by the big open fireplace. Cornelia... Theodore wasn't sure it would affect Cornelia, such was the burden of being a Broadwick.

'Cat ears got your tongue all of a sudden?'

Theodore snapped back to attention, ignoring the part of him that was desperate to get going. (He was always desperate to get going these days, filled with a sense of urgency that was not his but could not be ignored.)

He was in the room. He was present in the room. There was a fire in the hearth, two burgundy wing-backs pulled up beside it. One had a little iron-filing blanket tossed artfully over its arm so Theodore could luxuriate in the heat of the fire, offsetting the coldness of the presence of humans. Or human, in this case.

(It made him wonder who was haunting who, if the living left him cold.)

The fire made up for a distinct lack of other entertainment in the room.

Well, that wasn't fair. There was an Edwardian bookcase stuffed full of readable volumes. He enjoyed books more than the average ghost – he wasn't sure there *was* an average ghost, but if he took himself as the average and projected it onto a limited population of—

'And here's me thinking you were never going to shut up.'

'I wouldn't *have* to talk to myself if *you* would talk back to me even a fraction of the time,' Theodore said haughtily, instead of anything else he'd been thinking about.

It was better that way. Never let them know your next move.

'That… is a less than ideal way to speak to the person who has come to your rescue. More than once, I should remind you.'

It was true. It was also unfortunate, and Theodore didn't like to dwell on it. If he dwelled, he'd have to talk about it, and Mallory was the only person in the world who might listen to this particular predicament and not judge.

The first time he'd set foot in this place had been without an invitation, over a year prior. He'd been on the run after trying to give the Undetectables safe passage to a party-gone-wrong at Oakpass Manor, and had found himself in desperate need of a place to hide out until the police and the Ghoul Council got bored of looking for the culprit (which usually took as little as forty-eight hours, but he had seen them give up on investigations into spectral activity within five, and so he was probably being overly-generous with his caution).

Theodore had not expected that the owner of this hotel might find him a day later, or that the hotelier in question would be someone who both owed him a favour of monumental proportions, and had grace enough to not report him. A right place, right time meeting that would be serendipitous, if Theodore believed in such things.

'Where have you been, anyway? The hotel has been cold without you.'

'You should start paying your heating bills. To me. Deposit them in any crevice in this room and I will gladly accept your offering,' Theodore said.

'Oh, let's not quarrel. Come here.' There was the sound of a foot tapping against the hearth.

Ugh.

Theodore threw himself into his wing-back, his hand over his face so he could only see the foot, encased in a loafer. He moved his fingers and let his gaze travel up the almost-casual trousers, to the soft cashmere jumper tucked into them, to the (irritatingly) handsome face of his once-nemesis, now… not-quite-nemesis, Grey Quinn.

'Are you listening to me?' Grey demanded.

'No, I am despairing,' Theodore said mournfully.

'I need you to conclude the desperations and *listen.* If you're going to be living here with me, you could at least—'

'I cannot *believe* you'd be this insensitive!' Theodore pressed a hand to his chest.

'Poor wording on my part,' Grey said dryly. 'If you are going to *reside* in this property with me, I require you to be party to my meetings. It saves me having to recount them for you. You know how I hate questions.'

'*You* don't even reside here,' Theodore mumbled.

Grey Quinn officially lived in an apartment he said was, quote, 'deeply of the twenty-first century' and Theodore would explode the electrical components the moment he set foot in the stairwell.

'Be that as it may.' Grey lifted a glass of something dark and amber to his lips and tipped it back.

He had a nice mouth, in Theodore's opinion. His general dislike, nay general *distrust* of Grey could not alter the bare facts.

'The meeting went terribly, thanks for asking.'

'And is that my fault? It's not like I can be at *every* meeting.'

'Why not?'

'Because,' Theodore said.

Many reasons, none of which he could elaborate on, and so he did not.

'Whatever, I don't care,' Grey said. 'The short version is the UML and the Ghoul Council are up to something.'

'Something more than hunting me? I'm a social pariah and the scapegoat of the century, in case you hadn't noticed. Theodore Wyatt, Social Scapegoat Pariah, at your service.' He affected a mocking bow that made his cat ears momentarily slide off his head, only to materialise back into place a second later.

'All the more reason to attend my meetings.' Grey rolled his neck, stretching until there was an audible *pop*. 'That immutable fact aside, it's the moves they've been making lately. Things are changing in Wrackton. Within Occulture. Through the grapevine, I've heard… worrying developments. Not to mention how they're closing in on my empire. First the Broadwicks resign without warning, then investors start dropping like flies.'

Theodore had known this, but not why. No amount of trying to check up on the Undetectables had enlightened him.

'There is *something* going on up there. Nova Khan wasn't next in line to take over the Ghoul Council after Ezra and Imogen, and I had not thought Olivia Reid capable of such staunch support of Khan as a leader, but politics are so mercurial. Any alliance can change, in the right conditions. Dorothy died, did you know?' Grey tipped a decanter and dispensed himself a generous measure.

Theodore did know this, but he wasn't sure if he was meant to. The oldest member of the Ghoul Council, she'd been practically an aunt to Cornelia. Before he'd betrayed his friends, he'd gathered she'd been unmasked as the Wickermere Reaper, though he hadn't much of a sense of how that particular showdown had gone. He wished he'd thought to ask before blowing up both his life and Broadwick Mansion basement. 'Oh nooo, not Dorothy! Poor Dorothy. Who is that, again?'

'Never mind. The point is, not only have the Broadwicks resigned, they are *missing*. Utterly incommunicado. Believe me, I've tried. Second, third phonelines. Emails, letters. Nothing. I never thought I'd say this, but Vincent Van Doren was clearly holding this place together. Two years out and his death has brought nothing but a cascade of trouble my way. And now they're sniffing around Oakpass Manor.'

This got Theodore's attention.

'Sniffing around how?' He sat up, forcing himself to look at Grey. It had been months – over a year, really – but he still found it difficult to overcome the urge to claw his face off while hissing. 'Or is it a secret?'

'I'm always game for secrets,' Annoying Voice said, and Theodore hid a wince with great difficulty. This voice was very much inside Theodore's head, was very, very much inescapable, and the existence of it was not something he could readily, or, indeed, at all, share with anyone who wasn't himself. (And Theodore had already talked to Theodore about it on a number of occasions, noting that Theodore was deeply displeased with the unfolding of events.)

So many secrets, so little time to dissect them.

'Oh, I've been expecting it.' Grey poured another drink – he was doing this more and more often, Theodore had noticed. Some days Grey stayed in his wing-back all night, staring into the fire with increasingly blurry vision until he passed out. 'I thought the Broadwicks would be leading the charge. Not enough noise was made at the time about the discovery of the Larkin family's bodies—'

'Not that I know anything strange about that,' Theodore said.

'—and there is so much in Oakpass that the Ghoul Council should want to get their greedy little hands on, even I'm surprised I got this far. They're trying to claw it back as a "heritage site", which suggests something worthwhile is in there, and I'm going to get to the bottom of it.' He took another generous sip. 'In the nick of time, as they say.'

'Nick of time for what?'

'Nothing for you to worry about. My old friend Hollis Hadley – you know, the writer' – Theodore did know, and knew Grey had had something of an on-again-off-again romance with him over the years – 'convinced me there was something special about Oakpass. Maybe I'll look through his things. Most of his writing was left to me.'

Grey kept talking but was largely not conversing with Theodore, his theories uninteresting and his points unfocused, unknowingly vying for Theodore's attention with a sense of urgency he was unable to shake as he forced himself to sit and listen, his body vibrating with a need to move, move, *move*. A need that was not his own.

'—of course he *did* get things right, like the time Wrackton was dug up because people were looking for the bodies of the Ternion. I've never really believed they're buried in the memorial garden, no matter what my grandmother would tell you. And she'd tell you all sorts of local history, because she was half-sauced. But you'd know all about digging things up, wouldn't you?' Grey bit the rim of his glass with his stupid nice mouth. 'Are you ever going to tell me what you did with those bodies, or shall I just assume the worst?'

'*No more games. Time to go,*' Annoying Voice urged, and Theodore felt an agonising pull towards the door. The need to complete a task at war with his urgent need for a moment's peace. Oh, to be a Samhain ghost who got to sit next to a reasonably-quite-very attractive demon and have him constantly rip the piss out of him! But alas.

Perhaps something on his face indicated his sudden need to leave, because Grey stopped talking – or had finished talking, Theodore wasn't sure. He'd been nodding intermittently in a manner he hoped appeared 'normal'.

'And how are they?'

Theodore flinched. 'How is who? How are who? Who are we talking about here?'

'Don't make me elaborate. I am fond of them, you know. Not… hugely. But a betrayal is a betrayal is a betrayal, and I suspect they're worse off than I am, business-wise.'

He meant the Undetectables. Theodore arranged his face into a frown, masking his relief. 'I find it odd you think I'd know,' he said airily. 'I'm Wrackton's most wanted.'

'And yet you check in on them with alarming frequency.'

It was a statement of knowledge that would've made sweat prickle the back of Theodore's neck had he been capable of such human tells.

'Don't bother, I have my sources.' Grey raised an eyebrow.

'Sources! Don't we all have them! Like rivers! Like our unfortunate origins!'

'You talk to yourself quite a bit,' Grey acquiesced. 'I know you've been skulking around, watching them. You keep talking about "tiny tattoos".' The three of them had returned to Wrackton with matching star tattoos between thumb and forefinger and it had baffled him from the moment he noticed. It made sense for Cornelia to succumb to that kind of impulse, and maybe Diana, but he could not fathom Mallory agreeing to something so permanent without a full-scale consultation.

'It's not doing any harm,' Theodore protested.

'No harm to *them*. It's not helping you. Therefore, it's not helping me.'

He balanced his glass precariously on the arm of his chair. Theodore watched a bead of condensation drip down the side of it. If things had been normal, he'd be in the lab right about now, watching the rest of the Undetectables work through case theories or agonise over client emails.

'*Theodore!*' Annoying Voice whispered, growing in insistence, demanding his attention. A constant companion he hadn't signed up for.

'I have to go,' Theodore said abruptly, stepping through the wall. Leaving Grey and his nice mouth behind, scheming alone.

That made two of them.

(Schemers, not owners of nice mouths. Though Theodore couldn't possibly be impartial on the latter.)

THREE

Also NOW – Evening of Tuesday, 29th October

On the other side of Wrackton, at approximately the same time, the PI agency formerly known as the Undetectables had given up the ghost.

Thanks to the Besiegement Curse that Mallory had been forced to activate to stop the Wickermere Reaper from killing them and releasing a tide of ghosts on the unsuspecting souls of the Lake District, they were set to die in just over forty-eight hours.

Mallory Hawthorne was taking this about as well as one might expect. Curled up on a sofa in her childhood home, a blanket tucked over her lap and her laptop balanced on a cushion on her knees, Mallory typed and typed, thirty-six tabs open that she flicked back and forth between, checking referencing structures, describing methodology and experimentation, and the successes she'd had with both the Sprinter – a terrible nickname for the innovative spell database she and Theodore had invented, modelled on an Apparent forensic fingerprinting database – and the Magic Magical Machine – a terrible nickname for a GC-mass spectrometer she and Theodore had adapted to be able to identify and colour code traces of magic.

Music pounded through the floor above, the shouts and scuffles of people having a very good time utterly at odds with her private moment of feverish determination. She had tasks to do, and not a lot of time to do them.

Task the first was to write a comprehensive guide to, and articles about, the machines she had built and the advances they posed for magical forensics – a field so obscure as to not exist at all outside of her former lab in Broadwick Mansion.

She'd spent years in relentless chronic pain, but she'd been repeatedly reassured it wouldn't *shorten* her life. That she'd have time to be the person she wanted to be, even if it took longer than she'd have liked. Accustomed as she was to that pain, it was a particular kind of ache to think that she was due to have her body possessed by a ghost. That all her attempts at making something of herself would simply vanish. When the clock struck twelve on Samhain, it would be goodbye Mallory (and Diana, and Cornelia and the rest of the Broadwicks), hello… someone else, who looked like her and perhaps talked like her, but would be wearing her face.

Task the first was easy, as she'd pulled most of the files from Broadwick Mansion before she left, and difficult, because it meant thinking about Theodore even more than she had been, which made a pit grow in her stomach that pulsed in time to the music.

He had betrayed her.

Worse than that, he had ended the Undetectables.

Five months ago, when Theodore announced in the

basement that was home to their former headquarters that he was the Wrackton Digger – a nuisance case he had been leading the investigation on, secondary to the Wickermere Reaper case that was set to kill them in two days – their credibility as a PI agency shattered. Nobody wanted to hire them. Any time a new offer of a case pinged into their agency inbox, it was ruefully rescinded hours later, presumably after the client had done a modicum of research. And as awful as that had felt, Mallory couldn't blame anyone. Certainly not more than she blamed herself.

She heard a *whoop!* from upstairs and scrunched her eyes shut, her head spinning from concentrating so hard for so long. She pulled her notebook with her to-do list from between the seat cushions. A short thing:

1. MMM and Sprinter: case studies and guide
2. Tell Cornelia

Even writing their name felt too revealing, so Mallory scribbled over that item until it was illegible.

It wasn't like they hadn't *addressed* what happened when they'd plunged into Lake Wickermere to rescue a Ternion goddess (a sentence Mallory never thought she'd think, let alone say aloud). She'd hallucinated kissing them at the bottom of a boat and her ever-logical mind had come up with a real-world way of testing it: her otherwise-unexpressed preference for one sugar in her tea, over the usual four Cornelia had dumped in there.

She'd been too scared to drink the first cup Cornelia had

made, and so had continued to think for at least a month afterwards that it had all been, for want of a better word, a dream.

Until Diana got sick of being on tea duty.

'Why the *fuck* am I always in charge of making tea? Mallory has an excuse, but *you,* Cornelia, have denounced the Broadwick name. You're a commoner now. A lowly little tea maker. It's your turn,' Diana had said, in response to which Cornelia had summarily hexed her silk pyjamas a slightly different, but displeasing, shade of lavender.

They'd been sitting on the very couch Mallory was on right now. Cornelia beside her, Diana standing with her hands on her hips, her girlfriend, Taylor, resting her chin on Diana's head.

She remembered opening her mouth to say to Cornelia, 'I'd really like a cup'. She remembered how it felt like a confession.

She remembered Cornelia lifting their face, their eyes finding hers.

'One sugar, isn't it?' they'd said.

Mallory's world fell away. Diana and Taylor did not exist. Her parents' living room, with its tasteful beige treatments and porridge-coloured couch, vanished. It was just her and Cornelia in the bottom of a boat, promises spoken, confessions made, Cornelia telling her they were in love with her, too.

It was a month wasted. Years.

Mallory drank the tea, electrified. And when Diana and Taylor went to bed, Cornelia had turned to her. They took her hand. Mallory couldn't make herself say anything. Words were gone. She was just… alive, despite the death sentence.

'Taylor and Diana are clinging to each other like the world

is ending,' Cornelia had said to their clasped hands. 'I couldn't bear to watch you die.'

Mallory had nodded. The words cut through her, clear as anything. Cornelia didn't want it to happen like this. Not on these terms. Not with the few months they had left.

If someone had asked Mallory what kind of love she thought she deserved, she'd have said none. But even still, there was a part of her that *wanted* it anyway. That wanted to love, and be loved. That craved peace in cups of tea and hanging out with her best friend who she was in love with.

And she could have all of that for a few more months, without saying a word. She could have those things without asking for more. Without asking for the impossible, and making it painful. Cornelia had been clear; Mallory would have to accept it.

And so Mallory nodded. They'd sat side by side, wordlessly, for at least an hour. And then Cornelia had made another cup of tea.

And they hadn't mentioned it again.

Another thump from upstairs shook Mallory back into the present. The blinking cursor. She had no idea what she'd say to Cornelia about any of it – that she disagreed? That they'd made a mistake?

She moved her pen to the next line.

Task the third was long-standing, and had, in fact, been on her to-do list since she was fourteen, at the very beginning of the Undetectables. It was as simple as it was hard:

3. Solve Theodore Wyatt's first murder

Last year, during the Dollhouse Murderers case, Katherine the Samhain ghost (who was currently trapped inside the Mayoral Offices with no way out, thanks to the Ghoul Council and the Unified Magical Liaison, both of which seemed to have no idea she was there) had shown them a memory where it appeared that the Broadwicks had killed Theodore, and Mallory had thought they were finally getting somewhere. But when Cornelia had confronted the Broadwicks about it, they had seemed *baffled*. Aside from the word of a Samhain ghost who did not always seem to know what was going on, they had no evidence to support the accusation, and so it was still unsolved, officially. Even though Theodore had betrayed her, she still wanted answers for him.

He'd betrayed all of them, in the end. The revelation he was the Wrackton Digger had ballooned into a sick feeling she carried in the bottom of her stomach.

Since he'd shattered the glass in the Broadwicks' basement and forced them to move out, posters were plastered around Wrackton, urging people not to approach him if they saw him. Someone had dug up a pre-cat ears photo of him and drawn on his various feline adornments, and his face stared down at Mallory whenever she left the house. His messy blonde hair, his warm blue-green eyes, his elfin features. They were referring to him as the Notorious Theodore Wyatt, as though he was some sort of monster. Or a particularly tragic white rapper. Wanted for grave-robbing, possession of Apparents, and in connection with possible murder. The only person that could have helped Mallory complete this item was public enemy number one.

Not that it mattered. Without a lab, they had nowhere to

work. They weren't able to bring big forensic machines to Mallory's house, and asking the Broadwicks to help was so far out of the question, nobody had dared to suggest it. Cornelia maintained they were utterly finished with the Broadwicks as an institution – though Diana had gone to great pains to get them to agree that if the Broadwicks found a way out of the Besiegement Curse, Cornelia would accept it. Imogen and Ezra Broadwick had been Besieged at the same time as the Undetectables (as had Agatha and Ethel Broadwick), which had simply cemented Cornelia's certainty that they wanted nothing to do with the Broadwick name, or the Broadwicks themselves. They had seen an undeniably ugly side to the former leaders of the Ghoul Council during the Wickermere Reaper case. Cornelia maintained their friends were their real family. Mallory had no arguments there.

She hadn't even bothered writing the last item down, which was, simply

4. Find a way to not die

Despite how adamant the Broadwicks had been that they'd find a cure, and despite them ceding control of the Ghoul Council to do so, Mallory was sure such a cure was not forthcoming (particularly as they had been unable to disseminate what that would entail, should such a thing exist) and that they were actually trying to find a successor to the Broadwick fortune, as their entire lineage was about to be wiped out in one fell swoop. With Cornelia utterly disinterested in maintaining a familial relationship after returning to

Wrackton, and Mallory unwilling to overstep that carefully drawn line on their behalf, they'd convinced Diana to put in an exploratory phone call. Imogen and Ezra Broadwick had tersely promised that they were promising nothing but their best – a statement that was best interpreted by the former half, rather than the whole. In a similarly unhelpful vein, the Ghoul Council did nothing but email them once a fortnight to ensure they were continually aware that on the hour of midnight on Samhain, her body would no longer be hers, and to ask about 'symptoms' without providing examples of the sort of thing they were meant to be documenting. Diana and Cornelia had both expressed 'anger', 'dismay' and 'chagrin' once too often, and now all correspondence was directed to Mallory.

Everything, as they say, happened so much.

She slammed her laptop closed and massaged her temples as a particularly loud shout tore through the floor. She should go hang out with them – Cornelia and Felix and Kingston had been having non-stop parties for the last few months, to the point that Mallory was unsure she had seen Cornelia fully sober since the day they'd moved into Mallory's house together. Diana had elected to take the box room, as she was spending most of her time in Taylor's apartment in Oughteron, though she was upstairs now too, having a nice time.

Exactly as Mallory should be. Making memories for the living to carry with them for ever.

She didn't know if the ghost was going to live in her like a skin suit until she died a natural death, if they'd run her into the ground, or if they'd discard her upon realising her body didn't work the way other people's did.

Mallory laughed into her hands. This is what things had come to: worrying that a ghost wouldn't think she was good enough when it literally killed her and wore her like a hat.

An email pinged onto her phone and she hated the little feeling of hope that stirred in her stomach, the anticipation of a case, but it was just Nova Khan, acting head of the Ghoul Council, confirming receipt of Mallory's confirmation that the Undetectables did not know Theodore's current whereabouts, or the whereabouts of any Samhain ghost, in the vicinity of Wrackton. The less they knew, the better.

Most lies were better with a little truth in them. On one hand, Mallory truly did not have any idea where Theodore was – though she constantly imagined he was there, out of the corner of her eye, or flitting past her as she walked. Sometimes she'd wake up in the night, the room warm and filled with a soft crackle, and then her eyes would open fully and there'd be nobody there. On the other, Mallory *did* know the locations of not one, but two other Samhain ghosts.

'MALLORY!' Felix shouted. 'ARE YOU GOING TO STOP BEING BORING NOW PLEASE? UNLESS YOU'RE NOT FEELING WELL, IN WHICH CASE, PLEASE REST!'

Mallory smiled and pulled herself to her feet, checking the time. It was a little before nine p.m.; they'd agreed to cut off the noise before midnight. It gave her a chance to slip out and do what she needed to do.

She pulled on her coat and padded upstairs in search of a hat.

Felix ran towards her as though they hadn't seen her a couple of hours previously. 'You're here! Are you joining us?'

Mallory shook her head as Felix tried to tuck her under their armpit, despite being only a few inches taller than her. They were wearing a denim flared catsuit and a pair of 70s-style boots with cherry-red flames up the sides, and they were very, very drunk. Mallory allowed herself to be squished in a gentle hug for approximately thirty seconds.

'I have to do something,' she said.

Felix planted a kiss on the top of her head. 'Love you lots, wish you'd hang out with us more.'

Mallory's breath caught in her throat. Felix Cole was a faerie and they could not lie. She'd watched them lose a best friend, back at the start of everything, and now she was going to leave them too. Felix had no idea. It had been the longest one-sided goodbye she could imagine having to endure, and she'd hated every second of it. Hated the hole she was going to leave in everyone's lives, even as she actively tried to shrink the hole down to nothing.

'I love you too,' she said instead.

Felix pressed their fingers to her forehead. A solemn faerie custom that she felt down to her bones.

'Where are you off to? Do we have a case?' Through the doorway of Cornelia's bedroom Mallory saw Diana lean on Taylor to pull herself to her feet.

'Watch my hat, you eejit,' Taylor said, as Diana stumbled and pulled Taylor's cat-eared beanie down over her eyes. Taylor adjusted it so it sat neatly over her green hair, and Mallory smiled as her heart sank at the inadvertent reminder of her cat-eared ghost.

Taylor was the only one who knew they were dying, and

she was sworn to secrecy. She was doing an excellent job of pretending, but Mallory could feel waves of sadness coming off her whenever Diana turned away.

Taylor turned the music down as Cornelia and Felix protested. Felix's boyfriend Kingston swayed in the centre of the room with his eyes closed, dancing to music no one else could hear.

He often offered Mallory a bit of whatever he was on (besides blood; Kingston had mastered the vampiric art of micro-dosing blood, even though it was strictly against the Unified Magical Liaison's post-Vampire Wars Do No Harm charter) but she privately suspected his ability to achieve substance-driven peace was a personality-based quality she lacked. As tempting as it had been, many times over the last few months, Mallory had swerved the call of oblivion.

'We haven't had a case in months.' She leaned on the doorframe, feeling awkward in her coat.

'The Undetectables are no more,' Cornelia said solemnly, and then Kingston shoved them and Cornelia burst out laughing, collapsing in a heap with him on the floor.

'I have to go do… the thing I do every week,' Mallory said.

'I'll come too,' Taylor said. 'I won't lie, I am being nosy as fuck here and Diana won't tell me what you do be up to.'

Mallory waved a hand, hoping it seemed airily dismissive and not a rejection of spending time with Taylor. She liked Taylor a lot – liked how good she'd been for Diana – but this was a secret the former Undetectables couldn't share with anyone. They'd agreed Mallory would make the weekly trips alone, and once the group was distracted again, she snuck off.

She took the walk slowly, glad for a break in the near-constant cover of rain. If she had to describe Wrackton in one word, it would be 'wet'. If she had two, she'd add 'neon'.

Mallory unlatched the side gate into Broadwick Mansion, trying to appear casual in the event there were any passers-by who might see her go in. A vaguely familiar car passed and Mallory looked down at her phone until the rear lights disappeared around the corner. She'd quickly learned this was the best time for her weekly visits – not so late as to arouse suspicion, but late enough that the streets were largely empty. Once the coast was clear, she slipped into the back garden.

Theodore had blown the floodlights along with everything else so it was fully dark, Broadwick Mansion itself silent since they'd vacated it. The Broadwicks were still in Wickermere, and while they'd mentioned wanting to throw one last Samhain ball – a final hurrah – Mallory had seen no signs of that going ahead, likely for the same reason she hadn't yet told her parents or any of her friends she was dying: it would make the Besiegement too real.

Bracing, she used her shoulder to push the sundial in the middle of the garden aside, the grass wildly overgrown and resisting her with every step.

One final shove revealed a trapdoor. She pulled it up just enough to crouch, her back screaming in complaint, and descended the stairs.

'Oh, you're back. I thought you'd died already,' Blair the Ternion goddess said.

It was perhaps one of the strangest achievements of her short career as a private investigator that Mallory could say she had the ghost of one of the goddesses of Occulture locked in a bunker in the garden of her best friend's house. Especially as none of the former Undetectables had even realised they'd brought her from Wickermere to Wrackton until Theodore had blown up the lab and Blair was standing before them, confused and missing her heart.

The impact was somewhat undercut by the fact they'd just been cursed by (Mallory was sure) the ghost of the goddess Elisabella, and by the fact it was not strictly legal to harbour a ghost without informing the Ghoul Council. Add in the extra fact they were keeping her in the grounds of Broadwick Mansion without permission of the Broadwicks, and Mallory was breaking a number of rules. Between finding Elisabella (and throwing her back into Bonemarrow Lake) and unearthing (then re-earthing) Blair, they were just missing Hexana wandering around to make it a Ternion trifecta. Though Mallory didn't particularly want that to happen – if she was being honest with herself, she was getting quite sick of Samhain ghosts.

Mallory inhaled for three seconds before speaking. 'Nope, still here. I just wanted to see how you were doing.'

'I would be faring much better had I not been moved from one prison to another,' Blair said, touching the wall of the bunker.

It was deep enough that Mallory could leave several feet between them, iron-lined enough that Blair couldn't leave unless Mallory let her out, and solid enough that it had been around for at least a century, and was still going strong. Mallory had no idea why it existed, other than, perhaps, a relic of an Apparent war, or perhaps pre-electricity food storage. It had been Cornelia's idea to use it for Blair. The last sensible idea they'd voiced, before they'd totally checked out of anything other than partying.

Blair fixed her with a gaze, and Mallory felt herself stiffen with anxiety. The salt in her pocket didn't feel strong enough to stop Blair from hurting her, though it hardly mattered when death was a few dozen hours from welcoming her.

'Do you need anything?' A perfunctory question; Mallory's weekly visits were solely intended to ensure Blair was where they'd left her.

'If you happened to have the sweet release of death on your person, I would gladly accept the offering.'

There was no good answer to that. Cornelia would've said, 'Can you get that in the weekly shop?' Diana would've offered her a little death instead, and Theodore would've... Mallory didn't know what he'd do.

'I'm sorry about all this,' she said instead.

'Your sorry does not offer me the comfort you might imagine,' Blair said. 'Have you news of my sister Katherine?'

Blair had, in a previous life, been known as Rosemary Vane, and Mallory had, at a previous time, made an inordinate effort to locate her grave at the behest of the aforementioned Katherine, who was yet another Samhain ghost Mallory had the misfortune of being acquainted with, who transpired to be Blair's sister.

'No,' Mallory said, for what felt like the hundredth time. 'Sorry.'

Blair crossed the space between them in two rapid steps, her face in Mallory's, static crackling around them both. Mallory wrenched her eyes up from the hole where her heart should be. The skin visible beneath her dress was slashed badly. Mallory did not need her forensics training to know someone had hacked into her while she was still alive.

'I know she's near.'

'How?'

'I sense her,' Blair whispered. 'I know. Something... Something is coming. And you can't stop it.'

Mallory closed her eyes, unable to avoid jumping when she opened them to Blair centimetres closer to her face.

'What's coming?'

'You need to let me out,' Blair said.

'Or what?'

'Or... I will kill you. I will end your pathetic little life.'

Mallory exhaled, deliberating. She looked at the walls of the bunker, at Blair, whose expression was unreadable.

It was likely a trick. Lying, trying anything to get Mallory to let her go.

So instead of digging further, and fighting against all of her instincts, she took to the stairs, glancing back at Blair who stared at her across centuries of death and oblivion. 'Haven't you heard? I'm already dead.'

She shut the gate behind her after waiting for a dog walker to pass by, unsure if they glanced her way and feeling wildly paranoid about it, before heading home. The streets were empty, lit only by neon witchlight lamps high above. Mallory pulled her coat around her, the October chill settling deep into her bones. As she did, she felt a whisper of warmth spread across her limbs.

She whipped around, half-expecting Blair to be behind her with a knife in her hands, but there was nothing. The air crackled next to her ear and she froze, waited thirty seconds, sixty, ninety, until all she could hear was her own heart and her own breath. An unfortunate hazard of spending so much time with mercurial ghosts was imagining they were after her.

The house was empty when Mallory let herself in and she climbed into bed with her coat still on, letting sleep overtake her gratefully.

Her phone rang and she fumbled for it, squinting at the name on the screen, expecting it to be Diana or Cornelia saying they'd forgotten or lost a key, but what she saw there made her sit up, heart pounding.

'Hello?'

'I need you to come to the Observatory. Now,' Detective Inspector 'Sully' O'Sullivan whispered. 'It's happening again.'

PERIMORTEM I

She was climbing out of the hole bad choices had landed her in when she died.

She'd be the first to tell you that she'd been enamoured by the idea of power since the day she was born, but had been gifted a recent change of heart.

Perhaps it was being told her whole life that she was beautiful and exceptional, only to learn that both of those things were gilded cages meant to keep her on a certain path.

Perhaps it was the untimely death of her boyfriend – significant other, really, for he was neither 'boy' nor 'friend', and lacked the selflessness required to be a 'partner', and really the respect for her to be a 'husband' – who had promised her the stars in the sky.

This too was a cage, more ornate than the first. Frying pan, fire.

The external changes to her life upon realising that rich men could offer no lifetime security if they died too soon led to internal changes, and she'd given herself over to a life of politics.

Not because of him – she was sad he was dead, had really loved him (in her own way) but would not give him sole credit for her change of heart – but because, in her grief, she'd made some friends. The three of them had worked together against a shifting tide of uncertainty within Occulture, trying to make Wrackton better. It was exciting. It was daunting.

It was not her problem any longer.

She had felt very good about her choices right up until she found herself in the roof of the Observatory, staring up at the delicate star-painted glass, thinking about reaching for them herself as her throat slowly constricted, her teeth biting down on her tongue.

After that, she thought of nothing ever again.

FOUR

Many years of being told what to do, where to go and how to be had left Theodore trembling on the precipice of *utterly done with everything.* The latest orders from Annoying Voice were means to a great ending (for him, anyway), but it didn't mean he particularly enjoyed taking them.

Especially when the call was coming from inside the house, so to speak. What haunts the haunted.

'I should keep workshopping the haunted house metaphor,' Theodore whispered to himself. 'I both unlive in a haunted house, and have become one.'

It was the closest thing he could imagine to possession without someone taking over his physical form completely. He was effectively a semi-corporeal puppet on strings, and while the terms and conditions were admittedly very good, he was forbidden to tell anyone about the Voice, about what the Voice wanted him to do, or about what the Voice had promised him.

'A ghost who is haunted is no ghost at all!'

'*Focus.*'

This was not, strictly speaking, a command from Annoying Voice, for the owner of the current voice in Theodore's head had two distinct *moods*. While the everyday chatter of Annoying Voice made him fervently wish he had a tail to twitch in annoyance, this variant made him want to cry. It was the memory of a stomach ache, a constant sense of malaise. It was pure terror, and it took him by surprise every time he heard it. There were moments where he could convince himself that Annoying Voice did not have as much power over him as Theodore feared it did, and these moments were infrequently swallowed up by a few guttural syllables echoing around his mind. He was never sure if the Voice could read his thoughts, if it could see through his eyes, or hear what he could hear. It watched him closely, almost always present, making him do things he did not want to do.

He was never safe, not even in his own mind.

'*Now*,' Terror Voice commanded, as if on cue.

This instruction came unbidden from some place on high that Theodore couldn't ignore if his life depended on it. (Or, as the case may be, if someone else's did.)

Theodore crouched down further behind the Ternion memorial monument, deep in the Memorial Garden he had never had much reason to visit. He refused to make himself invisible for as long as he could help it, waiting for Terror Voice to speak again. Sparks fizzed as he rested against the joined marble hands representing the three goddesses of the Ternion – Elisabella, Blair and Hexana.

Directly in front of him was tonight's target: the Observatory. A great rotunda with a half starry, half clear painted domed roof and a wide segment of stained glass nestled in the brick wall that gave him a funny turn whenever he looked at it, the pattern intricate and familiar even from the outside. The gardens – where he was huddled in wait – were to the rear, well-manicured with seasonal plants and a spindly, ancient-looking elder tree. A tool shed that had probably been a cottage at some point or other that Theodore, glumly and belatedly, realised he could've tried to live in instead of Grey's hotel. *Que sera, sera annoying.* (He didn't *hate* living in Grey's hotel, exactly. Grey paid attention to where he went sometimes, and it was nice to be missed. To be remembered. He just wished Grey would ask the right questions, poke at the right things Theodore said, and then he'd have someone to talk to about all of this without breaking any rules or suffering any consequences.)

Terror Voice urged him forwards, and Theodore spent one last second taking in his surroundings. A tiny rebellion that wouldn't go unpunished. What he wouldn't give for a moment's peaceful contemplation. He hadn't known a single one since his first death.

(This had all, in a way, happened before.)

He pulled his cardigan tightly around himself, trying not to think too hard about what was being asked of him. It was a point of particular chagrin that the wool refused to stretch with the action. The cardigan wasn't dead, after all.

Although, now he thought about it, when he'd had the Apparent gravediggers dig up his corpse that time, he'd thought he wouldn't look at his remains, but he did. The image – ha! – haunted him ever since. In an admittedly silly, romantic way, he'd expected his cardigan would be wrapped around his bones, encasing his skeleton in a cozy embrace, but decay had claimed the iconic purple as quickly as it had ravaged his body, and it saddened him. He'd been so naive when he'd first died. Completely unaware of what the core of Occulture was about. How rotten the whole thing was.

But that was then. Before all of this. Before he'd died a second time, and had been confronted with his true purpose.

'Now, Theodore.'

Constant. Neverending. Instructions galore. Theodore wished he slept, so he'd have a few hours' respite from Terror/Annoying Voice's incessant attempts to control his every waking thought, despite having hundreds of them a second.

If he had to concede to there being any benefit in being dead, it was the fact he never tired of his own stream of consciousness. It was, of course, no use when he couldn't web search anything, or make spreadsheets, which somewhat devalued it as a benefit, but he took his wins where he could get them.

And, as established, Theodore Wyatt was not known for winning.

'NOW!'

This command pushed him forwards. He whimpered, checked for witnesses, and entered the Observatory unseen.

A second almost-benefit of being a ghost was his ability to pass through doors and walls and ceilings and whatever else have you, provided they had not been reinforced with anti-ghost measures (really anti-creature-from-the-Mayoral-Offices measures that didn't *fully* work on him, but he'd had good reason not to expressly point that out to either Night Mayor), which the Observatory did not have. (Theodore suspected this was in an effort to encourage ghost visits at séances, but also probably due to Council laziness, or arguments over funding, or both.)

He'd been here once before, when he'd first died. He had been struggling to contend with the fact he was not going back to his only-okay apartment in Oughteron, that he was never going to buy another shirt, that he would never watch another film, that he was never going to leave Wrackton, and he had come in the middle of the night to speak to Observer Johnson.

Or rather, he had come in the middle of the night out of desperation, and Observer Johnson had been the only one available to talk.

Observer Johnson didn't say much, apart from some niceties about the Ternion wanting this for him – ha! – and that, whether he liked it or not, as a Samhain ghost he was now Occult. In level tones he told Theodore he had an opportunity to embrace the Ternion, and the goddesses Morrigan and Hecate, as part of exploring the history of his new people.

What that history was, Observer Johnson seemed troublingly uncertain. While Theodore had known the basic mechanics of the formation of Samhain ghosts – died on Samhain, soul becomes detached from body, and, theoretically, some kind of spark as simple as static shock and so on and so forth – if a man in charge of disseminating the histories of Occulture could not tell Theodore where Samhain ghosts originated, could not give him even a *hint* of his beginnings, then Theodore was evidently in more trouble than he could possibly fathom.

It had not been easy, waking up beside his body, facing three ostensibly confident witches who'd transpired to be young teenagers scared out of their wits. And it had not become any easier after spending the first night in the basement of Broadwick Mansion with his own thoughts, and discovering that he was not, in fact, 'alone' in the strictest sense of the word.

A voice appeared in his head, asking him for help. A voice that baffled him, as it belonged to someone he had met. A soon-familiar voice that whispered instructions to him while Wrackton slept, who guided him in his navigation of the world, reaching through the thin veil that separated him from humanity and speaking to him inside his brain.

(A voice whose owner he could barely remember. Any direct thoughts he had of its owner were fuzzy and grainy, like an old photograph. A shape, more than a memory. A feeling, more than a certainty. A name, unspoken. A secret, unshared.)

It was a ghostly cliché, to have unfinished business. The familiar voice would not tell him why, or even particularly *what*, so he'd tried his best to find answers. To solve a mystery he couldn't mention or face or speak about directly that probably held clues to his death, but that he couldn't sift through no matter how hard he tried. He and the familiar voice had made it work. He'd balanced being a ghost and being a person with reasonable success.

And then he'd died again.

That familiar, seductive (in the persuasive sense) voice was gone, replaced with the never-ending carousel of Annoying-to-Terror-and-back-again Voices. A head haunting he had not asked for, but one that promised him something. Though it was not a gift; Theodore had to earn it.

'*Remember what's at stake here*,' Terror Voice boomed as

Theodore weaved through red-curtained hallways, cat ears quivering with unexpressed fear.

The Observatory was empty, and so Theodore stole up to the room inside the domed roof – no need for the ladder, no need for a door. He lay the pieces out as instructed, trying to remind himself that this was all a game. That pawns were always sacrificed to make bigger moves. That he was, ultimately, doing the right thing. It may not be the best thing, or the most-advised thing, but he was in it now. Only way out was through.

He just wished it didn't involve traps. Or anything so permanent as murder.

'Easiest way to make the medicine go down is to take it in the first place,' Theodore muttered as he worked, wishing someone living was around to appreciate his wisdom.

'Not like that. Do it how we discussed.'

Annoying Voice was firmly back in place. Theodore shook his cat ears violently, wishing the voice would *SHUT UP* every now and then. Goddess it was so *annoying* to have a constant little detractor muttering in his head at all times.

'I'm doing my best,' Theodore said archly. 'Surely we can admit that I am, in fact, doing my best? Or is that too hard for us? Do we need to throw a party? Should we invite the Ternion, and then we can maybe tell the truth to ourselves?'

Annoying Voice didn't reply, and Theodore felt a small frisson of satisfaction.

That, or he'd just accidentally brushed off the Observatory roof.

He waited until he felt the threads of Annoying/Terror Voice's attention fading, suggesting it was occupied elsewhere, and tacked on his own little flourish to proceedings. Another rebellion that wouldn't go unpunished, though it was not as if the Voice would *know.* Not unless he accidentally told it. Or it read his mind, which Theodore was 91.6% certain it couldn't, but there was a scary margin for error.

Satisfied he'd laid out all the pieces as planned, Theodore clambered back down and out, trying to ensure he remained hidden as he travelled across Wrackton. He could hide in plain sight for as long as he actively remembered that's what he was meant to be doing. He had, on many an occasion, become distracted and given away his position. Thankfully, the living were both often stupid and subject to disbelief. He'd lived among the inhabitants of Wrackton for *years* and still their first port of call, even with full knowledge of the Notorious Theodore Wyatt – they'd used a *terrible* augmented photo of him on the posters and made him look very sad and pathetic – was to assume there was nothing there.

Everyone except Mallory.

He'd been sure she had seen him earlier outside Broadwick Mansion. The way she'd stood stock still while he cursed and retreated, trying to keep himself hidden. It had been easier in the summer, when she was less likely to notice the warmth he brought with him.

He'd never tell him this, but Grey was right; it didn't help to follow Mallory, or Diana or Cornelia, but he couldn't stop himself. He'd just wanted to see what Mallory was up to. Figure out if she was still mad at him. Samhain was fast approaching—

'*Time to get moving.*'

Theodore swore under his breath – a long, inventive chain

of insults he directed very hard in the direction of Annoying Voice – and headed back to base.

'*The lightbulb,*' Annoying Voice reminded him as he walked, feet dragging in the general direction of Grey's hotel.

Theodore gritted his teeth and pulled anxiously at his cat ears. He didn't want to go there.

'*You chickened out earlier,*' Annoying Voice pointed out. '*Wasted time looking at Mallory, who doesn't want to see you. She's the enemy now. They all are. Get the lightbulb. You know you want to.*'

The lightbulb. The object he'd been holding when he died – the physical cause of his death. A clue trapped in the oldest filing cabinet the Undetectables had in the basement of Broadwick Mansion. Theodore's old lab. Theodore's home.

'*I'm starting to doubt you're as up for this as you said,*' Annoying Voice taunted, and Theodore told it in no uncertain terms to fuck off.

The idea was in his head though, like a terrible metaphor. The lightbulb could solve his murder, which could help him to explain why he's Like This, which in turn could fix everything. Maybe not excuse his actions, but surely if he could understand *why*, he would be able to explain *what* had driven him to all of this. He could solve the ultimate unsolvable mystery: himself.

But it was impossible, on his own. (Voice aside.)

'I never blamed Mallory, you know,' Theodore said to Annoying Voice. 'She tried, but she didn't have the right tools. The right context. I can't… I can't quite remember what came before. Every time I try to think about what led to me dying, I feel strange. Panicked. I'm always panicked, that's nothing new, the world is so very frightening and I'm but a little guy and so forth. But with this… every time Mallory got close, I'd scare her off. I don't know why.'

'*You do. You know the answer.*'

There was a strange push on his mind and an image unfolded before his eyes, unbidden, of the owner of the familiar voice, from his previous death. A person he could not, for reasons of magical tomfoolery, name, and only refer to (mentally or otherwise) as *Her.*

He shuddered at the fuzzy, unfocused sight of *Her*, feeling his whole body flicker as electricity pulsed through him, hoping once again that the Voice could not read his mind. 'Fine! I'll get the lightbulb. Just not now.'

He had no intention of ever doing it, and he suspected Annoying Voice knew it. The idea of accepting help from the Voice – beyond what the Voice had offered him, the bargain he'd struck – rang alarm bells even he couldn't ignore.

There were two paths available to him, and he had accepted the more dangerous one. Trying to exonerate himself hadn't worked in the past; he'd be able to do it in future, when this was all over. He was about to be part of something huge. Something that would change the Occult world.

He hated himself for choosing the coward's way out.

A painful throb passed through his head – more the concept of pain, than an actual pain response – and Theodore pawed at his face.

He opened the door of the bunker and let himself in, taking care to leave the door ajar behind him.

He'd find a way through all of this, one way or another.

FIVE

Wednesday, 30th October

A single text was all it took for Diana and Cornelia to leave the Larix, where they had taken their revelries, and swing by Mallory's house in a taxi to pick her up. She was still fully dressed and had just managed to drag a brush through her hair before clambering into the back and directing the driver to the Observatory.

'What did Sully say?' Cornelia kept asking, leaning gently against Mallory while she passed the kit bag to Diana and tried to settle in.

Mallory shook her head, a wordless gesture that meant 'Not in front of the driver' – a witch, who kept glancing suspiciously at them in the rearview mirror.

'But what did she *say*? Diana, do you know?' Cornelia asked again. Diana attempted to kick them, missing and hitting the footwell.

'The Observatory, at this hour?' the taxi driver asked, and Mallory pasted a smile on her face.

'Just getting some pre-Samhain Observation in,' she said,

hoping the lie didn't sound as obvious as it felt leaving her mouth.

'Sooo many people we know have died,' Cornelia said.

This, apparently, was the key to getting the driver to stop asking questions, but it also reminded Mallory that she was in the rather unideal position of investigating a murder scene – if it was murder – with two thirds of the available Undetectables absolutely off their respective trollies. She couldn't tell if they were drunk, high or both, and she felt tension seeping into her jaw. She was tired, and sore and didn't want to do this. *They* didn't do this anymore.

That, and Cornelia casually pressing their leg against hers – gently, she realised – was very distracting.

Diana and Cornelia bickered as they clambered out in front of the Observatory, swaying unsteadily the way people who are trying very hard to appear sober tend to do. Mallory pressed her palms into her eye sockets.

The Observatory was silent, not a soul around. No sign anything out of the ordinary had happened. And yet, Mallory felt the familiar frisson of a true case settling on her, and knew that as much as she wanted to call the taxi back, she wasn't going home. Her curiosity wouldn't let her.

That left two options. One, she go in alone.

Or two…

'Which one of you has the hip flask?'

Cornelia cheered until Diana clapped a hand over their mouth, and Diana handed over a flask full of well-matured whiskey, presumably liberated from the Broadwick stores when they'd moved out. She took a deep sip and felt the warmth of it seep through her limbs as it burned down into her chest. It didn't kill the pain, but it felt easier to be in her body.

This was, of course, entirely against crime scene protocol. Every bit of her body was screaming at the blatant flouting of their agency rules.

'There is no agency,' she mumbled aloud, and took another long sip, wincing, before passing it to Cornelia.

Their fingers brushed and Mallory flinched like she'd been shocked.

Diana raised an eyebrow, but didn't comment. 'What *did* Sully say?'

'She said "I need you to come to the Observatory now, it's happening again",' Mallory said, her head warm and fuzzy.

Impaired, the part of her that always followed rules whispered. It was both judgemental and correct, but Mallory shoved it away.

'Then she hung up on me and wouldn't answer when I tried to call back. Her car isn't here, so she could be on foot, but—'

A car rolled up beside her, window wound down, and it took Mallory a second to recognise it as the taxi they'd just vacated.

'You forgot this,' the driver said, and passed Mallory her kit bag.

The kit Diana was supposed to be holding.

Mallory waved him off with a grateful thanks and threw the kit down, crouching beside it even as her knees screamed in protest.

'Torches, gloves, booties once we get to the door. We've no idea what we're going into, and should assume it's a crime scene.'

The Undetectables staggered through the door of the

Observatory and Mallory and Diana did a sweep of the ground floor, calling softly for Sully.

The Observatory was dead silent, red divider curtains motionless as they padded over red plush carpet, their steps soundless. The main atrium with the stained Ternion glass window sat ready for visitors, and Mallory averted her gaze from it as she always did, its pattern of circles, lines and stars as sickening as it had been when she'd seen it carved into the stomachs of the Whistler's victims two years ago.

She caught sculptures and artwork in the spotlight glare of her witchlight. Reams of Occult decadence collected through the ages that spoke to a rich history Mallory didn't know. The whole world had been waiting for her, and she would never have a chance to discover it.

Diana's witchlight grazed over a faceless statue of Morrigan that had been poorly modelled on the Apparent *Birth of Venus* – Occulture liked to think it invented everything worth remembering, but either the Apparent greats were actually Occult, or Occulture needed to put a pin in their obvious elitism – and the beam hovered over Morrigan's bare form.

'I am going to guess no one has ever before said what I'm about to say in the Observatory, but: the artist really assumed she had cracking tits, didn't they?'

'Diana. Are we going to stand here discussing the endowments of a goddess of Occulture, or are we going to find out why the fuck we're here?' Mallory hissed, and Diana grinned, turning the witchlight back on her own face.

'I love it when I piss you off in *exactly* the right way,' Diana said happily.

'Hey,' Cornelia called from the hall.

Mallory did one final, furtive sweep of the room before going to meet them.

'Ladder's down, even though the hatch is closed,' Cornelia said, pointing up at the ceiling. 'Someone's been in the roof.'

'I'll go first,' Mallory said, her foot already on the smooth bottom rung. 'Diana, can you grab a cushion from the tarot room and put it beneath the ladder, in case one of you two take a tumble?'

She was halfway up before she heard Diana shriek as she lost her footing, and a soft *thump* as she and Cornelia hit the ground, collapsing into giggles.

Despite herself, Mallory smiled and pushed open the hatch, clambering inside.

The first thing she took in was the smell. She clamped a hand over her nose and mouth, looking around with her eyes watering. The night sky through the Observatory glass was a half-turn away from matching up perfectly with the constellations on the half-painted dome. She'd remember this later, when she replayed the scene in her mind's eye.

The second thing she took in was the body.

For all that her senses had tried to tell her that there was a case, she hadn't really believed it.

She didn't know what she was expecting to see, but it was not a charred corpse. Supine, featureless, utterly, utterly dead.

Mallory's hands shook as Cornelia and Diana noisily made their way up the ladder, Diana gagging as the smell hit her too.

The floor around the corpse was blackened, the carpet melted, but everything else in the room untouched. There was no soot up the walls. Everything about this was controlled, deliberate, concentrated on the body.

The smell should've permeated the whole Observatory.

'Oh, *fuck*.' Diana grabbed Mallory's arm.

Cornelia had gone white as a sheet and for a second Mallory worried they were going to throw up. Instead, they tugged Mallory's kit bag open and rummaged around, finding a small pot of something that they daubed under their nose.

'I bought this last year,' they said, handing it to Mallory. 'Helps mask smells. I heard Izna asking Dr Ray about it one of the times we were in the mortuary – Dr Ray was most dismissive of the concept, of course. Apparently smells are all part of medical examination. Sounds fantastic, can't wait to die so I don't ever have to do it as a job.'

It was strong menthol, and it did mask the scent, though Mallory was sure she'd have the smell of burnt corpse in her nose for the rest of her life.

That is, for the next forty-something hours.

'Nothing like a burnt corpse to sober you up,' Diana said, similarly composing herself.

Together, as though they'd never stopped, the Undetectables snapped into crime scene investigation mode.

Diana took photos and Mallory and Cornelia walked the perimeter, away from the body.

'What are we looking at here?' Cornelia asked. 'Apart from a body, I mean.'

'I am specifically looking at the burn patterns,' Mallory said, her head clearing slightly. 'There should be soot up the walls, signs of the fire spreading in some way. I'm most interested in the fact it's so concentrated – nothing else in the room burned bar the body, and I didn't notice any burn patterns on the ceiling, or smell smoke inside the Observatory.'

'Which…?'

'Suggests it could be of magical origin,' Mallory said grimly. She was used to magical murder – undetectable methods of using magic to kill were so baked into everything she and the Undetectables did, nothing should come as a surprise to her. And yet. 'I had never considered the *possibility* of magical arson before. However, there are multiple, non-magical situations that might allow for a body to burn, but not its surrounding area. See the scorch marks there?' Mallory pointed to the charred pieces of red carpet around the body. 'And how it hasn't spread further than an inch or two from the corpse? Wool doesn't burn very well at all unless its soaked in some kind of accelerant, and lots of carpets are specifically fire-resistant. This indicates there was a deliberately set fire. But I can't be fully certain without testing – we'll need to take sections of the carpet away to see.'

'So we're taking the case, then?' Cornelia said.

Mallory looked at them askance, but their eyes were bright. She didn't answer, and took a steadying breath while Diana finished photographing the scene, and they took turns combing the ground for any evidence of the killer. Any evidence anyone had been here at all.

'Hexana help us, it's going to be hard to pull any evidence from the body, assuming it isn't utterly destroyed. This poor person. Their positioning suggests they weren't alive – usually the body will curl up involuntarily – but we can't be sure yet,' Mallory said, mostly to herself.

There was a suspiciously witchlight-shaped object in the body's hand, soot-covered but unmistakable, and Mallory grimaced.

Even if the killer came in via the ladder, they likely didn't exit that way.

'There's some hair here.' Diana crouched at the head of the corpse, her expression unreadable. 'Still attached to their head. Not much, just a few strands.' She gently lifted a small lock of long, strawberry blonde hair from beneath the corpse.

Mallory carefully crouched to bag the hair, which curled in the evidence bag as she sealed it up and handed it to Cornelia, who stashed it immediately.

Her eyes scanned the body, taking in the witchlight in the body's hand. Her gaze caught on something shiny on the body's wrist. 'Get a photo of that bracelet, then bag it – could help ID them,' Mallory said. 'Until you found the hair, I was worried it was Observer Johnson.'

'Who is famously bald,' Diana said unnecessarily, for nobody's benefit.

'Thanks, Diana,' Cornelia started. 'I—'

But whatever they were about to say was lost amid the sky lighting up. Flashing blue lights illuminated the scene and their faces, and Mallory felt a strange sense of relief settle in her stomach.

'Sully,' they said in unison, and Cornelia leaned over the hatch as the Observatory door opened with a crackle of walkies and heavy footsteps.

Sully's call had worried Mallory, as had her absence.

'Sully! We're up here,' Cornelia called.

Diana had just finished packing her camera away as footsteps sounded on the ladder.

'I don't want to alarm you, but we think it could be—' Mallory started to tell the familiar figure who emerged through the hatch, but the rest of the sentence caught in her throat.

It was not Sully, but Detective Chief Inspector Nathan Tate looking back at her, his hand pressed over his face as the smell hit him. They'd run into him two years prior when they were investigating the Dollhouse Murderers case, when he was brought in in an attempt to oust Sully from her job. He'd fucked off back to whence he came once he'd failed to apprehend the killers, or prevent them drugging half of Wrackton.

And now he was here.

'You'd think a DCI would be better equipped to cope with an odorous crime scene,' Cornelia said.

'Shut up,' Tate said, somewhat fairly. He did not like the Undetectables at all, and the feeling was mutual.

'Where's Su— Detective Inspector O'Sullivan?' Cornelia demanded.

'I'm the Wrackton DCI. Why are you here?' He gestured to someone behind him as he climbed into the roof properly. 'This is a closed crime scene, and you're on private property.'

'The Observatory is publicly owned and managed by the UML,' Cornelia said. Diana elbowed them, and Cornelia looked at her sharply. 'What? The concept of property being "private" is, at its core, theft. We aren't going to enable the police to continue protecting the desires of the wealthy to claim ownership over whatever we want, are we? Plus, the Observatory is open twenty-four hours, even if there's no one here.'

Mallory both knew that they were right, and wanted desperately for them to stop talking.

'Does right now feel like the best time for a monologue on socialist policies?' Diana hissed.

'Where's DI O'Sullivan?' Mallory tried again.

'She's downstairs.'

'Well bring her upstairs, then. Fixed it for you,' Diana said.

There was a point where, while intoxicated, Diana went from witty and brilliant to borderline incoherent, and she'd passed that point many, many hours ago.

'I'm going to give you one more chance to answer. Why are you here? I should have you arrested for trespassing – this particular part of the Observatory is not open to the public without a prior invitation from a qualified Observer.'

He said it so snottily that Mallory was having trouble not getting angry herself. She was saved from having to prevent Cornelia from reacting by Diana stepping on their foot in silent warning.

'Understood,' Mallory said. 'We'll leave.'

'Hand over anything you've taken from the scene—'

'We haven't taken anything!' Cornelia said, stepping in front of Diana as she quietly and quickly spelled away their sample jars. The camera was, thankfully, hidden.

'It's an offence to lie to a police officer.'

'I think the burden of proof is on you, buddy,' Cornelia said, in a manner that suggested they'd temporarily, conveniently forgotten they weren't a Broadwick in the strictest sense of the word anymore.

'What Cornelia means is,' Mallory started, hating herself

for reverting to old ways of talking for Cornelia. Smoothing out the wrinkles, trying to keep the situation under control. 'That we aren't doing anything wrong. We stumbled into a crime scene – quite by accident – and were expecting a police officer to be in attendance.'

'Is that why you're wearing gloves and booties? Stumble around crime scenes a lot, do you?' Tate asked, and amid the embarrassment of making such a poor excuse, Mallory felt a push on her brain, persuading her to tell the truth.

Demon magic.

'We've solved our share of murders, both in Wrackton and beyond,' Mallory said carefully. 'But as you're the scene officer, we'll leave. There's clearly been a mistake.'

A second elapsed. Two. Voices were shouting, radios in the hallway crackling. Menthol and burnt flesh marinaded in Mallory's nose and she hardly dared to breathe as Tate's expression did not change, calculating, deciding, wasting their time.

He stepped aside and Mallory exhaled. He gestured for them to pass, his eyes scanning their faces. Cornelia chose that moment to allow a level of drunkenness to wash over them, becoming unsteady on their feet, and Mallory saw the way Tate's eyes rolled over, taking Cornelia in.

Mallory climbed down the ladder as quickly as she could, clenching her jaw.

'Sully!' Mallory said, spotting her standing at the glass front doors.

Diana and Cornelia clattered down the ladder after her and Sully looked up from her clipboard.

'Did you see her? Did you—' Her eyes widened, and she looked over Mallory's shoulder. 'Not here,' she whispered. 'Not now.'

'O'Sullivan,' Tate said, appearing down the ladder. Mallory jumped.

'Team have set up a perimeter,' Sully said flatly. Her eyes were pink, her expression hard. 'I'm keeping track of who's coming in and out.'

'Scene wasn't secured, O'Sullivan. These three were trampling around upstairs.'

'I was unaware, Tate.'

He coughed.

'*DCI* Tate,' Sully ground out.

'Go home, O'Sullivan. Get some sleep.'

'What?'

'What?' Diana said.

Tate swivelled to look at her. 'I thought I told you to leave.'

Mallory hesitated, but Sully stared at the ground, a single tear hitting her boot, and Mallory made a directorial decision.

The glass Observatory doors slammed behind them. Police lights flashed in the reflection and cast shadows across the concrete pavement as they approached the perimeter line some officers were setting up. They stepped underneath it, ignoring the searching looks from the officers, Diana clutching Mallory's kit bag tightly to her chest.

They walked around the side of the building and past the Ternion memorial before they stopped, inhaling the cool night air.

Mallory closed her eyes, grateful to be outside, utterly shaken by what she'd seen. All murders were horrific; as fascinated as she was by the mechanics and the processes of murder, as determined as she was to get answers, each murder case they'd taken had been worse than the last. Burning someone – making it difficult to identify their remains, obliterating them – that would keep her up at night, if she'd had more nights to stay awake.

They waited to see Sully climb into her car, and watched as she drove off.

'I assume we're going to Sully's now,' Diana said after a moment.

Mallory nodded. That had been her exact thought process.

'Good. I've already ordered us a taxi.'

Mallory grinned at her – the first real smile she'd allowed herself all day.

'A last hurrah, before we go?' Mallory suggested. 'Not that—'

'Murder is bad,' Diana said firmly. 'But we love what we do. And we're so good at it.'

It felt to Mallory like she didn't just want to solve this murder: she had to.

And then she heard a camera shutter sound.

It was distinctive and unmistakable, crisp in the October night air.

Mallory whirled around to see a wiry man, black curls cropped close to his head, crouched awkwardly beside a stone planter hosting an overly-manicured shrub. He casually lowered the camera, though it was clear he had been pointing the telephoto lens at them.

'What the fuck are you doing,' Diana said. It wasn't a question.

'Nothing,' the obvious liar replied, standing. He tucked the camera against his side, as though that would make it invisible.

'Nothing,' Mallory repeated. 'Let's pretend that's true. Why did you take a photo of us?'

'I'm sorry. Really. There's just something going on here,' the liar continued, though this wasn't a lie, more a clear observation of facts, 'and this is what I do.'

'Take photos of people?' Cornelia demanded. 'Unawares?'

'Unfortunately it's part of my job. Paparazzo.' He paused, a brief look of confusion passing over his features. 'Usually, I mean. Sometimes, if the situation requires it, I sell in photos of crime scenes. Man has to eat somehow. Sam Bridewell,' the man formerly known as the liar said, holding out the hand not holding the camera. 'It's a pleasure to meet you. Honestly, people don't usually notice me. Makes a nice change.'

'I'd love to say it was mutual. I won't, but I'd love to.' Diana smiled sweetly.

'So what's—' Sam started, but the taxi pulled up and the Undetectables clambered in.

As an afterthought, Mallory handed over an agency card she dug out of a pocket in her kit bag. 'If you saw anything of note tonight, call us.'

'And delete any photos you took of me that aren't flattering,' Diana shouted out the window. 'Otherwise, we were never here.'

Sam's brow furrowed as he glanced between the card and back at them. Mallory held up her hand in a half-hearted goodbye, feeling strangely sorry for him. He didn't appear to know who they were, or what they were doing. He was just trying to do a job.

She glanced back to see him still watching them, his camera trained on the car, until the taxi turned a corner.

'What the *fuck* are paparazzi doing in Wrackton?' Diana asked. The taxi driver – a different one this time – glanced at her, and then averted their eyes, clearly deciding not to get involved.

'Technically paparazzo, if there's only one,' Mallory said absently.

'If opportunistic photographers are the biggest complaint you have about this town, I think you're going to die very happy,' Cornelia said.

The taxi closed the distance between them and Sully's house, the smell of death strong in Mallory's nose and lungs.

Murder kept finding them, no matter what else was going on in their lives. But this was it. Their last gift to Wrackton. Mallory's last chance to make something of herself.

She'd do whatever it took.

SIX

They say the first sign of madness is talking to yourself, but Theodore considered that claim scientifically dubious.

If he were to catalogue the 'signs of madness' he'd displayed over the last two years – over the last eight, really, if he was being honest – they would be endless, and they would serve to make him more 'other' than he already was.

'It's called sanism, I believe. And it's a terrible way to look at the world,' Annoying Voice said, and Theodore, much to his alarm, agreed.

'I dislike the notion there is a "right" way to operate in the world, and that everyone needs to conform to that,' Theodore said magnanimously. 'There is a world in which I did not do musical theatre and anthropology as a joint discipline, and became Doctor Wyatt, Clinical Psychologist.'

Alas, he'd known what choice he was making when he'd forgone that particular path – in his experience, the type of people who did psychology degrees were people like Cornelia's dickhead, now dead, ex-boyfriend Beckett Kingston, and if

Theodore were to produce a Venn diagram of 'people he liked to spend time with', 'people who did psychology degrees' and 'Beckett Kingston', he would have a hard time letting the circles intersect.

Sadly, his chosen career path wasn't without perils, and Beckett was dead, and Theodore was maybe, possibly, responsible for it.

He hadn't realised he was speaking aloud until Annoying Voice said, '*Moralising again, are we?*'

Theodore shook it, and the thought, away. He was perfectly capable of being judge, jury and executioner for himself without anyone else weighing in.

That said, perhaps the true second sign of madness was standing in front of Broadwick Mansion with intent to break, enter, and steal files and evidence, all to placate an annoying voice that really enjoyed telling him what to do at all hours of the day. Especially when he really hadn't planned on it.

'*It's not really "breaking" if you're just "entering".*'

He double-checked there was no one around, keeping himself invisible, before taking a deep, unnecessary breath and descending the stairs into the basement of Broadwick Mansion.

He wondered if Mallory knew yet. If she'd been to the Observatory. If she'd seen what he had done. If she understood.

He lifted a hand and a solitary witchlight glowed dimly. He may have spent his time in the shadows, but he still needed to see. At no point in his various existences had he been able to walk into any room without wanting to be in the light.

The basement was a sorry state of affairs. The Undetectables had swept up the glass he'd exploded, and taken down the glass and iron partition, covering the sofas and desks in dust sheets. They'd ransacked their store of books – some of Theodore's were gone too, he noted, and he felt a pathetic surge of hope at that. Maybe it meant Mallory didn't despise him after all – and the shelves had gathered a surprising amount of dust. The snack cupboard was empty, the tea cups they used for guests stacked haphazardly to the side. They'd left most of their machines covered in plastic. Very little of the lab equipment had been taken.

The most glaringly absent piece was Diana's Wrackton diorama she and Taylor had spent ages building. It was a perfect miniature of the entire town that she could animate for tiny crime scene reconstructions. A few months ago, she'd used it to map out what ultimately transpired to be the Crimes of Theodore Wyatt (he was workshopping potential memoir titles, and he currently favoured this one). The vivariums Cornelia had wall-mounted were empty, and Theodore supposed that if he went up to the Bug Room, it would be devoid of life too.

He was all alone in a shell of a house. Haunting it again.

'If I was Mallory, which I am not but if I was and I was smart and organised, and even if I was dejected and hated me, Theodore, who I am not being for the purposes of this exercise, where would I hide the lightbulb?'

The Voice was quiet, the thread of connection between them crackling but otherwise silent, which pleased Theodore. It was off doing something monstrous, no doubt.

He found a filing cabinet pushed back underneath the lab benches, and reached a hand through the locked drawer. The mechanics of reaching *through* objects interested him to no end, like the way light refracted through other things, or the way radiation could permeate obstacles. His current hypothesis was that in the moments where he passed through or held another object, electrons temporarily moved aside to accommodate him. Maybe there were changes on a micro level. Maybe every touch left an invisible, metaphysical trace, one no machines could detect. Maybe it was memory. Maybe that's all that he was.

'That's rather morbid, Teddy,' Theodore admonished himself, his hand passing through what felt suspiciously like evidence bags. He fumbled around until the cabinet unlocked. There, *TU #001* stamped clearly on the outside, were all the notes and evidence bags to do with his original murder.

It was unimaginably strange to be in the place he'd died, and even stranger that it was a place he'd come back from the second-dead – only to realise, in a slow-dawning cascade of horror, that he wasn't *back*. He wasn't himself, and he never would be again.

Not to mention the lying-by-omission.

'*Touch it*,' Annoying Voice said helpfully, meaning the evidence bag that contained the lightbulb that had ostensibly killed him.

Theodore jumped. He'd been enjoying his moment of solitude.

'I won't,' Theodore said. Not because he didn't want to – some part of him did. He was drawn to it, moth to a flame. Moth to a… lamp.

Maybe in a former life, he'd died this way too. A former insect, forced to live out a sad human life for twenty-odd years, and then forced to continue existing anyway. He'd missed his thirtieth. He would miss his fortieth. He might see Mallory celebrate all of those without ever—

'*NOW. Listen when I tell you things. Don't make me do the scary voice, I know you don't like it.*'

Theodore drew his shoulders back, and touched the light-bulb for only the second time in his full existence.

The last time it had been in his hand, Mallory was gently taking it from him at his crime scene to bag it. She'd been so young then. The three of them had been just children. Diana and Cornelia were nervous – Cornelia especially – but Mallory hadn't even hesitated, taking the reality of him in her stride. He'd got to see them grow up and become adults, become his real friends, people he knew inside out.

If there was one thing he knew, independent of anyone else, it's that in the face of the worst things imaginable, no matter how things looked or how much pain Mallory carried around with her, she was the strongest of them.

Betraying her had hurt him the most. The look on her face when he smashed the glass, the fact she was hearing but not *seeing* what was in front of her—

'*What does it remind you of?*' Annoying Voice cut in.

'Dying,' Theodore answered shortly. 'Dying a death I don't remember. No pain, no… anything. I was alive, I was laser-focused on fixing the bulb.'

'*A reminder of your mortality.*'

'What's with the tone?' Theodore asked. 'You're using the tone you take when I'm missing something obvious, and I am registering my objections to it. See! I object!'

The Voice didn't reply and Theodore huffed in annoyance. He tucked the file and the evidence bag into his pocket, kept the bulb gripped in his hand, and stormed out.

He'd perfected the art of storming. If he got it really right, he could make the air swirl behind him and papers would flutter to the ground in his wake.

Here, he did just enough to ruffle the dust sheets, unwilling to leave a trace behind, no matter how much he wanted to. *I was here*, he wanted to say. *I mattered.*

'Why did you want me to get this, again?'

'It's a reminder that you're dead,' Annoying Voice said. *'That you were mortal, once.'*

'Which means... what, exactly?'

Silence. A particularly smug silence, Theodore felt.

'Hello?' He twirled on the spot, looking for the Voice in the corners of his brain.

'Time to head home. You can try to figure this out another time, it was just important you have it in your possession. Wouldn't want anyone else to have it,' Annoying Voice said idly, and Theodore felt a physical tug on the connection between them, urging him back to the hotel he was calling home.

His body flickered, his mind swirling. This state made him particularly susceptible to suggestion, which he, understandably, resented.

Another voice – his own, this time – whispered to him to resist.

A gut instinct, as Cornelia would say. A hunch, as Diana would say. An untested hypothesis, as Mallory would say.

Annoying Voice didn't *help*. It bargained and made up rules and little games and put Theodore's innermost desire on the table as a prize. But it did not *help*.

Theodore was going to get a step ahead of it.

'Oh, fine. I'll go right back to the hotel-hovel I call "home",' he said aloud, and the tug on his semi-corporeal state stopped.

He ambled in the direction of the hotel, remaining hidden with the aid of a song he'd made up. It consisted of chanting '*Remember to run! Remember to hide! That's how you evade capture, when you're outside!*' in the shape of whatever familiar tune he could catch.

He'd always felt it was one of his more charming attributes. If Theodore sang a song and no one was around to listen, he'd still perform it with all his might.

The hotel swam into view, and Theodore felt the Voice back away completely, clearly satisfied Theodore was being compliant. The hotel – if one must call it that – was in poor condition, nestled in a very old row of townhouses on the relatively abandoned outskirts of Wrackton, windowpanes shattered and boarded up, stone facade cracked, staircases and paintwork in disrepair. Grey had said he'd got it for a steal, but Theodore was of the unexpressed opinion that Grey was the one who'd been robbed.

He waited a second. Two seconds. Then turned on his heel.

He was going for a walk.

Theodore's favourite place in Wrackton was the faerie Redwoods. Here he could forget about the hiding song – if anyone saw him they'd think they'd seen a ghost, and they'd be right, but they wouldn't know it was *him*. The static blowback from passing too closely to trees, plus the constant contact of old leaves and twigs meant that Theodore was not particularly *visible* in the strictest sense of the word. A few carefully-timed 'oooOOOOoohs' and he'd be alone again before too long. Apparents were the worst for being easily spooked; he supposed it wouldn't be long before the Redwoods were set upon by Apparent ghost-hunters or paranormal surveyors, or what have you – though the latter had para-anthropological crossovers that he could get behind.

It just struck him as odd that Apparents were so desperate for proof of something he *was*. Big Foot probably felt the same.

Lost in his thoughts, Theodore didn't notice until he'd taken a step over the place where the Redwoods became, officially, Oughteron, and unofficially (but still officially, it just wasn't marked on an ordinance survey map) the limits of Theodore's haunting radius.

'Shit,' he said, hopping on one foot. He closed his eyes, prepared to be immediately propelled back to the basement of Broadwick Mansion, but nothing happened.

He opened one eye and dipped his head forwards, letting his cat ears graze the invisible boundary. Nothing happened, so he placed a foot down. Then took a purposeful step. And another. And another.

Nothing happened.

Theodore was standing outside the boundaries of Wrackton. *Outside* his haunting radius, an invisible boundary that he'd been ruled by since his first death eight years prior.

Until now.

He glanced down at the bulb in his hand, twitching his nose. He'd seen in the mirror once that it gave him the distinct aura of a cat considering their next move. (Or perhaps he'd just imagined doing so, he couldn't remember.)

He walked back over the boundary line to Wrackton, and *ran* full-tilt over it, passing through an Oughteron tree a good twenty feet from the boundary, eyes screwed shut in trepidation for being thrown back to the basement, but still nothing happened.

Elation flooded him. He found a sharp rock and a bark-stripped tree and assembled rough columns, measuring distances by eye and finding a second tree when he'd completely populated the first with his scrawled numbers. It had been a while since Theodore had had to use mathematical equations for anything and it showed. The null hypothesis repeatedly, statistically proved itself as nothing happened.

He experimented over and over, trying as many different parts of the boundary line as he could – for all he knew, someone, somewhere could've redrawn the Wrackton boundaries and that's why he could move, but he also felt sure someone would've complained about that. He'd have heard faeries say something, or Dr Ray mention some sort of ceremonial 'Wrackton has more land, yay!' ceremony. *Grey* would've had something to say about investment opportunities, won or lost. He'd know.

This wasn't a boundary issue.

He was the dependent variable. The environment was the same, but *Theodore* was different.

He looked down at his hand. At the lightbulb.

He imagined it illuminated – just for an illustrative second. A bubble of excitement built somewhere around his middle. (He no longer had a stomach or intestines or throat to situate his feelings, so he had to settle for vague descriptors to get his point across to himself.)

'If the Voice asks, I changed my mind on going back to the hotel. Because it was… draughty. Bad for the constitution. Okay. Let's think this through logically. We want to know what this is for. It's a reminder of my mortality. Well, literally. It *did* kill me, by proxy. But that can't be what it meant. Can it? Was I just supposed to contemplate my death? That seems particularly cruel. Haha! Hilarious. I'm so funny. *Cruel*, as if—'

He coughed and looked around, as though the Voice was going to jump out of the trees.

'Okay, Theodore. You are a scientist. You need to find the test parameters.'

At the edge of the boundary, he set one foot carefully over the invisible line, then crouched as low as he could. Static flew between his body and the ground and he was glad no one was around to see him do his best impression of a crab.

He set the lightbulb down and slowly, carefully, one digit at a time, let go of the bulb, tensing in preparation for being immediately whipped back to the Broadwick Mansion basement, but *nothing happened.*

'Fucking HEXANA!' Theodore shouted.

The lightbulb was in Oughteron. *He* was in Oughteron.

He nudged the lightbulb carefully back over the boundary line, leaving himself standing in Oughteron, the bulb in Wrackton, but the second he lost contact he felt that familiar rushing sensation of his body trying to propel him back to the basement, and he snatched up the lightbulb.

The rushing stopped.

He did it again and again in as many permutations as he could imagine and then some. As long as the lightbulb was within the same boundary lines as Theodore, he could travel there. He could travel without having to touch it, leaving it tucked in the pocket of his cardigan as he ran several feet in every direction, jogging back to update his Tree O' Calculations II until it, too, was full of numbers only comprehensible to Theodore.

'Fuck me,' Theodore said. 'Fuck *me*. I can leave Wrackton. I can go *anywhere*.'

He had more questions, ones he couldn't fully answer during a single set of experiments, but the start of answers to a long-held question were flowing around him, changing his electrons permanently, giving him something he hadn't felt in a very long time: hope.

He cradled the bulb to his chest and ran as fast as he could, body blurring and gliding over the ground until he was back at the ramshackle hovel he reluctantly called home. He couldn't wait to talk to Grey face-to-face.

SEVEN

For the majority of her career, Night Mayor Dr Priyanka Ray had kept her personal life as private as she could hope to in a gossipy town like Wrackton.

Which was to say, not very secret at all.

Despite being private investigators, it hadn't taken any skills for the Undetectables to know when Dr Ray and Sully started a relationship, or to hear through the grapevine when they'd moved in together mere weeks later. Consequently, they knew exactly where to find them – and it helped that Sully's car was parked outside. Cornelia insistently pressed the doorbell, leaning against the boundary fence for support. The house was tucked in beside the late-night wine bar Diana could never locate first try, though it was less 'late night' and more 'open for everything', just as the Larix was. Wrackton was a town that didn't sleep, it just went about it with a sense of decorum.

With the effects of her mouthfuls of whiskey but a pleasant distant memory, Mallory fought back a tear at the idea that visiting Sully and Dr Ray at home for the first time was one of the last first times she'd ever have again.

Dr Ray wrenched open the door and, despite herself, Mallory smiled at the sight of her. She'd grown so fond of her over the years, and while she didn't think Dr Ray considered them *friends*, Mallory was quietly confident Dr Ray reciprocated that fondness.

Then Mallory focused on her face. Dr Ray had been crying, her nose pink and her eyes swollen.

'Get in. Don't let anyone see you.'

She ushered them into a sage-green sitting room – first and last time they'd see it – where Sully was hunched on the green velvet sofa. Her hair was pulled back from her face and she too had been crying, her slender arms wrapped around her knees.

'Did you see her?' Sully asked, her voice rough.

'See who—' Cornelia started, at the same time as Mallory said, 'We couldn't confirm a positive ID—'

Dr Ray's brow furrowed. 'What do you mean?' she said, at the same time as Sully said, 'I saw Hayley Eason dead in the roof of the Observatory, what the fuck crime scene did you go to?'

'Alyssa,' Dr Ray said gently, and Sully closed her eyes.

'I let Hayley go. I told her to, in fact. Night Mayor's orders,' Dr Ray said, tears forming in her eyes again. Sully stood up and pulled Dr Ray to her, gently stroking her thumb over her cheek, speaking a million unspoken words through her eyes.

'Okay, back it up,' Diana said firmly. 'Hayley Eason is dead?'

It barely computed. For a moment, Mallory was sure she'd misheard Sully's phone call, that they'd gone to the Observatory by accident and happened to see a second murder.

'She was right there. In the roof of the Observatory. Lying on the ground, carvings in her stomach. That's why I called you, it's why I— it's happening again! The Whistler murders. Someone's killed Hayley,' Sully said, her usual composure gone.

'Hayley Eason is your aide,' Mallory said, though it wasn't a question. She had met Hayley precisely once, in Dr Ray's office, though she'd been tangentially aware of her for some years. The former girlfriend of the former Night Mayor of Wrackton, she'd been Vincent Van Doren's convenient alibi back when they'd thought he was using his Mayoral powers to commit the Whistler murders.

A simpler time, really.

'She's our *friend*,' Sully shouted.

'Your friend, yes,' Mallory tried again, trying to make sense of it. 'Unfortunately when we arrived at the scene, we were unable to visually confirm it was Hayley. We have collected a hair sample that could potentially confirm the victim's identity – it's several strands, so there's a good chance, but it isn't a strong provider of DNA. I mean, you know all this,' Mallory added quickly, remembering she was talking to a police officer and the literal medical examiner. 'The remains were so badly burned, we—'

'BURNED?' Sully and Dr Ray said as one.

Mallory blinked in confusion. 'Well. Yes? We searched the Observatory and went up to the roof—'

'You didn't really give us much to go on,' Cornelia added.

'And we found the remains. A body. What do you mean, carvings?'

'That's what I saw! I saw—'

'For the love of Blair,' Dr Ray said, kissing Sully's hand before standing. She fixed them all with a very level, very professional gaze, visibly swallowing her grief. 'What do you need to know?'

'Everything,' Mallory said. 'We need to know what she saw, how she saw it. What time she saw it at.'

'We sent her there to look for particular records for the Ghoul Council,' Dr Ray said. 'At about quarter past eight this evening, she left the Mayoral Offices.'

'What happened then?'

'I was due to start my shift at nine. She'd been gone about forty-five minutes and her phone was going to voicemail. We thought— DCI Tate has been hassling her about… well. About both of us, and the work she does for Priya. I assumed… I don't know what I assumed. So I drove over to check on her,' Sully said. 'And I couldn't see her anywhere. The place was deserted – Observer Johnson wasn't around.'

'What time was that at?' Mallory prompted.

'Just after nine p.m.,' Sully said quickly, wiping her face. 'What do you mean, *burned*?'

'Let's stay on what you saw,' Mallory said smoothly. Professionally. 'As much detail as you can.'

It struck Mallory then that it was possible Sully had never worked a truly personal case.

'Hayley was our friend,' Sully said again. 'She was our friend, and…'

She swallowed hard, a sob working its way up her throat. She took several deep breaths, and Mallory lowered her gaze. She hated this part – hated asking people to ignore their feelings. She did it often enough herself that she knew how it started to rot you from the inside if you didn't take a minute to feel them.

'I did a sweep of the Observatory, but it was silent. I saw no one. I stupidly thought she maybe had earphones in or something – maybe she couldn't hear me calling. I rang her phone again, but it went straight to voicemail. I noticed the ladder was down and climbed up, pushed open the hatch. And there she was, spread out on the floor of the Observatory.' A low sob escaped her and Sully took another moment to compose herself; Sully the person melted away, and DI O'Sullivan emerged.

'At the scene, Hay— the victim's eyes were open. There was a dribble of blood on her chin, her body supine, limbs spread. I checked for a pulse, checked her mouth, but it looked like she'd bitten her tongue off. Purple witchlight in her right hand. I checked for signs of an intruder and then lifted the hem of her blouse, visually confirming carvings we'd seen before, in the Whistler case. Looking for too long made me nauseated, as it did in the original Whistler murders. In my professional opinion, there wasn't a single thing about this murder that looked different to the Whistler murders. It could've *been* another Whistler murder.'

'And as Jacob fucking Gabbott is dead, that's impossible,' Cornelia snapped.

Mallory resisted the urge to take their hand, to reassure them.

'Which begs the question: are we looking at a possible copycat killer?' Dr Ray said.

'We could be, if not for what we found.' Mallory described, in as sparse detail as she could, what they found in the Observatory. The burnt body. Possible signs of an accelerant.

They sat in silence as they digested this fact. This horrible, horrible fact.

'At least she was dead before she was burned,' Cornelia said. 'So there's that.'

It wasn't much, in terms of comfort.

'So you arrived just after nine p.m.,' Mallory said. 'And you called me after midnight.'

'Yes,' Sully said.

'Why?' Mallory asked. 'Just trying to establish timeline.'

'First chance I got. I had a shift, and Tate's been on my arse since he's rolled back in.'

'And she would've spent some time examining the body. She called me, then left the scene,' Dr Ray said.

'What time did she call you?' Mallory asked.

'Not sure,' Dr Ray said. 'Would have to check. It was a quick call from the squad car.'

'Speaking of Tate – why's he back?' Diana asked. 'I thought we got rid of him ages ago. He's far more annoying than you are. Sorry. I think I'm still drunk.'

Mallory didn't want to move the conversation on – she wanted to stay on timeline, stay on trying to understand how Hayley could go from lying on the ground killed in the way Sully described, to burned by the time Mallory got to the scene – and why.

Sully sighed, massaging her temples. 'Everything's changing. The Broadwicks leaving the Ghoul Council has had a domino effect on the UML, on Wrackton, on the structure of Occulture as a whole.'

'My role as Night Mayor has devalued in influence over the

past five months,' Dr Ray said. 'Practically ornamental now. A planned influx of tourism while there's an active hunt ongoing for a potentially *very* dangerous Samhain ghost is *not* my idea of public safety, and yet the UML is determined to step up the *Visit Wrackton* campaign. Create a tourism hub, put Wrackton on the map, save its reputation from all the murders.'

'A genius idea, if it wasn't so spineless,' Sully spat.

'Having to attend committee hearings on campaign colours has successfully prevented me from attending – or being invited to – UML or Ghoul Council meetings, or hearing what's going on in my town. I suspect by the time re-elections roll around, I'll... well. I don't know what'll happen,' Dr Ray said. 'In short, Tate has been transferred back to Wrackton in an effort to deal with the Theodore problem and our surprisingly high homicide figures, and he thinks Alyssa is a factor in these problems. Despite my best efforts to convince everyone otherwise.'

'And if your wife the Night Mayor can't do something to stop that, what's the point?' Sully said.

Mallory paused, and Cornelia's face crumpled ever so slightly in silent devastation, their unending devotion to Dr Ray a very open secret.

'Sorry,' Diana said incredulously. 'Not sorry. WIFE? You didn't invite us to the LESBIAN WEDDING OF THE YEAR?'

Dr Ray stared at her until her face returned to neutral.

'No,' she said shortly. 'It was a beautiful ceremony, made much better by you three not being there.'

Mallory could accept that, despite the sudden stab of longing for one final opportunity to see Cornelia in a tux, and to have Diana pick a dress out for her.

Sully laughed, her eyes wild and unfocused. 'Sorry. It's just… I left her, and someone came back, and… burned her. I left our best friend on the ground, dead, and I went to work, because I didn't want to lose my job. My fucking *job*, that I'm going to lose *anyway*.'

'We still need to positively ID the body,' Mallory said. 'I mean, someone has to. We have hair, as we said.'

'And a bracelet!' Diana said, opening Mallory's kitbag. She took out a marker and carefully wrote the time on the front of the evidence bag, then opened it so Sully and Dr Ray could see it.

It was covered in soot and Mallory thought it was nothing short of a miracle that it was still intact. Flashes of metal through the tarnish gave her a picture of what it might've looked like – silver, with a heart-shaped tag on it.

'Oh, goddess. That's hers,' Dr Ray said.

'How do you know?'

'Read the back of the tag.'

Mallory nodded and Diana pulled on a pair of gloves to hold it up to the light, squinting.

'FOR MY SHINING STAR. FONDLY, VVD.'

'Van Doren. What a romantic,' Cornelia said. 'Top notch work there.'

'She wore it all the time. Afraid to take it off, because he was dead,' Sully said.

Mallory still wanted to forensically check, despite not having a lab to do so in.

'Do you think you'll do the autopsy?' *Can* you, she wanted to ask. Can someone autopsy a loved one?

Dr Ray pursed her lips. 'It's out of my hands. The Ghoul

Council will make that decision – the UML have positioned the Ghoul Council as the de facto organisers of *any* locale where there is a ghost on the loose. Which is to say, Wrackton and Wrackton alone. Until Theodore Wyatt is caught, our hands are tied. Van Doren and the Broadwicks made the decision to keep Theodore here instead of containing him. These are the natural consequences. Have you had any contact with the Broadwicks, Cornelia? They've been frustratingly quiet.'

'No,' Cornelia said baldly. 'But I also haven't tried.'

Dr Ray didn't so much as blink. 'All right. We'll need you to take this case, and quietly.'

'What, officially?' Mallory asked. She had already accepted the case was theirs, but the idea of an *official* Undetectables job, this close to death, felt impossible.

'No, Sully called you to rubberneck at the scene, and we allowed you to come in and gawk at us in our time of grief,' Dr Ray said archly. 'Obviously officially. This is what *you* do. This is who you *are*.'

Mallory needed this. She needed to solve this, to prove to Wrackton that she was worthy. She was being handed a chance, an opportunity to rescue the social standing of the agency. There was just the small matter of a clock ticking over their heads.

'I'm just… surprised,' she said finally, unwilling to explain the whole 'almost dead' conundrum.

'Do you think we have many other options? You don't know where Wyatt is, do you?'

Mallory shook her head.

'I believe you. We're asking, as colleagues. As… as…'

'As friends,' Sully said.

Mallory glanced at her friends. Something defiant burned in Cornelia's eyes – Mallory could only imagine how difficult someone copying the Whistler was for them, after what Jacob had done, how lasting the effects were – and there was something akin to resolve in Diana's.

'We'll do it,' Mallory said. 'Officially.'

One last case. No fading; she would leave Wrackton with a rocket-loud bang.

'The deviation from the original Whistler murders doesn't make sense. It's already got frightening implications – one being that the circles cut into Hayley's stomach are suggestive of there being another death blade, for example,' Mallory said fretfully as they waited for a taxi to bring them back to Mallory's house. It felt strange to not go straight to the Broadwick Mansion lab, to sweep in and refresh the murder board and be reassured by Theodore quipping away in the background. '*One* horrible specially-made glass blade for harvesting souls was enough,' Diana said. 'A *second* one doesn't bear thinking about.'

'Then burning the body *after* Sully saw it just… doesn't make sense. Why change the original murder method?' Mallory mused. 'If it was meant to be a copy of the Whistler method, why change it?'

'We need to wait and look at this sober.' Cornelia reached under the frame of their glasses to rub their eyes.

As if they had time to wait: it was creeping up on two a.m. They had just forty-six hours left.

'I wish there was a way to see what happened at the scene,' Diana said, drumming her fingers on the windowsill. She'd perched against the fence of the wine bar in a way that appeared nonchalant, but that Mallory highly suspected was an attempt to not fall over. 'Like what we did in Wickermere with the Lyreflies, using them to listen to the scene for us.'

'Oh, did I not tell you? There is,' Cornelia said.

'What?' Diana and Mallory said together.

'I thought they were super rare? Super hard to find? Super the whole thing that held us up and led to us enacting the Besiegement Curse that is going to guarantee our deaths in less than two days' time?'

'And they are,' Cornelia said.

Mallory didn't often get frustrated with Cornelia, but they were being frustratingly obtuse, so it felt okay in the circumstances.

'Explain,' Diana demanded. 'Or I'll...'

'What? Kill me? Oooh nooo,' Cornelia said, and Diana hit them with a hex that almost knocked them off their feet.

They squabbled until a familiar voice behind them shouted, 'Mallory? Diana? Is that you? GUESS WHAT! The neeeecromancer is BACK!'

The Undetectables turned as one, in varying levels of delight, to see a familiar blonde actor emerge from the bar beside them. Mallory broke into a grin at the sight of several-time prestigious award nominee, gay icon and former suspect in the murders on set of *Undead Complex*.

'Sandi Clementine!' Diana and Mallory said in unison.

'Shhh, I'm here undercover! We're hiding from the

paparazzi' – she pronounced it 'paper-razzy', for no discernible reason – 'and there's no neeecromancy here, sadly. How ARE you?' She swept forwards and pulled Mallory and Diana into a hug in turn. She stopped when she got to Cornelia.

'You! You're the person from the historical society! And I think I saw you in a well, once,' she added knowingly.

'I'm good for hugs, thank you,' Cornelia said, but their words were swallowed up by Sandi pulling them close.

'The smartest person I've ever met. So much knowledge. Hey, maybe you can help me figure out some heestory in relation to my grand-mom!'

'She's late,' another voice cut in, emerging from the wine bar.

A tall, handsome man with bleach-blonde hair wearing designer sunglasses. The fact it was the middle of the night did not seem to be an issue for his eyesight.

'MALLORY, and so on,' Sandi beamed. 'Have you met my fiancé?'

'Hi. Mallory,' Mallory said, taking his hand.

'Remington,' he said warmly. He was whippet thin, pale and blonde, but his voice was deep and resonant. 'A pleasure. Friends of Sandi's?'

'He's an actor,' Sandi whispered. 'But you knew that.'

Mallory, sadly, *did* know that. A dearth of cases and a tendency to tire easily when typing up her case studies meant she was turning to daytime television for comfort, and had found herself watching a lot of press junkets for films she was never going to get to see. (It had also been somewhat soothing to make connections between actors, directors and production companies, the patterns around ostensible overnight successes emerging like easy puzzles she could solve. So easy, she had gone to lengths to not tell anyone she was doing it.)

This was Remington Davis: former English stage actor turned Hollywood B-lister.

'The rumours are true,' Sandi continued in a stage whisper, though nobody had asked. 'We are totally engaged. But we're on the deee-ell. That's "down low". Undercover, you know.'

'Eighth husband-to-be lucky,' Remington said, winking at Diana, whose face crumpled in mild disgust. He wrapped an arm around Sandi, checking his phone again. 'Really must be going, darling.'

'Oh, but I haven't told them about our heeritage tour!' Sandi said, ignoring everything Remington had said. 'We're in Wracktoon to learn about Reemington's heeritage. I'm not really Occultical – that was my grand-mom, but I was probably confused about whether she was really a neeecromancer or, you know. But Remington's basically a witch! Isn't that so exciting! A real live witch!'

Mallory bit back a smile as Remington visibly winced. 'Darling, don't bother the Occult folk with my silly heritage. Grandad was a witch, which I suppose makes me... Sandi, they're calling me again, my love.'

'Why don't you come with me!' Sandi exclaimed, taking Mallory and Diana's hands. 'Oh, what a FABULOUS idea. Mallory, Diana, heestorian – come with me to the Leerax.'

'Do you mean the Larix? We were just there,' Diana said. 'They were setting up for—'

'TAROT NIGHT! Yes! I'm doing a special appearance.'

Sandi beamed, clearly unaware that being on the 'dee ell'

and making a special appearance in the heart of Wrackton were contradictory.

'This has been a lovely reunion,' Cornelia said, glancing at Mallory. 'But we should probably be going. Murders to—'

'Oh, you can't leave!' Sandi insisted. 'When am I going to get to see my favourite Occulticals ever again?'

It was a question that hung awkwardly between them, and Mallory didn't know what to say, or how to say it.

'Taylor's still there, with Kingston and Felix,' Diana said quietly. 'And we did say we'd come back.'

'But we have evidence to—' Mallory stopped, and the Undetectables exchanged glances. Mallory wanted, very much, to go and work on the case they'd just been handed. The very sad, very close-to-home case. She was sure she smelled of burnt corpse.

'We could do both?' Cornelia suggested *sotto voce*. 'Go have a last few hours of fun with our friends and Sandi. Solve the murder tomorrow.'

Mallory felt herself wavering. They had so little time left to live; it would be wrong to stop them.

It would be wrong to deny *herself* this side quest.

Pain be damned, she could do everything. This was her last chance to live.

'I think that silence means they're in,' Remington said, grinning. He lowered his sunglasses to fix them with a piercing, twinkling stare. 'Let's go. Before anyone else pops up and tries to take photos of us.'

EIGHT

Theodore was halfway through both a third symphonious shout of 'GREY!' and the front door when he caught sight of something jammed in the letterbox and pulled it free, squinting at the Ghoul Council logo with distaste and perhaps a hint of fear. He had yet to receive anything good from those people, but they'd so far been unable to find him. Wrackton wasn't a big town – the Council just weren't very good at looking for him.

That, or the Notorious Theodore Wyatt really *was* a criminal mastermind, hiding in the last place they'd expect him to be.

VISIT WRACKTON SAFETY ADVICE

Your comfort and safety is a priority for Wrackton. In the unlikely event that you encounter a Samhain ghost during your visit, DO NOT engage with it. Please call **0808-7264246** and retreat to a place of safety.

Emergency salt bags will be distributed to every dwelling and business by no later than the afternoon of 30th October.

– **NOVA KHAN**,
acting head of the Ghoul Council

On behalf of the Unified Magical Liaison

'Even the Broadwicks wouldn't have stooped so low,' Theodore said acidly. 'Next they'll be posting ghostlights through everyone's front door and offering a reward for my capture. Nobody do that, if you somehow heard me say it.'

'Salon,' Grey said, a full three minutes after Theodore had stopped calling for him.

Theodore felt the elation of his lightbulb discovery flood him again as he bounded inside, where he found an uncharacteristically tousle-haired Grey on the floor, next to a crystal tumbler and a trunk – an actual, honest-to-Elisabella *trunk* – with papers and drawings and books scattered around him.

The strangest thing of all was a little table with a beautifully carved chess set, intricate pieces shifting and shimmering on a smooth black and white board, sitting next to Theodore's wing-back like it had always been there.

'Are you *reading*?' Theodore asked.

'Is that so unusual?'

'We have nothing but books and ourselves for entertainment, and yet I've never seen you do it voluntarily. Too busy looking at yourself in the mirror, usually.'

'And yet you desperately wanted my attention. What is that?' Grey nodded at the note in Theodore's hand. His gaze lingered on the lightbulb, but he didn't comment on it, even when Theodore folded an arm so he could hold it more aloft.

'Oh, you know. Warrant out for my arrest, Mayoral Office trying to protect the tourists they've demanded descend on the town. Bureaucracy 101 suggests that this combination of things – a manhunt and inviting vulnerable Apparents into town – neither go together, nor are they overseen by someone who gives enough of a fuck to figure out how to prioritise the obvious issue. If *I* still worked in the Mayoral Offices, no doubt this would trickle down to me in the form of tedious paperwork that someone would take and then throw in the nearest bin. Not even the recycling bin, just any bin at all.'

'The perils of civil employment.' Grey took a sip from his glass.

His arms were surprisingly strong, his elegant hands matching the lean muscle in his forearms, the curve of his biceps, and Theodore realised that he'd never *seen* Grey's arms before. Grey had taken his blazer off and was sitting in a soft black T-shirt and his usual tailored trousers. He'd removed his loafers and was wearing a pair of socks patterned with—

'Are they *ghosts*? On your socks?'

'Tis the season.' Grey didn't look up, sifting through a pile of drawings. 'Don't take it personally.'

Theodore didn't know how to take it at all, so he didn't.

'What are you doing?' he asked instead, some of his haunting radius excitement deflating. 'And what's this chessboard?'

'Hollis left me this trunk,' Grey said. 'By which I mean, he left it in Oakpass when he passed. Possession is nine-tenths of the law, as we know. Hollis appeared to believe that Occult goddesses have special objects that tether them to the earth. He had a silly name for them, I don't remember what it is, but they're basically objects that were important to them in life. Obviously this is all buried under analogy and so on, but… perhaps that's what the Ghoul Council are after. There are a lot of things in Oakpass Manor. Who's to say one, or three, of those things aren't of incredibly historical value?'

'Who indeed,' Theodore lied, his mind immediately going

to the ring he knew Diana had hidden in a diorama somewhere in Mallory's house. Blair's ring, at the very least, was very real.

'Hollis was talented,' Grey was saying, and Theodore tried to tune back in. 'He had an uncanny aptitude for circling the most obscure concepts and weaving them into a narrative. I'm not sure even he understood what he was doing half the time, or if he really knew what it meant. However, I don't know if he's *right*. The Ghoul Council could be interested in Oakpass Manor again because they think they should be. They could be interested because it's a closer base to Wrackton than whatever dump they have in Wickermere. But… I don't think that's the case, do you? I think there's something in there. I think I have something they want. So it's just a case of figuring out what it is. Staying a step ahead.'

He looked excited; his face was flushed, his eyes bright, a confidence overtaking him that Theodore hadn't seen since… Since he'd placed cat ears on Theodore's head. Or perhaps the many times the Undetectables had asked him for favours. He hadn't noticed its absence because he didn't really *know* Grey, but now it was like seeing puzzle pieces were missing when everything else was in place.

'Any ideas?' Grey prompted, and Theodore shook his head, wrenching his gaze from Grey's lips.

'Could be something small! Spooky, naturally. A small, spooky object. Like a… planchette. Or… a chess piece.' He waved the lightbulb pointedly at the chessboard, but Grey didn't take the bait.

'Oddly specific examples, but perhaps. Obviously I can't *ask* Khan or Reid what they're sniffing around for, because I don't want them to think I know what I have. I want to undermine their efforts. Best bet is that the Council believes I am deeply unaware I have something of value, and I allow them to wrap themselves up in red tape.'

'Sounds great. Just one question, though,' Theodore said, raising a hand. 'What is the point of that?'

Grey sat back on his hands, a boyish grin ripping through his features and making him look almost… pleasant.

'You've got so much to learn,' he said.

Theodore sat down in his wing-back, holding the lightbulb aloft again.

'Great work. Fascinating. Scintillating, even. Looks like we both had news to share today. That's good to know.'

He sat with the lightbulb above his head, waving it side to side.

'What are you doing?' Grey asked finally, after what felt like hours of him shuffling through papers and muttering to himself, steadfastly ignoring Theodore, the lightbulb and his burning desire to know what the chessboard was *for.*

'I'm adopting the universal "ask me about my lightbulb" stance.'

Grey looked back at his papers.

'Oh, fine. If you're going to be so insistent about it, I'll tell you everything.'

In the middle of the stupid salon (which had done nothing to personally affront Theodore) with his stupid blazer neatly placed across his wing-back and his stupid ghost socks and his stupid tousled hair and his stupid, expressive eyebrows, Grey Quinn laughed.

'Why are you laughing? What's happened? Did I tell a joke? Did you misunderstand the point of my story?'

'I'd say I was sorry, but… Theodore, this is *pathetic*. Even for you.'

Theodore resisted the urge to place a fist right through Grey's middle. It wouldn't do anything except make both of them feel very strange, and he hadn't quite built up to throwing objects around their house.

Grey's house. Grey's place.

Theodore had just performed a full-scale re-enactment of finding the lightbulb – cleverly leaving out the bit where he went to the Observatory for fear of being eaten by the Voice (as had been threatened more than once), and the other bit where he was starting to think his existence as a Samhain ghost had a higher purpose that he could never actually say aloud, for fear of being locked up and studied like a bug.

In order to cleverly avoid the truth he couldn't speak, he'd lied a bit. Embellished. Said he'd accidentally found the lightbulb when in his old basement lab while looking for things that might help exonerate himself. He thought it had been quite effective. The whole tale was well-told and should've inspired *awe* and *chagrin* and *emotional complexity*, not… pity and insults.

But perhaps that's what happens when the only friend you've got left in the world is Grey Quinn, hotelier on the edge of a full-scale breakdown.

Punching him wouldn't achieve anything.

Instead, Theodore drew himself up to his full, relatively

diminutive, height, stilling the swell of dramatic indignation.

He was a good actor, he knew that. Everyone who met him knew he was calm and collected. His dramatics were known to be well-contained.

'What could *possibly* be pathetic about what I've just said?'

'You're Wrackton's most wanted, and you didn't know you could leave this whole time? Every minute of every day you've lamented your lack of freedom, and it was right there this whole time. Locked up inside some lightbulb. I *am* sorry, actually. It's just too good.'

'Fuck off, Grey,' he said, as plainly as he could. 'I've spent *eight years* thinking I can't leave the bounds of this town. Eight miserable, tiresome, *wakeful* years trapped inside Wrackton. Where I am, as you well know, a wanted ghost. I've been inside your walls Grey, and I could've been in anyone's walls. I could've gone ANYWHERE IN THE FUCKING WORLD, but I've been *here*.'

Grey paused, glass halfway to his mouth.

'Don't say that,' Grey said after a moment. He stood and padded to where Theodore stood, gently taking the lightbulb from his grasp. The air crackled at the contact.

'Say what?'

'*Here,* like that.' He held the lightbulb up to the firelight before handing it back. 'If you hadn't been here, you'd never have had the pleasure of my company.'

Theodore's fist lashed out and through Grey's stomach before he'd had time to make it a conscious action. A shock passed through both of them and Grey's head fell back in surprise.

'Did you just *punch* me?'

'If we're to be accurate about it, I'd say I passed my fist through you. I fist— hmm,' Theodore said.

Grey's face remained impassive, studying him. 'And you're sure it works? Your lightbulb escape route.'

'I've tested it enough to know I can cross over into Oughteron, yes.'

'So you don't know if it's the entire world, or just the bounds of the world beyond the Redwoods? Not very scientific of you.'

'Well. No.' Theodore faltered. 'My study obviously had limitations, given that it was just me and the trees. If I cross the line sans lightbulb, I get thrown back to the Broadwicks' basement and have to start all over.'

'Almost fascinating. And *risky* – I did hear through the grapevine that the Broadwicks are planning to return. Something about a Samhain ball. They've been gone so long, I thought they were dead. Unlucky for you.' Grey crossed to a polished glass mirror and adjusted his hair while Theodore hovered behind his shoulder.

Not literally hovered. His two feet were firmly on the ground. It was more his cat ears came up to Grey's shoulder and he couldn't peer over it properly like they used to do in films when characters had serious conversations without looking directly at each other, and what Theodore wouldn't give to watch a *film* right now—

'But I haven't decided if I'll attend. Part of me wants to know why they so abruptly resigned, why they've been silent as Khan and the UML have ushered in so many terrible changes to Occulture as a whole. Part of me is desperately interested in what happened to Dorothy, as they are being *very* tight-lipped about it – even our own Night Mayor hasn't a clue, though I suppose that's to be expected. No disrespect to Dr Ray, of course.' His gaze flicked to Theodore. 'These are all things I'll learn in due course – part of my survival requires adjusting to the new world order, as and when it happens.'

If only he knew the half of it.

'Did you mean Samhain as in, less than days from now, Samhain?' Theodore said, instead of anything else.

'I've thrown together a party in minutes, sweetheart. Speaking of adjusting to the new world order – you've twisted my arm. The chess set is for you.'

Theodore blinked at him.

'I thought it might give us something more… cerebral to discuss. And that you'd hesitate before throwing a board into the fire. I have not quite forgiven you for the cards incident.'

'It's not *my* fault Granny Wyatt taught me the wrong rules to gin rummy!'

'Nonetheless. I'm willing to give you a second chance. And it's your move.'

'Where did it come from?' Theodore allowed himself to look at it closely, marvelling at the detail, at the fact the pieces were clearly magical.

'Oakpass. An Appoccult Society speciality – the pieces can look like anyone you want. Clever little design I can't quite figure out.'

Theodore knew the answer. An innocent little plant that could be quite deadly in the wrong hands. Or the right hands, if the wrong Voice was watching. A magical plant that had the power to shift and change a person's appearance, if they ingested it (or wore it on their person) and the power to kill if taken in high enough doses.

He plucked up a pawn and saw it change into something with cat ears. Glaring at it, he made his move.

Grey pivoted away from the mirror and casually moved a knight, which shimmered and was now sporting a cravat.

'Interesting. You see yourself as a pawn, I see myself as a dark knight,' Grey said.

Theodore felt the Voice stirring at this, and whirled away from the chessboard, feeling Grey's eyes on him in the mirror.

'I thought we'd take the game slow. One move a day. And maybe answer a question for every piece taken.'

'Fine. Sounds great. Thanks,' Theodore said, though he was secretly delighted at this obvious attempt at enriching his enclosure.

'We could begin with a free question, to begin. Indulge me. What do you want most in the world?'

Theodore's eyes snapped up to meet Grey's.

'You don't normally ask me such bald questions.'

'I don't normally want bald answers. But this is the game.'

The bald answer was that he wanted to be human. He wanted to experience humanity again. He wanted to feel his heart sink, he wanted to feel real joy in his limbs, he wanted to do over the life he'd lived before he'd died and then some.

'I want to solve my first murder,' Theodore said instead.

Grey raised an eyebrow and slowly turned towards him. 'I wasn't expecting that. Why?'

'I think it'll answer why I exist, and if we can answer that, we can work on exonerating me. Explaining why I did or didn't do certain things that made me notorious. I prove my innocence, and I can enjoy my newfound freedom. You could help.'

'Why would *I* help?'

'You don't need to hole up in here,' Theodore gestured at the salon. 'You won't be harbouring a fugitive anymore. Wouldn't that be nice. I'd just be some guy again!'

Grey's eyes flicked over Theodore's cat whiskers – the ones he'd hand drawn – and back up to his eyes. Looking into them was uncomfortable at the best of times, but Theodore held his gaze.

'And why wouldn't I just kick you out right now, when you've proven you can fuck off to another town without a moment's thought?'

'Because I imagine that whatever ulterior motive you had for taking me in hasn't evaporated. I think you need me for something.'

A slow grin spread across Grey's face. 'I couldn't say that was the case before, but now you mention it, there *is* something you could help me with in return.'

'Of course there is. What is it?'

'I think if you tuck your little lightbulb under your fingers and walked through the Redwoods following the signs for Oakpass Manor, we could find a nice little arrangement for ourselves. You uncover the truth of what the Ghoul Council thinks I am harbouring up there – besides you – and I'll help you solve your murder. Deal?'

'Deal.'

Theodore paused.

'There's just something I need to do first.'

NINE

They'd been here before.

Although the Undetectables had visited the Larix several times since the Whistler killed their friend Ben in the basement, Mallory hadn't been back at night since, and she had the strangest sense of déjà vu.

Sandi had gone on ahead, ushered in by a stressed-looking faerie, and Remington had nodded to them, his arm around Sandi, as they were swallowed up by the neon glow within.

Mallory rubbed her eyes, feeling massively underdressed, conflicted at leaving Sully and Dr Ray in their grief for a night of revelry. Hayley Eason was dead. There was a killer at large again. Instead of throwing everything into solving a murder, Mallory was at the club.

Her phone buzzed in her pocket and her brow furrowed at the newest notification – a breaking news bulletin that had just aired.

She hit play, turning the screen so Diana could read the subtitles.

'—reports that Detective Chief Inspector Nathan Tate, head of the Wrackton police force, has today issued a reward for the whereabouts of the Notorious Theodore Wyatt. Mr Wyatt, who is a Samhain ghost, is now additionally wanted in connection with a murder that took place in the early hours of this morning. Further details will be released in due course. Citizens are advised that he is dangerous and must not be approached. A dedicated hotline—'

'They think Theodore killed Hayley,' Mallory said, staring at her screen until it faded to black.

'I suppose it's possible,' Diana said. 'Not to agree with Nathan fucking Tate on anything, but it would track. Theodore said he's the Wrackton Digger, and we couldn't get him to confirm he *didn't* kill the people he later dug up. Why not murder in a different way? Let's face it, Mallory. We don't know him at all. We never did. Whatever we thought he was – friend, mentor, colleague, trustworthy... all of that was a lie. This could be more of the same.'

'But why? What would make him murder in exactly the same manner as the Whistler case – and to what end? Jacob's goal with the Whistler murders was to join the Ternion. Theodore hardly wants that. And why would he go to all that trouble, then burn Hayley's body? I'm not seeing the motive.'

The troll bouncer on the door glanced at them, but said nothing.

'Why did Theodore do *anything*? Why did he dig up those bodies, and run away, and why has he been acting weird for years at this stage? And most importantly, why did he leave you thinking you'd brought him back wrong?' Cornelia's tone was unusually uncombative, like they didn't actually want answers to those questions.

But something akin to determination was flowing through Mallory, alongside the earthquake-shake of the bass beneath her feet. She thought of Dr Ray and Sully's faces. Of the fact that in just under two days, there'd be no more Undetectables, no more Broadwicks, no more Wrackton as the epicentre of Occulture. The world would change in a slow, inevitable chain reaction, and Mallory had a sinking feeling it would not be for the better.

'I don't know! I don't understand anything Theodore was doing. But I *do* know that he helped us with our research. He helped me with my machines. We have no evidence to suggest that, up until the Digger case, he was doing anything *but* helping.'

'Tate picking Theodore as a target does have an unmistakable bang of "we have no other leads, so let's blame him",' Diana said fairly. 'It's exactly the sort of thing you'd do if you were being given a second chance at the whole head of police thing. We can figure all of this out.'

'I can call the taxi back—'

'Tomorrow,' Diana continued gently. 'Tonight, let's just have some fun. I want… I want Taylor to have this memory with me. With us.'

Mallory closed her eyes. It was an inarguable point.

'Later,' Cornelia agreed.

There was no later. But Mallory nodded, and followed her friends into the Larix, letting herself get swallowed up in the wall of noise and comforting darkness.

'I thought Sandi said this was a tarot night?' Mallory shouted as they entered the main room of the Larix.

The stage was draped in black velvet, a table covered in shiny metallic fabric in the centre of the stage, a gossamer curtain obscuring one of the chairs, leaving a grandiose throne on display. A projector screen screamed *LET US READ YOU* and *TAROT TIME WITH SANDI CLEMENTINE* and *VISIT WRACKTON* in rolling ornate font.

'Oh shit,' Cornelia said, and made a beeline for a faerie holding several stacks of cards in front of the stage, grabbing him into a hug.

Langdon Ericsson looked up once they released him, saw Mallory, and smiled. Diana had promptly disappeared – presumably to find Taylor, who had texted her no fewer than a hundred times – and Mallory allowed herself to be hugged by her friend.

'I didn't know you—'

'Did readings?

'Gotta do something when we're home from tour, or I'll go stir-crazy.'

'You're in a band?' Remington asked, appearing beside Mallory. He had lowered his sunglasses and was appraising Langdon in a manner that was not befitting of the fiancé of Sandi Clementine.

Langdon grinned and launched into an explanation of Crown and Hemlock, the band he, Felix and Kingston were in – 'they should be around here somewhere, you'll love them' – and Mallory felt a sort of second-hand flip in her stomach at how easy it was for some people to just... connect.

She looked at Cornelia as Langdon and Remington chatted – flirted, really, but Mallory was staying out of it – letting the lights and sounds and noise wash over her, fading away so it was just her and Cornelia and the memory of Cornelia's mouth on hers, their hands on her hips, how easy it had been to let it happen. How easy it would be to do it again.

How easy it would be to ask to do it now.

She raised a hand to tap Cornelia lightly on the arm. Uncertain, stumbling words formed on her lips. She'd ask Cornelia to come to a quieter spot of the Larix where they could be alone. Maybe, if they seemed amenable, she'd put a hand on their cheek, tilt their face up towards hers. Wrap her other arm around their waist. And if Cornelia didn't want it, Mallory could simply melt into the shadows of the Larix, head home and pretend it never happened.

'Cornelia—'

The music changed. The house lights dipped, and the room erupted with cheers.

Sandi clambered on stage with a silver megaphone, dressed in a black, sparkling gown and a hooded cloak.

'THE NECROMANCER IS IN. I'M SANDI CLEMENTINE, AND I DECLARE IT TAROT TIME!'

Mallory had limited experience of tarot – she and her friends had done readings for each other, and she'd been aware of the existence of private reading booths and parlours and the general interest it held in Apparent circles, but this was not quite what she'd envisioned.

The crowd swelled around the stage as a live faerie quartet played over a dance beat. Langdon shuffled and pulled cards for guests who filled the shrouded chair one by one, as Sandi offered laconic commentary. The projector screen behind him showed the cards as he worked – a beautiful deck with drawings that related to Morrigan, Hecate and the Ternion (a Blair-themed card made Mallory's stomach do an unexpected flip. If only everyone knew she had a Ternion goddess in a bunker) that must've been specially commissioned for the *Visit Wrackton* campaign. The participants were unmic'd, so even right in front of the stage, Mallory could only hear Langdon repeat their questions.

'I'm getting in on this,' Diana said in Mallory's ear, and she and Taylor bolted towards the stage, where the same faerie who had ushered Sandi into the building shepherded Diana around to the side of the stage.

'What do the next forty-eight hours have in store for you?' Langdon said, repeating Diana's question, and Mallory suppressed a sad smile. He pulled Diana's first card.

'The Moon,' he said, holding it up. The crowd howled.

'Things are *very* uncertain,' Sandi said ominously.

'That's right,' Langdon said, clearly getting into the whole thing. He had a natural showmanship. 'You're on a dark path, things don't feel clear to you. But this card—' He pulled the next one. 'Wheel of Fortune.'

A leer broke across the crowd. Someone gently touched Mallory's shoulder and she turned to see Felix and Kingston, the latter of who was looking at her with an amount of concern that was beginning to make *her* feel concerned.

'WHEEL OF FORTUNE! WHEEL OF FORTUNE!' the crowd chanted.

'I fear things are about to turn full circle,' Langdon said finally, flipping over the last card. 'I fear you are in for a betrayal.'

'Betrayal. Betrayal. Betrayal,' Sandi whispered, her voice distorting in the megaphone.

'And I fear it's someone close to you. Three of Cups reversed. This suggests the next forty-eight hours will be fraught. Someone you know may be out to get you. Maybe someone in this very room.'

The crowd leered as Diana stepped away and Langdon did another, vaguer reading for an obvious Apparent who wanted to know if her boyfriend was ever going to propose, and one for someone who wanted to know if they'd ever finish writing a book.

Mallory barely heard anything else that was said. Diana and Taylor whispered in a corner together, and Mallory's skin prickled, worried, her head full of the hunt for Theodore. She caught Cornelia's eye, but didn't get the sense Cornelia was particularly concerned about it, either.

Her own opinions on the lack of scientific explanation behind tarot aside, tarot readings were a big part of Occulture, and, well… they had to mean *something.*

Despite the questions being less exciting, Langdon and Sandi kept the energy up for an hour until they took a short break, the quartet seamlessly intensifying as the house lights came up halfway.

The crowd dispersed and Diana materialised beside her, making a beeline for the bar. Mallory followed, though she had little choice in the matter as Diana had her hand in a vice-like grip. Diana dipped and weaved until she was in the eyeline of the bartender, and Mallory hung back, watching for Cornelia following through the crowd. She wished she'd been able to grab their hand, too.

She found an empty table and hovered beside it, her mind full of betrayal, full circle. Langdon *couldn't* know Hayley Eason had been found with Whistler carvings in her stomach, that the Undetectables were nursing a sense of déjà vu over just how full-circle things were feeling. And if Langdon had seen the news bulletin about Theodore, he wouldn't have put Diana on the spot about betrayal like that. If she was being honest with herself, she had so many doubts about Theodore that warred with her implicit belief that he was fundamentally good. If she was being utterly honest with herself, she did not want Theodore to be responsible. She did not want to think he'd killed anyone, that he was out there murdering people again.

A movement to her right caught her attention and she spotted Remington – sunglasses still firmly on – slip away from Sandi, weaving through the crowd on the phone, arguing with someone.

'—obviously don't want to be here. But how else do you expect me to put myself on the map? Nobody even knows I'm— Don't say *one of them* like that, only *I* get to say it like that. Magical *bollocks*.'

When Mallory looked back, Sandi was gone, and she felt guilty at the sense of relief that flooded through her. Sandi was great, but was not how she wanted to spend the last forty-odd hours of her life.

'Oh, and here's our fucking stalker again. Laters,' Remington said, and hung up, weaving his way through the crowd.

Mallory turned to see Sam Bridewell by the wall, his camera in his hands, not even bothering to hide that he'd been photographing Remington and Sandi.

She considered approaching him, asking him again what he'd seen at the Observatory – how he'd known there was something to see, if he was following Sandi and Remington around Wrackton. A camera provided a good cover for a multitude of sins...

Just as she was pondering this, Diana arrived back with Cornelia, Taylor and an armful of drinks in tow.

'Sorry we were gone so long, I realised there were things on the menu I'd *never* tried, can you believe that?' Diana handed Mallory a tall glass of something violently yellow that she insisted was called 'Honey Bee's Knees'.

'Sam Bridewell is here,' Mallory said into Diana's good ear. 'It looks like he's following Sandi and Remington around town. I'm wondering how he ended up at the Observatory right when a murder happened, before it was even on official channels?' Diana repeated it for Taylor, who repeated it to Cornelia, who said, 'Where?'

Mallory gestured, but Sam had vanished.

'THE READINGS WILL RECOMMENCE IN THREE MINUTES,' a pre-recorded voice boomed over the Larix's PA.

The lights flashed twice, the quartet simmering down into something anticipatory again. Mallory felt her heart racing. She was having a good time. This was okay. Her pain levels were low-ish. It was worth being here to see Taylor smile adoringly at Diana, to see Cornelia look like they were, for once, unafraid to be outside. It was worth it to feel like she was giving herself a good send-off, even if it felt dream-like and impossible.

And then, like a recurring nightmare Mallory could not shake, the screaming started.

VIVISECTION II

Samhain, eight years ago

We return to the night it all began.

Back to the miniature Broadwick Mansion, where the ballroom scene plays out in earnest.

Watch as a miniature Theodore Wyatt is approached by an equally-diminutive Grey Quinn – utterly intoxicated, barely able to stand.

Grey Quinn is attempting a flirtation that, in reality, did not go as smoothly as he believes, his actions less sweet, more mocking than he had imagined.

But there was, ultimately, a *reason* he was drawn to our Apparent scientist. A *reason* he approached him. At a loss for what that reason was, so far gone he could not recall, his mind filled in the blanks. Attraction was the reason he accepted most readily. Flirting was the obvious move.

But there remained a deeper motivation. Something he was meant to give Theodore (not a good time; make no mistake, Grey Quinn was known for his forwardness, but not at parties full of Wrackton's elite. He played the game well. There were few beds he had not found his way into, and fewer still who did not now owe him a favour. Rather, it was something he was meant to relinquish control over.)

Pass the baton. His only instruction.

But Grey did not perform as expected that night. Instead, we watch as he finds a pen in his pocket, and draws cat whiskers on Theodore's face.

He's gentle; the movements are delicate, Theodore is too consumed by horror and indignation to see it. He takes the pair of cat ears that had been foisted upon him by a passing witch (who had not, much to his amusement, seemed to notice he was gay), and discovers they make an excellent makeshift costume for Theodore. We can't see his thoughts, but know Grey had considered Theodore to be sort of *sweet*. Standing there, accepting the costume good-naturedly. He was sure Theodore was laughing along. Apparent–Occult relations in full swing. He was sure, dimly, mockingly, that Vincent Van Doren would be proud.

Fact the first: the 'baton' was something physical. An object.

We already knew this.

Fact the second: Quinn utterly failed this task.

Instead, he goes looking for a bathroom shortly after this interaction, stomach churning, skin on the back of his neck prickling with anxious sweat. He doesn't make it. We see him push past Van Doren and Ezra Broadwick, who are deep in hurried, pressured conversation. He does not notice either of them looking up to notice his stumbling. He ignores Imogen Broadwick, who places both a kind and warning hand on his arm and asks him if he is okay. We see him dip behind a red velvet curtain just in time to empty his stomach contents onto the highly polished ballroom floor.

We see the lights go out.

And I can tell you that, by this point, the object is no longer in his pocket.

I can also tell you that later he will find himself in a taxi, and the urgency of handing an object to Theodore Wyatt had evaporated. Any memory of the necessity of doing so had utterly deserted him, and Grey Quinn neither knew nor was curious about the specifics of Theodore Wyatt's death until, over six years later, he saw for himself the cat-eared ghost, and his mind granted him a dim recollection of a jovial exchange.

His path would cross with Theodore's again and again, but this is where his involvement in the murder ends. He was a piece that did not make the expected moves, forcing a pivot elsewhere.

Three key players remain. One of them is the killer, in the practical sense.

The object – the real murder weapon, in a sense – is already known. Always has been.

But what does it mean? What does it tell us?

All in good time.

TEN

Mallory often had nightmares where she woke to the sound of someone screaming. It was a specific kind of scream – one audible over loud, thumping music. A scream that changed her life two years ago (though she'd accepted that change had been coming long before she'd opened the letter inviting the Undetectables to take on the Whistler case).

But the thing about nightmares is that you usually wake up from them. No matter how real they feel, how long they linger, your eyes snap open to weak sunlight streaming through the window as confirmation: here endeth that particular unpleasantness.

This was not a dream.

The lights went out and the quartet stopped, leaving a thumping, gothic reverb playing through the Larix speakers as the backing track for someone screaming and screaming and screaming. Mallory moved towards it, her body reacting where her mind had not. Diana snapped out of her horror first, grabbing Cornelia and Mallory by the arms and forcing her way through the crowd until they got to the stairs to the Larix basement.

This, too, had happened before.

'Everyone stay here!' Diana called, gesturing for a troll bouncer to stand in front of the stairs, an action that would hold back curious folk for approximately thirty seconds.

They ran down as quickly as Mallory could manage and found Sandi on her knees, the scream pouring out of her practically choral in how she was sustaining it, how loud it was. It was pitch dark, every light out but the witchlight emergency exit signs over a black painted door Mallory had never been through, but supposed led to some sort of sub-basement.

Sandi, her face bathed in the red glow of Diana's witchlight, paused screaming just long enough to wail 'He's *GONE*!'

'Who? Who's gone?'

'The… the ghost. I saw the Samhain' – pronounced *Sam Hane*, for reasons Mallory could not begin to unpick – 'ghost.' Sandi's eyes were wide. Terrified.

Mallory's stomach dropped. 'Where?'

Sandi raised one shaking finger, pointing into the closest storage antechamber.

Diana summoned Mallory's kitbag as Cornelia hit the light switch nearest to them, but nothing happened. 'Fuse must be gone.'

The Undetectables moved as one, holding witchlights high as they rounded a stack of boxes.

The chamber was full of haphazardly stacked cardboard boxes, a drinks fridge that had gone dark, condensation building on the glass front, and nothing else.

Nothing but an envelope on the ground, with *Undetectables* written on it, lovingly placed beneath an extinguished witchlight.

'Sandi?' Remington shouted, clattering down the stairs. 'Are you okay, love?'

Sandi's knees gave way and she collapsed in a heap on the floor. Remington caught her after she fell, and knelt beside her.

'What's happened?'

'I saw SAM HANE!' she shouted. 'The ghost they want! He was so... so big. The *ears.* He had so many legs, Remmy. So scary. So... spooky. None of my necromancy magic worked on him, he just looked at me.'

'So many legs?' Cornelia asked, but Sandi raised a hand to cover her face, shaking her head.

'No,' she moaned. 'I can't... I can't explain further.'

'Is this some sort of joke?' Remington demanded. 'Like a Halloween thing, scare the Apparents?'

'We joke about many things,' Mallory said firmly. 'But Occulture takes ghosts very seriously.'

More footsteps clattered down the stairs as Felix, Langdon and Kingston pushed their way through, faeries and trolls and Apparents all peering down the stairs.

'What's going on?'

'THERE WAS AN INTRUDER!' Sandi wailed.

'Everyone stay back,' Mallory said grimly. 'This is a crime scene.'

'We think,' Cornelia added.

'We need to call the police,' Remington said.

'No,' Felix and Langdon said sharply.

'Why not?' Remington got to his feet. 'Surely you're not suggesting you're... *lawless*?'

'I'd rather this lot than the police. Fuck, my uncles are going to kill me,' Langdon groaned. 'I promised there'd be no hassle.'

Langdon's uncles were, possibly, kingpins of an underground faerie-troll mafia, and Mallory had steadfastly looked the other way. The Larix was, in some ways, a front for the other business, but they genuinely seemed to like the place. Faeries and police just didn't mix.

'Give us five minutes,' Cornelia said.

'What on earth could you do that the police couldn't?' Remington demanded.

'Everything,' Diana said, at the same time Mallory said, 'We're Wrackton's foremost magical private investigators.'

'You ARE?' Sandi gasped, wailing forgotten. 'Oh, *wow.* I had no idea!'

'Stay here,' Cornelia commanded. 'Don't move. Don't touch anything.'

There wasn't much of a scene to process, and so Diana took photos once more while Mallory examined the perimeter of the scene. She wanted to touch the envelope, the witchlight. See what any of it meant.

'Do we think Theodore has been here?'

'Apart from the fuckarse description of him having too many legs, whatever that means – the electricity is off, and a witness insists she saw something.'

'Photos taken. Go for it,' Diana said, and Mallory pounced

on the envelope. She carefully tore it open. Figures and letters wriggled across the single page within, taunting her with its obvious magical code.

Without having to ask, Cornelia was at her elbow, a sound beetle in their hand. It glowed green and chirped as soon as its tiny tarsi touched the paper. Like living litmus tests, they changed colour and made a sound in the presence of a magic trace. Mallory would for ever – until tomorrow – be grateful for Cornelia's insect discoveries.

'I can decode that,' Cornelia said, and did. 'Basically the easiest code there is.'

The letters wiggled into the correct order.

Q1. WHY DID THEODORE WYATT DIE?

A. TO GET TO THE OTHER SIDE

Q2. WHY?

A. ????

Mallory flipped the paper over, revealing more lines.

(HINT: Find the answer, stop the apocalypse)

Tick tock!

See you soon

'I do not like this,' Mallory said. 'I do not like this one bit.'

Her heart would not believe Theodore would make a mockery of the Whistler murders like this.

'Are we *sure* Theodore was here?' she asked. 'This is typed. He can't type, it would explode in his hands. Unless it's a mechanical typewriter. In which case, he can. But where would he get one of those?'

'Only one way to find out.' Cornelia produced a box from Hexana-knows where and opened it.

Diana shrieked. 'Cornelia, what the *fuck* is that?'

Cornelia frowned. 'The Lyrefly hybrid I told you about?'

'First of all, you *didn't* tell us about these, you were infuriatingly smug and evasive about it. Second of all, *that's* not a Lyrefly. Lyreflies are small and kind of goofy-looking beetle fly things. *That* looks like it's being actively eaten by a massive, fuck-off spider!'

'Don't be silly,' Cornelia said scornfully. 'Lyreflies will reproduce with *Portia malus ferro*. Quite readily, in fact. The offspring are like mules in that they can't reproduce, and not all of them have Lyrefly-like abilities, but the spiders lend them a longer lifespan and they've so far taken on spider-like properties. It's quite interesting, actually.'

Mallory blinked. All this time, she'd thought Cornelia had been on a non-stop bender, but instead they'd been working on something hugely useful and potentially revolutionary for forensic entomology.

'And how did you make that disgusting discovery? "*Does the Lyrefly fuck?*" is an interesting research topic to dedicate the last few months of your life to,' Diana retorted.

'It *is* interesting! It turns out the poison from steel silk spiders is essentially pheromones to the Lyrefly—'

'Spiders are venomous, actually,' Kingston said. 'Sorry.'

'No, no, you're right.' Cornelia pushed their glasses up their nose. 'Just in the case of *Portia malus ferro*, the *silk* is poisonous if ingested. It's got a very low pH, so it's also corrosive. They themselves don't contain any venom. Easy mistake to make.'

They scooped the monstrosity out of the box and Mallory got a good, unfortunate look at it: a spider with wings, its bulbous back ruby-red and shiny. Without another word, Cornelia released it, and it went straight for the letter, wings twitching.

Mallory's skin crawled.

There were the sounds of camera clicks on the stairs and Diana's expression turned mutinous, clapping her hands for attention. 'Okay, seriously. Everyone out. Could one of the faeries also please call the Night Mayor—'

'I'll do it, when we're done here,' Mallory said.

They lingered until they heard sirens approaching, then ran to join everyone up in the bar. Langdon had managed to get the houselights back on, and was trying to slowly siphon faeries and trolls out the side door when the sirens resulted in a mass exodus, leaving Sandi and Remington, the Undetectables, and their friends.

And one Sam Bridewell, making his way to the exit.

'Keep an eye on Remington and Sandi,' Mallory said, and Diana and Taylor scampered over to talk to them.

Cornelia ran ahead to intercept Sam, and he turned at the touch on his elbow just as Mallory reached him.

'Hello again. Fancy seeing you here,' Mallory said coolly.

'Ah, hello. Thought I'd come check out the local culture a bit,' Sam said.

'Did you see anything interesting at the Observatory after we left?' Cornelia asked idly.

Sam's brow furrowed in confusion, then he shook his head.

'Load of police standing around. They hadn't even brought the body out by the time I left.'

'What time did you get there, would you say?' Cornelia continued.

He checked his watch, frowning. 'Not sure. Why?'

'Just wondering what you saw, or didn't see.'

'I heard there were a number of tourist events going on in Wrackton this weekend. I knew Sandi and Remington were in town, and I wanted to get some candids of them doing touristy things. Photos nobody else would have, that I could sell. I have a contact sitting on a big story about them, so just waiting for the right time.'

Mallory couldn't control the vague look of disgust that came over her.

'They call us to come to these places themselves, most of the time,' Sam said quickly. 'I know how it sounds, but someone close to Sandi asked me to come, make sure I photographed the pair of them. I was planning on coming anyway – my mother was a witch, which I guess makes me… half Occult?'

'It does, yes,' Cornelia said. 'Congratulations. Welcome to the family.'

'Thanks,' Sam beamed, completely missing the flat delivery. His brow furrowed. 'Oh hey, I don't know if this is relevant, but last night I was asked—'

The side doors to the Larix were thrown open and Nathan Tate swept in with uniformed police in tow. He took in the scene, and the people in it, his gaze uncomfortably shifting over Mallory, Cornelia and Diana in turn.

His team pointlessly asked the calmly gathered crowd

to stay calm, and after a bouncer pointed to the stairs, they clattered down, crime scene investigators in full overalls close behind.

'What were you saying?' Mallory began politely, but there was a shout, and a loud bang, and an alarm screamed.

'FIRE!'

The crowd scattered, running for the exits. The Undetectables didn't need to be told twice to leave, Taylor holding Diana's hand for dear life as they spilled out into the cool night air.

'Time really is a flat circle,' Cornelia said, as Mallory eased herself onto the sofa, her arms still locked around her kitbag.

'We should run the samples,' Mallory said, her head swimming, the uncomfortable reminder of Diana's tarot card reading floating into her head. 'Somehow. Maybe we can figure out a way to—'

'In the morning,' Diana said firmly. Taylor had fallen asleep standing up, head tucked against Diana's shoulder. 'We can spare a few hours.'

'She's right, you know,' Cornelia said gently. 'And I don't say that lightly. Rest now, science later.'

There was barely a 'later' to science in, but Mallory's body demanded rest, and she relented. 'Eight a.m. latest,' she said, and just about made it up to bed before crashing completely.

ELEVEN

Theodore stashed a bag in the hollow of a tree and took a moment to collect his thoughts. These were largely that, if he was human, he'd be panting and sweating and everyone would know that he had something to hide.

Grey was expecting him to arrive any minute, the instruction of 'first light' something Theodore had been playing very cavalier with. It wasn't *entirely* his fault – he'd had to spend way longer at the Larix than he'd wanted to. First, he'd been afraid of breaking the Larix sound system with his presence too soon and giving the game away – not that he'd *wanted* to break anything, it was just an unfortunate side effect of existing in a semi-corporeal Samhain ghost state – and then someone had, inexplicably, called the police. Then he'd had to wait around even longer to make sure he'd finished the job, though he doubted the Voice would say he'd done it well. (In a way, he hadn't done it at all.)

Then he'd waited even longer still, just in case. He couldn't quite say what he'd been waiting for. (For Mallory to understand.

For Mallory to see what he was doing and make everyone else understand. To feel the relief he was chasing. To know there was a life worth living on the other side of all of this.)

'Okay, Theodore. Teddy, old boy. You need to do this cleverly. Inconspicuously. Intelligently. All your main values,' Theodore said to himself, ambling towards the border between Oughteron and Wrackton, lightbulb clutched in his hand and that hand tucked into his pocket – nonchalantly, of course – and swaying casually as he walked in case anyone saw him, despite there being nobody around.

And it made him feel better.

'Okay, let's think. Think aloud. Think, think, think. It takes me an hour to walk there, even at my fastest pace. Grey REFUSED to set me up a witchlight without me having visited first, as if I would break something by erroneously transporting myself into the toilet or wherever, so on foot it must be. It's fine! Everything is perfectly fine. I'll tell him I stopped for ice cream. No, that won't work. I'll tell him I had a bassoon recital. That'll only hold if he doesn't ask what a bassoon *is*. I'll tell him I got caught up at work. Or somewhere. Obviously by the time I'm at Oakpass Manor, I will have thought of the perfect excuse for my whereabouts. An alibi, as it were. One my only living ally in the entirety of Wrackton will readily believe.'

Theodore walked, the satisfying autumnal crackle of trees and leaves rustling as he passed, until his mind conjured a most horrifying thought – one so horrifying, he couldn't be sure it hadn't come from the Voice.

Why don't you tell Grey the truth?

'This is obviously an impulsive thought. No, intrusive.

No, the— The one where you get a thought you don't want to act on. Because that's *ridiculous.* Even if I *could* explain any of this. Even if I fully comprehended what was occurring here, inside my own head, and also out there in Wrackton at large, why would I go and blurt the truth out to *Grey*, of all people? Ha ha! Ho ho! Imagine just walking up to Grey Quinn and telling him to his objectively not-unattractive face that I, Theodore Wyatt, Notorious and Most Wanted, have the voice of— OUCH.'

There was an audible *WHUMP* as he felt himself flicker, splintering momentarily like someone had slammed him against a brick wall.

'*Stop*,' Terror Voice said simply, the words crackling around him like Theodore was inside a very dark, echoing tunnel. He waited for his vision to clear, for Terror Voice to disappear again, and shook his head violently.

'And evidently I can't, because of whatever the hell that was.'

He was unsuitably excuseless by the time he strode through the gates of Oakpass Manor. He'd seen it in scale the year before, when Diana had brought home an astounding miniature crafted by mother of forensic science Francine Leon's very hands, and he permitted himself a generous five minutes of marvelling at its life-size counterpart.

He marvelled at the way ivy tried to choke the life out of the window frames, the way the black stone walls were lit in an eerie green. He spared a marvellous second to notice half the building was covered in scaffolding, dark construction tarp fluttering in the breeze. He took a deep, marvelling breath, imagining he could smell the open air – or perhaps the scent of old history – but the night gave him nothing. If he didn't have a scent memory for it, he couldn't recall it in his semi-corporeal state.

He concluded marvelling by noticing multiple parked cars outside the manor – one belonging to Grey (that he was forbidden to be closer than forty paces to) and two he didn't recognise.

Perhaps there really was a meeting.

Singing his invisibility song softly to himself, he walked through the walls and followed the sounds of voices to the dining room. Grey was lounging at the table, loosely clutching a champagne glass, while a short, beautiful person with immaculately groomed facial hair sat on his left, and a tall, dark-haired woman who reminded Theodore of Mallory if she was older on his right.

'You have to admit, Nova, that this entire thing feels underhanded because it *is*,' Grey said.

Theodore knew that name. Nova Khan, the new acting head of the Ghoul Council.

Nova picked at the stem of their glass. 'Any underhandedness is a direct result of your refusal to engage with us. The terms of purchase of this property included allowing investigations by the Ghoul Council—'

'Should you deem them necessary, appropriate, *and* such notifications of intent were lodged before we broke ground on renovations. You did not do that, yet I *still* complied with the original investigation into the Larkins family's remains. I let you come in here and dig up anything you wanted, I did not complain, I did not interfere. It's been well over a year since that – eighteen months. Every *single second* of that time, I have been haemorrhaging money on this investment.'

'Which we understand. Should the Council make any findings relevant to Council proceedings, we will reimburse you partial costs,' the woman said.

Grey turned to her. 'What *happened* to you, Olivia?'

Olivia Reid, Theodore realised. The more he looked the more she reminded him of Mallory – tallness and dark hair aside, she had a quietly bright gaze that seemed to take in everything, cogs turning behind her eyes. He'd heard all about Reid and Khan taking over the Ghoul Council from Grey – largely that the pair of them were by the book in a manner that everyone found even more tedious than the Broadwicks. If 'everyone' meant 'Grey and people like him', which Theodore supposed it did.

He drifted closer, hoping someone would bring up the Broadwicks. He'd dug up bodies and they'd disappeared from Occult society; it wasn't something he'd readily admit to Grey, but a tiny selfish part of him wondered if they'd quit the Ghoul Council because of him. Notorious Theodore Wyatt, the scandal that rocked Broadwick Mansion basement. The alleged killer on the loose.

'As you are aware, the Ghoul Council originally wanted to purchase Oakpass Manor and we were in an informal agreement to do so before you… acquired it,' Olivia continued, ignoring the question.

'For sentimental reasons, yes,' Grey said, touching a finger to his ubiquitous pocket watch. Theodore wondered if he knew he'd done it.

'Understood, of course. But that was then. We don't *want* things to come down to a compulsory purchase order, and we can avoid that with your cooperation. A former member of the Council compiled some evidence before her death—'

'Dorothy, wasn't it?'

'We're not at liberty to divulge that information,' Nova cut in smoothly. 'All we can say at this point is that there is quite evidently a link between Wrackton, the Ternion, and Oakpass Manor – a deeper link than we previously thought possible.'

'And one that could save a number of people's lives, to be perfectly frank,' Olivia added.

Theodore had to place a hand over his own mouth to prevent himself saying, 'But I thought your name was perfectly Olivia' out loud.

'Strange that this is just coming up now,' Grey said, his expression unreadable. 'I've chatted to the Broadwicks recently. Strange they left when they did.'

Sometimes he switched back into hotelier mode, his movements dangerously controlled, his expressions smug, and Theodore wanted to punch him again.

'Is it?' Nova reached to refill their glass from a violently orange pitcher on the table – Grey was fond of a citrus-based cocktail, and Theodore strongly suspected mimosas.

Olivia hadn't touched hers, likely on account of it being barely eight a.m.

If anyone asked – which they wouldn't – Theodore would say that one of the most fascinating parts of being a ghost was that hiding in awkward places to eavesdrop only became uncomfortable if he thought about it. It was amazing what the brain would and wouldn't allow the body to do when it came to boredom, and listening quietly was boring. Feeling an impending Category Five Ghost Reveal, he spotted a strange-shaped vase in the corner of the room – probably ancient, probably worth squillions and almost certainly meant to be in a museum in its country of origin – and crouched down inside it, hoping if he did spark static that he neither cracked the delicate, patterned ceramic, nor drew attention to himself.

'*I think you should go to the chamber now. Leave this nonsense.*'

A terrible feeling of dread overwhelmed him at the unexpected sound of Terror Voice. It was a feeling that only got worse as Terror Voice was suddenly *there* with him, present in his reality instead of off doing untold hideous, evil things.

Theodore was quite sick of the dichotomy of his existence – lonely in his endless waking hours, but craving solitude from the person that sought to plague him with its malignant thoughts whenever it so desired.

(Even if it wasn't a person anymore, in the strictest sense.)

'What chamber?' Theodore whispered, as quietly as he could manage. He was sure that he could talk to Terror Voice *inside* his head as it did to him, but he was afraid of thinking the wrong thing at the wrong time, or giving it access to his every complicated thought. Nobody wanted that less than Theodore.

'*You know how it works. You know how to find it. The bunkers are everywhere. There's one here, one there, one anywhere you look. A network, ready-built for us. Elder and oak, willow and red. Larch the fifth...'* Terror Voice sang, a tenor that reverberated through Theodore with a bass rumble, and Theodore's entire body felt like it was on fire with horror.

'*Go now. Go. Now,*' Terror Voice commanded, and Theodore shook his head violently.

The meeting conversation had changed direction. Nova was sidestepping Grey's probing questions about the Broadwicks, and Theodore fought to keep listening as Terror Voice got louder and louder, filling his head until there was little room to use any of his senses.

'—back to Wrackton, for a final ball.'

'*Final?* Rather morbid,' Grey said. Nova and Olivia stilled, and Grey set his glass down. 'Surely not.'

'We aren't at liberty to say,' Olivia said.

'Surely they mentioned it, in your recent "chat"?' Nova said, in a voice that said they didn't believe half of what Grey said. (Fair, in Theodore's opinion.)

'What is it? Illness? Can't be both of them, surely. Unless they're terribly unlucky.'

'*Now,*' Terror Voice said again, tipping back into an Annoying Voice whine as Theodore kept shoving back, forcing his attention to the conversation, waiting for his name to be said. He needed to know. He needed answers.

'The Broadwicks are old friends, I am sure they wouldn't mind—'

'They were Besieged five months ago,' Olivia said shortly. 'I'm afraid the Curse concludes tomorrow night. Hexana's mark is in play. That's why they've stepped down.'

'Olivia, this is against protocol—' Nova protested.

'If they weren't trying to find a cure, they'd be here instead of either of us having this argument with Mr Quinn,' Olivia said firmly. 'We can't keep hiding the truth. It is not in our interests. And now Grey understands our interest in Oakpass Manor, and why we want to act on the information we have. We want to save the Broadwicks' lives, and the lives of the other affected civilians.'

Theodore's head spun, tuning back out, Terror Voice a frightening force that pushed and pushed and made his hands twitch and his body flicker, static spraying from him, blue light building somewhere in his chest and none of it important as his swirling thoughts.

If Ezra and Imogen – his once-hosts, his once-landlords, two people he did not particularly like – were Besieged, and it had happened five months ago, that meant it lined up with the Wickermere Reaper case, which meant that three quarters of the Undetectables—

Theodore mouthed *no* as softly as he could, only to discover he hadn't quite whispered so much as bellowed the word at the top of his once-lungs.

Nova, mid-sentence, fell silent.

'What was that?'

Grey stood up. 'Speaker in the wall. As my renovations are incomplete, I've had to resort to letting Apparents do haunted property tours, graciously yet poorly funded by the *Visit Wrackton* campaign.'

Nova raised an eyebrow while Theodore pushed himself back through the wall, unable to see if they were buying Grey's pathetic excuse.

Mallory Diana Cornelia Mallory Diana Cornelia Mallory Mallory MALLORY

A sob crawled up his throat. It was the memory of one, really, rather than any actual tears. (The last time he'd been able to cry was when the permanent tear tracks on his face appeared, and he generally didn't like to think about that.)

'*Now*,' Terror Voice said, either oblivious or unfeeling towards the horror spiralling through Theodore as he stood in the foyer of Oakpass Manor.

Or else Terror Voice really couldn't feel what he felt.

Swallowing in an entirely performative manner, he looked around to get his bearings among the marble pillars, knowing which parts of the manor he had to touch to get the floor to open. To get to the chamber.

Elder and oak, willow and red. Larch the fifth and buried again.

As he spun around, stalling, the dining room door opened. Nova and Olivia filed out, exchanging glances, but holding their silence.

Old friends, then. Allies. Theodore missed having those. (They were going to die.) All he had was Grey, and he wasn't entirely sure what to make of him (his friends would cease to exist for ever).

The front doors slammed shut behind them and Grey pivoted in the foyer.

'Where are you?' he asked flatly. 'And why did you feel the need to shout in the middle of my meeting with the fucking Ghoul Council, and what took you so fucking long to get here? I wanted to get you in a good position to listen, maybe feel around in Olivia's head for me.'

He could tell Grey this much. He could tell him his friends were dying and nothing else mattered. That everything he was doing was rendered worthless, because he'd assumed at the end of it all, he'd be able to win back their forgiveness. That he could look Mallory in the eye and make her understand what was at stake.

'I got some bad news,' Theodore said sullenly. 'They've discontinued my favourite newspaper. Had to process this, hence my delay.'

'Tremendously sorry for your loss,' Grey said. 'The Broadwicks are dying and whatever information old Dorothy had for them *has* to be about the Ternion. I was right. Do you understand what this means? Either I hold the items they want to ransom, or I force their hand in buying this place off me. I'll be free of it. I can recover— I can focus on other aspects of my business. Hollis Hadley was *adamant* this was a special place – he's written so much about the Ternion, though in typical Apparent fashion, it's all piecemeal. I always had the sense he was circling something true. Something real. But I could never quite put my finger on it, as though it just floats away from me whenever I try.'

Hollis Hadley *had* been circling something true with his necromantic comics – the *Undead Complex* had a real-life counterpart ritual that was, incredibly, also known as an Undead Complex. It involved combining the souls of two dead people into a large insect for reasons Theodore understood to be a kind of non-traditional necromancy. The Undetectables had had a showdown at this very manor over a year ago to stop an egotistical little man from doing precisely that.

'The Ghoul Council have shown their hand – they want this place, Theodore. They *want* it.' Grey ran a hand over one of the pillars, lost in thought. 'Hollis and I spent many an hour wandering around here before I bought it. I knew it was a mistake, even then, but the things one does for love… I would rarely put myself on the line for someone else. That's not how I survive in this world. And now I'm paying for it, and I don't even have my dear, idiot friend around to make up for it.'

Theodore didn't know what to say to that. He felt like a poor approximation of a stand-in for Hollis Hadley, a man Grey had clearly adored. For a brief, uncomfortable moment, he envied him. At least Hollis got to be properly dead.

'I believe this is what the children call a "situationship",' Theodore said. 'As you were in many situations. What was he like?'

'What?'

'Hollis. You talk about him a lot, but I never knew him, never knew his work' – not adding that the only thing he knew about him was the work the Undetectables did on the TV set of the *Undead Complex* pilot, and the plot had not made much sense to him, even then – 'and I feel if I am to hear many a monologue on the thoughts of this fellow, I should know his mettle.'

Grey dropped his hand and moved to the credenza behind him, rifling through a stack of papers. 'Hollis was a bumbling little fool. That's what I'd first thought of him. You know how it goes, with first impressions.'

Theodore thought he did, but for once he said nothing. He was dimly aware Terror Voice had disappeared, which meant it would only be a matter of time before it renewed its efforts to get him into the very floor Grey was standing on.

'His head was always in the clouds. Always reading something or other, talking incessantly even when nobody was listening. Until I realised that was only how he was around *me.* I had a window into his soul that nobody else had. He made me like my own company. I felt… at ease, around him. Of course, his successes did not make up for the fact he was Apparent, and that he was always going to be on the outside of my world. He didn't get the politics, didn't quite understand my family, my ambitions, the demonic urge to persuade.'

Theodore could picture Grey Quinn at school, with celebrated comic book author-illustrator Hollis Hadley following him around like a nightmare dark academia novel.

'We only fitted together when circumstances allowed. I hurt him, and he hurt me in turn. There were… goddess, there were *years* where we didn't speak and I did whatever I could to make sure I didn't think about him. I think that's when… with you…'

'With me what?'

Grey gestured at his own face, making hand movements suggestive of stroking whiskers. 'I was not myself that night.'

Understatement of the year, in Theodore's opinion.

'Anyway.' Grey rested a hand on the papers. 'They're circling. I trust you heard all of that conversation? By the time you deigned to arrive, I mean.'

'Oh, well. I wouldn't say I heard *all* of it,' Theodore said primly. 'I was visiting your beautiful hotel, on account of suddenly being able to freely travel through space after almost a decade of being trapped in the confines of Wrackton. I can't even say for certain they're sure there's anything of interest here.'

Grey raised an eyebrow. 'They're far more interested in Oakpass Manor now than they were when the Larkins were discovered, even with that whole business with the giant millipede that escaped from the Mayoral Offices, or whatever it was. That was your area of work, was it not?'

Theodore laughed in what he hoped was a casual and aloof manner.

'I know nothing about it. I mean if I think about it a lot – it was quite a while ago – I suppose I recall a... memo, or some such about a giant creature that was probably a centipede and not a millipede.'

'They gave up searching for the centipede after about twenty-four hours.'

'They were shutting down my role at that point,' Theodore said archly. 'I was, as they say, being rendered unnecessary to Mayoral Office operations.'

'Fascinating. Anyway, they've been continuously cock-blocking my attempts at making *any* fucking money from this place, and now it's our turn.'

'"Our"?'

'We have an agreement. I help you, you help me.'

'But there's clearly nothing here,' Theodore said dismissively, pulling his cardigan around himself for comfort from his own lies. He could not tell the truth. He *could not* tell the truth, even if he wanted to.

'*Yes, misdirect. Very good*,' Annoying Voice said, and Theodore shook his head.

'Shut up! I mean, not you. Me, shut up. Sorry. I'm saving you from yourself. There's nothing here. Cut your losses.' *Run*, he added silently. *Run away.*

'But you'll look for me.' It wasn't a question. 'Think of it as a deposit towards the gargantuan PR machine you'll need to rehabilitate your image over the next half-decade. If the wolves stay away from my door, they stay away from ours. Have a gander.' Grey walked to the front doors, throwing them open with a flourish. Weak morning light filtered in. He looked back at Theodore, half his face bathed in green light. 'I'll leave you to it.'

Theodore emerged into a spider-riddled corridor and followed a tunnel into a damp stone chamber that he imagined smelled like death to someone with a normal nose. There was no feeling of coldness, nothing to suggest a single soul was down here with him, just a stained stone plinth with rusty outlines that once held the bodies of the Larkin family. Two more tunnels branched off out of this chamber and he chose with his heart, humming the same tune Annoying Voice had lodged in there months ago. *Elder and oak, willow and red. Larch the fifth and buried again.*

This was oak.

He found himself in an antechamber set up like a living room, though one that had seen better days. Moss and lichen rose up the walls in mottled blooms and smashed glass coated every available surface, glittering in the pale morning light that shone through the open roof through the gaps in the tarp half-heartedly laid over it. He was quite sick of the concept of living rooms. He'd long felt they were named in a discriminatory fashion. If there was going to be a living room, there should be a dying—

He moved to the wall beside him and placed his hands on it, the stone flags slimy and sparking at his touch.

The wall shifted, and opened, revealing another tunnel.

Theodore walked and walked, time stretching and distorting around him, until he came to another wall, where he placed his hands on the dirt. Clods broke away and fell around his feet as he pushed, his mind feeling for the catch, then the barrier fell away, leaving him standing in the middle of a bunker.

A bunker that was not empty. He averted his gaze from the body – the *bodies* in front of him, a small sad pile that made him feel… wrong.

'Oak,' Theodore said definitively, and tensed as he sensed the rattle of movement. 'I know you're there,' he added.

Tiny little peals, almost *clacks*, rattled over the metal floor as something moved around the bunker behind him. Hundreds of them, over and over, as it approached.

Theodore didn't turn around. Not because he was a coward, but because he couldn't bear to face it. It was so much better when the Voice was just inside his head.

'*Look at it*,' Terror Voice said, and Theodore did. He wrenched his gaze back to the sad pile of bodies, letting his eyes lift up and up until the body lying spread-eagled on top was in full view.

A body, with unseeing eyes staring up at the clouds through the shattered skylight.

A body he knew well.

A body he remembered inhabiting.

'Your choice is easy, Theodore. This is what's at stake.'

Theodore choked back another sob. He could not let Terror Voice see him cry. Could not let Terror Voice see how much he wanted this. How much he hated himself for it.

'It's almost time. Soon, everything will be different. You will be different. We will have changed the world, together.'

This was the promise he clung tight to, this belief that everything he was doing could be forgiven one day.

The human part of him, desperate to be redeemed.

The *clacks* moved closer, until he could feel the coldness of something living against his back, and he lifted his chin, cat ears quivering.

'*Samhain approaches*,' Terror Voice said softly in his ear. '*You know what to do*.'

TWELVE

Mallory contemplated her preliminary investigation material from beneath her duvet on the couch, hindered by the groaning soundtrack of a very hungover Cornelia and Diana trying to bring themselves back to life. Her body was one giant ache. This was how she was going to die: on little sleep, with history repeating itself obnoxiously.

'What's the plan?' Diana yawned, handing Mallory a stack of toast. 'Start with the murder, then go onto the note, or assume they're connected?'

'I think we can safely assume Theodore is our main suspect,' Cornelia said. 'The note suggests that.'

'And like, no disrespect, but I can't think of anyone else who'd care enough to have his murder solved.'

'We can discuss that,' Mallory said, meaning that she did not agree. 'Let's begin.'

Diana set up the murder board as they ran through what they knew about their victim.

'Are we taking the hair and the positive ID of the body's

bracelet as a positive ID of the body?' Mallory asked.

'Sully did see her before she was burned,' Diana said.

'And are we taking what Sully said as the truth?' Mallory continued.

Cornelia tilted their head. 'Are you not?'

'I just think it's all very strange,' Mallory said quietly. 'Do you not?'

Cornelia adjusted their glasses, thinking. 'I don't know,' they said finally.

'Neither do I,' Diana said. 'But if Mallory thinks that the body is actually Hayley Eason's, based on the limited evidence we have—'

'And taking into account we can't wait for an autopsy—'

'We don't have to,' Cornelia said, checking their phone. 'Tate's released her name. They were able to ID her with her teeth. It's Hayley.'

Mallory closed her eyes. Perhaps it was her own impending death, but the humanity, the *reality* of the victim was eating her alive. That Hayley had been alive until sometime last night. That someone had snuck in and killed her, in the way the Whistler once had. Then burned her body to a crisp.

'Okay. Hayley Eason was in her mid to late twenties—'

'Twenty-eight,' Diana said.

'And she was the aide to the Night Mayor. She was in the Observatory from around eight p.m., Sully dropped by at around nine p.m., and then we have a gap of three hours in which she could've been killed and burned. Now. Why would someone kill Hayley?'

'If it's a copy of the Whistler murders, maybe she was just

in the wrong place, wrong time,' Cornelia suggested, their voice faltering on the word 'Whistler'.

Mallory bit her lip, afraid to ask what this was bringing up for them, if they were also reliving those days two years prior when people died around them until they unmasked Jacob Gabbott. Until he'd died in front of them.

Cornelia scribbled on their makeshift murder board, which was a whiteboard Mallory's parents used to write weekly meal plans and gentle reminders to each other on. It had been so long since it had been used last, Cornelia had to forcibly scribble over the stubborn remnants of SPAGHETTI BOLOGNESE.

- FORMER GIRLFRIEND OF VVD

'Former girlfriend of the former Night Mayor of Wrackton, who was killed by the Whistler. Could that be the connection?' Mallory said. 'Someone tangentially related to the original case?'

Diana nodded, gulping her tea and pouring a second cup. 'That's a logical assumption for now. She was digging into something for the Ghoul Council, according to Dr Ray – could that be motive?'

Cornelia wrote up:

- AIDE TO CURRENT NIGHT MAYOR, GHOUL COUNCIL
- FORMER MD AT QUINN HOTEL GROUP

'She used to work for Grey Quinn and we used her alibi, and

Quinn's verification of her alibi, in the Whistler murders, if I'm recalling correctly,' Cornelia said.

They teased out as much of her history as they could, then Mallory got out her kit bag, going through the evidence they'd gathered last night and laying it out on the kitchen table.

'I was thinking we start with the samples we took, see if there's any trace evidence to go on, then we can look at potential witness—' Mallory started, silenced by the look on Diana and Cornelia's faces. 'What?'

'There's the little issue of the Theodore-themed note,' Cornelia said.

'That little issue, yes,' Mallory said slowly. 'There's something bothering me about it, and I think it's that we need to consider that it is, perhaps, *too* convenient that all roads seem to lead to Theodore.'

Cornelia sighed and Diana took an aggressive bite of toast.

'What?' Mallory looked between them, an uncomfortable pit growing in her stomach.

'We thought you might not accept he could be involved,' Diana said. 'Not that there's an *issue* with that, it's just… not unexpected.'

Mallory frowned. 'So you both think this *is* him?'

Cornelia put down their cup. 'I think we don't have a clue, and we don't have the luxury of not thinking about it. We need to know, conclusively, as soon as humanly possible and preferably before midnight tomorrow night, who is mimicking the Whistler, and we also need enough time to communicate that knowledge to someone living.'

'A notion that seems unlikely.'

'Not likely, but not impossible. Let's look at the facts,' Mallory said. 'For old time's sake.'

They finished breakfast, Cornelia made a second round of hot beverages, and Diana brought in her Wrackton diorama and plonked it down on the coffee table.

It was a perfect miniature of the town – scaled buildings and graveyards and grasslands, cobbled sections of the streets, witchlight street lamps, the Mayoral Offices, the Larix, the Redwoods, the Observatory, Mallory's house, Broadwick Mansion. All perfect, all tiny, all exactly as they were. Sometimes she liked to imagine that, inside their old lab, a miniature Theodore was working away on an experiment like nothing bad had happened. Like nothing had or would ever change.

'Hayley Eason died in the Observatory.'

'Whistler-style,' Cornelia added, their voice a tad too glib to be genuine.

'Witchlight in her hand. Then in the time it took Sully to call us and leave to avoid a run-in with DCI Nathan Tate, her body was burned.' Diana lit a tiny witchlight that glowed red over the Observatory, hovering above the Ternion Memorial Garden. Mallory peered closer and realised she'd managed to replicate the monument in miniature, right down to the Ternion's clasped hands.

'And before we looked at our samples from that scene, a note was left in the basement of the Larix – the same place a victim of the Whistler murders was killed.'

'We find the note, and the fire alarm goes off before we can conclude questioning Sam Bridewell, who was at both scenes.' Diana lit the second location in the diorama, and whispered another spell that made a thread of light connect the two murder scenes.

'Both of those are places Theodore could easily go,' Cornelia said.

'I know,' Mallory said. 'And I'm not discounting the *possibility*, I just… want none of this to be true. I also want to be sure we haven't decided the killer before we investigate. Anyone could've been in the Observatory, and anyone could've left us that note. There were witchlights at both scenes, and everyone knows about witchlight travel now. If this killer is copying Jacob Gabbott's Whistler method, it's to get our attention. Hence the note. Additionally hence the narrow window of time between killing Hayley and leaving that note.'

'But not hence the fire. That's the bit that doesn't really fit.' Diana frowned. 'And the fact the lights went out, and Sandi's insistence that she *saw him*, suggests we do need to look at Theodore a bit closer.'

'We haven't even run the sample.' Mallory dropped her head into her hands, the fight going out of her. 'Okay, for argument's sake, let's say it *is* Theodore and this entire thing is to draw us in. The note wants us to solve his first murder – so let's do that. We keep on looking for other evidence, but if we solve his first murder, and if it's him, maybe he'll stop. I know we don't have a proper lab, but we proved in Wickermere that we don't need one. Not a magical one. We can do this with regular, analogue forensics.'

'You want to play the killer's game?' Diana asked incredulously.

'What else can we do? "Want" doesn't come into it. We have to play it. Learn the rules. Beat them at their own game.'

Diana and Cornelia exchanged a glance, one that spoke volumes, and Mallory fought the urge to snap at them. She was asking them to spend their last few hours alive solving a case that had thus far proved unsolvable.

'Okay,' Diana said. 'Two crime scenes, one agency.'

Mallory looked to Cornelia, who held her gaze before nodding assent. 'We're with you to the end.'

Under Mallory's direction, while Mallory tried to stretch out her aching back, Diana and Cornelia set up a chromatography station so they could conduct a manual test for magical traces. It had worked before – the colours separated out to show an otherwise invisible trace of magic. Something to work from.

Mallory took the letter, its letters shifting and shimmering, and lay it flat on a serving tray. While Diana and Cornelia – mostly Cornelia – finished testing the samples from Hayley's crime scene, she dusted the paper and envelope for fingerprints with a large brush and red print powder. It came up clean.

'Could one of you—' Mallory started, but Cornelia had already muttered under their breath so the code solved itself, the words visible again.

Q1. WHY DID THEODORE WYATT DIE?

A. TO GET TO THE OTHER SIDE

Q2. WHY?

A. ????

Diana pinned it to the murder board, and scrawled up the text from the back –

(HINT: Find the answer, stop the apocalypse)

Tick tock!

See you soon

'Do we have the—' Mallory started again, but Cornelia had already squeezed their arms into a doom stack of various boxes, bags and bug-related paraphernalia that had taken up residence in the corner of Mallory's sitting room. Mallory had been pretending it did not exist to avoid getting stressed about it.

Triumphantly, Cornelia pulled out a tote bag.

'The Sprinter, my beloved. How useful you've been,' Diana said affectionately. 'I still don't really understand how it works, but I love science and your brain, Mallory.'

The Sprinter was a magical fingerprinting machine of Mallory and Theodore's creation, which contained a known database of every single spell they were able to get their hands on, for identifying magic samples from their cases. It had the same unfortunate limitations as Apparent fingerprinting technology, in that it could only recognise the spells already known, and not anything else. Otherwise when shown an unfamiliar spell, it would say—

'Inconclusive. Undetectable,' Mallory said, deflating slightly. The machine beeped again and Mallory straightened. 'It doesn't know the spell, but it has suggested a match to another sample we showed it in the Whistler case! The one from the coded letter we found at— At Ben's crime scene.'

'A thing Theodore knew about,' Diana pointed out, and Mallory deflated further, eyeing the Sprinter. It could only match what it already had access to. Someone was using the same spell Jacob had used before. When they'd had to go before the UML to talk about the Whistler case, they'd kept it simple and hadn't mentioned the note. It was an Undetectables-only piece of information. Even still—

'It's not enough,' Mallory said. 'How're the chromatography samples coming along?'

'I'd like to run it again,' Diana said quickly. 'I'm not sure—'

'Diana,' Cornelia said reproachfully.

'What is it?' Brain fog, rustiness and her general annoyance at her friends' unwillingness to properly throw themselves into the investigation had Mallory doubting herself, but she looked and looked at Diana and Cornelia's results, scarcely able to believe her eyes.

Mallory and Theodore had devised a method of identifying magic samples by colour – it wouldn't say *who* had cast the spell, but it could help identify if they were a witch, a demon, a faerie, a troll, a vampire or a combination thereof.

She ran the test again without saying anything, pleased she had the correct solvents and dyes to hand, and was not relying on her own memory to pull things together.

Before long, she had two clear chromatographic results that made her heart thud painfully in her chest, and made Diana and Cornelia look more than slightly ruffled.

'Is that...?' Cornelia asked, but Mallory knew they knew the answer. They all did.

The dye was a solid pale pink.

'A witch with Apparent heritage,' Mallory said slowly.

'Just like the Whistler case,' Diana said unnecessarily. 'This is our killer. We're looking for a witch with Apparent heritage.'

'So it's *not* Theodore, then?' Cornelia asked.

Mallory wanted to say no. She wanted to say the evidence suggested it wasn't, and that he couldn't do something like this. That he wouldn't.

But Mallory was a scientist, and their agency motto – besides 'helping you detect the undetectable!' – was 'no stone left unturned'.

'I think… we can't discount Theodore's involvement, somewhere. It would be silly of us, after the Wickermere Reaper case – Dorothy was using ghosts to kill. Theodore has previously possessed – or *encouraged*, or however you want to put it – two grave diggers to dig up bodies in Wrackton cemeteries, for as-yet-unknown reasons. So even if Theodore is pulling the strings: whose strings is he pulling?'

It was a question that made Cornelia write *PUPPET MASTER??* on the murder board.

'Wait. Are you suggesting Theodore has some sort of… ghost apprentice he's ordering around? A pre-Samhain ghost? Learner ghost?' Diana said, evidently struggling to think of something witty. 'Let me have it, I have a splitting headache.'

Mallory smiled in spite of herself, but somewhere beyond her, while time was trickling through her hourglass, another timer had started up. Something big was going on, and she needed to get to the bottom of it.

'I don't know. It might just be an enthusiastic witch-Apparent apprentice. And we've got lots of those around. Even more than usual, thanks to the enormous success of the *Visit Wrackton* campaign. Cornelia, you had an… erm… insect, at the Larix?'

'Yes! I did!' they said, brightening. 'I don't know how Lyrespies would respond to ghosts, actually, so if he was there we might just have a bunch of static. But let's find out, shall we?'

'Lyrespies? Please don't give your monstrous hybrids a cute name, when they are literally nightmare fuel.' Diana shuddered.

'That's not a very nice way to talk about Norman,' Cornelia protested.

'NORMAN?' Diana shrieked, but Mallory raised a tired hand, and Diana didn't continue. After a moment's hesitation, Cornelia got the Lyrespy out.

In proper light it was, for want of a better word, revolting, and that was coming from someone who had been in semi-unrequited love with a forensic entomologist for a very long time.

'Okay, Norman. Do your thing.' Cornelia waited expectantly.

Norman's terrible face and terrible body stared up at them, before he shot a small length of steel silk webbing that thankfully landed on Cornelia's sleeve and not on their bare skin.

'Fucksake, Norman,' Cornelia said crossly. 'Just tell me what you heard.'

To Mallory's surprise, Norman replayed an eerie echo of what occurred at the crime scene. They listened intently to what sounded like Langdon and Sandi shouting into a microphone, then music, footsteps on the stairs. Shuffling, a small exclamation of surprise, more shuffling.

Then it began to hum a strange tune Mallory had never heard before. One that ended in a piercing whistle that made her clap her hands to her ears and screw her eyes shut until it stopped.

Mallory opened her eyes, assuming Norman was finished. Then the sounds of Sandi's screaming filled the room, making them all jerk backwards, and Norman fluttered its wings as if to say, 'and how did you like them spiderous apples?'

Cornelia patted Norman on the head with their little finger until it finished.

'I didn't hear any static,' Mallory said. She knew it sounded like a pathetic attempt to excuse him. 'What are we calling this case, by the way?'

'The New! Whistler,' Diana suggested.

'The Imitator,' Cornelia said.

Mallory had a better idea. 'If it's okay with you both, I think we should call them the Copycat.'

The others nodded, and Mallory felt a small sense of satisfaction curl in her stomach.

'Okay. So. Even with no audible static from Norman. We have Theodore as a suspect. We also have Sam Bridewell, who was at both scenes. We have Sully—'

'Sully? Really?' Cornelia said, then considered it. 'Fair do's, actually. No stones, et cetera.'

The Undetectables had trusted before, and had that trust broken.

'Even if my belief that Theodore is' – *being framed? Being forced to do all of this?* – 'not the only possible culprit, there's a bigger picture we're not seeing. There has to be a *reason* to copy the Whistler, both the murder and the coded note. It's been two entire years. He's dead. Why would someone start this up again?'

'To get our attention. To puppet master someone else

into getting our attention.' Cornelia paced back and forth, deliberately placing their feet in line with the floorboards that stretched across Mallory's living room. Theodore had always hated that rooms were called that.

'Langdon texted,' Mallory said, glancing down at her phone and typing quickly. 'He's got the Larix's CCTV from last night for us. I said we'd come get it soon. We need a second murder board.' Mallory grabbed a table cloth from the sideboard for Diana to hang next to the first murder board.

Mallory took up a pen.

- WITCH TRACE ON LIGHTBULB
- WITCHLIGHT IN BASEMENT

'Allow me to spell out the obvious for a moment. We were shown a memory by Katherine Vane last year that suggested the Broadwicks killed Theodore,' Mallory said, reaching through the tangled threads of her own exhausted memory. 'But when Cornelia confronted the Broadwicks, they were…'

'Confused,' Cornelia said. 'Incredulous.'

'And the motive was never clear. They kept Theodore around to study him after he died. Why would they kill him in the first place?'

'So that they could study him?' Diana suggested.

'I mean, maybe. But the variables involved were so risky, and they're so risk *averse*, that I simply don't buy it. The letter the killer – we assume – left asks us to look at *why* he was killed. So who else do we look at?'

'We know Van Doren, the Broadwicks and Grey Quinn

were there that night, from Theodore's own accounts of his movements. We've tried to talk to all of them,' Cornelia said. 'To no avail, if you recall.'

Mallory did, in fact, recall. At age fourteen (and again at sixteen) she had written polite emails and made polite phone calls, and none of them had resulted in satisfactory answers. At the time, it had felt like they were never going to be taken seriously as an agency. Time really was a flat circle.

'Is there any point in trying to appeal for new information? Given that he's now Notorious Theodore Wyatt, and folk will be foaming at the mouth to prove how much of a wrong 'un he always was?' Diana lifted her phone, holding it over her face as a charm with the letter 'T' on it dangling in the air. ('T as in Taylor?' she'd asked when Taylor gave it to her. 'No,' Taylor had said. 'T as in try not to fucking die before your time is up.' Mallory had had to leave the room, both to stop herself sobbing at the brutally honest thoughtfulness, and because Diana had proceeded to try to unbutton Taylor's jeans while Mallory was still present.)

'Hold on – the person who cast the spell that killed Theodore *has* to be a witch, but it doesn't mean there weren't other people *involved*,' Mallory said, the cogs turning.

'Another puppet master situation?' Cornelia said.

'I mean, maybe? We're trying to establish a link between Theodore's murder and Hayley's. Maybe the reason we haven't been able to solve it is that we haven't been thinking laterally enough.'

'And not because it's an eight-year-old cold case that happened when we were literal children and had no magical forensic technology at our disposal,' Diana said, but Mallory was undeterred. The cogs were still turning as she turned her gaze back to Hayley's murder board, her eyes catching something.

'Wait. Hayley went to the Observatory at eight p.m. There was no one around. Why not? There's always someone in the Observatory.' Mallory hobbled to where she'd left her coat the night before, shrugging it on.

'Diana. Are you sober enough to drive?'

THIRTEEN

Theodore heard them before he saw them.

He'd thought about nothing else on his long walk out of the Redwoods, having made sudden sense of their tiny matching hand tattoos and apathy. Their overwhelming collective lack of a sense of self-preservation – Mallory had been visiting a *ghost* in a *bunker* that wasn't *him*! – had a clear reason, and it cut him to his core. The Undetectables were Besieged. His (ex-)friends were dying.

He'd made the decision to walk by the Larix, largely because he was curious to see if it had burned down completely, and there they were, as if he'd manifested them.

The Undetectables were huddled with their friend Langdon Ericsson, who was talking emphatically, pointing back into the Larix. Theodore watched him hand over a small object and Cornelia said something and Diana made a face and everyone laughed and Mallory checked her watch, wearing a look of determination that Theodore knew well.

One of his favourite things was studying the people around

him like they were anthropological curios, and he'd had the privilege of seeing Mallory grow from a brave – albeit nerdy – fourteen-year-old, into a shadow of herself, and then into someone even braver. This Mallory, with this look on her face, was as familiar to him as breathing once was, and his heart would've ached with the memory of being in the lab, the mundanity of working side by side examining forensic evidence, if he'd still had one. (Everything he was doing was in an effort to earn it back.)

Langdon slipped through a door beside the Larix and Mallory gestured to Diana's obnoxiously yellow car. Mallory's head turned, eyes searching, and her gaze landed square on the place Theodore was standing. He'd allowed himself to drift closer, feeling the coolness of the living on his semi-transparent skin, and he froze in place, not daring to move an inch in case he sent up a spray of telltale sparks. (*Remember to run! Remember to hide!*)

'What?' Diana looked through Theodore as though he wasn't there.

Which, if he was performing his song correctly, was true.

'You look like you've seen a ghost,' Cornelia said.

'I have,' Mallory said softly, taking a step towards Theodore. (*That's how you evade capture, when you're outside!*) She held her hand out, her fingers shaking. 'Feel this? It's warm here.'

Theodore gritted his teeth, willing Terror Voice not to choose this second to ask him a question. He had to focus, he had to focus, he had to—

'Mallory…' Cornelia said uneasily. 'There's nothing there. He's not there.'

'I thought I saw him before, at your house, but I convinced myself—'

Cornelia's phone buzzed and Theodore ran the second Mallory looked away. 'It's him. He says he's there now and he's up for talking. Apparently, gruesome murder notwithstanding, we are not to consider this "a personal favour", but actually "his job".'

'Theodore?' Mallory said softly, not acknowledging what Cornelia said. 'We found your note. Talk to us. We want to know what your murder and Hayley's murder have in common. Help us out here.'

'Mallory!' Diana said, aghast.

'It's Theodore. It has to be.'

Fuck. Shit even. *HEXANA DAMN HIM—*

Theodore ran. Blurring in the general direction of the hotel, panic overtaking him as he darted out of the road past the Larix and back onto the footpath, the desperate need to put space between him and Mallory making him careless. He passed through someone who had just stepped out of a taxi, and he and the person stumbled and swore.

A familiar person.

'Grey!' Theodore yelped, and dragged him down a side alley, sparks flying.

'What, and I cannot stress this enough, the *fuck* are you doing?' Grey asked, wrenching his lapel free from Theodore's ghostly grasp and smoothing it. He had a folder under his arm.

'Shh! Shh! Be quiet!' Theodore said, clapping a hand over his mouth. He had to lean up to press Grey against the wall behind him.

'My suit,' Grey protested, but it was muffled against a roar of static that had built up between them.

'I was almost spotted,' Theodore hissed.

'Dangerous, seeing as you're now extremely wanted for murder. Something you're not telling me?' Grey asked. 'Also – didn't I leave you at Oakpass?' He hadn't pushed Theodore away again, and Theodore felt waves of cold emanating from him.

'Obviously not! Murder? Me?' Theodore laughed. 'What a silly thing to say. And I'm clearly on my way back there, to do a second sweep.'

'It's fascinating how you're never at home or where I need you to be, despite not having a job or any friends or really any other place to go. Unless, of course, it's that you truly don't enjoy spending time with me.'

'Well I *never*.' Theodore pressed a hand to his chest, his other still resting on Grey's – surprisingly solid – upper arm. He'd never seen him lift anything, or do anything that could resemble exercise. 'What a scurrilous accusation.'

'You *do* have this awful habit of running off right before something terrible happens in this goddess-forsaken town, and one might be led to believe that you had the ideal opportunity to, say, murder a woman, or, say, set fire to the Larix.'

Theodore blinked. 'Why would you think that?'

'Setting fire to things feels like a very *you* solution to your problems. As does revisiting the scene of the crime.' He pointed down the street towards the Larix. 'Saying that, whoever set that fire may have just done me a favour. The Larix owners agreed to meet with me to discuss a potential buy-out.'

'Oh. Great. Wonderful how things work out for you,'

Theodore said, not really meaning it. 'She got a note,' he added bluntly.

'Who?'

'Mallory. A note that means police will be doubly after me for…' he gestured around himself. 'All of this.'

'So tell her the truth,' Grey said.

'You know I can't do that!'

Theodore felt in his head for the Voice's reaction, but it wasn't there.

'I don't, actually. I am finding this level of honesty very disturbing. Tell her, don't tell her. I have a meeting to get to—'

'I *can't*,' Theodore said, pressing his hands against Grey's shoulders. Grey tilted his head down at him, his eyes softening. He had a really nice mouth. There were inches between his and Theodore's mouths, actually, and he could just tilt his head up and—

Theodore sprang away, dragging his cardigan around himself.

'You're serious,' Grey noted. 'Okay. Then if you *can't*, why not… persuade her?'

'I'm not a demon.'

'And?'

'I can't persuade.'

'Come on, Theo. You're not *listening*.'

'I am! Enthralled. Bewitched. Do go on.'

'You can persuade her with the power of possession. I did not joke when I suggested you could enter the Ghoul Council's heads – why not just rummage around in hers, convince her of the truth?'

Theodore's mouth dropped open.

'I want to convince her that I'm not a bad person, and you think the answer to that is to *fucking possess her*?'

'I could do it,' Grey said casually. 'Just a little nudge, to give you a chance. Hear you out.'

This was somehow even worse than the idea of Theodore doing it himself, and he didn't dignify it with an answer. His expression must've been enough to convey all of this, because Grey changed the subject abruptly.

'Well what does the note say, then?'

'I don't know.'

Grey actually, literally, rolled his eyes, and commenced dusting off his suit.

This was what it had come to. Theodore, rendezvous-ing in an alley with his only ally – the Alley Ally – who had no real suggestions for him, who could not know the full story, who would not understand why he was doing it, or would make the wrong assumption about it.

Mallory, of all people, would understand why he was doing what he was doing. She'd understand the stakes! She'd make everything okay again, by sheer virtue of being his friend! Theodore needed a friend. He needed an *ally* – a true one, who cared about him, who wanted good things for him, who did not make him come to meetings or play games of chess or make terrible suggestions in alleyways.

An ally could help Mallory understand him again, as she always had, before she'd started looking at him like he scared her. Like her world had come crashing down around her ears. If he could just make her understand that all of this – the murders, the grave digging, the Voice, the plan – were bigger than Theodore. That it was bigger than all of them. Things would improve. He could be better.

But he couldn't.

'If you don't want my help—' Grey began, and Theodore felt a prickle of anger.

'I am terminating this correspondence,' Theodore said archly, aware that the prickle of anger was rising into something else.

Rage. Loathing. Fury. Feelings he hadn't permitted himself to feel all rose to the surface. He did not want help. He did not want to be a victim. He wanted to *live*. He wanted to be *human*. He wanted to make mistakes. And he wanted Mallory to help him.

'Have it your way. I'll see you at home,' Grey said.

As soon as Grey turned his back, the answer hit him. A closing door moment of inspiration.

'Wait!' Theodore darted in front of him. 'You're right.'

Grey's mouth twitched into an involuntary smile that he couldn't push away. 'I always am. But what about, in this instance?'

It was a risk to say anything the Voice might catch wind of, but he needed to try.

'I need to convince her.'

Grey spread his hands. 'Then by all means—'

'NOT magically. I can tell her the truth without telling her. With a series of *clues*. She's a detective! Well, she's a private investigator, which is a distinct role compared to that of a—'

'Don't care,' Grey said, albeit gently. 'And far be it from me to tell you something's a bad idea, but are you capable of such subtlety?'

Theodore waved a dismissive hand. 'I've got it. Enjoy your meeting. Go, go! Good luck with your empire.'

Theodore stood in Mallory's living room. He heard the distinct sound of a laptop battery exploding from his proximity, but he ignored it, checking the rooms for signs of life. (If he touched the laptop it would make it worse, and then where would he be? Somewhere much worse off than he had been moments before, no doubt.)

There was nobody home. He maybe had minutes before Mallory, Diana and Cornelia crashed through the front door.

He felt around in his head for the Voice, but the line was busy.

Thank fuck for that.

'Okay, Theodore. If we need her to independently think of the questions that need to be asked – such as who, and what, and where and why – we also need her to have the means to answer them. Without tampering with her mind or memory or doing anything that would bring harm to her, we will leave her clues. We as in me myself and I, and nobody else.'

He circled back to the dining table, where there were abandoned chromatography samples that showed an Apparent-witch magic trace.

'Perhaps she *is* asking the right questions,' he said.

He didn't need Grey to help him with this part. He didn't need anyone to help him. In his recently-reformed opinion, there was nothing more human than a healthy distrust of others.

It hit him again, the truth of what was going to happen to Mallory, Diana and Cornelia. The Besiegement Curse. Certain death in thirty-seven hours. 'Oh, Mallory. What did you get yourself into?'

Theodore spent five careful minutes looking through the Undetectables' evidence, giving the Sprinter a wider-than-normal berth. (The iron screens in the lab had been more useful than he'd given them credit for.)

He approached Diana's diorama of Wrackton. Someone had lit witchlights over the Observatory and the Larix, a thread connecting them.

Good. Smart. The perfect place to start.

He got to work. Small, subtle hints that would point them in the right direction. Tiny clues that would make them think, and puzzle and ask the right questions.

Surely they'd notice a red light over the Ternion Memorial Garden, a pencil ring drawn – apologetically – around the Ternion monument that Diana and Taylor had captured in perfect miniature. They'd notice a red light over the Redwoods and one over Broadwick Mansion. Surely they'd notice the Observatory and the Mayoral Offices had swapped places, that they were no longer as they should be.

Surely they'd see the paper he'd found on the Ternion with their names circled, the word *ALIAS* written in what was unmistakably his hand. They'd lift it and find the case file on Katherine Vane he'd pulled up, *Vane* underlined three times. Clues he knew Mallory would put together, even if the other two remained sceptical.

She'd be home soon, and she'd find the answers herself.

He stood back and admired his work, his eyes falling on a tray with a paper sample Mallory had been working on, telltale signs of red fingerprint powder dusting the edges. Some letters still shimmered with magical code, but he could read enough of it.

Q1. WHY DID THEODORE WYATT DIE?

A. TO GET TO THE OTHER SIDE

Q2. WHY?

A. ????

Theodore glared at it, knowing he was risking summoning Terror Voice, but he had something to say and he was going to say it.

'It's not even a proper fucking pun, is it?'

FOURTEEN

'It's not beyond the realms of possibility that Theodore is following us around,' Diana said carefully, pulling into a space in front of the Observatory. 'Especially if he is involved in the Copycat murder. But I didn't see anything. Cornelia didn't see anything. He's not exactly known for being invisible, is he?'

Mallory slapped her hands against the dashboard. 'Diana, I FUCKING KNOW IT DOESN'T MAKE SENSE. I feel absolutely out of my mind even *considering* it, but *he was there.*'

'I didn't notice my hearing aid crackling, and I didn't feel a temperature change. That doesn't mean you didn't, of course, but I'm just saying. Evidence wasn't there.'

'I didn't see anything, but thinking back on it, the air did feel warmer,' Cornelia said. 'A presence of some kind.'

Mallory closed her eyes, gratitude flooding her.

'He might've been checking up on us, seeing if we're investigating. Seeing if we got the note,' Cornelia continued. 'And maybe Samhain ghosts can be invisible. We don't really know what his powers were, apart from breaking electronics.'

It made sense to Mallory, even if Diana still looked sceptical.

Diana pulled out the thumb drive Langdon had given her and Cornelia put it into their laptop. They paused while scanning through the footage, giving Mallory a moment to collect herself. 'CCTV footage for the whole night after about midnight is all static mess, just as Langdon said.'

'Can you see anything at all through the static?' Mallory asked.

'Basement lights went out at about midnight, rest of the lights went when we heard the scream. Before that, you can see us leaving to come to you when you called, but there's nothing of us coming back in with Sandi and Remington.'

'And if Theodore can make himself invisible, we probably wouldn't have seen anything anyway,' Mallory said.

'It could also be a different ghost,' Diana suggested after a moment. 'Not in the basement – following us around. A manifestation of the Besiegement, making sure we don't harm the vessels until the Curse has completed.'

'That's disgusting, Diana. I contain too many multitudes to be a mere vessel.' Cornelia slammed the laptop shut.

'Tomorrow, we're all ghost meat! Might as well accept it.'

'Maybe,' Mallory said, rubbing her eyes. 'To the Curse part, I am not commenting on the use of "ghost meat".'

'Are you okay to do this?' Cornelia asked. 'We can drop you home and Diana and I can take care of the interview.'

She felt the urge for rest overtaking her, but instead pulled out the bag of snacks Diana had picked up at a garage – time trickling away with every little decision – and milled a packet of crisps, cracking open a violently pink can of energy drink.

The prospect of Cornelia handling this particular interview was mildly alarming, but Mallory also wanted to be there.

'No point,' Mallory said, crunching. 'I'd just be staring at our evidence.'

'And it's not like secret elves will have snuck in and showered us with extra clues while we were gone,' Diana said.

As Mallory slid out of her seat, Cornelia handed over a packet of disposable heat patches. 'Grabbed these when we were in the shop. Thought you'd need them.'

They studiously looked at their phone before Mallory could say anything.

The Observatory still had crime scene tape stuck over the doors, but before Mallory could wonder how they'd get inside, Observer Johnson rounded the side of the building, his robes brushing the stained-glass windows.

'This way. The police – and the UML, and the Ghoul Council, as they all had to be consulted – have agreed to not formally close the building as it is a public space, and we need to leave a place for folk to grieve. We can't go into the roof, as even if it wasn't a crime scene it's not been cleared structurally, but I am permitted to use the rooms to the rear. Dreadfully sad day.' His face was creased in a manner that appeared defeated. 'Hayley came by regularly. She was researching something for the Ghoul Council. It, sadly, make me think of you three, and Jacob Gabbott. And now here you are. Here we are. I can't understand what forces would cause such a horrific thing to happen in Wrackton again, but I have a terrible feeling you're here to ask me about it.'

He didn't wait for any of them to formulate a response as

he led them into the Observatory through an emergency exit next to the Ternion glass. Mallory felt a swoop in her stomach as she looked at it, a familiar nausea she wished she'd never known. A reminder of what the Whistler had done, and what the Copycat was doing.

'Now,' Observer Johnson said, situating them in a red-curtained room that looked very much like all the other red-curtained rooms Mallory had been in. She sank gratefully onto a red sofa. 'Explain.'

'Hayley came here looking for something, last night. What was she looking for?'

Observer Johnson levelled Mallory with a stare. 'I ordinarily do not divulge the secrets I'm trusted with.'

Mallory waited for him to continue, but quickly realised it was a full sentence. A diplomatic no.

'Let's rephrase that, shall we?' Cornelia said. 'Hayley Eason came here last night looking for something, and we think it got her killed. What was it?'

Observer Johnson took in a very deep, very slow breath. 'The Ghoul Council tasked the office of the Night Mayor with digging up records pertaining to the Ternion. More specifically, pertaining to the conditions required for the Ternion to walk the earth again.'

'Like the Whistler case,' Mallory whispered.

'Every time I see you, it's for a terrible reason,' Observer Johnson said. 'Yes, like the Whistler case. I believe your issue with Jacob Gabbott was a belief he was trying to summon the Ternion – that he was carving up poor, poor local folk to harvest seven souls that would somehow manifest the Ternion. Yes?'

That was roughly the story as Mallory understood it.

'We have reason to believe someone is trying to duplicate those murders,' Mallory said carefully.

'But Hayley was burned.'

'Yes. She was. But she also had the Ternion's sigil cut into her – circles, lines and stars.'

'Like the Whistler murders.'

'Yes.'

'But Jacob Gabbott is dead.'

'And I thought *I* liked to state the obvious,' Cornelia said, a wisp of fear wavering their voice.

He ignored them. 'So someone came here last night and killed Hayley. Because she was looking into something they didn't want her to see?'

'Perhaps. Isn't there usually someone here all the time?' Mallory asked.

'Usually, yes. But more often than not it's just me here. And I have to rest occasionally. Not that that occurs to anyone,' he added, *sotto voce*.

'Would anyone have known you weren't here last night?'

He grimaced. 'I've been wondering that myself. I left at approximately half past eight yesterday evening – I can't tell you how irritating it has been to deal with tourists. Especially tourists with cameras. Flash going off in my face at all hours of the day without so much as *asking*. There was a particularly loud American actor here yesterday afternoon – she kept insisting she was undercover, asking question after question about Oakpass Manor and her great-grandmother, as if I was that old. I knew her face, of course, just can't remember her name, and I couldn't think what it might be over the sound of her asking if I was "Occultical". She had a young man with her – a pompous prick in sunglasses – asking the most inane questions. Both of them irritated me into a migraine, so I left, took medicine, went to sleep, woke to missed calls, and came back here at around five.'

Mallory exchanged glances with the others. While it was hard to verify the truth of a migraine, he was describing an encounter with Sandi and Remington so perfectly, she could not imagine he was lying.

'Did everyone leave when you left?'

'I suggested they'd be more comfortable coming back when there were Observers present. The sunglasses man was very taken with the Ternion glass, but I believe they left before me.'

'Did you see them get into a car, or anything?'

'Migraine,' he repeated. 'I was focusing on not throwing up or passing out.'

'Yes. Totally with you. So that leaves a massive window for the killer to have come in, if they weren't here already by the time Hayley arrived,' Diana said.

Observer Johnson bristled. 'We have an open door policy. This is a place of worship, I cannot be expected to sweep my surroundings for murderers—'

'We aren't blaming you,' Mallory said quickly. 'Just trying to establish facts. I wanted to ask you about something else, actually.'

She laid out, in the barest terms possible, what she wanted to know about the night Theodore Wyatt was killed.

'Is this linked somehow? Did he kill Hayley?'

'We don't know,' Mallory said honestly. 'But we need to know, before midnight tomorrow, what really happened that night.'

'What's the rush?'

'We're Besieged,' Cornelia said unceremoniously, before Mallory could stop them.

Observer Johnson paused.

'It's us and the Broadwicks. Tomorrow night. Ghost meat,' Diana said. 'So we're on a time crunch – we need answers to who killed Theodore, and we need to know, definitively, if that answer sheds any light on why Hayley died.'

'I have always suspected he was murdered,' Observer Johnson said. 'I met him once, back when it happened. He was so scattered, so scared. And I wondered… well, I wondered if he was an experiment of sorts. Murdered, to see what would happen. And I've wondered why we know the concept of Samhain ghosts, but have not met any. Or many, in your case.'

He nodded to Mallory, who stared at him, a stab of terror lancing through her that he somehow knew the Undetectables had Blair locked in a bunker in the Broadwicks' garden, until she remembered the last time she'd been to talk to him.

She'd had to tell him about Katherine Vane, when Katherine had insisted Mallory help her find Blair. At the time Mallory had assumed she meant Blair's grave. It felt like a lifetime ago.

'Oh! Yes. That.'

'That?' Diana asked. 'What else could—'

'I asked him questions about the Mayoral Offices,' Mallory said quickly.

'If there was any chance we didn't know about the secret

Samhain ghost in the Mayoral Offices, you've done a terrible job of hiding that from us,' Cornelia said, barely suppressing a grin.

Observer Johnson did not smile back.

'You said Hayley was looking for the consequences of the Ternion walking the earth again,' Mallory said, something terrible occurring to her.

'I said conditions,' he corrected. 'Which could cause potential consequences, such as a resurgence of the Vampire Wars.'

'What if – and this is a big, long leap – but what if the conditions didn't require the Ternion to be living?'

'You mean if their remains were located?'

'I mean, what if they came back as Samhain ghosts?'

Observer Johnson sat back, thinking, as Diana and Cornelia stared at Mallory in horror.

'You don't think…' Diana said.

'I don't know what I think,' Mallory said, standing. 'All I know is that the Whistler case links to Hayley's murder links to Theodore's. I know Theodore came back as a ghost.'

'And you're wondering if it's possible if the Ternion could, also?'

'That's already—' Cornelia started, but Mallory talked over them.

'I'm wondering if it happened before. In the…' Mallory trailed off, the words Vampire Wars on her lips, just out of reach, her mind swirling the way it did when she looked at the Ternion glass.

'Sorry, what were we talking about?' Observer Johnson said.

'Theodore, I think,' Mallory said thickly, her mind

swimming. 'You don't know who killed him. We thought— it was suggested to us, via a witness, that it was the Broadwicks.'

'I did consider that. Once. I considered he was killed on purpose, to research him.'

'And what made you change your mind?'

'Your parents were highly influential members of Occulture. Still are. The scandal of Theodore dying in their home rocked the boat very, very hard. Vincent Van Doren – dear old Vinny,' he added with a rueful smile, 'pulled strings, smoothed things over with the UML, made sure to declare how happy he was to host Theodore in Wrackton, to continue to employ him. But I understood the Broadwicks would never, ever have allowed for something so publicly damaging to happen in their own home if they had something to say about it. All of which is to say – I believe there were smarter ways to kill Theodore if he was to be a Ghoul Council test subject. And so I believe it was someone else. Someone with more to gain. And more to lose.'

'That's essentially what we've concluded,' Mallory said.

'But if it's something higher – something bigger – then we're talking about the Ternion. Again. Right?' Diana said. 'That all of this boils down to something happening with the goddesses of Occulture tomorrow night, AGAIN. Goddess, I'm so sick of this shit. Why can't we just have a nice party?'

'Because we're going to die, Diana. And historically, parties in Wrackton? ALSO end in death,' Cornelia said.

'Think about it,' Mallory said. 'If Jacob was trying to join the Ternion, and if someone is now copying the Whistler murders, it is possible that someone in Wrackton thought of it years before Jacob got the idea into his head. And that someone could've tried testing things out on Theodore. Killed him, to see how it would work.'

'Like an invisible ghost mentor? Someone who could've shown Jacob the way two years ago, and now... what? Has a new apprentice? I was *joking* when I brought it up earlier!'

'And now that we know of the possibility of invisible ghosts – or have at least considered the hypothesis – perhaps it is a joke that has merit,' Mallory said. 'I'm just saying, no stone unturned. Our suspects could still very well be involved.'

Diana threw her hands up. 'Do you have an opinion, Observer Johnson?'

'I think Mallory is right. There are secrets in Wrackton – secrets so hidden that I would never in a million lifetimes uncover them all. I have tried, of course. I have thought about Jacob Gabbott and the murders he committed often over the past two years, and my conclusion is that he was either a man of terrifying intelligence, or he had some assistance. Perhaps Theodore has acquired that same assistance. Or, indeed, is providing it.'

Mallory closed her eyes. 'Thank you so much. We'll leave you be. Really sorry about Hayley.'

Observer Johnson nodded, and looked at each of them in turn, as though he was committing them to memory.

'I've seen a lot of death, over the years. Countless celebrations of life in varying magnitudes. I've witnessed singular burials, I've witnessed families dying. I can't comfort – it's not in my nature to offer kind words where a gesture is more impactful. More meaningful. I cannot give everyone what they ask for, only what they need in the moment. You want to be saved, and

I cannot save you. All I can say is that I won't forget your faces. I won't forget you.'

He swept towards the door.

'Wait,' Mallory said, as Observer Johnson crossed the threshold.

'What?'

'I don't know your first name.' She felt her cheeks flush. Such a pathetic thing to have to admit.

Observer Johnson smiled softly and stuck out a hand. 'Julian,' he said. 'It's been something to know you all these years.'

FIFTEEN

For the second time in twenty-four hours, Theodore was crouched outside the Observatory, waiting. The day was overcast, weak sunlight replaced by rolling cloud bank.

'*Good, you're here,*' Annoying Voice said. '*We have some things to discuss.*'

'Like what?'

'*I think you know. Someone's lit a little fire under you, haven't they?*'

'I have absolutely no idea what you're talking about. Fire? What fire? I know nothing of fire. Or flame!'

'*Oh, don't give me that. It's just you and me here. Two friends. You want friends, don't you? You miss your old ones.*'

'Please stop that,' Theodore said. 'Please. Constantly yammering in my head, reading my personal private thoughts like they're LETTERS, shouting at me, telling me what to do.'

'*Read your thoughts? It's not at all like that. I'm trying to help. Sometimes I think you don't even like me, despite all I do for you.*'

Theodore did not dignify this with a response.

'Very, very soon you'll be able to walk round and round the garden, like a teddy bear. Eyes on the prize.'

'I cannot believe I'm about to say this, but for the love of Hexana, would you *FUCK OFF!*' he hissed.

He heard sounds of life from the rear of the Observatory and pressed himself back against the wall, his hand on the Ternion glass.

He wanted so badly to smash it. Smash it, reveal himself, end this whole thing.

Once again, Theodore watched from a distance as the Undetectables emerged, keeping far away this time. If Mallory felt his presence here, it was game over.

No body, just crimes.

'I know how badly you want them to accept you. The new, improved you.'

Theodore pursed his lips. Another rare instance of Annoying Voice being correct.

'It won't matter, will it? They'll hate me for what I've done.'

'I don't see what the big deal is. Schrödinger's Cat Ghost – they either will or will not accept the things you've done as a means to an end. They either will or will not understand your desires.'

'They aren't desires! It's… yearning. A specific kind of yearning.'

'Yes, the yearning for humanity, isn't it? Years and years of adjusting, of complaining until the yearning fell to numbness, to habit. You crave the concept of human touch. Of human love, a shred of which you gleaned from your friendships, but now their time on this earth is fragile and fleeting. Amid the sadness and the terror, you want. You, Theodore Wyatt, WANT.'

'STOP READING MY DIARIES,' Theodore shouted, then slapped a hand over his mouth.

Nobody heard him.

He watched Mallory, Diana and Cornelia drive off in Diana's alarmingly yellow car, and tried to take a mental picture of them. To remember them as they were.

'*See you in a moment,*' Annoying Voice said.

The mental connection between them severed like the snap of a spiderweb, and Theodore composed himself just as a long shadow flitted through him, though all shadows that passed through him were long and he still hadn't figured out the mechanics of it, despite trying for years.

This long shadow was more like a physical manifestation of the darkness he'd lived under. The lies that had felt so sustainable, even as the Voice got louder and louder with promises that his part in this would be over soon if he just did *one* more thing.

And one more thing.

And one more thing.

He was in it now. So it goes.

'*Are you ready, Theodore?*' Terror Voice rumbled.

Theodore nodded, not looking at it. Refusing to set eyes on it. He hated how easy it had become to accept what the Voice was doing. To accept the things he would never have as a human, or during his first afterlife. It had all been so incremental. A pot boiling as he sat in it, lonely and sad and desperate to find a way back. Hoping a young witch could save him by solving his murder. Hoping he'd find a way out.

And yet, even with the lightbulb in his hand, he couldn't escape the Voice.

'I realise you may be contemplating your newfound freedom,' Terror Voice said, once again not disproving Theodore's fear it could read his thoughts. *'But we are in this together. You accepted that, when you accepted my terms.'*

As if Theodore had really had a choice.

'I'm contemplating nothing! My mind is a blank slate. I showed up, I've done what you asked, it's all ready. Can I go home now please?'

'There is more at stake than one little skeleton, five foot six. You think it is the most important thing to you, but there is more. I don't take kindly to displays of ingratitude.'

Terror Voice clacked closer. So risky, in broad daylight. So terrifying, not underground.

'You're right, sorry. T-thank you. For not destroying my skeleton,' said Theodore the coward. Theodore, the desperate to please. Theodore, the notorious sycophant.

'How many times, Theodore? I am benevolent. I will be *benevolent. I just hope you don't have to apologise to me again, because your acting skills leave a lot to be desired. I know you're not sorry, but you will be.'*

'What?'

A figure Theodore would recognise anywhere stumbled up the path, face blank, suit rumpled, face handsome, witchlight in hand, and Theodore felt a curious sensation, like he was falling.

Like there would be no one to catch him, when this was all over.

PERIMORTEM II

Julian Johnson had given his life to helping other people, and he'd resented every second of it.

There were those who wanted to be helped, whom he could not. And those whom he could help, who rejected it. There were ceremonies he took pride in that were taken for granted, and there were teachings he would never master in a lifetime of attempts. His whole world had opened up when he'd joined the Observatory – he was a scholar, an academic. A man with good intentions.

The Johnsons had two paths they could go down – like much of his family, Julian's brother had fallen into the Occult underworld, caught up in a wheel that would only cease turning if death claimed him. Julian broke the cycle. Changed the narrative.

Moments before he died, he was taking a steadying breath, still shaken by the death of Hayley Eason only hours before, now reeling at the idea of losing the stalwart presence of the Broadwicks. Of losing the young, occasionally idiotic investigators who kept darkening his door.

He had tried to stay beyond the petty nature of Occulture – the *who's who* of politics and capitalistic greed that destroyed Apparents over and over, that Occulture had barely adjusted for by throwing money at its problems, so Julian didn't have to feed his people as well as save them – but the Broadwicks were at the epicentre, and were unavoidable, and he had, much to his chagrin, genuinely liked them.

At the precise moment he died, he was thinking about Vinny Van Doren. The first time he'd met the man, he'd thought him trouble. But he'd also thought him charming and affable and found him ready to throw his weight at other social issues Julian encountered in his workplace.

Vinny's end had been so violent, but perhaps not that surprising. Another wheel that would only stop with death.

So naturally, Julian didn't see his own coming.

He did not hear the sound heralding the end, but his body felt it and reacted accordingly. Muscle wrenched from muscle via involuntary mastication. Stomach slashed by someone unseen.

Mirroring the death of Hayley above him, he stared up at the red-curtained room, one of many that had been a second home to him.

Eyes open, no more life to give.

SIXTEEN

Mallory’s phone ringing woke her with a jolt.

‘’Lo?’ she croaked.

The weight of that morning, and of the night before, hit her. She stifled a groan, her back completely seized.

‘There’s been another one,’ Sully whispered.

Mallory could hear sounds of people talking, wind blowing against the speakers. She pressed her face against her pillow. ‘The Larix? We processed that scene already.’

‘No. The Observatory again. Another murder.’

‘What? We were just— Shit, that was five hours ago.’ It was well into the afternoon. She was going to die tomorrow. She put her weight on her elbow, her spine screaming. ‘What’s happening?’

There was a burst of static, Sully’s voice lost in it. ‘—get back in.’

‘You’re breaking up, could you repeat that?’ Mallory closed her eyes, a cloud of brain fog taking up all available space, stealing her words, her comprehension.

‘—Ternion—’

'What? Sully—'

Sully hung up.

Mallory flopped back on her pillow and blinked at the ceiling, experimentally wiggling her toes. She was hungry and thirsty and sore, but thought that with a bit of fortification she could manage to get out of bed.

She texted Diana and Cornelia, who had also slept, which made Mallory feel less bad about wasting an entire afternoon. Diana brought tea, water and a bag of fresh pastries – Mallory's favourites – and Mallory told them what Sully had said.

Attempts to call her back were futile.

'Anyone talking about it online?' Cornelia asked, and Diana shook her head.

'Stories are still focused on Hayley and, to a lesser extent, the Larix fire. The Ghoul Council have reissued statements reminding folk not to approach Theodore. They're absolutely convinced he's the at-large culprit. If there's been a second murder and they still haven't caught him after five months of searching, this looks truly terrible for them. And they know it – Nova Khan has floated the idea of a curfew. Not to mention the sacks of protective salt that are sitting at every front door. RIP Wrackton tourism, we hardly tolerated you.' Diana threw her phone down on the bed.

'If someone was killed in the Observatory *again*, that's in broad daylight, unless we somehow missed a second body while we were there,' Cornelia said.

Mallory lifted her face, a cold sensation flooding her limbs. 'The only living soul in the Observatory five hours ago, apart from us, was Observer Johnson.'

'You don't think—' Cornelia started, but Mallory was already struggling into a pair of compression socks.

'I don't know how close we'll be able to get to the scene. If Tate's there already we'll have no chance of slipping past him, so unless we're fast enough...'

Diana smiled, a wicked grin that lit up her entire face. 'Don't worry, Mallory. I'm way ahead of you.'

Diana's plan was as genius as it was outlandishly ridiculous, and Mallory supposed that eventually had to circle back around to genius again. Dressed in a white forensics suit, her face covered with a mask and goggles, Diana slotted right in with the crime scene team moving around the Observatory as Tate barked instructions to his police officers, sans Sully.

Crime scene tape fluttered in the breeze. The magic number of murders required for a sacred space to be officially closed to the public was, apparently, two.

Cornelia and Mallory sat in Diana's car, parked as close as they could manage. They peered through the windscreen into the evening gloom, where Mallory had resigned herself to the fact there was absolutely nobody other than Tate's CSI team and a couple of Apparent uniformed police officers around. No Sam Bridewell, no Sandi and Remington, no Sully, no wandering tourists. Cornelia's arms were hooked over the steering wheel as they leaned forwards, a listening spell doing absolutely nothing to help them hear what was happening at the scene.

'And that's a no on Sully again, straight to voicemail. Also,

I do think the nature of the stake-out requires you to sort of... appear to not be on the job,' Mallory said.

Cornelia grinned, reaching a hand over to drop the seat back so they were practically horizontal, putting their arms behind their head.

'Nonchalant enough for you?'

For a split second, Mallory imagined herself climbing into their lap. She'd look to see if their pupils blew the way they did in the lake. She'd carefully run her thumb over Cornelia's jaw and she'd wait to feel one of Cornelia's arms snaking around her waist, for them to adjust one of their knees so that it—

'I probably shouldn't be doing this, either,' Cornelia said to the car roof. 'But I can't seem to make myself care about being caught looking, or drawing Tate's attention to us. I should be angry at them pushing Sully out – you know my feelings on the concept of policing, but Sully tries her best in a rotten system, and pushing her out in favour of actual rot seems counterintuitive to progress. I should be absolutely besotted with rage, and there's just nothing where my usual fire should be.'

'Nihilism,' Mallory said, forcing her gaze away. 'The last defender of apathy.'

'Do you think we have time to put together a book of very uninspiring quotes before we scuttle off the immortal coil, or whatever that Apparent fellow says?'

'It might get in the way of solving our case,' Mallory said. 'But while we're sitting here, I also don't see why not. What else have we got?'

'Yellow cars: if you want to be seen, they're not a PI's dream.'

Mallory laughed. 'We could also try "Costumes: not just for Samhain".'

'Fuck, that was such a Theodore thing to say.' Cornelia paused, their smile fading. 'I wanted to talk to you about that, actually. Terrible segue, but here we are.'

'About Theodore?'

'About the note. I've been wondering if it isn't a case of—'

Their phone buzzed in their hand and they vaulted into a sitting position.

Diana
It's Observer Johnson
Carvings in stomach, whole shebang
(And I do)
(Sorry)

'Shit,' Cornelia said again, rubbing their face as Mallory felt the colour drain from hers. 'If it didn't already feel personal...'

'Let's think about this logically.' Mallory willed herself not to start crying, despite crying seeming like such a logical conclusion these days. 'The Copycat murderer has now killed two people. Left us one note. We have just over one day until Samhain, as the note threatened. What is the Copycat doing, and why?'

'If we take Theodore into consideration. The bodies he dug up last year – that was Paul Blackburn, and Freya Evans. Himself. And... Jacob Gabbott.' They said his name carefully, like it hurt. 'Add to that Hayley Eason and Observer Johnson... does the Copycat need to emulate the Whistler exactly? Does the Copycat need seven souls?'

'Do Theodore and Jacob count as souls? Theodore didn't kill Jacob, and we know he didn't kill himself. Right?' Mallory paused, a sudden terror overcoming her.

'We found a witch trace,' Cornelia said patiently. 'He was Apparent. He didn't kill himself, and couldn't have manipulated someone else into doing it for him. Magically, anyway.'

'Oh yes. Sorry, temporary lapse in conviction. Okay.' She took out her notebook, keeping a weather eye on the Observatory for Diana to return, and drew three columns.

WHISTLER MURDERS	COPYCAT MURDERS	THEODORE MURDER

'What do they have in common?'

'Magic. Untraceable magic.'

'Magic that we were able to trace in the case of the Whistler murders,' Mallory said. 'Magic we were able to trace at Hayley's scene. Magic we were able to trace from Theodore's lightbulb.'

'Okay. What else?'

'A witch was involved in all of them. A witch with Apparent heritage in the case of the Whistler and Copycat murders, and a witch-for-many-generations witch in the case of Theodore's.'

'There aren't many multi-generation witches in Wrackton,' Mallory said. 'It hadn't occurred to me before. Do you still have the list of attendees?'

Cornelia did – in an utterly unprecedented moment of organisation, they'd taken a photo of the attendees list they'd taken from the night Theodore was killed, though they had to scroll through hundreds of irrelevant screenshots to find it. Mallory scanned the photo and made a note of a small handful of names. 'It leaves us with the Broadwicks – including you, Agatha and Ethel – Diana, me... and Vincent Van Doren.'

'Okay. So realistically, it's between my mother, my father and Van Doren,' Cornelia said, and Mallory's heart swelled at how objective Cornelia was being.

'Realistically, yes. Imogen and Ezra Broadwick, and Van Doren. One of those three people killed him. But. Perhaps they're not aware they did it.'

Mallory looked at her list again.

'Perhaps all three of these murders have something to do with the Ternion.'

'Elaborate,' Cornelia said.

'This is a total stab in the dark – but Theodore is a Samhain ghost. What if the "walk the earth" thing the Ghoul Council has everyone so stressed about is actually just the idea of calling the Ternion's souls back to walk the earth... as Samhain ghosts? I think I tried to say this when we were with Observer Johnson, but I couldn't get the words out for some reason. We have now met, and have one held semi-hostage, two of the three Ternion. We know there are other ghosts – what if Katherine was someone's past attempt at bringing back the Ternion? Goddess, what if *Blair* did it?'

'Killed her sister, to see if it would work?' Cornelia frowned, chewing it over.

'We should go talk to Blair. Shit! I forgot, when I talked to her before' – somehow not even a day ago, but a lifetime had passed since – 'she said something I meant to tell you, but I clean forgot all about it. She said, "something is coming, and you can't stop it". There was something else too, about—'

Diana rapped on the window, startling them both. She checked no one was coming and pulled the overalls off before throwing herself in the back of the car, exhaling heavily. She had an evidence bag clutched under her arm with the Wrackton police logo printed on it.

'I see we've reached the "be gay, *do* crimes" portion of the case,' Mallory said drily.

'It's not like they're going to figure it out in time to arrest me before I die. Let's go home. Wait, this is my car. Move, Cornelia.'

Cornelia clambered over the driver's seat as Diana got out, but before they managed to fully extract their legs from the front of the car, Diana shoved them. Cornelia sprawled with their face between the seat cushions, swearing at her but laughing at the same time.

'Mild comic relief before I say that was definitely poor Observer Johnson. By the way, not one person questioned who I was. Tate's team are worse than I imagined.'

'Did Tate see you?'

Diana shook her head, starting the car. 'He left quickly – someone on his team mentioned to one of the other CSIs that he was off speaking to a judge, urgent business. Anyway, it was fucking brutal. Exactly like the Whistler murders.'

'Poor Julian,' Mallory said. 'This is so unfair. We might've been the last ones to see him alive.'

They sat in silence as it sank in. Julian was a man they'd known their whole lives. He'd begrudgingly helped them time and time again, despite never wanting to. He'd made it quite clear he did not enjoy their company or the trouble they brought with them all too regularly. But he'd done it all the same.

'You just missed Mallory suggesting we go talk to Blair,' Cornelia said, and Mallory filled Diana in.

'Let's say we do talk to her – what are we going to say? "Hi, we think someone has been orchestrating a bunch of murders in your name. But quick question, are you involved in some way, and did you kill your sister and is that why you keep asking about meeting her even though we've explained over and over that she's been bricked into the Mayoral Offices permanently because the Ghoul Council and the UML are very, very bad at their jobs? Thanks babe."'

'I think we'd put it a bit better than that,' Mallory said, flushing. 'But you maybe have a point.'

'I'm all for talking to a literal goddess of Occulture, I just think we need a stronger case first. We could look at the scene samples I lovingly collected. I even used one of Cornelia's disgusting beetles without being spotted,' Diana said.

Another silence fell between them, pauses speaking volumes more than Mallory could hope to articulate. A clock ticking down and down and down. Time passing no matter what they did.

'I suppose we have to ask another question,' Cornelia said. 'And apologies for being serious. But. Is all of this… our fault?'

Mallory wished there was a simple answer.

'Yes, in the sense that whoever is killing really, really wants our attention. No, in the sense that we can't be personally responsible for who the Copycat chooses to murder.'

'It just all feels so similar. Like, yeah it's functionally the same method. But it feels like we're going full circle. Being dragged around by a serial killer who's watching us. Maybe there'll always be Jacobs, even after we're gone.'

It felt true, no matter how much Mallory didn't want it to be. It felt like someone was watching them and laughing while they stumbled around the facts of the case, trying to piece together motive and means and opportunity while the Copycat was puppeteering them to their end. They had nothing more than a witch magic trace, and—

'Maybe the answer is right in front of us,' Mallory said, sitting up. 'Maybe the answer is sitting in the Broadwicks' bunker.'

'Mallory, we just discussed that, remember?' Cornelia said gently.

'No! I mean maybe the answer is to *make Blair go away.* Help her pass on!'

'That feels about as likely as ending the Besiegement,' Diana said. 'Not to dismiss your great idea. But even if we make Blair pass on, someone's still murdering.'

Mallory pressed her fingers against her eyes, forcing back a prickle of tears. 'I'm enjoying this honest questioning hour, though, and I have another one: is this our legacy? Folk dying around us until we die too?'

'I have honestly no idea,' Cornelia said. 'I'd like to hope not.'

'Then let's stop hoping,' Mallory said fiercely. 'We make our own legacy. We're the Undetectables. Dying won't make that untrue. For the last time, let's unmask a killer.'

SEVENTEEN

'Tut, tut,' Grey said as Theodore arrived back to their— *the* hotel, wishing, not for the first time, that he had a literal tail to tuck between his legs.

'Me?' Theodore looked around as though there were telltale signs of his misdeeds on his hands. 'No body, no crime, as they say!'

'Oh, you're home.' Grey looked up as though he was just noticing his presence.

He had pulled a large desk into the room from goddess-knows-where and was sitting on an oxblood leather swivel chair, stacks of colour-coded pages laid out in front of him.

Theodore made a move on the chessboard, his knight now facing Grey's. Annoyingly, his knight had sprouted a cravat and he glared at it, willing the cravat to go away. 'Yes. I have returned to the secret den of scheming and contemplation that I have been granted temporary access to. It is not my home, and I was not aware there was anyone else here for you to talk to. What are you dressed up for?'

Grey was resplendent in a grey suit and a thin-knit black turtleneck, his pocket watch tucked into the recesses of his blazer. He looked more like his old self than Theodore had seen in months, the alley-rumpled suit from earlier gone.

'You've even brushed your hair,' Theodore said suspiciously. 'You didn't look like this earlier.'

'Earlier I was accosted in an alleyway, on my way to a meeting, by a fugitive ghost. I take your point that I have been less sartorially consistent these days. Hurts the heart. And I've decided that there is little the heart wants more than to be human,' Grey said, as if that answered anything.

'I thought the heart wanted Tortured Dark Academia Professor with early signs of alcoholism,' Theodore said. 'But I digress. Did… Do you remember where you went, after Oakpass, and your alleged meeting?'

'I came back here, smashed a glass, had a glorious bath, dressed' – he ticked these off on his fingers – 'and then you showed up, in a decidedly less panicked state than when you dragged me backwards through an alley.'

'Well. Needs must,' Theodore said. 'Why didn't you go back to your state of the art apartment for a bath?'

'Speaking of Oakpass,' Grey said loudly, ignoring him. 'What did you find for me?'

Theodore paused, unsure if he should press. What business was it of his where Grey removed his clothing? 'A lot of nothing.'

'And?'

'Dirt. Spiders. Opulent excess. A lackadaisical attitude towards hoovering. It's your turn.' He gestured to the chessboard. 'That's all you did earlier? A meeting?'

Grey made a move without looking at the board, his eyes piercing Theodore's.

'And I got dragged backwards through an alley by a possible murderer.'

After an agonising few seconds passed in uncomfortable silence, Theodore said, 'As I am not a murderer, it must've been some other guy. Anyway, moving on from where you were, or weren't. *Whom* were you tutting at? Given that we can ask questions after chess moves. This is your game. You should probably answer, lest you wish to be thought of as a... a scoundrel,' Theodore added primly.

Grey's lips twitched. 'Hollis,' he said shortly. 'He was holding out on me. In one of his stories, the characters find a secret passageway beneath the floor of Not-Oakpass.'

'Which is probably also full of dirt.'

'In his version,' Grey went on, ignoring him, 'the necromancer queen Ruthless Monroe finds a secret stone or some bollocks that allows one to summon the trapped goddess within. A fancy-cut rock, disguised as something else. They called it the Obsidian.'

'Does that ring a distant little bell in your overstuffed mind?' Annoying Voice asked.

He didn't respond, because he wasn't sure what Annoying Voice meant, and if he wasn't sure what Annoying Voice meant, he wasn't giving it the satisfaction of not knowing something, nor the gratification of helping him.

'This might sound absolutely bizarre, but I have come to the conclusion that the Ghoul Council want whatever real-life item the Obsidian corresponds to. If I can find it, I'm sure I can use it to either nullify the agreement and approach other buyers, or force their hand. Cash. I'm sure there's a loophole in the wording.'

Theodore dragged his cardigan across his body, hoping this would be the time the woollen fabric would slice him in half so he could cease having this conversation.

'Be that as it may,' Theodore started, realising two seconds too late that that was precisely the wrong thing to say.

'So you agree? You think that, festering among the "dirt" of Oakpass Manor is something monumental, and I've been wasting my time trying to turn it into a fucking luxury hotel?'

'I couldn't possibly say,' Theodore said, wishing it was clear how much he meant it.

Grey tapped a stack of Hollis's writing. 'You know something else? We don't talk about Hecate and Morrigan as much in Occulture,' he continued, without waiting for Theodore to speak (presumably mistaking the fact Theodore had closed his eyes to wish for a way to undo everything that had come before now for a rare bout of active listening). 'I assume it's *because* of the Ternion in some way, because you'd imagine Occulture would be fascinated by the idea of some sort of summoning rock.'

'Like a ghostlight, but not terrible,' Theodore said, opening his eyes again. 'Anyway. Have you ever played bridge? I think we should start a bridge club. Just the two of us! It won't be at all like the gin rummy or the poker or the go fish or the Monopoly or the Guess the Person games, or even like the chess game you can't stick to the rules on. It would be totally different.' Theodore absently picked up a witchlight from one of the bookshelves, the air crackling as he tossed it hand to hand. 'I wouldn't throw the cards into the fire this time. I mean. I never resort to fire. Ever.'

Grey watched him, a thoughtful expression on his face. 'I've been thinking about that night.'

'Which one? I've experienced many in their entirety over the last eight years, so you'll have to be more specific.'

'*The* night. The night you and I met, and you met your fate. I've been trying to recall why I ever even approached you.'

As he had previously implied it was as a distraction from heartbreak, Theodore felt this new rewriting of the narrative to be bordering on offensive. He bristled, his cat ears quivering.

'Is the idea that you *wanted to* not good enough?'

'It doesn't quite explain my lack of memory,' Grey said. 'I'd enjoyed myself thoroughly at the free bar. I remember seeing Vincent Van Doren and the Broadwicks. But I had this sense of... a job to do. It's just every time I think about it, it floats out of my head. The witchlight reminded me, but it's an idea on the tip of my tongue.' He paused. 'I clearly wasn't in my right mind. It was as though someone else was making decisions for me.'

Theodore knew all about that.

'For what it's worth, I always thought it was Van Doren,' Grey said. 'That you'd got in the way of one of his plans somehow, and he took care of things. I can't imagine it would've been the first time. He had an unfortunate tendency to sweep things under the rug until you could no longer walk on it. It is entirely his fault Jacob Gabbott did what he did.' Grey poured a generous measure into his almost-empty glass. 'Things could be so different now. I wouldn't be here, for example. But then, neither would you. I always thought your little friends would figure it out for you, but they got wrapped up in that mess. A pity they'll die. I am fond of them, don't get me wrong. But there're only so many times you can bail someone out. Saying that, I also wouldn't be surprised if the Broadwicks had you killed. The heads of the Ghoul Council having a pet ghost? It's practically poetic and desperately ironic. Too ironic, in fact, to not consider it was deliberate. Now, where were we?'

Theodore felt something burn through him, a crackle of fury he hadn't felt in years. Grey's callous dismissal of the Undetectables, as though their deaths were inevitable. As though all of this was *inevitable*, and not some manufactured series of events designed to make everyone feel powerless to stop them, designed to inspire apathy and permissiveness.

'*Careful, Theodore. You're getting sentimental in your cowardice*,' Annoying Voice whispered.

'I am NOT a coward,' Theodore shouted.

Grey blinked. 'I think you'll find I never suggested anything in the slightest. However, if the shoe fits…'

Perhaps it was the mention of the Undetectables, or the unwarranted mention of That Night, or the fact Theodore wanted so, so badly to be able to tell Grey he was better off running screaming from looking for Ternion-related objects and never looking back. Perhaps it was the fact that Grey had made no move to help him solve his murder despite his promises, or the fact he was not *interested* in the concept of Theodore's notoriety. Perhaps it was all of these things, or none of these things.

But something that had been pulled taut inside of Theodore for days, months, years, almost a decade, snapped.

'Fuck off. FUCK OFF, Grey. I am grateful you gave me a place to hide, but I don't need it anymore. I can go anywhere in the world. There is nothing stopping me leaving.'

'Do it, then.' Grey crossed to the door and held it open. 'Leave.'

Theodore tossed his head so the cat ears wavered. 'You need me more than I need you.'

'I thought you needed to be exonerated?'

'I can do that alone. In fact, I can do *anything* alone. Totally alone, with not a single voice in my head! I could get on a cruise ship and hide in the hull. Maybe commandeer a boat and float somewhere distant. I can go *anywhere in the world*, Grey. I can go anywhere at all, but you're the one who can't leave Wrackton.'

Grey laughed, his stupid, handsome face twisted in surprise. 'That's a preposterous statement, I hope you're aware.'

'It's not! Hexana help you – you have the *freedom* to leave, but you're trapped here, in the epicentre of Occulture. Your empire ties you down. You might think you can get on a plane and start over, but you're tethered to your hotels and your businesses, your contacts and the people who owe you favours, your alliances, your failures, your debts. But most of all, you're tethered to Hollis Hadley, an Apparent man who scribbled things on paper for a living, and he's a puzzle you can't solve. You're chasing ghosts and living among them.'

Grey blinked at him and Theodore felt like he was levitating. He had to check his feet were firmly on the ground twice before he concluded that the feeling was a dizzying sense of relief. Relief at having spoken his mind without exploding anything. Without incurring the wrath of the Voice.

'Hollis was my friend. Everything that happened between us happened a long time ago,' Grey said slowly. 'It's reasonable to mourn the dead.'

Theodore hit the chessboard with a bolt of static, pieces scattering across the room, the board cartwheeling dangerously close to the roaring fire. Grey watched it, unmoving.

'And there's been nothing and nobody for you since! You're here rummaging through boxes of his inventions trying to find meaning in them, when it's all fiction – a magic *rock* called "The Obsidian"? *Really*, Grey? – and you're searching for him in the bottom of a bottle. Chasing the high of something that's increasingly harder to reach. Is it Daddy's approval? Is that it? Some sort of internal need to be the most special boy the world has ever seen? All your friends are dead,' Theodore said, and felt a sob choke him. 'All your friends are dead, or about to die and you are— I am all you have left. I'm all there is. You need me more than I need you.'

Grey closed his eyes, pressing the whiskey glass against his lids.

He may have been crying. Theodore wasn't sure and thought asking would ruin the moment.

'You've made your point. What do you need from me?'

'I need a murder board. AND markers. Good ones, not squeaky ones. And I'll need paper. And a hot cup of tea.'

'I'll call the maid.'

'Thank you.' Theodore sniffled unnecessarily. 'And for what it's worth, I think you're onto something with the whole outside forces idea—' He broke off, throat constricted, and fell to the ground, gasping. It was not the sense of air being cut off, but a strange sensation of something pressing, pressing, *pressing* on his form, sparks flying, his brain insisting he was dying.

'*Enough*,' Terror Voice whispered.

The pressure lifted and Theodore panted on the ground. Air passing through, air leaving. Static settling as he reoriented himself. He felt a cool sense of humanity nearby and looked up to see Grey crouched over him, hand lifted like he was going to try to touch him.

'I'm good. Really could do with that tea,' Theodore said, as Terror Voice slinked away. An idea popped into his head and he'd spoken it aloud before he could talk himself out of it. 'Also, could you reach into my head and do some demon magic manipulation?'

Grey's teeth sank into his lower lip, suppressing a grin. 'I thought you'd never ask.'

'I mean it. I need a safe... *pocket* of my mind, where I could believe I was able to process my thoughts, so if anyone wanted to reach in and read them, they would be persuaded into believing they could not. Additionally, could you ask me no questions about it?'

'I've done a lot of things with a lot of men, Theodore, but I'd have to say this would be a first.' Grey moved closer. 'We'd have to combine our magic – ghost and demon would have to work in perfect tandem. There is no room for error. It would be an utter act of mutual trust.'

'Shall we have a safe word? We could try "armchair", perhaps.'

'Better make it something dangerous. Let's try... "fire".' He lifted his hand, inches from Theodore's crackling skin.

Coldness radiated over him, and he could swear he felt the long-dead hairs on his arms raise in anticipation. 'In order for me to get inside your head fully… I'll have to risk you getting inside mine.'

Theodore considered this. He had never possessed anyone – not properly. He'd somewhat convinced the gravediggers to dig up those bodies, but it was tremendously *easy* to do so when the Apparents in question were both incredibly dim and trusting, and predisposed to digging graves. He'd tried to get inside Mallory's head once, in a last-ditch attempt to tell her what was happening to him, but he had waited for permission she did not grant. Ghoul Council rules aside, full-throat possession had always seemed too dangerous. He knew what it meant to have someone else's voice in his head, and did not wish to be that voice for anyone.

This would be different. Grey would be working in Theodore's mind. He'd be letting Grey in.

'Shall I tell you a secret?' Theodore asked softly.

Grey raised an eyebrow.

'I've never done this before, either.'

A flicker of a smile passed over Grey's lips, and he nodded once, moving back to the centre of the room.

Theodore closed his eyes. They were feet away from each other but they could've been touching, the walls of his consciousness warping with dizzying speed as Grey gently pressed against his mind, the pressure building and building until the dizzying sense fell away and Theodore felt as though he was in a room full of vaults.

In careful, soothing tones that made Theodore feel as

though he was floating, Grey persuaded Theodore to step over the threads of connection between Theodore and the Voice – webbed and strange in his mind's eye – and towards a hidden door in the metaphorical hall of vaults that made up Theodore's mind. He could not see Grey, but he could feel him, cold wisps of air that tickled Theodore's neck and jaw and made him feel at ease. He was unclear what was his magic and what was Grey's.

'Is this okay for you?' Grey murmured. Theodore's eyes flicked to him; his eyes were unfocused, his hand raised and fingers twitching like he was moving through a filing cabinet. As he moved, Theodore felt a thrill shoot up his spine.

It was nice to have him in his head. He felt for the threads of Grey's connection to him, finding persuasive tendrils, and pulled them closer, simultaneously feeling Grey's mind resist, refusing him entry as an ornate doorway appeared before him, Theodore's vaults disappearing as he stepped closer and closer to the door, aware of Grey's breath catching in surprise.

'If I open the door, what then?' Grey whispered.

'I could step inside. Read your thoughts.' He placed his hand on the door and Grey inhaled sharply. 'But the way you're in my head, I think you could read mine.'

Grey blinked, like he understood something, and Theodore desperately wanted to ask what he wanted, but then the door disappeared and Theodore was back in his own vaulted mind. He stepped through the doorway of the hidden vault and the door closed behind him as Grey whispered encouragement.

'You are safe here,' Grey murmured, and Theodore felt a euphoric sense of someone running fingers down his face, down his chest, a palm flat against his stomach. 'And if you wanted to share any of those thoughts aloud, well. You'll just have to make a game of it.'

As quickly as the sensation had appeared, it vanished, and the vault door closed behind him.

It did feel safe. Like all his thoughts in there would be his own. Like the Voice could not reach him here.

'*You have more free will than you think*,' a voice said in his head, but it was not the Voice, and by the time Theodore thought to reply, he was fully back in the room, Grey was opening the door to head to the underused kitchen, and it was like nothing had happened (chess pieces thrown asunder aside).

For the first time in two very long years, he felt in control of his own thoughts. Clear-headed and… not free. But capable of consequence-free action.

There was one thing he needed to do. One thing he could do, as a fail-safe. In case something went wrong tomorrow night. In case the Voice needed some persuading of its own.

'Murder board, wasn't it? Great. Thank you. While you're sorting all that, I'll be right back – I have to go pick up something. A metaphysical object. Hypothetically.'

And once again Theodore exited stage left, pursued by a bugbear.

EIGHTEEN

The names of the deceased shone wetly on their fresh murder board, next to slightly blurry photos of Observer Johnson that Diana had sneakily taken on her phone.

HAYLEY EASON. JULIAN JOHNSON.

Mallory pulled her notes together, frowning as Diana settled cross-legged against the wall and Cornelia commenced their ubiquitous pacing. Her things weren't left the way she'd thought – the diorama was in a slightly different place, old notes that had nothing to do with anything pressing were scattered around the room. It had the air of being disturbed.

She pushed it aside, aware of the pendulum swing of time getting faster and faster, closer to ten p.m. than she was comfortable with.

'Okay.' Mallory pointed to the scene photos of the victims. 'Julian Johnson was killed in the manner Sully reported Hayley Eason was killed. Only Hayley's body was burned. There was a five-hour window after we left the Observatory in which someone could've come in to kill him. There's a reason he wasn't set on fire – or specifically, there's a reason Hayley was.' Mallory sighed. 'We need Sully for this, she's our common denominator.'

Diana waved her phone. 'Still trying to get her. Really curious why she wasn't on the scene at all, even after Tate left, but still let us know it was another murder.'

Mallory grimaced. She hated suspecting people they knew, people they liked. Hated both the idea of Sully acting of her own free will, and the even worse idea of Theodore being the one pulling the strings.

It all had to mean something.

'You're thinking.' Diana picked up a rubber band ball and passed it from hand to hand. Mallory noticed that she'd changed into a leopard print dress and platform Mary Janes, her hair in an immaculate half-up, eyeliner perfect. She realised with a jolt that she was trying to make sure that if she died in her current outfit, she wasn't running the risk of a Theodore-style ghost costume.

'I'm thinking you look fabulous.'

Diana blew her a kiss, and resumed her anxious ball-passing. 'Okay. Suspect list. Sully, obviously, because we know an Apparent-Occult individual is involved *and* she was at the scene.'

'In the first murder, yes, and it's reasonable to extrapolate that the same person was involved in Julian's,' Mallory said. 'Chromatography station is working on those samples you took from the scene for us, so we should be able to say definitively in the next few minutes. Pending replication tests, of course.'

Cornelia picked up the marker again and wrote:

ALYSSA O'SULLIVAN
REMINGTON DAVIS
SAM BRIDEWELL

'Okay,' Mallory said. 'Means?'

'Witch-Apparent heritage,' Cornelia said.

'Great. I knew that, but hearing it out loud makes it worse. This is all nice and vague.' She had the overwhelming sense they were barking up the wrong tree. That Remington, Sully and Sam were convenient suspects. That she was trying to grasp handfuls of sand and coming up with nothing. She couldn't make Theodore working with any of these people fit, because she couldn't make Theodore being involved fit in the first place. It was unthinkable, even in the face of their limited evidence.

'I'm getting real undetectable vibes from this Undetectables case,' Diana said. 'Shall I check the Observer Johnson scene samples? Did you know this is the first time I processed an *entire* scene by myself? And the last, obviously, but still!' She squinted at the chromatography station. 'It's not ready yet. No real colour I can see. Just muddy.'

'Okay, back to our suspects. Why would Sully do this right now? Whether it's attached to Theodore or not,' Mallory added hastily. 'But let's assume that Theodore is only part of the puzzle. We have to consider personal motives too.'

'Observer Johnson thought that Jacob had had some sort of help,' Diana suggested. 'Maybe she's always been in on it, and we just missed it first time around? Plus, she could be angry about Tate kicking her out of her job for good this time, and decided to start things up again by herself?'

'Is it enough?'

'People are generally pathetic,' Cornelia said. 'Jacob did the whole Whistler thing because he was mad at his dad. Any motive's good enough if you're able to convince yourself you're right.'

'Incredible that we've all been spared your wrath, then,' Diana said, and Cornelia flipped her off.

'The one thing giving me pause is that we have used Sully's magic sample in the Sprinter before, and have samples on file. And while the Sprinter gave us a match to the same spell used in the Whistler case, it didn't offer any *other* matches,' Mallory said. 'But we don't have a magic sample from Remington.'

Cornelia snapped their fingers. 'I'll be right back!'

They ran off upstairs and thumped around for a few minutes, coming back down dressed in their favourite oversized jumper and ripped jeans.

Mallory blinked.

'What? Diana got dressed up for death, I decided I should too. Anyway, Sandi made him give me this business card last night, before they went into the Larix – she really cannot grasp who I am and got it into her head that I'm a director? He didn't seem to mind, though. It's going to be weak sample, but we should be able to pull magic from it.'

They cleared a space at the table, keeping a careful distance from the chromatography station as they hummed.

'Are you sure?' Mallory asked after a minute.

'If you don't trust me, do you trust Lawrence XI?' Cornelia triumphantly held up a sound beetle, which was resolutely green.

Mallory grinned. 'Great work.'

'I'll run that sample too,' Diana said, as Mallory turned back to their list. 'Doesn't it sound so official when I say it? Why didn't I do this before, science is so much *fun*.'

'It really seems like Sully is the most viable suspect on the list, doesn't it?' Mallory said softly. 'I like her, I like Dr Ray, I like that she's tried very hard to resist the general order of police in Wrackton, but as we say, no stone unturned. Diana? What's happening over there?'

Diana had gone oddly still.

'What's wrong? Is the sample contaminated?' Mallory turned around in her seat, straining to get a proper look.

'It's blue,' Diana said, her voice strained.

'What?' Mallory said, at the same time as Cornelia said 'No fucking way. *Demon* magic?'

'It's absolutely, definitely, 100 per cent blue.'

Mallory didn't know what to make of that, couldn't factor in the implications of a demon involved in the murders.

'This is— Do you hear that?' Mallory sat up, listening to the sounds of shouting right outside her front door.

It sounded like several men trying to break up a fight, until the doorframe splintered and a uniformed police officer ran into the sitting room where she sat, frozen, staring at him.

She couldn't move, and not because of magical interference. Every bit of her was frozen in a combination of terror and surprise, unable to reconcile hearing shouting with someone forcibly entering her home. It was slow motion, utterly impossible. This was her parent's house. She'd grown up here. There had never been so much as a break-in in all her twenty-two years, and that was even with leaving the house empty for most of the last two, because Wrackton was governed in such a way as to eliminate the *need* for this kind of anti-community behaviour. They just had petty grievances and murder.

There was something akin to irony in the fact that the first person to attempt a break-in was this police officer, and Mallory felt an overwhelming urge to laugh.

The papers. The diorama moved. Second break in.

She illogically worried it had been Cornelia and Diana's focus on partying that had brought them to this, or this to them. Maybe Kingston had stashed something particularly illegal in one of the rooms and they'd found out somehow.

Seconds passed while these thoughts raced through Mallory's head.

'I have a search warrant. Stay seated,' the uniformed officer said.

He was followed by a stream of people in plain clothes, Nathan Tate at the rear, his expression unreadable. Tate directed the stream of people into rooms they were already entering, like this was planned, gloves on, careless hands tearing at bookshelves and entering Mallory's kitchen and upturning their murder board, papers scattering further.

'Who are all these people?' Cornelia demanded, trying to snatch a book off the uniform who immediately got in their face, demanding in turn that they calm down, while Tate looked at them like they were an idiot.

'They're police. We're all police,' he said slowly.

Mallory felt her stomach bottom out, staring at Cornelia and Diana but unable to say anything other than, 'I think I'm going to have a panic attack.'

And then she did, while the police ransacked her house. They weren't careful with the dioramas.

'What does the warrant say? What is the warrant *for*?' Cornelia asked, but Tate held up a hand.

'Remain seated, or I'll have to take you in.'

Cornelia snatched the warrant out of his hand, their hands shaking. 'This is a warrant for this property *and* Broadwick Mansion. Where we don't live. And you're looking for "items or documents pertaining to an open investigation". What the *fuck*? On what grounds?'

'Reasonable belief,' Tate said.

'Have you spoken to Imogen and Ezra Broadwick? I'm sure we can get this sorted out,' Diana said sweetly.

Tate raised an eyebrow. 'We are under no illusions that Mx Broadwick's relationship with their parents has been strained in recent years. We know *everything* about you, Cornelia Broadwick.'

'Do you? Interesting. Maybe you call tell me what I should wear to my funeral, I'm still wavering between my favourite jumper and—'

'Specifically, I know your proclivity for wriggling out of trouble.'

Cornelia scowled at him. 'I have no idea what you're talking about.'

'I've heard about you. Broke a sacred vampire covenant two years ago and bribed a uniformed officer not to press charges by offering him a ticket to a ball, wasn't it? He's been binned since, and we have no grounds to reopen that investigation, seeing as the vampire in question – Beckett Kingston, wasn't it? – is dead, but step another *toe* out of line, and—'

His walkie crackled. 'Found something in the garden.'

'Go on,' he barked into it, eyes on Cornelia.

'Bunker. Signs of recent activity. Called in the Ghoul Council to open it. Khan and Reid said to wait.'

Mallory felt her blood run cold. She was melting into the sofa, barely able to move. Someone must've tipped them off about Blair. The Ghoul Council must've figured it out somehow. Of course it would all come out in the wash, and Cornelia would be blamed because it had been Mallory's idea to hide Blair in their family's home.

It didn't quite explain why they had a warrant for Mallory's house too, unless they had that wrong, somehow.

Tate said a few more things into his walkie, his eyes never leaving Cornelia, a slow, sadistic smile crossing his face. 'I've got you now,' he said quietly.

'I don't know what you're talking about,' Cornelia said. 'This whole fucking thing is ridiculous. It's entrapment, for starters. What judge okayed a search warrant with that many parameters? And on what grounds? Who ordered it? The most general, reaching, suspicious piece of shit I've ever seen—'

His walkie crackled again and he stepped away to speak into it as Cornelia shouted after him, making less and less sense as they got angrier and angrier.

Mallory had never actually seen a Cornelia versus the police confrontation, but it was no less than she'd expected, and the force of it was helping to melt her own terror. They could explain away the bunker. In fact, there was nothing to say Blair had come from anywhere – except Blair herself, but would they believe her? Would Blair turn them in, only to end up back in a ghostlight by herself? There was a clear path out of this. Mallory could see it. They just needed to stay calm—

'And get your fucking *ugly shoes* out of my house too, while you're at it!' Cornelia shouted after Tate as he walked down the hall.

'Shut up,' Diana said quickly. 'Shut the fuck up right now. I'm so serious.'

Cornelia did. Tate came back with the uniforms, who looked so excited they were sweating. They blocked the doorway, as if any of them were going to run.

'Fucking do it then,' Cornelia said, standing between Tate and Mallory.

Mallory stood slowly, putting a warning, pleading hand on Cornelia's arm. Cornelia pushed their sleeves up, their hands balled into fists that they seemed to force to relax, though their legs shook. 'Do what you came here to do.'

Tate nodded, then gestured for Cornelia to step aside.

Mallory felt compelled to sit down again, persuasion magic in her head telling her not to run, the look on his face telling her everything she was afraid to hear.

'Mallory Hawthorne,' he said, not bothering to hide the smile in his voice as he spoke. 'I'm arresting you on suspicion of the murders of Hayley Eason and Julian Johnson.'

NINETEEN

Theodore had once lamented how unseen he was in his day-to-day existence, and now realised what a fool he had been to wish it away. Being the most wanted man in Wrackton – in all ways but, he noted with a tinge of sadness, carnally – meant that standing in the lobby of his former place of employment was a particularly dangerous activity that could've benefited from a bit of being looked through. It should be easier to do things he did not want to do at all.

It was an even deeper misfortune that the Mayoral Offices no longer closed on the days around Samhain for the safety of the town. How Theodore would've loved to have been a fly on the wall for *that* meeting. Ignore the giant insects that keep 'escaping' from the Mayoral Offices! Ignore the ghost at large! Spend money in our town!

Instead of a clear path between him and his (incredibly risky, probably stupid and maybe even illegal) objective, he was amid hordes of Apparents and out-of-towners and locals trying to appear nonchalant as they toured the premises, which had been decked out with pumpkins and spider-webs and all manner of ghoulish things Theodore associated with Apparent Samhain and not Occult Samhain, which was much more sophisticated (Occult Samhain would never concern itself with hats and T-shirts that read *APPARENT-LY IT'S REAL MAGIC.* It would have good puns) and much more respectful of the dead (puns included).

His eighth anniversary was tomorrow night.

'Where's the fucking union on this? This was a three-day holiday last year!' an Office employee said to their companion as they rushed past.

'I could really do with a creature escaping right about now.' The companion swerved around a group of Apparents, and the employees, Theodore's former colleagues, a symbol of the ways he used to belong, disappeared into the recesses of the Mayoral Offices.

Theodore only vaguely recognised them – the Offices either had four employees or four hundred, and Theodore had wiled away many days without seeing anyone at all – but he wanted to grasp them firmly by the arms and tell them that the 'creatures' they so carelessly conjured were not what they thought. That he alone – excluding the Voice and, to an extent, the Undetectables – knew the truth, and was bestowing that truth upon them like a benevolent goddess. (*Stop screaming, why are you screaming?* he would say, and they would run and run and run and Theodore would have to take up residence in the nearest toilet and his life would be even more miserable than it was now.)

It had been to his benefit that his job was incomprehensible to anyone living. He'd responded to a call-out for 'an anthropologist with paranormal interests' to deal with what they called a 'five-year annual problem' of large, armoured creatures escaping from the Offices in the run-up to Samhain. But they – Vincent Van Doren, and the united face of the Mayoral Offices, plus the Ghoul Council, plus the UML, and probably some other random suits who'd stuck their oars in – had then taken great pains to make sure Theodore was never able to get close enough to figure out what they were, or what function they posed.

Then he'd died, and his job became mostly paperwork. And then he'd died a second time, when the Whistler… did what he did, and he found he was able to get much closer to the creatures than he'd bargained for. It was hilarious, really. Chortle-worthy. The answer was so obvious once he'd been clued in. If the Offices and the UML and the Ghoul Council had *asked* what they were, had really let him do his job, there'd have been an entire taskforce. An uprising. An army.

But there was just Theodore.

He drifted down the corridor towards the Night Mayor's office as a second group of tourists passed through him, and Theodore heard the telltale *POP* of several phones meeting an untimely end. Theodore had recently suggested to Grey he start a 'Tournion' business, leading groups around the Observatory and the Memorial Garden, which received one glare and half a laugh, which was an indication that Grey not only loved the idea, but would remember to credit Theodore down the line for such an obvious money-making hit. He would need to add a phone repair shop to the list of related start-up businesses.

He slid through a wall to hide while the Apparents flapped

and complained about their sudden loss of devices and found himself in a storage cupboard. He waited for the coast to be clear again, his face halfway through the door, while a faulty witchlight above the door of Dr Ray's office flashed maliciously at him. It could sense him, even if people couldn't.

He checked for the Voice and felt a faint flutter of connection. It wasn't gone. It would never be *gone* (until tomorrow night, that was) but it meant his and Grey's magic-melding attempts had actually worked. The Voice could not reach Theodore's most secret thoughts, and he had them aplenty, along with a litany of facts he'd prefer to keep to himself until the time was right.

The fact Mallory, Diana and Cornelia had chosen the bunker to hide Blair was good. The fact they did not seem to understand the bunker was even better.

The fact nobody in the Mayoral Offices seemed to understand anything about the anatomy of the building was better again. The fact they thought bricking up a wall was sufficient to prevent a 'creature problem' was only to his gain. There was someone in here who could help him. Someone similarly dead. Someone who was, unbeknownst to Her, guarding an object Theodore now needed. An object thrown in a grave. Not knowing the object's importance, but knowing the Voice was looking for it, he'd stolen it, just in case. In case the Voice changed its mind about giving Theodore what he'd bargained for. If it came down to it, it could be a bargaining chip. This object in exchange for his skeleton. For his future life. An elder solution to an old problem.

The door to Dr Ray's office cracked open and he watched Detective Inspector Alyssa O'Sullivan slip through the door.

He pressed closer, listening hard, dipping into the office and taking care to remain near a radiator so he wouldn't blast too much inexplicable heat into the room. He was becoming a master of hiding. A master of disguise.

'—any luck finding him?' Dr Ray asked.

Theodore felt a jolt of fear until Sully shook her head.

'Slipped back to the scene when Tate left, but he was gone. Fucker won't answer his phone now that he knows I'm looking for him. I should've—'

So not Theodore, then.

'You can't. Tate's going to keep this up for as long as he can, all you have to do is keep your nose clean. If you can get to Bridewell, I'm sure you can go over Tate's head. Maybe go back to the boys in Oughteron? They like him even less than you do. I can go with you. Leverage with their Mayor.'

Sully slumped down in her chair. 'Leverage with what? There's no evidence. We just like him for this. He was there, he's got Occult heritage.'

It took Theodore a moment to realise they were talking about Sam Bridewell, a name he'd seen scrawled on Mallory's notes when he'd broken into her house.

Mallory. Maybe she'd figured it out by now. Maybe she knew the truth.

The conversation drifted into uninteresting logistics, and Theodore resumed his journey to the centre of the earthly institution known as the Mayoral Offices, until he reached a point where invisibility was no longer an option, such was the strength of the Offices' magic. The walls became solid to him, his magic became weak. Semi-corporeal with all-corporeal limitations. No matter how strong he was, the Offices were stronger. Otherwise he'd have found a way to free Her a long time ago, as he was once meant to.

Here he was, exposed and ready to commit further crimes. Such was the life of the Notorious Theodore Wyatt.

And then he heard the distant strains of living people, talking as they came closer.

'—the neeecromancers lived *here*, I *heard*. My dear friend Hollis Hadley, rest in pieces, dollface, said that there were neeecromancers all *over* Wrackton' – the owner of this familiar voice curiously pronounced this as 'Wrecktune' – 'and he *was* right about *so* many things. Except the part where he died, of course. Rest in *pieces*, as I said!' the voice concluded.

'Fascinating, sugar kitten,' a second, bored voice said.

There was nowhere to run. Nowhere to hide. And it was all his own fault. He scurried up the corridor as the voices drifted ever-closer, bearing around the corner like they were stepping into frame, and found a statue of the Shroud of Morrigan (literally a statue wearing a poorly-rendered shawl) to cower behind. His plan was in tatters, when he was so close. If he was spotted now, that was the end. No body, so many crimes. A one-way Isolation trip to Bonemarrow Lake, where he would remain forever.

Which was, to state the obvious, a very long time.

'Oh wow,' the so-called Sugar Kitten said, 'a statue! Remmy, hold the bag. Hold the bag! Yes, yes, thank you darling. Okay let me pose with this statue. That could be my great-grandmom's statue and we wouldn't know!'

'Sandi, darling,' said the alleged Remmy, his voice no

less bored. 'It says on the base here that this is Morrigan. Apparently.'

'Oh, you're right, Remmy. I don't think I'm related to her. Take the picture!'

Theodore stayed as still as he could, feeling static charging through him. He had no control here.

'It doesn't say Clementine either,' Sandi continued, and Theodore placed her voice with a barely-concealed yelp of surprise.

Veteran gay icon Sandi Clementine. He hadn't seen her in any films in years, on account of his being dead, but he'd know her anywhere.

He wished he could tell Diana about it. Share a story, like she had when the Undetectables had worked on the Undead Complex case. Back when they trusted him. Back when they didn't understand.

'Film it. Film it! Hi, I'm Sandi Clementine, here with my friend Remmy—'

'We're meant to be undercover, sweet pea.'

'Yes but they won't *know* you're my fiancé, darling! Again! I'm Sandi Clementine, here with my dear platonic friend Remmy, and we're at the site of the neecromancer's home – Ruthless *Monroe*, that was me. Well not *me*. I'm here on a mystery *research* tour, getting in touch with my family *roots*. This moment… wow. I'll be drawing on it forever.'

It had been less than five minutes, and Theodore wondered how anyone in the world had ever thought Sandi Clementine was a wise iconic figure. She just said a bunch of random things that sounded vaguely deep.

'They've arrested someone,' the bored voice – Remmy – said.

'Gosh! Who?'

'A girl. Twenty-two.'

'Oh, I worked with her for a time! Genius. Very talented. Will go so many *places*.'

'Such as jail,' Remmy said.

He was starting to get a sinking sense she was talking about Diana, only because Cornelia's not-girl status would disqualify them from such an assertion.

He reached out a small, gentle tendril, feeling around the surface of Remmy's mind – Remington Davis, another actor, how fascinating! How terrible that he was notorious and not able to mingle with the Apparent elite! – as non-invasive as a ghost could get, and had barely seen the name before he blasted past them, all thoughts of the object that could save him from the Voice forgotten.

Sandi and Remington stared after him in shock, a combination of rapture, and perhaps, desire on their beautiful actor faces.

Or so he would allow himself to ponder, when he wasn't in a state of all-out panic.

It couldn't be Mallory.

It *couldn't* be.

TWENTY

Seconds after Mallory was put in handcuffs, Cornelia threw a book at the uniforms and was promptly arrested too. Mallory had just enough wherewithal to take it in, between her shock and horror and the sensation of cold metal against her aching skin. That, and Diana screaming at Cornelia that this wasn't going to help anyone, and to remember agency protocol.

The protocol being: shut up and don't say anything.

Neighbours poured out on the street as Mallory was marched from her house. Mrs Blackburn was there with her ratty dog, like something out of a nightmare.

Mallory blinked and she was in the police station, being shown into a bare questioning room, furnished with a metal table and chairs bolted to the floor. They used to do policing differently in Wrackton, she'd heard – tea and biscuits and a casual chat. This was new and unfamiliar and terrifying.

She blinked again, dazed, then realised she hadn't blacked out – they'd travelled via witchlight, which explained why she felt like someone had repeatedly punched her in the stomach, a wave of pain and anguish rolling over her.

Theodore had been wrong about that – witchlight travel was *not* getting easier.

They left her sitting for at least an hour, her mind racing, afraid to move, to fidget. Thousands of hours of Apparent police procedurals, countless thrillers and dozens of lectures she'd attended virtually told her that this was by design. This was a high-pressure, high-profile case. They needed to put someone behind bars. Anything she did could be picked over for signs of guilt. Of culpability.

Mallory picked a corner of the room to stare at, panic a sharp claw in her chest as she tried to breathe and remember the facts. To think logically. The look on Tate's face as he'd delivered the blow – *Mallory Hawthorne, I'm arresting you* – suggested that he was going to do whatever he could to keep her for the maximum holding period before he tried to charge her.

If he could charge her.

Finding the bunker, correctly determining there was some sort of ghostly activity within it, was just the icing on the cake. They thought they were going to get Theodore. Instead they would find Blair, and Mallory would be accused of harbouring a goddess of the Ternion. Of trying to replicate what the Whistler had wanted to do two years ago.

They'd raise the alarm, and she'd be well and truly fucked.

More time passed. Every second, every minute, was utter agony, and not just for her body. Adrenaline had lifted much of her general pain away, but a sharp ache ran from the base of her skull into her shoulder, flickering fluorescent lights making it worse by the second. She wanted to lie down.

She had no idea what time it was – she'd thought it was after ten p.m. when they'd brought her here, but there was no clock, no window, no way of telling.

An age passed before the door opened again. Mallory tensed as a lawyer walked in – a troll Mallory didn't know, who introduced themself as though Mallory should've been expecting them.

'Janne,' they said again, and when Mallory looked at them blankly, they leaned in closer and said, 'I'm a friend of the Ericssons.'

Mallory closed her eyes. Diana must've called in a favour to Langdon's uncles, who were the only people she could think of who might even *need* criminal lawyers.

'We're going to answer their questions very plainly.' Janne tossed back their curls. They were wearing a glittering navy suit with a pair of studded stilettos, their blue-grey skin as glossy as if they'd just stepped out of a magazine. 'If there's anything I feel you shouldn't answer, I will give you a signal, and I will ask them to stop and clarify anything I feel is not clear. I can't promise you it'll be okay, but we will go for a combination of honesty and simplicity.'

Tate threw open the door unceremoniously and Mallory jumped, fighting to rearrange her face while Janne whispered several more things Mallory didn't hear. He'd probably been watching her through the glass the whole time, waiting for the right moment to burst in. He sat on the other side of the desk and two more officers walked in carrying boxes. One stayed, leaning against the wall behind Tate.

'Where were you on the night of Tuesday 29th October, into the morning of Wednesday 30th October?' Tate started. Straight down to business.

Both Tate and his lackey watched Mallory with an intensity that she knew was designed to make her anxious and was, unfortunately, working.

She looked askance to Janne, who nodded once.

'I was at home. Asleep. I got a call just before midnight, asking me to come to the Observatory.'

'And you just went.'

Mallory said nothing, for it wasn't a question.

Janne winked subtly in approval.

'Okay, what did the caller say? Did they identify themselves?' Tate pressed.

'No, they didn't.' True: just because Mallory knew it was Sully didn't mean she'd actually *said* it was her.

'What did the caller say?'

'They said something was, quote, "happening again", and asked me to go to the Observatory.'

'Just you?'

'I took it as an implication that the caller meant my entire PI agency.'

'Former agency, I thought?'

'Soon to be, yes,' Mallory said.

'Why's that?' the other officer asked. Too eager, Mallory thought. They were warming up and he was jumping in too fast. Tate obviously thought so too, because he silenced the officer with a single glare.

Tate asked the same questions in slightly different words, and then asked again, more casually, about why the Undetectables were winding down.

'You've done a lot of work locally in recent years. Seemed to have won the approval of DI O'Sullivan and the Night Mayor, despite your lack of legitimacy. Why would you stop that all of a sudden?'

Mallory weighed it up in her head. Not telling him didn't help her any more than telling him did.

'You can answer that,' Janne said quietly.

'We're dying,' Mallory said simply.

'Yes, the Besiegement Curse,' Tate said, his tone still casual. 'I heard about that.'

Janne's eyes widened, and Mallory tried to ignore them.

Tate flicked through a file box in front of him with HAWTHORNE, MALLORY written on the side, taking great pains to ensure Mallory could see just how full the box was. Despite the Undetectables many run-ins with the police and their general allyship with Sully, and despite the files Cornelia had found in Ghoul Council HQ with their names on it, there was no way Wrackton police had anything that amounted to one single file folder, let alone the many file folders that would necessitate the multiple boxes Tate had had brought in.

This was a tactic. It was also, sadly, working; Mallory could feel doubts creeping in.

'When does that activate, again?'

'Tomorrow night.'

'Samhain,' Tate said slowly. 'Anyway, you got a call. Did you decide to go?'

'I did.'

'And who came with you?'

'My friends.'

'Their names, please.'

Mallory paused.

'You can answer that,' Janne said again.

'Diana Cheung-Merriweather and Cornelia Broadwick.' Which Tate already knew.

'And you brought them to the Observatory. This was at what time?'

'Midnight, or there abouts.'

'And how did you reach the Observatory?'

Mallory felt, with a heavy sense, that she was going to be here for hours answering drawn-out question after drawn-out question. He was going to try to wear her down, and if her pain levels ratcheted up a notch or two she'd start slipping.

'By taxi.'

'Do you normally travel around Wrackton by taxi?'

'Occasionally.'

'Yes or no.'

'It's not a yes or no question,' Mallory said calmly. 'Sometimes I do, sometimes I do not.'

'How often would you say you get taxis?'

'I consider them whenever it's more than a five-minute walk.'

'Nobody to give you a lift?'

'Sometimes.'

Tate levelled his gaze at her. 'I'm trying to help you out here, Mallory.'

Mallory said nothing.

'My client has already answered how she gets around Wrackton,' Janne said.

'So you got a taxi that night. Did you call it, or did someone else?'

'I can't recall.'

'I see. And did you go anywhere other than the Observatory that night?'

'We went straight from my house to the Observatory.'

'And where did you go then?'

Mallory hesitated. 'We went to visit a friend.'

'All of you together?'

'Yes.'

'Who is this friend?'

'Alyssa O'Sullivan.'

'For the record, that is DI Alyssa O'Sullivan,' Tate said.

Mallory swallowed. Her throat was so very dry, the light was so bright, Janne was not helping in the slightest—

'Did you find anything at this scene?'

Mallory paused. To admit she took samples may get her in more trouble; to not, when they saw the murder board and her samples out on the table, was pointless.

'We took non-invasive samples from the scene.'

'I see. On whose authority?'

'Our own. That's what we do. Help you detect the undetectable.' Her cheeks burned with embarrassment.

'And what did these samples say?'

Janne nodded assent again.

'We got one from Hayley Eason's crime scene that suggested the culprit was a witch with Apparent heritage.'

'And how does one narrow this down?'

Mallory explained how the Magic Magical Machine worked, how she was making the same determinations with manual chromatography, how the samples were giving good data, just not as complete.

'Fascinating,' Tate said, and Mallory felt relieved. Maybe he'd let her go. Maybe he believed— 'Fascinating that nobody has called into question the validity of your machines. You built them with Theodore Wyatt, didn't you?'

Mallory felt her face drain of colour. 'Yes, but—'

'And they're not peer reviewed? Not been subject to any kind of verification, beyond the alleged expertise of Theodore Wyatt?'

'Well no, but—'

'And you yourself haven't been to university, or have any formal training in forensics, beyond the teachings of Theodore Wyatt?'

'I've been taking classes,' Mallory said.

'You know, last night I got a very interesting call,' Tate said, leaning back in his chair. His eyes briefly left hers as he stretched, cat-like, then rolled his neck on his shoulders. 'A taxi driver saw the news about a death at the Observatory. It struck him as interesting – he said he dropped three witches off at the Observatory at a very strange hour. Two of them were deeply intoxicated, he said, and he'd worried about his upholstery.'

Mallory focused on not moving her face.

'He told me he dropped the witches off and drove away some distance, only to realise they'd left a bag behind. A kit bag, he said, that he believes contained what he termed "instruments". Ringing any bells?'

Just one very large, very loud alarm bell that wouldn't stop sounding no matter how much Mallory tried to make herself breathe through it.

She let silence elapse.

'I'm going to need you to answer that, Mallory.'

'My client doesn't have to answer that question,' Janne said.

'That's okay. We found the "kit" in Mallory's house. All sorts of jars and gloves and solvents. Care to explain what it is?'

Janne nodded again and Mallory wanted to ask them to leave.

'I'm a trainee forensic scientist. I co-founded a PI agency. Sometimes we investigate scenes. There were swabs in there too.'

'What did you talk to O'Sullivan about?'

'What we saw in the Observatory.'

'Why did you go to O'Sullivan?'

'You kicked us out of the scene.'

'Ah, yes,' Tate said, stretching. 'The scene. What were you doing there, when you arrived?'

It went on and on and on like this, Mallory answering every second question with nods or interjections from Janne. She was acutely aware at least an hour if not much more had passed by this point.

'—As you say,' Tate said, and Mallory realised she'd taken a micro nap and had no idea what she was alleged to have said. She blinked a few times. 'The body was burnt, and there were several items in your kit bag that have been taken into evidence as possible sources of accelerant.'

Mallory bit her tongue, knowing that pointing out that

their everyday kits were dry and contained only powders, lights, evidence bags, brushes and various jars would not be taken as correcting the record, but as her trying to assert her innocence. It was up to them to prove in court that she had something that could be used.

It would never get as far as the courts.

'Then of course, you and your friends fled the fire at the Larix. Suspicious, in the circumstances.'

Mallory realised she didn't quite care what would happen anymore. They'd decided she was guilty. They'd hold her for as long as they were allowed to, and it was longer than she had.

'Is it?'

'You didn't remain at the scene.'

'Mallory—' Janne started, but Mallory shook her head.

'There was a fire alarm, we left the building. We weren't instructed to remain.'

'Of course, this isn't the first time you've been involved with fire,' Tate said, and Mallory blinked.

'I need to talk to my client—' Janne started, but Mallory shook her head again.

'What?'

'I have it on good authority that the Witches of Bonemarrow Lake died in a fire earlier in the year. And you were the one who called the ambulance.'

'There are members of the Ghoul Council who will assert that that was the work of Dorothy Early,' Mallory said.

'What members?'

'The… The Broadwicks,' Mallory said, faltering. The rest of the Council hadn't witnessed the showdown at the lake.

'Interesting. Would you say your impending death has made you more reckless?'

'No,' Mallory said shortly.

'You know, I've wondered something for a while now. Speaking as we were of Theodore. You worked with him, didn't you?'

'You know the answer to that.'

'Yes or no.'

'Yes,' Mallory ground out.

'And last year, Mr Wyatt stole bodies from Wrackton graves, isn't that correct?'

'It is a matter of public record,' Mallory said. 'Yes.'

'Interesting. You claim you haven't a clue about that, but I find it very strange that you would have had *no* idea what he was up to.'

Mallory said nothing.

'It's strange nobody has really pressed you on this, either. You were instrumental in catching the Whistler – aka Jacob Gabbott, weren't you?'

'Yes. And the others.'

'There were the Dollhouse Murderers, though I recall we were the ones who issued the arrest.'

The uniform behind him smirked.

'And Dorothy Early,' Mallory added. 'The Wickermere Reaper.'

'You were involved in all those cases and didn't know to stop Theodore digging up bodies? Somehow missed that he was killing folk in Wrackton?'

'Allegedly. We don't know if he killed anyone or if he just dug them up—'

'Quick to defend him, aren't we?'

'It's not fair to accuse him when he's not here.'

'Just like Jacob Gabbott.'

'What?'

'He died before anyone could really verify that he was the Whistler, didn't he? You and your friends were sole witnesses to his demise. You and your friends found Vincent Van Doren dead in his office, heart ripped out and left on a plate. Very different to the other murders. Very personal. Who's to say you didn't pin that murder on Jacob?'

'Van Doren was Jacob's *father.* He had a specific parental-based gripe with Wrackton and his own lack of power, and he took it out on Van Doren.'

'So you say. But let's talk about something else. We found something very interesting in the Broadwicks' back garden. Did you know there was a bunker down there?'

'Yes,' Mallory said, as Janne said, 'My client doesn't have to answer—'

'And have you visited it recently?'

'No.'

'Strange,' Tate said. 'I drove past the Broadwicks' yesterday evening. Could've sworn I saw you closing the gate behind you.'

Mallory froze. It wasn't a question. She kept her mouth shut.

There was a glint in Tate's eye, one that said *I've got you now,* wolfish and hungry, and Mallory was powerless to stop him.

'So I ask again. Was that you?'

'I—'

Tate's walkie squawked into life. '*—Empty, Boss. But you won't believe—*'

Tate pressed a button on the walkie. 'Repeat that.'

'Bunker's empty. Ghoul Council are furious, but Alan's just got to Mayoral Square and you're going to need to see this. Right now. Hawthorne can't have done—'

Tate turned off the walkie, vaulting to his feet. 'Interview concluded.'

The first sign of doubt crossed his face before he carefully smoothed it away. He motioned out the door for someone to bring Mallory to a cell. Janne was sent elsewhere, and Mallory couldn't help but feel relieved.

The cell door clanged shut behind her and Mallory burst into angry, frustrated, terrified tears. She tried to think of the facts again, even though the facts were 'I'm in a cell', 'I've been accused of multiple murders', and 'if Janne was my lawyer for real I'd be going to jail', followed by '*the bunker is empty*'.

Blair was loose somewhere in Wrackton.

'Cornelia?' Mallory called timidly, unsure if they'd been released or if they were here somewhere, in a neighbouring cell. 'CORNELIA?'

Someone slapped her cell door twice.

'No shouting,' an officer said, and Mallory sank down on her bunk, pulling her knees to her chest.

She could feel panic building. Tate seemed to think she was the ringleader. The orchestrator. The Copycat Murderer. Or party to Theodore, in some way. The whole thing was both ludicrous and also, sadly, inevitable. Someone had to be the Copycat Murderer, and Tate did not care about being right in his accusations.

She lay down and closed her eyes, trying to count the

minutes as they passed but occasionally slipping into sleep. Her head and body ached. This was it. She was done for.

The door unlocked and Mallory scrambled to her feet as Sully poked her head around the door. Mallory almost knocked them both down throwing her arms around her in relief.

'Okay, okay, are you okay?' Sully asked, pushing her away gently. Mallory felt a flush of embarrassment and tried to recompose herself, remembering that Sully was a key suspect in the Copycat Murders and that her presence was not as much of a relief as it should be.

She tried to recalibrate, put herself back on guard. The real killer was still out there. Could be standing in this room.

'Yes. No. I'm fine. Why are you here?'

'Cornelia called the Broadwicks, who called me. They plan to return to Wrackton – the Ghoul Council were snooping around in their back garden earlier, and they've had enough. They're filing a case against Tate, but it's going to take some time – Imogen and Ezra are under the impression every bit of this is down to Theodore. In the meantime, they're pressuring Tate into either charging you quickly, or letting you go, given your… situation.'

And theirs, Mallory wanted to say.

'The Wrackton station still sees the Broadwicks as having some authority, and nobody wants to go down with Tate if he's overstepped. They've been all too keen to accommodate me, but I don't have long.'

A good enough answer, if a little too *full.* Mallory blinked a few times, trying to clear her head. 'Are Cornelia and Diana okay?'

'They were both questioned and let go hours ago.'

'Sully,' someone called. 'Chop chop.'

'What time is it?' Mallory asked urgently.

'It's just after one a.m.,' Sully said, lifting her phone screen. Mallory's heart sank.

Twenty-three hours to death.

'It could be late tomorrow evening before the Council manage to convince them to let you go on bail,' Sully added quickly. 'They don't believe you were harbouring Theodore in the bunker. The Broadwicks think it's impossible, and they're refusing to allow anyone to investigate further. I've never seen them this adamant. Anyway, we'll get you out. Hang in there. Okay?'

'Okay,' Mallory said weakly.

Sully patted her gently on the arm. The expression on her face was one akin to the look someone got when meeting a particularly pitiful animal on its last legs.

'Sully! Let's go!' someone rapped on the door and Sully excused herself.

The door clanged shut behind her, voices fading.

Alone in her cell again, Mallory lay on the bunk and waited for morning, her suspects flitting through her head. Sully. Remington Davis. Sam Bridewell. The demon sample that threw everything into question. Theodore.

It always came back to Theodore.

She turned on her side, pain ripping through her and she stared at the floor, lost in thought.

And then she saw a movement across the bottom of her cell door.

TWENTY-ONE

'*Arrested?*' There was a note of alarm in Grey's voice that made Theodore feel a bit like he might cry.

He could feel his tear tracks shimmering wetly on his face, made worse by the fact that, in his absence, Grey had rotated Theodore's wing-back to prop up a brand-new whiteboard. He'd written *TW: MURDER* in the centre alongside some bare facts ('lightbulb', 'dead', 'Broadwick Ballroom'), and had provided heavyweight flash cards, red string, fancy pens and a neat stack of photographs.

'It's even less likely than *you* being the culprit.'

'I think we'll find that crucially, they *do* think I've been doing it and there's been a ransom out for my arrest.'

'How much was that again?'

'Not enough to save a crumbling empire,' Theodore said. 'I don't know why they've pivoted to Mallory, but they're blaming her for my— I mean, for *the* murders.'

'Tate's panicking, clearly. Suggests he's not as in with UML as he wanted everyone to believe. I suppose not being able to capture one measly little Samhain ghost would do that.'

'I've never had the measles,' Theodore protested. 'How dare you.'

'I've known Tate far too long, this is going to haunt him. No pun intended. Let's face it, policing in this town has been lacklustre at best. Your little friends only started doing what good old Vinny Van Doren refused to. While Tate's difficult, he's doing what should've been done back when the first spate of murders occurred.'

'Arrest a twenty-something-year-old, who is one of the only people actually trying to find out what's happening?'

'Take things into hand,' Grey corrected.

'And you agree with this?' Theodore asked incredulously. 'You think Tate should march into Wrackton and arrest people. That *that's* taking things into hand?'

'I don't recall expressly stating if I agree or disagree with it,' Grey said silkily. 'My dear Theodore, when will you figure this out about me? My livelihood is determined solely by my ability to be a contrarian. You will never know what I'm really thinking unless I tell you. And even then...'

'Oh, fuck off,' Theodore snapped. 'The whole town thinks I'm a monster, and you take me in out of the goodness of your heart, something you *keep* trying to convince me you don't have, and then my frie— my... Someone important to me is arrested and you just throw your hands up and say, "Oh well"?'

'I think you'll find my hands have remained firmly by my sides,' Grey said, twirling a marker. He was back in comfortable clothes and Theodore felt the need to avert his eyes.

'YOU KNOW WHAT I MEAN!'

'Temper, temper,' Grey said, as Theodore started crackling. 'I am merely saying that I can see where Tate is coming from. Whether that's something I agree with is up for debate.'

'You were going to build a for-profit prison here,' Theodore said accusingly. 'You *do* realise the only thing worse than believing wholeheartedly in a punitive system of stripping people of their rights is being so utterly *spineless* that you don't have an opinion on it outside of potential profit?'

'Now we're getting somewhere,' Grey said pleasantly. 'Good.'

'Fuck off,' Theodore said again, pacing. He pulled his cat ears off and threw them so they appeared on his head again, and did it a handful more times until the rage that was building in him dissipated.

'You need to help them. You need to help *her*. Someone… someone needs to do something. They can't die, she can't be in *jail* for this. Scapegoated, because of me! Because their original scapegoat was too good at 'scaping, and now they need a second goat! SHE IS NOT A FUCKING GOAT, GREY.'

Grey stopped twirling the marker. 'Theodore,' he said quietly. 'There's nothing we can do.'

'HOURS ago, you were all for helping me out. You were going to help me solve my murder. You put a very kind trigger warning in the centre of the murder board— wait, those are my initials. Regardless! You were going to help. I was gone an hour, and now you're Mr Defeatist?'

'I got a call while you were gone, from an advisor. The creditors on this place are out for my blood. I'm out of time to do anything clever with Oakpass Manor. The apartment sold last week.'

Theodore blinked.

'Come now, let's not pretend you didn't know how dire things were. The Ericssons have proposed one offer, no negotiations, and I'm tempted… but I've been thinking about packing it all in. Starting over somewhere else. Free myself from all of this. Stop letting a dead man dictate what I do with my one precious life.'

Theodore spluttered. 'You're giving up?'

'I was rather thinking you'd come with me, but if you want to put it that way, so be it.' He waved a hand. 'My gut feeling is that Oakpass Manor is important. Perhaps the most important asset I've ever owned.'

'Nonsense, you're the biggest ass I've ever met.'

'But I'm prepared to let it go if it comes to it,' Grey continued, as if he hadn't spoken. 'To walk away. My time here feels like it's coming to an end. Not because of what you said, but because it's a truth I should've faced a long time ago. Can't you feel it? The change in the air?'

'That's called the final vestiges of autumn,' Theodore said primly. 'Normally happens when the earth rotates further from the sun. Do they not teach you that in demon school?'

'I went to an Apparent boarding school, as you well know,' Grey said lightly. 'I saw you nosing through my old journals when you thought I was asleep.'

'Fuck off,' Theodore said a third time, the power gone out of it completely. He had, in fact, done that, while Grey slept in front of the fire, a woollen blanket pulled up to his nose. He'd looked peaceful. 'Are you going to help Mallory or not?'

'I can't,' Grey said. 'If she calls me, I can try. Maybe I'll send a text to Diana, see if there's anything specific she's thought of. But I don't have that kind of power anymore.'

'Is that *it*? Forget it! Don't wait up.'

Theodore blasted out the door, ignoring Grey calling after him.

He didn't stop, a moving blue blur, until he passed through the door of Mallory's house and made every effort to be invisible. This had all gone far enough. He could throw himself on their mercy. Ask for temporary amnesty, for Mallory's sake.

'—you *cannot* be fucking serious,' Diana was saying. 'No. Absolutely not.'

'It's the best idea I have.'

'Better than running to the Broadwicks?'

'You're only out here because I did that! I can't do anything else. We *have* to get her out. We don't have enough time to wait around for Imogen and Ezra or the Ghoul Council, even if they argue that the Besiegement Curse is going to end her life in a matter of hours. You heard Tate, he doesn't care.'

'He expressly said that to *you*, after you told him that he, his colleagues and everyone in the institution of policing was, quote, "a bastard".'

'Am I fucking wrong, Diana?'

'Besides the point! I don't see how *spiders* are the answer to this, or indeed, anything!'

'*Portia mallus ferro* are the answer to *everything* right now. I can't do this without Mallory. I can't die without her here. I *can't*, Diana.'

'Oh, but of course you don't have any feelings for her,' Diana sniped.

Cornelia was silent.

'Wait. What have I missed? Apart from the pair of you being *really* weird ever since you went into that lake. Are you... Did you... Did something...?'

A sigh. 'She didn't want it to happen like this.'

Diana screamed.

'Stop. STOP! This isn't the time for— I just need her here, if we're going to die or we're going to solve a murder or figure out what the hell Theodore's been doing—'

'Wait. Did you draw on my diorama?' Diana interrupted. 'We'll go back to the Mallory thing in a second, I just want to know what the fuck—'

'Obviously not. I wouldn't do something like that! Can we focus on the important thing here?'

'No, we can't. Someone's drawn a big ring around the Ternion memorial. This is— There's something else off about it as well, I can't—'

'Maybe it was Mallory,' Cornelia said. 'We can ask her when my spiders get her out.'

'It's not going to work!'

She was right. It wouldn't work. This was a terrible plan.

'None of this would be happening if it wasn't for Theodore,' Cornelia said quietly.

'I know.'

'I just wish we could go back in time. That we'd paid attention.'

'How were we supposed to know he was an evil mastermind? He looked and behaved like the former-human equivalent of a wet kitten!'

'Bit harsh,' Theodore mumbled.

'What was that?' Diana said, stilling. She fumbled with her hearing aid.

'What was what?' Cornelia looked up sharply, some sort of *hideous* creature walking across their hand. It was sort of cute, actually, the longer Theodore looked at it. Like *Portia mallus ferro* had a baby with a fly.

'It's… crackling,' Diana said, whipping around. 'Theodore?'

Theodore backed out of the wall as slowly as he could.

'THEODORE? If you're here, you better show yourself,' Cornelia said. 'She's been arrested and it's YOUR FAULT!'

Diana listened, her head cocked in concentration as Theodore's nose was the only thing still in the room, the rest of his body outside Mallory's house.

'It's stopped. Maybe it was just adjusting to us shouting at each other. I'm not trying to be cruel, I just don't think using spiders to break Mallory out of prison is…'

Diana's voice faded.

Theodore stood very still, thinking. If Mallory was in prison because they thought she was a murderer, he both needed to prove she couldn't have done any of them by virtue of being locked away, and he needed a very large distraction. Something to draw everyone out and convince them she wasn't a killer. He'd need to go big. Some sort of display in a very public place. One that said, 'I'VE KILLED AGAIN', perhaps using real body parts. No, that would take too long. He needed something smart, and quick.

He couldn't make Mallory see that he was innocent, but he could save her.

This one time, he could save her.

TWENTY-TWO

Thursday, 31st October

The air around Mallory filled with warmth and the crackle of static as Theodore Wyatt stepped through the wall of her cell.

'Hello, Mallory,' he said, holding his arms out. 'You are going to die.'

She shrank back.

'I see you're in prison,' he continued, looking around.

He looked the same as ever; cat ears on his messy blonde hair, marker-drawn whiskers, permanent tear tracks, oversized cardigan, check shirt. His eyes were wide and hopeful and full of concern.

And all her brain said in response to this familiar, wonderful, inexplicable apparition was *danger danger danger danger.*

'Quite the pickle. A devious conundrum, one might say.'

'I'm in a holding cell at the police station,' Mallory corrected, finding her voice. 'You've been in a holding cell at the police station too, if I recall correctly.'

'You do. You do recall correctly. Wonderful, smart, *brilliant* Mallory, who always sees the bigger picture of things!'

Mallory bit her lip, angry at herself for feeling such a rush of fondness. She knew why he was here. Should've known all along.

This was someone who used to be her friend. Who used to be kind. Who used to be so nice to her.

But then, they'd met so many killers who had seemed nice, who were otherwise just people. His appearance here, in her cell, was confirmation of what she couldn't accept before. What Diana and Cornelia had been worried about, what they had tried to get her to see. It was obvious now: this was how it would end. If he didn't kill her, the Besiegement Curse would. It would hurt more than anything to not have officially solved the case.

'Just get it over with,' Mallory said. She was tired, and sore, and the cell was chilly despite his warmth. 'You're going to anger a bunch of Besiegement ghosts if you try to take my soul because they want my body, but that can be your problem.'

'What?'

'Kill me. I am going to die – I'm dying anyway. Just do it.' She closed her eyes, the image of his concerned face burned behind her eyelids. The last thing she'd ever see.

She waited. And waited. And waited some more.

She opened her eyes. Theodore hadn't moved, though his expression was no longer concerned, but in the realm of alarmed.

'The— You— ah.' Theodore nodded slowly. 'I see. You think *I*... which really suggests you have *not*... okay.'

'What?'

'I was hoping you'd had a chance to peruse the clues I—'

There was a clamour in the hall, the sounds of voices.

Someone said 'Cell three', which Mallory knew to be the cell she was currently sitting in, accused of murder and of aiding and abetting Theodore, the most wanted man in all of Wrackton. The case they'd so easily fabricate if she was caught with Theodore. The conclusions they could so easily jump to. The same conclusions Mallory herself might jump to, if she was not in possession of discernment.

Theodore seemed to consider all of this himself, a stillness coming over him, until he pointed at Mallory triumphantly.

'Time's up. New plan! I have a proposal.' Theodore reached into his cardigan pocket. He held up a lavender witchlight, the shade he had always been so partial to. 'But I can't tell you what it is until we get out of here.'

'To go where?'

'Can't say, unfortunately,' he said cheerfully. 'But the question remains: Mallory Hawthorne, do you trust me? Or better, *can* you trust me?'

Footsteps drew closer and Mallory felt her blood chill. She couldn't do this. She couldn't be here with him, but she also couldn't waste the last precious hours of her life in this cell. Either she would die at Theodore's hands and her friends would avenge her, or she'd die from the Besiegement Curse. Being a sitting duck was not an option. Staying here was not the answer.

Theodore held the witchlight out to her, the edges fuzzed and crackling the way objects always did in his hands. She hadn't had enough time on earth to know why it happened, or how his touching objects changed their molecular structure. She hadn't had enough time to understand Theodore.

Mallory extended her hand, fingertips quivering. There

would be a Wrackton-wide search party for her. A hunt. There was nowhere Theodore could take her that would be safe—

The cell door swung open. Mallory didn't register who was there as her fingers connected with the light. The room disappeared around her, along with shouts of dismay at her empty cell.

She tumbled into nothing, into darkness.

TWENTY-THREE

Mallory stumbled, body jarring on impact.

Her hands touched soft grass and ferns, decaying leaves. Pure darkness surrounded her as she blinked and blinked, her stomach roiling, willing her eyes to adjust to the gloom.

She got her knees under her and took several deep breaths, familiarity striking her along with a sense of déjà vu.

Woodland. A forest.

‘Redwoods?’ Mallory asked with difficulty, pulling herself to her feet.

Her eyes were adjusting, details pulling themselves into dim focus. She could see a treeline that gave way to a muddy expanse she did not recognise, interrupted by a line of red witchlights, where they’d presumably emerged from. Across the expanse she could see a heap of something strange and blocky, stacked haphazardly as though they’d been cleaned up after an explosion.

A stack of old TVs. A stack she’d seen before, at the side of a lake.

A lake that, the last time she'd seen it, had been teeming with the telltale static hiss of so many ghosts.

'Try again,' Theodore said gently.

'This is Bonemarrow Lake. In Wickermere. Which is not in Wrackton. It's actually so far out of Wrackton. But you can't leave the surrounds of Wrackton. Can you?'

It was one thing to sense him following her around Wrackton, but another thing entirely for him to be able to leave.

Theodore reached into the pocket of his cardigan and pulled out an object Mallory knew very well. She had studied the lightbulb that had killed Theodore over and over, though she had not physically handled it in two years, when she pulled the witch magic trace off it. She had thought about it every single day since the Besiegement Curse had been activated.

The lightbulb wavered in his hand. There was a tiny glow from the filament inside, one that should've been utterly, irreparably dead.

'How?' Mallory said finally, unable to formulate a better question. The answer was beyond her comprehension, but she knew she'd accept it when she heard it.

'I simply had to remember I was mortal,' Theodore said grandly. 'Have bulb, can travel. The answer was on file, inside a filing cabinet, all this time.'

Mallory's mouth opened and closed, but no sound came out.

'Wards!' she blurted eventually, gesturing to Wickermere at large. A town that was heavily warded. That should not have let Theodore in.

'The Ghoul Council weren't interested in warding against

ghosts,' he said, almost apologetically. 'I have a… erm… friend, who had inside help to verify this.'

Mallory reeled, trying to understand. She had always known Theodore to be honest – in so much as someone who had lied to her, a lot, could be. She had thought herself able to tell when he was not being honest – because his tells were so strong – and had no reason to consider he was lying right now.

Except for all the things he had been accused of. And the things he had admitted to. And all the lies that hung in the air between them, complex and fragile as spider-webs.

'Why?'

'I'm… not sure, actually. The idea popped into my head.'

Theodore smiled uncertainly at her and Mallory took an involuntary step back, which forced her to take in her surroundings properly. They were in the clearing where Dorothy had forced them to enact the Besiegement Curse, except instead of the hissing lake, there was an expanse of wet mud. Even in the stillness of night, birds called to each other over the treetops. Naturally, Mallory felt she must be dreaming. That Theodore had tried to kill her in the cell, and this was her brain desperately trying to bring her some kind of peace.

This must be how every single one of the Copycat victims felt. How every Whistler victim felt. Alive, then nothing. Awake, then dreaming. Her body on the hard bunk of the cell, her mind detaching itself to save her some pain.

Except she was still in pain. Her body, in this dream-place, still hurt.

No. She was alive. She was sure of it. She took a deep breath, trying to think of the facts. He had admitted to digging up bodies in Wrackton. He was wanted in connection with the murders of Hayley Eason and Julian Johnson. She did not know if he had killed the people he dug up. She did not know if he had orchestrated the killings. She did not know if he had involved Sully or Remington Davis or Sam Bridewell in said killings. If he'd got a demon involved, somehow. She had agreed to trust him. She had let him break her out of prison (a holding cell, really, but semantics were not important here).

But now he'd taken her to a secondary location. Nobody knew they were there. He could kill her and Cornelia and Diana would never find her body.

Why hasn't he killed me?

She took another step backwards. She was so sore, so stiff, but she could run. She could hide. She could dig up a witchlight and get back to Wrackton. She wasn't going down without a fight.

Her hands tensed.

Theodore drifted closer. 'I have so much to explain to you, but I can't. I can't tell you anything, no matter how much I want to. And I do! I really do! I—' he broke off and shook his head violently. 'STOP IT. LEAVE ME ALONE. Sorry, Mallory. Where was I?'

Mallory paused, Observer Johnson's words coming back to her. If Jacob Gabbott had a helper, someone stronger controlling him… maybe someone was controlling Theodore, too. Maybe he wasn't a killer, but a sort of victim. One with a complex involvement that would take years to unravel.

'I take it from your silence that you are experiencing some sort of trepidation at my return, and overwhelm at what I have revealed to you thus far. I also take it that you're trying to ascertain if I am innocent or guilty or some combination thereof. Totally understandable. Virtually expected, at this stage.'

'Well,' Mallory said. 'A lot has happened. I might be currently in the last vestiges of death, and I'm not entirely certain our whole friendship hasn't been a lie.'

'Then try me! Ask me anything! Within reason,' he added hastily. 'Within much reason and at our— My! My own! Discretion, ask away.'

'Did you really not know you could leave Wrackton until recently?'

'I swear to you on… everything I have, which is not much. My word, let's say. On my word, I did not know until recently. That isn't to say that *someone* didn't know about it first, but I myself was utterly ignorant to the possibility. And look! Look where we are! Look where I've brought you!'

Mallory glanced around again and swallowed, trying to keep her face neutral, but she saw Theodore see her hesitation. Her fear. His face fell and he dropped to his knees, shuffling forward pitifully as he tucked the lightbulb into his pocket.

'Mallory please. Please understand, I have to do this. I can't *tell* you the truth. I meant it when I said… what I said. I have done things, but they're not my— WILL YOU SHUT UP!' He roared, tapping the side of his face a few times before his expression cleared. 'Sorry. So much I can't say freely.'

'Have you murdered all those people? Did you kill Hayley Eason, and Observer—' her voice caught. 'And Observer Johnson. And last year. With the Wrackton Digger stuff. Did you kill Freya Evans, and Paul Blackburn, then dig them back up?

Theodore blinked.

'I did not, with my own hand, kill any of those people.'

'That's not an answer! It's not an answer I can do anything with! It's a yes or no question, Theodore – *did you kill those people?*'

He looked at her sadly. 'I can't say.'

'So who *did* kill them?'

'You'll have to tell me,' he said, screwing his face up. 'I can't say.'

Mallory swallowed. If he wanted a denouement, she didn't have one. All she had were puzzle pieces that didn't fit together.

But she could try. 'We investigated the murder scenes of Hayley Eason and Julian Johnson – both at the Observatory – and obtained samples from each. The magic sample from Hayley's murder scene suggested the killer was a witch with Apparent heritage – just like the Whistler murders. But the magic sample we got from Observer Johnson's scene turned out to be demon magic. And I didn't get to look into it further, or really think about it, before I was arrested.'

'That's good. That's really good.'

'But what does it MEAN? I can tell you already – nothing! It means *nothing*, because without viable suspects, all I have are traces. My entire hypothesis evaporated before the police broke down my front door—'

'They didn't *knock*?'

'—and I'm angry! I'm upset my investigation methods are inferior to the magic we're up against. I can't even trust my methods EVER worked, because *you* worked on them with me!'

'Hold on. That's a little far-fetched, isn't it? Credit where credit is undue? I completely admire your ability to believe in the capabilities of others – it's one of your best attributes, of which there are many – but even if I was an evil genius – which I'm not, but *if* I was – then I'd hardly make it so that *everything* I helped you with was useless. What a waste of time that would be!'

Mallory threw up her hands and stalked away from him, rage ripping through her insides. Rage, and the certainty that she didn't have the answer. She had not solved the case.

'Mallory, hold on. I'm not trying to be difficult, I'm just… dealing with a lot here. I am not as involved as you might expect, but I'm not… *not* involved. It's not willing,' he added, his voice soft.

Mallory looked at him. Her old friend. A possible murderer.

'I don't know who you are anymore,' she said quietly. 'I don't know where you've been. It's been five months, Theodore. You've been following me around, but you haven't *been there.* Not in the way that matters to me. I've had so many questions – I've questioned everything I've ever known. Tonight, no matter what you do or don't do to me, I won't exist anymore.'

'The Besiegement,' he said. 'Yes, I heard. I wish I knew how to… How to stop it. Reverse it. You don't deserve that. No one does. I'm so sorry. For everything. And I'm sorry I wasn't there. That… I should've tried anyway. Consequences be damned. You deserved better. But I'm here now. You needed me, and I came, and I'm here. You don't have to forgive me! Not a single ounce of forgiveness is necessary! But I am asking – nay, *begging* – you. If you believe nothing else, believe I never, ever, *ever* wanted to hurt you. Ever.'

Mallory closed her eyes.

Part of her wanted to not believe him. Part of her wanted to be strong, and unswayable. To believe he intended to kill her. That this was the end, he was responsible, that the note was an attempt to misdirect her.

And the other part of her wanted her friend back.

But as with all things, there was no going back. There was only forwards.

If she was going to accept the alternative hypothesis – that Theodore was, somehow, not a killer, that she had been wrong – she needed evidence. She needed data.

'How does the lightbulb work?' she asked, changing topic. The note could wait. She needed him disarmed. Willing to talk.

'Like I said, I had to remember I was mortal. As long as it's within the same boundary lines as me, I can go anywhere. This is the furthest I've been in eight years. Isn't it *nice*, Mallory? The lake isn't much to look at, and it's dark so I can't fully appreciate my surroundings, but… Hexana, I feel so… so free.'

The smile on his face was so earnest, so *honest*, that Mallory thought she believed him. That all of this really was new to him.

'And by "remember you are mortal", do you mean in a sort of… Apparent memento mori kind of way? Like a talisman of sorts?'

'Yes! Precisely! I suppose not entirely *precisely* because it's not at all the function of a bona-fide memento mori, but that is the principle of it! A talisman! One that links me to the world. I believe that the lightbulb is the only reason I'm still here, and that our understanding of Samhain ghosts is completely wrong. It's not my *bones*, it's…'

'Your *raison de mort*,' Mallory said. 'The lightbulb. Your first death.'

'Yes! Oh, very good. Mallory, you have no idea how long I've gone without talking to someone who understands me the way you do, it's been very difficult. Of course that's not to speak ill of my *allies*, as it were, but it's so refreshing to be on the same wavelength as you again. I've missed this. I've missed you. My dear, sweet friend.'

She tried to stay afloat. In disarming him, she was disarming herself. Everything Theodore was saying *sounded* like the Theodore she knew, but she needed to know for sure.

'Why did you bring me here?"

'I dislike the idea of you rotting away in prison for something you didn't do immensely,' Theodore started, then his shoulders dropped, and the truth of it uncoiled in Mallory's stomach. 'And I have a little task to perform, one I rather need your help, specifically, with.'

'So not to help me, then. To help yourself.' *To kill me.*

'It sounds callous when you put it like that. I meant it as a gesture of... Of mutual benefit! I swear. I only want your help. I have no desire to harm you. I don't know how to be any clearer. Perhaps the medium of interpretative dance?'

He extended his arms to his right, fingers splayed, and performed a complicated-looking full body wiggle.

'I need more than this,' Mallory said, sitting down. The grass was damp beneath her legs, and moisture seeped into the fabric of her jeans but she didn't care. Sitting was good. Sitting was necessary. 'I need a reason to help you. I need you to give me something. A clue.'

'Mallory! I've given you so many clues!' Theodore exclaimed, mussing his hair with his hands. 'I tried leaving you— You know what, never mind. Okay. A clue.'

'Why did you leave me the note?'

'I can't tell you.'

Mallory snorted softly. 'Great.'

He paused, nibbling his lip. 'I… left it because I was meant to. It had a specific purpose, that was not useful. But I think… it *is* useful to you. In finding answers.'

Mallory searched his face for a lie, but there wasn't one.

'It asked us to solve your first murder. You can see how we wouldn't find that helpful.'

He nodded once.

'But it's meant to be helpful?'

He nodded again. 'It *can* be, if you look at it the right way and not, say, the way that was designed to get you arrest—' He stopped talking abruptly.

Mallory held his gaze. He was trembling yet determined and she really, really wanted to believe him. He had no reason to lie about the circumstances that led to her arrest; she had a sense that she'd walked right into a trap.

'Is the answer to all of this' – Mallory gestured around her – 'in solving your first murder?'

'I… believe so. I know how that sounds! Something… big is coming tonight. Something we can't stop ourselves. Something *I* can't stop.' He was whispering, his voice lifting away on the wind.

'But if we find out why you died – if we find out who wanted you dead – it will magically unravel the mystery of the Copycat Murders?'

'I think it's the answer to everything. But I can't elaborate.'

Mallory shivered and realised she was continuously shaking, adrenaline seeping away from her and leaving her cold.

'I can't do this.' She dragged an arm across her face. 'I just want peace, Theodore. I don't want to die. I don't want to become a vessel for someone else. I want *my* life. I want to be all the things I promised myself I could be. I want this to be over. I want to share my work with the world and I want to keep helping folk with magical cases, but I want to live life on my own terms.'

'I want that too,' Theodore said softly. 'More than you could know.'

'Then help me,' Mallory pleaded. 'Help me understand. I can't do this without you.'

'Okay. Okay! Let's—' Theodore froze, juddering.

'Theo?'

'Yes,' he said eventually, not to Mallory. 'Okay.'

'What's happening? Theodore, who are you talking to?' Mallory waved a hand in the air, waiting for a second Samhain ghost – Blair? Katherine? Someone else? – to materialise beside them.

'No one,' Theodore said strangely, bending down again. He picked up a stick from the shoreline and kept nodding. 'Yes, I will bring her in,' he whispered. 'I know there are consequences for her, I know this. I'm doing what I can – just one clue, Mallory? – *I'm fully aware* of what I'm risking.'

He took the stick and carefully pressed it into the ground in front of him, babbling affirmations at himself. Mallory felt cold and frightened as he drew five dashes, a line, two dashes, a line, four dashes.

He handed her the stick and nodded emphatically at her.

A game.

She swallowed angry tears and wrote the letter A at her feet. He took the stick back in silence and filled in two letters, his eyes resolutely looking away from her, so it looked like

_A_ _ _ / _ _ / _A_ _

She tried E, and he drew a noose. She tried I, followed by S, and got the middle word. Then tried O, and with a jolt realised what Theodore was trying to tell her.

A truth that should've been impossible. A truth that took Occam's Razor and snapped it in half.

She filled in the rest of the letters, Theodore's eyes on the sky as he chatted and pushed back on someone she couldn't hear. He glanced once to check, and gave her a thumbs up.

She dropped the stick and scrambled back, the words swimming in her eyes, threatening to choke her.

JACOB / IS / BACK

VIVISECTION III

Samhain, eight years ago

At long last, here is the crux of the matter. The mechanics of the first murder of Theodore Wyatt parallels something greater that happened – and has been happening – in Occulture for the longest time. History is doomed to repeat for as long as there are people. Lessons not learned that will happen again, in time, if the right circumstances line up. That will happen at the stroke of midnight on Samhain, if all goes to plan.

To understand who killed Theodore Wyatt, one must understand who's killing in Wrackton today. You might think you've been handed the answer, but it is not as simple as that. It has never been close to simple.

But before that.

Theodore Wyatt went to the basement where he died with a lightbulb in hand, an object which became so important as to languish in an evidence bag for nigh on a decade.

He did notice the lamp, that's true. He did reach into it. He did die with the bulb in his hand. And when Mallory, Diana and Cornelia came downstairs to the basement in search of a mystery and stumbled upon his body, it set into motion things that *would've happened anyway.*

He was always going to meet our trio of witches somewhere, even if this part of the story isn't about them. It was pre-determined.

History, doomed to repeat.

Witches three, destined to do great things.

He was correct to question if it had been his idea to go down there – it hadn't been. We can say that for certain. Try as he might, he did not hear the footsteps that followed behind him – the heavy footfall of someone on a mission. Someone setting out to do what they were told. Who was not thinking of the consequences. (That would come later, alongside a tide of guilt, and confusion and, finally, rationalisation.)

The owner of the footsteps cast the spell, but it was not *theirs*. They were the vessel. Acting on higher orders. Unaware of what they were doing, only that they were to do it well. A simple spell to move the lightbulb out of alignment on the correct assumption that an Apparent would pause to turn on the lamp. To ensure they had correctly restored power to Broadwick Mansion. A simple spell to conceal the truth of Theodore's murder.

Back turned, coward's killing.

But we already know that the killer is nothing *but* a coward. He would not like to think of himself as such, but one learns a dark secret or two in taking a vessel. He has opportunity, means, and would-be motive, and he is enamoured with power. Drunk with it, spinning at the epicentre of Occulture like he knows anything about it. My vessel could access what others could not. He could open doors. He could reach me any time he liked, no questions asked. And that is how I silently beckoned him through a door. He remembers nothing – a blank spot in his busy day that ended in a routine party. He does not miss the memory of meeting me any more than he misses the free will I commandeered. He is as blameless as he is guilty. Only I know how easily he would kill if he understood the link between us, and how many centuries it spanned. That's the funny thing about lineage: how little it matters, until someone decides it does.

That should narrow it down. Three key players become two viable suspects.

Vincent Van Doren or Ezra Broadwick.

You may know the answer, but I daresay you don't understand why. Not yet.

Put it together, though, and the answer starts to open up.

You start to understand who I am. Who we are.

You start to understand Theodore's place in all of this.

And you start to understand what the plan has been, all along.

TWENTY-FOUR

It hit her like a train.

All this time, she'd been sure they were safe. That Cornelia's fears of going outside were understandable but ultimately illogical, because Jacob was dead. She hadn't even let herself entertain the idea he wasn't, because it was so ludicrous. People did not come back from the dead. Necromancy wasn't real.

And yet, the evidence suggested otherwise. They had faced down the Dollhouse Murderers intent on performing complex acts of raising the dead that could be called necromancy if Mallory had really thought about it. She had ignored the significance of the Wrackton Digger robbing Jacob's grave, worrying only about Cornelia's reaction to it. It had taken authorities months to find Jacob's body at the culmination of the Whistler case, and a full year to bury it. As far as she knew, the only person who knew where that body was now was Theodore. She had assumed it was insignificant because she had ignored what the evidence was telling her. Every touch left a trace. Every piece was important.

She hadn't been able to solve who was orchestrating the Copycat Murders because she had assumed it was an imitator, not the original. But it fit. It made sense. The Whistler was back. Jacob Gabbott was alive. Necromancy was real.

Her panicked stream of consciousness condensed into one single, inadequate word. 'How?'

'How about that *weather*, you mean?' Theodore said loudly, the meaning clear.

'How do we know... the weather is here?' Mallory tried.

'The weather makes itself known!' Theodore said frantically. 'The weather is *very*... chatty. Some might say the weather talks to me directly!'

She could not see what he was wrestling against, coming to the conclusion that it was an internal fight. Control from inside his head. Control that could hear him speak.

'Inside your head, you mean?'

'Just join the dots, Mallory, please! I can't say anything concrete or he'll... he'll...' He shuddered, face fracturing into blue fragments until he pulled it together, cardigan crackling with electricity. 'Try!'

Mallory blanched.

'I've tried so hard,' she said quietly. 'I'm sorry I wasn't good enough.' She had wasted five months not solving his murder. She had wasted eight *years* not solving his murder.

Theodore reached out a hand to her and Mallory stilled, her breath shallow, but he didn't touch her. His face scrunched, the tear tracks on his cheeks shining like they were fresh.

'There are things you couldn't have known. Things you were *prevented* from knowing, and things I'm not sure I fully understand. But if you look at the evidence, look at the town in miniature, you can zoom in on the details,' he said quickly. 'Do some… reading on the subject. History of the town. Goddesses of yore. And fore, but mostly yore. Wars, perhaps. Famous wars. Vampiric subjects.'

The Vampire Wars. The Ternion.

'Witches three aren't what they seem to be,' he said cryptically.

Mallory frowned. 'Do you mean Elisabella—'

'LALALALA isn't it fun to *singggg*?' His eyes were wild with panic. 'You are the smartest person I knowwwww. And I am beggingggg youuu toooo finishhhh the puzzzzzllle.'

'Iiii'm tryinggg my hardesttt!' Mallory sang back, feeling both frustrated and foolish. Here lies Mallory Hawthorne, who died doing what she loved: appealing to the every ridiculous whim of a Samhain ghost she had adored.

Theodore closed his eyes and spun around a few times, mumbling under his breath. He stilled, tilting his head like he was rummaging around in his own brain. His eyes snapped open and he spoke quickly, his voice barely a whisper.

'We have a moment alone. I, very crucially – and quite selfishly, admittedly, but if it's for the wider good can it *really* be selfish? No, I suppose it probably is – need your help, Mallory. If you do what I – *we!* – need, we can bring this whole thing to its foregone conclusion.'

Mallory wrapped her arms around herself. 'What sort of foregone conclusion?'

'One where things come to a complete *stop*, because they're complete. So if you were to *help me* complete it, we could bring it to a *stop* because it would be done. I besiege you – I mean, *beseech*' – at this he made emphatic eyebrow movements – 'to know what can be *ended*. Nobody has to die. Except everyone who has already met their demise, of course.'

Mallory was unsure what to make of this. It would be an incredibly cruel trick, but one she could not imagine Theodore playing on her.

You don't know what he's capable of, she reminded herself.

'You're saying that there's a way for me – for all of us – to not … expire?'

Maybe he was telling the truth, and there was a way for them to stop the Besiegement. Maybe she didn't have to die.

Or maybe this was a ruse. Maybe this was Jacob acting through him.

He froze again and vaulted away from her. His posture was frightened, very different from how he'd been moments ago. It took him several long minutes to walk back to her, his body splintering like he was pushing against some great force. He sucked in a deep and frankly unnecessary breath, and then his old smile returned.

'Sorry about that. Yes! Yes, we likely have an end to… expiration. I need three things. Two, actually, because you already have one.'

'What?'

He paused, really looking at her.

'Mallory, you're shaking! Do you need to sit down? Am I… am I not warm enough?'

His eyes were wide and full of concern, the way they had been hundreds upon hundreds of times before.

'What thing are you talking about?'

'It might *ring* a bell,' he said emphatically, and then shook his head again, like he was ushering away a fly.

'Theodore—'

'I ask again, because I am very concerned. Do you need to sit? Can I get you anything?'

Mallory did need to sit, as it happened. She had nothing in her pockets, nothing on her person bar the necklace Cornelia had given her years ago that contained one single binding spell. She was a fugitive, she realised with a jolt. She was a private investigator. She was dying. She was too many things.

'I'm going to need a phone.'

TWENTY-FIVE

It was good to have her back.

Mallory managed to pick the lock to a small house that looked to be the exact same as the big house Theodore could not stop staring at – Rowan House in all its glory. It was the most magnificent thing he'd seen in, goodness, *hours*, since Oakpass Manor. In another life – in his life – he'd been an old building enthusiast. The drama. The prestige.

Sometimes he thought he liked old buildings more than he liked people.

Mallory found a phone and called Cornelia and Diana, who witchlighted in immediately. Theodore waited until they were settled in the living room, shouting and talking over each other and expressing constant relief, before slipping through a wall, examining the space, waiting for the correct moment to reveal his presence. He didn't want it to be dramatic, he wanted it to be low-key. Limit the anger, or the surprise. Maybe, if he did it right, they'd even be somewhat happy to see him. The Voice had gone silent since he'd insisted he was on the trail of the

Ternion's memento mori – trusting him, the loyal solider, to carry out the plan as… planned. Grey's persuasive magic had held up to immense pressure. He had been able to tell Mallory the beginning of the truth, and nothing had gone wrong. No consequences for Theodore!

'We're safe here for a while. We can figure some things out while we wait,' Mallory said.

'Like how you got here in the first place, or why *here* at all,' Diana pressed. 'We support you, we will go anywhere you want to go – within reason, I'm not really a fan of anywhere colder or wetter than England unless there's a chance to see penguins, in which case I'll consider it – but you have to tell us *why* you came here. Surely even the Wrackton police are wise to the danger of witchlight travel?'

'I was accepting my fate in my cell, sure I was going to die in there. Sully came to visit—'

'Oh, she lives, does she?' Diana said acidly.

'She said the Broadwicks were trying to wrestle control of the Ghoul Council back from Nova and Olivia.' She shot a glance at Cornelia, who did not react to this news. 'And they were going to do their best to get me out.'

'Which they promised me, too, when I called them to demand your unconditional release,' Cornelia said, eyes carefully focused over Mallory's shoulder.

Mallory cycled through surprise and looking like she was going to cry. Theodore had only caught snatches of The Situation between Cornelia and their parents – something about them being willing to let Cornelia's sisters die for the sake of power and not giving in to a serial killer – and he'd understood Cornelia had spent the last few months as an orphan-by-choice. He was less sure of the significance of the phone call, but by the time he'd started wondering about it, Mallory had blinked a few times, and continued like nothing had happened.

'I thought that was it. I'd die there waiting. Then I heard a noise, and felt warmth, and...'

'I APPEARED. YOUR GAY IN SHINING ARMOUR!' Theodore announced, materialising.

Nice and understated, just as planned.

Cornelia vaulted to their feet and stood between Theodore and Mallory.

'What the fuck is going on?' they held up a hand, a most cursèd object clutched in their fingers.

'Please refrain from throwing ghostlights at me, we know what happened the last time you did that,' Theodore said mildly, adjusting his cardigan. 'I am here as an ally. An ally with a small agenda. An agendally. Honestly I've spent far too much time with allies in alleys lately, it's all quite a coincidence. And you know what I think about coincidences.'

'Outliers that shouldn't be counted,' Mallory said automatically.

'I'll let Mallory explain. Mallory?'

She did, and Cornelia relaxed slightly, until Mallory paused and wrote down what Theodore had intimated with his cleverly-coded phrasing, written in the sand. (It was actually silt, but sand in spirit.)

JACOB / IS / BACK didn't look any better written in a dusty hand.

'What the fuck,' Diana said.

'Shh, I'm processing,' Cornelia said.

The room fell silent and Theodore had another nose around while his (former) friends did their usual thing of looking at each other and intensely holding eye contact and thinking.

'Hey,' Theodore said, when he figured they'd had enough of a pause to take it all in. 'There're only two bedrooms here. You all slept here a few months ago. I assume Diana took the upstairs bed, because I've had the misfortune of overhearing her side of a... night time conversation... between her and Taylor. But that leaves only one bed for Mallory. Where did you sleep, Cornelia?'

Mallory flushed and Cornelia looked like they'd like to punch him. A new development in their relationship, as they'd previously looked a bit like they pitied him but were generally fond of him, the way people are fond of rodents. Theodore had liked rodents in life, of course, but he hadn't wanted anyone to compare him to a summer's Cricetidae.

'Explain,' Cornelia said, instead of addressing his question, which could either be fascinating and on purpose, or indicative of Cornelia's absolute refusal to entertain his whimsy with this little left of their life.

Both valid hypotheses.

Theodore felt around in his mind again for the Voice, but there was nothing. Not even a twitch.

He'd got away with naming J— *the Voice* for Mallory without *naming* the Voice.

Jacob. He'd got away with naming *Jacob*. He hadn't been able to say it aloud before, but maybe Grey was right, that he had more free will than he thought. And it wasn't like Grey would benefit from lying. An ally could only be an ally if they weren't contained in a ghostlight and thrown into a bush somewhere.

Even still—

Jacob! JACOB JACOB JACOB! JACOB GABBOTT WEARS A SILLY HAT AND IS BORING TO SPEND TIME WITH.

Nothing. No reaction.

A new hypothesis emerged for him – one where Theodore had, perhaps, been wrong about the extent of Jacob's power over his thoughts. Maybe he had to be paying attention to listen. Maybe he couldn't see through his eyes. He had not reacted at all to the words in the sand. That was good. That was positive.

Perhaps he could simply make another game of it. All or nothing. Tell Mallory as much of the truth as he could.

He closed his eyes and felt for the mental vault Grey had made for him. He opened the door and stepped inside. He listened for sounds of Jacob becoming aware of his treachery. He opened his eyes again.

'Let's play twenty questions!'

'I hate twenty questions,' Diana said. 'Just tell me the answer or make it more fun for me to figure it out.'

'So far, I've figured out that he needs the lightbulb to be able to travel, and it functions as a sort of memento mori,' Mallory said. 'That's all I was able to get out of him.'

'What else?' Diana asked.

'Let's play twenty questions!' Theodore said again. He looked at her expectantly and she sighed.

'Fine. Can other ghosts travel with your lightbulb?'

Theodore shook his head, excitement bubbling through him.

This was going to work. They were smart, they were clued-in, he could continue cleverly divulging information just by moving his head.

'Can other ghosts travel with objects of their own?'

Theodore hesitated, then nodded.

'Is this confirmed?' Mallory asked.

Theodore shook his head.

'So, theoretical?'

Theodore wobbled his head side to side.

'He doesn't know, but strongly believes it. Right?'

Theodore nodded. They were getting it! Everything was going to be okay!

'And it doesn't have to be lightbulbs?'

He shook his head vehemently.

'For other ghosts, is the theory that they're objects they were holding when they died?'

He wobbled his head again and Diana, Mallory and Cornelia looked at each other.

'So it's a significant object,' Mallory said in an aside that Theodore could hear perfectly well.

'Either related to death, or something that was important to them at death?' Cornelia suggested.

'Is the lightbulb the reason you're haunting Wrackton at all?' Mallory asked.

Theodore nodded. 'It appears to only matter if the lightbulb is in the town I am in, otherwise I am violently returned to wherever the lightbulb is.'

'So if there was no lightbulb, there'd be no Theodore?'

He nodded. It was a hypothesis he clung to like a life raft;

the idea that if the bulb was destroyed, he would cease to exist. It gave him hope.

'Interesting,' Mallory said, the cogs turning in her head.

'What are you thinking?' Cornelia nudged her gently.

'You know the old Apparent custom of memento mori?'

'When they put bits of dead people into necklaces and shit?' Cornelia asked.

'It was a nice practice,' Diana said reproachfully. 'Taylor wants some of my hair for a locket.'

'Sorry, you're right, it was very nice. But that was it basically, wasn't it? They'd cut off hair or nails, and stuff them in an object.'

'Yes. A very meaningful object, that would be passed down through generations. Treated like an heirloom. Decorative objects, usually,' Mallory said.

'Right, yeah.' Cornelia pointed their index finger. 'Like a necklace, or…'

'*Ring* a bell, you said, Theodore?' Mallory said, catching on immediately.

'Blair's ring,' Diana said, a smile crossing her lips.

'Are we on the right track?' Mallory asked, and Theodore nodded once, a strange, pleasant pressure in his chest.

He had missed them so much.

'So the three objects you need to stop the Besiegement – to stop everything, you said – were the Ternion objects. Which are their memento mori. Goddess, all the warnings about the Ternion walking the earth again – that's what they were afraid of. Blair's ring, Elisabella's blade…'

'Hexana's whatever-a-star-is,' Diana added.

'They're all tethering them to the earth. That's why we've met Elisabella. That's why Blair was able to come back from Wickermere with us to Wrackton.'

'That's why she hasn't disappeared from… you know where,' Diana said, eyeing Theodore.

Mallory winced. 'About that…'

'I do know about the dangerous presence you were keeping in the bunker,' Theodore said lightly. 'And I am mightily surprised at you, Mallory.'

'You don't get to be annoyed with her,' Cornelia said fiercely.

Theodore held up his hands.

'But also – what do you mean?' they continued, turning to Mallory.

'The Broadwicks opened the bunker. It was empty,' Mallory said.

'Shit,' Diana said.

'Shit,' Cornelia said.

'Shit,' Mallory agreed. 'But listen! We might not know where Hexana's object is—'

'Or even where to start,' Diana added.

'But we do know something. I don't think it matters if someone was *buried* in a place. Which means that when we were here last and Cornelia—'

'Idiotically taunted the Wickermere Reaper and got us into this mess by accidentally summoning Elisabella?' Diana cut in.

'I'd put it nicer than that, but yes,' Mallory said. 'When we met Elisabella here, we couldn't understand why she didn't immediately ping back to Wrackton, despite her remains allegedly being in the Memorial Garden. Her memento mori is here. Her blade. That's why you brought me here, isn't it?'

Theodore couldn't help himself. He grinned, delight filling him as he crackled happily. It was a joy to see his friends work things out.

'Correct,' he said coolly, regaining his composure. It would never do to let that fall by the wayside. 'So now we just follow the plan, and everything will be okay.'

'*What* is the plan, exactly?' Cornelia demanded. They looked pale.

'Find the objects. Save the Occult world. And yourselves,' Theodore said, somewhat ominously. He hadn't meant it to sound that way, but the whole thing *was* rather ominous from any perspective.

Still silence from Jacob. He chanced saying a bit more. 'We don't have long. Where is Elisabella's death blade?'

'How should I know?' Cornelia protested. 'It could be literally anywhere in the entirety of Wickermere. It could be buried somewhere. It could be stuck to a wall in a guest bedroom in Rowan House. It could be used for slicing bread for all I know. And we don't even know what it looks like. Sure we saw J— the Whistler's death blade, but how could we *possibly* determine if a knife is a knife is a death blade?'

'No,' Mallory said slowly. 'We do know what it looks like. Me and you.'

Clever girl, Theodore wanted to say, but Jacob was suddenly there as Terror Voice, closing around his throat. Like he knew Theodore had said something he wasn't supposed to, and he was punishing him.

But Jacob didn't know he didn't need to say anything else. He didn't know Mallory like Theodore did.

The hold loosened as Theodore remained impassive, and Jacob slithered away.

Cornelia had stilled, memories flashing across their eyes. Or so Theodore liked to imagine; without being able to reach a hand into their head to rummage around and see the memories for himself, he'd never know.

Their micro expressions suggested strange emotions, though. Conflicting feelings. Something else he'd seen in Cornelia's eyes a lot, but especially in the last few years.

'How do we know if we can trust you?' they said finally.

Theodore wished he had an answer for that. 'As I said to Mallory earlier, you have my word, for whatever that's worth.'

'Not a lot,' Diana said, but she looked resigned. 'Where's this stupid knife, then?'

'Last time Mallory and I saw it, it was bouncing around at the bottom of Wickermere Lake. Which is now empty of everything, including the hundreds of spectres that were tossed in there. So if you were the Ghoul Council, where would you put all the ghosts?'

TWENTY-SIX

If there was one thing Diana Cheung-Merriweather was good at doing, it was networking, and if there was another, it was sweet-talking members of that network into doing what she wanted.

Lucy Caldwell had worked for the Ghoul Council until earlier that year, and they had not been able to organise a replacement for her in that time. This meant, among other things, that the Undetectables had not been removed from the list of those welcome in Rowan House without angering the wards, and Mallory was keen to take the wins where she could get them.

Lucy unlocked the door to Rowan House and ushered them inside, sleep rumpled and mildly alarmed by the Undetectables' presence – apparently the Wrackton bulletins had reached Cumbria, and she knew Mallory was wanted for crimes she had not committed. She also knew they were due to die, and had immediately taken pity on them.

The air was crisp and cool, even inside the house, and Mallory shivered so hard that Cornelia rummaged around a storage cupboard in the entrance hall until they'd found an old oversized jumper and handed it over.

'It's got a worm on it,' Diana said as Mallory pulled it on, grateful when Diana shortened the sleeves with a spell.

'Yes it does,' Cornelia said proudly, as Mallory took in the scientific illustrations of various worms, beetles and a dragonfly. 'I thought it was gone forever!'

'Do you think he's okay out there?' Mallory asked, looking at the front door.

Theodore was outside, unable to enter Rowan House – or the grounds – without permission.

'I'm sure he's fine,' Cornelia said.

'You still don't trust him, do you?' Mallory asked.

'Who's fine?' Lucy asked.

Mallory shut her mouth with a snap, right as Diana said, 'Cornelia has formed an emotional attachment to an orphaned horned treehopper they found outside.'

'That's very sad.' Lucy clutched her chest, and on some level she must've genuinely felt this way because faeries could not lie. As exhausted as she seemed, her eyes were alert, taking them in.

'Can you still do this for us?' Mallory asked, ignoring Diana's attempts to signal to her to shut up. 'I'm aware we're implicating you by involving you, so if you'd rather not…'

Lucy paused before saying, 'Fuck it. Yes,' and manually approved access for Mallory and Cornelia to headquarters. 'They might hear about it – I often suspected the Broadwicks were notified whenever anyone passed through the doorway, so Nova and Olivia might be back here soon demanding answers.'

'And you're okay with that?'

'I'm just trying to do something nice for some poor dying people,' Lucy said fiercely.

'Mallory, are you sure you're up for this?' Diana asked. 'I can go instead of you.'

Mallory nodded, despite that not being strictly true. The prospect of the spiral death-trap staircase down to the underground Ghoul Council HQ was a lot for her, even when fortified by the three cups of tea Lucy had made for her since stepping over the threshold of Rowan House (some habits, it seemed, were unbreakable).

'Then I will use the time to try to figure out what Hexana's star might be. I'll start with Dr Ray,' Diana said. 'But also, Mallory, do you really believe… the horned treehopper… didn't kill Hayley or Observer Johnson?'

'Do you?'

'I think I shouldn't be listening to any of this,' Lucy said, and started humming loudly.

'I don't know. I'd like to think that at this point, he wouldn't lie. But I don't know.'

'Indirectly. He won't say yes or no. But if he's not lying, and Jacob is really back, then he wasn't responsible in the first place. Right?'

'Do you just want that to be true?' Cornelia asked.

Mallory didn't have an answer.

'Either way. He didn't seem to know who she was. And the way he's acting, I think Jacob's voice is in his head, telling him what to do.'

'If… Does that mean…?' Cornelia said slowly.

'That Jacob's been in his head since Theodore came back after the Whistler case? Yes. I think it does.'

They didn't really know how to process that. Lucy's humming got louder and louder until Diana cleared her throat.

'I'll make some calls, and I'll talk to him myself. Try not to take too long. We only have about eighteen hours of life left, so no pressure on finding the knife or anything.'

They hadn't gone far into the Ghoul Council the last time they visited – all they'd seen of the official headquarters had been one long, beige corridor with a ceiling full of twinkling witchlights, and the inside of two of the offices. With direction from Lucy, they padded past identical offices for what felt like at least a mile, until they came to an old-style lift with a manual door and a crank handle.

'Handy that she can't lie,' Cornelia said, pushing open the grille.

Mallory wrapped her arms around herself as Cornelia turned the handle and they descended one, two, three, four floors, nothing but rock face staring back at them, a single green witchlight the only thing keeping them from total darkness. Mallory's stomach dropped as the lift picked up speed, and she wished it was possible to go back in time and stop herself from ever choosing to go into the lake, given the hideous consequences that had accompanied that choice.

That was the thing about choices. There was always a trade-off.

The lift bumped to a stop in front of a stout metal door and

Cornelia pulled back the grille. Cornelia knocked twice and the door creaked open. They stepped out into another corridor, not unlike the one above, though this one ended abruptly after twenty paces in yet another stout door.

There was nothing else in this corridor but a cathode TV propped in the corner, static pouring from the back and sides.

Mallory tentatively touched her fingers to it, and snatched them away as a hand inside the glass tried to touch her.

'Fucking *Hexana*,' Mallory swore. 'Hello?'

The static grew louder, the hand vanishing.

'What was that?'

'There's a ghost inside it,' Mallory said, cradling her hand against herself like she'd been stung. 'Maybe more than one.'

'Can they tell us how to get in? This door's locked.' Cornelia rattled it, scrabbling at the edges. There was no handle, just smooth, deep green paint across panels that had to be centuries old.

'Can you help us get in?' Mallory asked the TV, feeling foolish.

The static rose again, and she strained to hear whispered words.

'Why… should we… let you in?'

'We're trying to stop the destruction of Occulture,' Mallory said.

'Like… I… give… a fuck.'

'Some… of… us… do…' a second ghost voice said. The static hissed louder and the TV popped loudly. Mallory and Cornelia jumped, and Cornelia's hand closed around Mallory's wrist. Mallory hoped they'd leave it there.

'I don't... like... these... bitches,' the first ghost said.

'Shut... up... Dorothy...' the second ghost said. *'Why... are... you... here?'*

'We're Besieged,' Cornelia said. 'Thanks to your pal Dorothy there. Fuck you very much, Auntie Dot, by the way. Stellar mess you've made of everything. And we have less than eighteen hours to save Occulture from some fuckhead who won't die. Also, the Besiegement ghosts said something about needing to "tie up loose ends", and I assume if we don't do this, there will be consequences of some sort. Did they say, Mal?'

'No idea.'

'Anger... rage... rampage... me...' the voice claiming to be Dorothy said.

'I contain multitudes, and I am not opposed to violence as a solution, but I don't really vibe with your cause. You should vibe with my cause.'

'Ha... ha...'

There was silence, static crackling quietly.

'Shit,' Cornelia said. 'How do we get them back?'

'We don't,' Mallory said, pointing with her free hand.

The door creaked open and Cornelia pulled Mallory towards it as the light above them changed from green to blue. They got briefly stuck in the doorway, and Mallory was emotionally back in the boat with Cornelia. Surrounded by endless blue, their mouth on hers sending bursts of electricity over her skin. Cornelia's hands cupping her face, her hips, the shared desperation that she'd thought had been a long time coming. Cornelia's pupils blown, lips parted in amazement, like Mallory had hung the moon.

Then they were in the room beyond, and Mallory snapped back to the present.

'Disappointing, after all that,' Cornelia said, letting go of Mallory's wrist.

Mallory tried not to feel extra disappointment, her skin tingling where Cornelia had touched it as she tried to orient herself.

They were in a massive storage room, stuffed with row upon row of iron shelves, some padlocked with bars, most bursting with unlabelled boxes, and all overflowing with haphazard stacks of rocks and bones, some organised but most discarded under sheets of paper with TO BE ASSIGNED PERMANENT HOME scrawled on top.

It also smelled *terrible*, red and green algae thick on the floor and the walls.

'It smells like the lake in here,' Cornelia said, wincing. 'And there is only one single reason I'd ever want to go back there. If you… If that's something you wanted. In a different circumstance.' They paused, and walked to the other side of the room like they were trying to compose themself.

Mallory squinted, uncertain. She remembered how close she'd been to kissing them in the Larix. It should be the easiest thing in the world to cross that line, the invisible boundary between them. The one that stopped them being friends plus. Where nothing would change, but everything would.

For a few hours, they could be perfect.

For a few hours, Mallory could feel complete.

'Cornelia…' Mallory started, and Cornelia crossed the room in two strides, sliding their arms around Mallory's waist.

They held her like that for a moment, Mallory's chin resting on top of their curls, their body warm, their breaths in sync with hers.

She could stay like this for ever.

'I guess there're no guarantees we survive,' Cornelia said into the hollow of her throat, and Mallory shivered, her heart filling with bittersweet sorrow.

This was a kindness, she realised. This was Cornelia trying to offer her something she needed.

And yet, this was all she wanted. Sure she *wanted* more from her life, beyond Cornelia. But if she had one wish for the rest of her life, it was exactly this. Contentment. The peace she'd been chasing her whole adult life.

Cornelia looked up at her, expression unreadable, and they ran their thumb over the back of Mallory's hand.

It would be so easy to close the distance now. To kiss them. To promise to save their lives so they could have thousands more kisses on thousands more days. So they could live to see another sunrise, and another.

'Cornelia,' Mallory said gently.

Cornelia pulled away abruptly, and Mallory felt a pang of inadequacy.

Stupid, to think Cornelia wanted anything different. To think maybe-not dying would change anything.

'Shall we split up and look for a knife?' Mallory said, turning her face as tears filled her eyes.

'Sure,' Cornelia said, their own eyes glistening.

Again, Mallory wasn't sure what they were saying.

'Let's get a move on,' they said, and they took a side of the room each, trawling through the stacks for any reference point. Finding a knife in a poorly organised lake stack was not an easy task, especially when everything looked so different not underwater. It was at least a frantic hour of semi-methodical searching before Mallory saw a skull with a faintly-glowing witchlight in its eye socket and recalled seeing it on the lake floor.

'I've got something!' Mallory gestured to the top shelf. 'I remember seeing this, right where we saw the knife. This could be it!'

'You're taller than me, I can't see up there,' Cornelia said, and Mallory grinned.

'I always assume you're much, much taller than me.'

'It's the multitudes.'

Mallory rotated her aching shoulders before reaching up and feeling around. She scrabbled around, increasingly anxious, until her fingers grasped a handle and she pulled it free.

A fragile glass knife, an oily sheen to the blade. She held it to the light, black shadows flitting across the surface.

'*Hexana*,' Mallory hissed, her eyes meeting Cornelia's. 'If this is Elisabella's blade…'

'Those are the original souls,' Cornelia said, a strange expression on their face. 'And that's not all: I found something else.'

They opened their hand, and a blue glow lit up the room. For the first time since her arrest, they were a step ahead.

They found Theodore and Diana outside Rowan House, Diana staring at Theodore without saying anything, but with an expression on her face that suggested she was ready to put him in a ghostlight at a moment's notice.

That, and they walked out to hear, 'I've been a sword lesbian once, I can do it again.'

Mallory had entrusted Cornelia with the knife in a moment of weakness she hoped she wouldn't regret, and they were waving it around enthusiastically.

'You're back!' Theodore said, spotting them.

'Where did you go? What did you get?' Diana was on them in an instant, checking they hadn't been possessed or murdered or something else equally awful.

'It was a big store room,' Mallory said, allowing herself to be poked and prodded by an increasingly suspicious Diana. 'We found it.'

Diana patted her on the shoulder approvingly.

'We got what we went in for,' Cornelia said. 'Didn't get murdered by ghosts or swinging anvils or whatever funhouse bullshit traps they usually set down there. So let's go.'

'Go where?' Theodore asked.

'We need to move. Find Hexana's object before someone else does,' Mallory said. 'And we have someone we can go to for help with that. We just need to find her first.'

TWENTY-SEVEN

If someone had told Theodore six hours ago that he'd be reunited with the Undetectables and that they'd be witchlighting the fugitive Mallory Hawthorne to Broadwick Mansion in order to try to find the Ternion goddess Blair who had mysteriously disappeared from the back garden when the Ghoul Council opened up the bunker the Undetectables had been hiding her in, well. Theodore would tell them to sit down and take a nap. And then he would've hovered over them, wondering if they were actually clairvoyant.

The familiar ache of loneliness he usually got going through a witchlight clung to him as they opened up the bunker. He walked ahead of Mallory, pulling his cardigan around himself. He twitched as the door clanged shut behind him, the space lit by Theodore's lavender witchlight.

Jacob was still silent, and Theodore was overjoyed Grey's interference had worked. This was all going to be okay. He could have his cake and eat it, with cake to spare. Tonight, everything would be different. He'd never have to feel conflicted again.

He would have options. He would never take for granted the ability of human connection; he'd connect with humans every single day.

He'd go to cafes and have stellar interactions with baristas. He would get on the dating apps – all of them – and not cancel last minute in favour of work. He'd take up knitting and join a club. He'd go to the cinema and become one of those people who talked incessantly about films to his various dates, and he would sit opposite these men in cafes and have them witness his stellar barista interactions, and they would be so charmed by his outgoing nature. Unless, of course, his date was *also* a barista, in which case he might need to think of a new first-date location in order to overcome delicious human jealousy. It would end in tears, the relationship between him and the cinephile barista, and he'd have to seek joy in a different cafe and remember not to mix drinks with pleasure.

It would be wonderful.

'She's not here,' Cornelia said.

'Thanks, Captain Obvious,' Diana said, feeling around the walls like Blair was hiding in them. 'Could you have left the door open, Mallory?'

'Of course not,' Mallory said. 'I mean… no. No. I definitely put the sundial back.'

'She did,' Theodore said.

They swivelled to look at him.

'I happened to be walking by?' he tried.

Cornelia bit their lip and Diana raised an eyebrow, but Mallory didn't react.

'There's no evidence she escaped through the bunker

door. So if she didn't go out the front…' She moved around the bunker, pushing the walls experimentally until she got to the back wall. Under slight pressure from her hands, the back clicked and slid away, revealing a dark tunnel beyond. 'There had to be another way.'

'What the fuck?' Diana and Cornelia said in unison.

'Now you see her, now you don't,' Mallory said grimly.

'Are we up for a walk?' Diana asked, peering into the tunnel beyond.

Cornelia hefted the death blade and nodded. Mallory, who did not look in any fit state for any kind of walk, nodded too.

'Theodore goes first,' Cornelia said. He stepped into the tunnel with the witchlight.

'I think there's another door there,' Theodore said, after what felt like far too long of walking in silence – or near silence, as Diana and Cornelia were whispering together, and Mallory kept whimpering in pain and pretending she wasn't.

The wall slid back under his hands and Theodore led them inside the bunker beyond.

Although 'led' was a bit of an overstatement, as initially Cornelia refused to follow.

'Usually when someone in cahoots with a known serial killer suggests you enter a secondary location, one should consider not doing that,' they said, folding their arms.

'You made me go first!' Theodore protested. 'Fine. I'll go into the bunker alone.'

'No! That's worse!'

'Cornelia,' Mallory said. 'Please let's stick together.'

It took some more convincing, but they walked in and the wall clanged shut behind them. Theodore lifted his purple witchlight, and brought the contents of this new bunker into bright relief.

Diana screamed, and Mallory inhaled sharply.

'*Not very nice*,' Terror Voice said, and Theodore froze at the sound of it. The voice came from Jacob Gabbott, present in the flesh.

If you could call—

'It's a fucking giant centipede!' Diana said, recovering from her bout of excessive noise-making.

It was, in fact, a fucking giant centipede.

'Is this the one that escaped from the Mayoral Offices last year?' Mallory asked. 'The one that escaped the day they happened to find Jacob's body?'

'***Well done. Very clever. I've never been wrong about you, have I?***' Jacob-as-centipede said, although it came out as a series of clicks that only Cornelia seemed to understand, and reluctantly translated for the room.

'*Good work*,' Jacob-as-Terror-Voice said in Theodore's head.

'*This* is the Undead Complex,' Theodore said weakly. 'From the *Undead Complex* TV show. But also from real life.'

He wanted to say things like 'run for your lives!' and 'now you understand what I've been dealing with!' and 'I didn't tell him to come here please don't withdraw the limited trust you had in me over the last few hours!', but he was too taken aback. Maybe Grey hadn't lied; maybe Grey was just wrong. Maybe Jacob was smarter than him. Maybe Theodore was completely and utterly screwed.

'I know what it is!' Cornelia exclaimed, at the same time as Diana said, 'Wait, walk me through this. Is Jacob *in* there?'

'With another soul,' Theodore said, desperately trying to keep them all on speaking terms. Perhaps if he kept talking, the Undetectables would figure out a way out of this situation and everything would be okay again. 'Remember how Hollis Hadley figured out this whole thing with major souls and minor souls and it was a whole thing in the Vampire Wars—shouldn't have said Vampire Wars, you've all stopped listening and honestly I've forgotten what I was talking about, haha! But yes, there are two souls in the giant centipede – *Chilopodea titanica* – and one of them is Jacob.'

'Which half are you? Like are you the arse half, or how does it work? Fifty pairs of legs for Jacob, fifty pairs for someone else?' Diana asked, having rallied impressively. 'Actually don't tell me, the whole thing freaks me out.'

'Is Blair in there with you? Is that how this works?' Mallory asked urgently.

'It can't be, this is the one that escaped last year,' Cornelia started, but the centipede clicked in warning, high-pitched and sharp.

Even without translation, 'shut up' was the general vibe.

'Did you know he'd be here? Did you bring us here on purpose?' Mallory turned to Theodore.

Theodore shook his head, frantic. 'I had no idea. I promise. Mallory—'

'*Shut up*,' Terror Voice said in his head, invisible hands constricting around Theodore's throat. '*I knew you were being too whimsical with your little games. I simply can't trust you when it comes to them. My mistake.*'

An unideal turn of events that, if he was being honest with himself, was beginning to inspire panic! in the bunker.

'***The knife is here, I can feel it. The Complex can be completed. Give me the knife. Mother Morrigan demands it,***' Jacob-as-the-centipede said aloud.

'Demands what? What are you fucking *talking* about, standing there with your big legs—'

'Tarsi,' Cornelia corrected.

'—And your stupid bug face. This has been terribly fun, but we're out of here. We know you've killed Hayley Eason and Julian Johnson and probably other people, and we're going to do something about it, but we can leave this bunker on a truce. Cornelia, do you have the witchlight?'

'***Sadly I can't let you do that,***' Jacob clicked. '***Hand over the death blade, it's mine.***'

'Get fucked,' Cornelia said, stalking towards the door of the bunker. 'We're out of here.'

'***Theodore,***' Jacob implored, and Theodore snapped to attention.

He hated this bit.

Where his body wasn't his, and the connection between them strengthened. When he was truly haunted, his actions not his own.

Despite the holes in his memory, the uncertainty about what kind of hold *She* once had over him, he knew *She'd* never done this to him.

Well. Not *really.* She'd made *suggestions*, but some of those suggestions were entirely of his own offering. He hadn't been persuaded into them, he just… knew he was meant to help Her. And sometimes that 'help' had looked like 'digging through the archives for information he wasn't able to connect' and sometimes it was 'looking for an object he didn't understand'. And something about a baby and lineage he hadn't cared to comprehend.

Jacob, on the other hand, pulled on the invisible string tethering them and made Theodore do his bidding as violently as he could. Two-handing the invisible line between them. Straight up jerking it, and by 'it', Theodore meant his free will.

He'd never been free.

He'd made a mistake.

He'd led them into a trap.

Jacob took a step closer, tarsi clacking over the concrete.

Theodore tried to react, but his body was unresponsive. His arms were not his arms, his legs were not his legs. He pushed and pushed against it, static and sparks flying in his vision.

'No,' Theodore ground out. 'Don't!'

'*Do it*,' Jacob said in his head. '*You know the consequences otherwise.*'

But Theodore wouldn't. He wouldn't do this. He'd just made Mallory halfway trust him again, he *couldn't—*

There was a blur of movement, and then the knife was in his hands, Cornelia's shock palpable as they fell from the force of Theodore knocking into them against his will. He was back beside the centipede in a blink, turning the blade over. Elisabella's death blade. The real deal, black glass reflecting shadows of centuries-old souls trapped, waiting to be released.

He looked up at them, glancing at Mallory, at the horror

and betrayal on her face, at Cornelia, who stared at their hands in shock.

'MALLORY, RUN! MALLORY CORNELIA DIANA GET OUT GET OUT OF WRACKTON GET OUT GET OUT GET OUT GET OUT GET—'

'That's quite enough,' Jacob said, and Theodore couldn't make another sound. 'Theodore, the knife.'

I'm sorry Mallory I'm sorry I'm sorry I'm sorry

He fought every step of the way, but the centipede opened its terrible mouth and Theodore, his arms jerking, his legs flailing, put the knife inside.

The centipede swallowed, and convulsed, its back legs flailing, its body whipping against the sides of the bunker with a terrible *CLANG! CLANG! CLANG!* as claws struck and Mallory and Cornelia and Diana huddled in terror.

The centipede exploded.

Blue blood washed the walls, fell in a spatter arc through Theodore, and covered Mallory and Cornelia in viscera. Diana, who had huddled beneath them, was largely unscathed.

The remaining lump of carcass in the middle of the bunker crackled.

'Hello again,' Jacob Gabbott (as Jacob Gabbott) said.

His curls spilled freely over his forehead, and he was wearing a long coat and his ever-present canvas shoes with the floppy laces. He twirled the death blade in his hands, static flying.

'Samhain ghost?' Cornelia asked, their face pale.

'Samhain ghost,' Jacob smiled. 'It's so *refreshing* to be around people my own speed again. No offence, Theodore.'

Theodore swallowed unnecessarily, a terrifying sense of

Jacob's power washing over him. He'd known it before, on some level, but now it was impossible to ignore. And yet, he also found himself able to be annoyed at him more, now that he had a regular amount of legs. 'I really don't know who ought to be offended by that statement, honestly.'

'Quite. My, it is nice to see you in the… whatever this is. Flesh? Centipede eyes don't capture reality the way I'd like them to,' Jacob said, stepping closer to Theodore.

He looked at him from under his eyelashes and Theodore grimaced.

Tonight he'd be human. Tomorrow, he could pursue baristas and lifeguards and lumberjack daddies to his heart's content. Otherwise, his pool of ghostly suitors began and ended with Jacob. And he wasn't really into murderers. Morally grey was more his speed.

'I can still hear your thoughts,' Jacob said, and Theodore babbled something incoherent, terror gripping him, before Jacob laughed. 'Kidding!'

'*Or am I?*' a distant voice whispered in Theodore's head.

Theodore quivered. He didn't like to be not in control, and at some point in the last five minutes, he'd completely lost all grasp of the situation.

'We can stop you,' Mallory said, pulling herself to her feet. 'We can still stop you summoning the Ternion again, or joining them, or whatever it is you're planning to do this time. There's still time before Samhain.'

'Oh, Mallory. My old friend. My one true rival. Sort of. Didn't you know that unmasking the so-called villain is only half the story? I know I've been gone a while, but I've heard through the grapevine that you've been running around and solving lots of little murders in the last two years. Made quite a name for yourselves off my back. And I don't blame you for it in the slightest!' He twirled the death blade between his fingers. 'But you've become so accustomed to pointing fingers and saving the day, it means you don't confront the bigger picture. You're assembling a jigsaw puzzle without looking at the box, because you're not even aware you're doing it. Tell me, Mallory. What is justice?'

Mallory didn't say anything. Her mouth opened and closed, but no sound came out. Theodore tried to jump in – he had lots of thoughts on what counted as justice, as he was well-versed in the Undetectables' attitudes towards the flawed Occult justice system, not to mention the Apparent one – which he would've, if he had been able to speak.

'I'll ask it a better way,' Jacob continued. He rolled his neck like he was stretching, though he had no need to, and he ran a hand over his curly hair, as though it would do anything.

Theodore hoped and hoped he had an annoying strand of hair over his eyes that would never move away no matter how hard he tried, and also that he would die.

'Is justice ending centuries-old inter-Occulture disputes? Apparent–Occult rifts? Is it starting new ones? What I tried to do two years ago by joining the Ternion was just the start. Imagine my surprise to learn that you've already started it, bringing Blair back and locking her in a bunker! It almost makes me feel like we're aligned in some way. Like you want what I want. Thanks for this,' he nodded at Cornelia, waving the knife. 'Hope there's not too much bad blood between us these days.'

'We don't want what you want.'

'I don't believe you. I look at the three of you and I see history repeating itself. Three witches who want something more from the world. You can have it, you know. Join me, like Theodore has. I can make great things happen for you.'

'We're Besieged,' Diana snarled. 'You can't do shit.'

'Can't I?' He smiled. 'For my friends, I would do anything.'

'If they plan to revolt, it will be your job to kill them,' Jacob said in Theodore's mind, making him crackle with static and terror.

Out loud, Jacob continued, 'I want you to think about this: how Wrackton didn't burn down when Vincent Van Doren died' – Theodore resisted the urge to point out that Jacob had been the one wielding the murder weapon – 'didn't burn when the more worthy Van Doren took his place – me, obviously – but instead... kept going. Got worse. The greed, the grabs for power. I could've stopped it all, as the fourth goddess. And the Ternion wouldn't let me. Didn't believe in my *right* to join, if you can believe that. But something has to happen. Something *is* happening, and you can either be on the right side of it, or you can enjoy the show. It's your last one, and it's a *doozy.*' He tossed the death blade into the air and caught it again, static flying.

'That's short for whoopsadoozy,' Diana said, lunging for the death blade. Jacob vanished, and reappeared at the back of the bunker, leaving Diana standing in a mass of centipede goop.

'That was pathetic, Diana, sorry. Theodore, we got what we came for. Samhain approaches. I will leave you to make a decision. Tick tock!'

Theodore cast a desperate glance at Mallory, who looked

betrayed by him all over again. He wanted desperately to reach into her head and show her every single thing, every thought, every facet of what he'd been doing and why, but he couldn't move. He couldn't speak.

He juddered, and Jacob released his hold on his throat.

'I'll even let you have the last word,' Jacob said in his head.

'Mallory… we're in the grey, now,' he said emphatically. 'It's where we've been hiding all along.'

With one step, Jacob closed the space between them. He grasped Theodore's arm, and the bunker vanished.

TWENTY-EIGHT

Mallory Hawthorne had spent months not wanting to die and now very much wanted the earth to swallow her whole.

'THEODORE?' she shouted, knowing the chances of him still being there were zero. They were alone in a dimly lit bunker, with only centipede guts for company.

This couldn't be happening.

Cornelia was alternating between hyperventilating and mumbling 'shit, shit, shit' under their breath.

'It's okay,' Diana said in her most soothing voice, gently rubbing their arm. 'I mean, it's not even a little bit okay. But I'm trying to be soothing because WHAT THE FUCK IS HAPPENING? Sorry. We aren't panicking.'

'No you're right, what the fuck *is* happening?' Cornelia said, eyes wild.

Mallory closed her eyes. 'I'm sorry. I'm so sorry he's back. I'm so sorry he's not dead. But I think he wants the memento mori because he's going to kill the Ternion instead of joining them. That's what that whole thing about starting a new dispute was. He got Theodore – unwillingly, I suspect, and possibly unwittingly – to get us to find Elisabella's memento mori so that he could take it and destroy it. He's going to destroy the rest of the Ternion. And then he's going to replace them.'

'Can you even do that? I'll confess I never understood what he meant by "joining" the Ternion the first time we had to deal with this prick,' Cornelia said, trying to compose themself.

'What is a goddess, anyway?' Diana shrieked, then cleared her throat. 'Not panicking. Just wondering if that's relevant. Like, do we believe in them and they become goddesses, or did the *Ternion…*' she drifted off. 'What was I saying?'

The whole conversation wisped away from Mallory, leaving her with the sense of a word on the tip of her tongue. 'Cornelia, are you okay?' she asked instead.

'What, with my worst nightmare coming back to life? Yeah. I'm fine. I feel strangely vindicated by the whole thing, to be honest. Like all the terror was worth it, all the looking over my shoulder. All this time I've been waiting for him to pop back up, and he's been out there. He's the giant centipede that saved us in the Dollhouse Murderer case. He's been under our feet. Hiding in plain sight.'

Mallory opened her mouth. There it was again, that sense that she was missing a big piece of the puzzle. That there was something just beyond her reach that she wasn't able to understand.

'I think this is a murder board situation,' Mallory said finally.

'We have twelve hours left before Samhain, and presumably twelve hours left to stop Jacob Gabbott from killing the Ternion. We have one Ternion memento mori' – she paused as Diana showed off Blair's ring like an old-fashioned game show host – 'and we had another, which has been stolen by Jacob. There is one more up for grabs.'

Mallory took a second to eat a couple of crisps. Diana had assembled a tray of all their favourite snacks, and it felt scarily like a last meal.

'Which means we just need to find the last memento mori,' Diana said.

'Yes, but. What do we do with it? We can hide it, but we die at midnight, and he'll find them again. He's already back as a Samhain ghost – I don't think he needs to wait until Samhain to destroy them.'

'Do you think Theodore was telling the truth about the memento moris helping us stop the Besiegement?' Cornelia asked Mallory.

Mallory tapped her fingers off the arm of the sofa, thinking.

'Yes,' she said finally. 'But I think it's more complicated than that – we still need to solve his murder to understand *how* to save ourselves. It's all connected somehow. And that also doesn't answer all our questions. Why is Jacob still killing people? What is he doing with them?'

'And who does he have acting for him?' Diana asked. 'Were we onto something with the witch and the demon trace – we hadn't cleared Remington Davis, Sully or Sam Bridewell before things got more complicated, and we have no idea who the demon could be – unless we want to start naming random demons we've come in contact with recently.'

'And if we *were* onto something, do they even know they're acting for him?' Cornelia asked. 'Does chasing them down help us at all? More to the point – did *Theodore* betray us again?'

Mallory rubbed her temples. 'I don't think he was in control of himself. I think Jacob is able to talk to him in his head, control his actions. Which is probably what happened to whoever killed Hayley and Julian. They may not even know they were involved.'

'Okay, so that leaves us with…' Cornelia uncapped a marker and wrote on the murder board:

DO SOMETHING WITH SOULS OF MURDERED (TURN INTO GHOSTS (?))

KILL TERNION

???

TAKE OVER OCCULT WORLD AS NEW GODDESS

'And what do we need to do before midnight tonight?' Diana threw a packet of pig-shaped sweets to Mallory, who grinned. They were her favourites.

FIND HEXANA'S MEMENTO MORI

SOLVE THEODORE'S MURDER

SAVE OURSELVES

SAVE OCCULTURE

Hesitating, Cornelia added:

FREE THEODORE (?)

'Unfair that our list is longer than Jacob's. Surely we can't be defeated by the forces of evil because of bureaucratic red tape?' Diana tapped her head against the wall in frustration.

'In good news,' Mallory said, holding up the ghostlight Cornelia found in Ghoul Council Headquarters. 'We found Elisabella.'

Diana snatched it from her, her eyes wide. It shimmered blue and they all stared at it, remembering the last time they saw Elisabella in the semi-corporeal flesh, her face hidden. Remembering her involvement in the Besiegement Curse.

It was a small victory, in light of what had just happened. Jacob didn't have her, but Mallory wasn't sure she particularly wanted to be responsible for her.

'She can be plan C, I don't really want to summon her again,' Diana said. 'Especially with Blair missing – it doesn't sound like they know where she is, but they know she's around. If we can keep a hold of Elisabella, maybe...'

'What, we can appeal to her goddessly sensibilities?' Cornelia asked. 'Sounds great. She won't be at all mad we threw her back into the lake, or that she was left to rot in a storage room.'

'Plan A is, obviously, finding Hexana's object,' Diana continued, undeterred.

'It might not be an object. She might not have one!' Cornelia said.

'No,' Mallory said. 'It wouldn't make sense, firstly. And secondly, Jacob seems adamant there's another object out there to find. Which suggests that he has information we don't.'

'Or he's an idiot?' Diana suggested.

'He could be, but he'd be an idiot with a vendetta, which is the most dangerous kind of idiot,' Cornelia said.

'I don't know how we didn't figure out he was back sooner. The clues were there.' Mallory's brain was mired with fog and threads of thought she couldn't hold onto, and she was past the point of being able to tell if it was fatigue or magic. 'I *knew* our suspects didn't have motives on their own, and I didn't believe Theodore was behind it. People kept *saying* Jacob was dead, but we had the note and the Whistler carvings. We knew how long it took to find his body, we knew about the possibility of an Undead Complex situation. We've known Theodore came back wrong since he returned two years ago! It was all staring me in the face, and it's like I was *unwilling* to put those pieces together. We should've known.'

'*How* could we have known? It shouldn't be possible. We watched him get torn asunder by the vengeful spirits of people he'd killed, it was perfectly reasonable to assume he was dead-dead and not ghost-dead.' Diana gritted her teeth. 'If anyone should've noticed, it was the Ghoul Council. Honestly I hope we don't have to speak to them because how are we meant to explain their catastrophic failures to them? "Hi, a serial killer has *come back from the dead* like this is a TV show starring Sandi Clementine and, oops! He's going to EXPLODE the Ternion, but you also should've known this would happen, you're just all too focused on bureaucratic bullshit to see it?" I can see that taking six to eight business months to resolve, which is time we don't have.'

'At least we didn't waste an enormous amount of time

running around after Copycat suspects who aren't Samhain ghosts and probably had no conscious participation in the murders at hand,' Cornelia said. 'Oh wait.'

'And at least the note we got threatened an apocalypse we can't stop. Oh, wait,' Diana said.

Mallory could feel the gears of her mind sticking as panic set in. 'What else was said in the bunker? Anything you can remember. Theo said something when we were leaving, didn't he?'

'Before his latest betrayal, you mean?' Cornelia said archly.

'I, and more importantly, *you*, do not believe it was intentional, and I know this because you've voluntarily written up there that we should save him.' Mallory smiled at them, and Cornelia bit the inside of their lip. 'He said… What on earth was it?'

'He says a lot of things. Something about hiding in the grey?'

'Meaningless Theodore theatrics, as usual,' Diana said.

'No it's not,' Mallory said slowly. 'I can't believe it didn't occur to me sooner.'

'What?' Cornelia demanded.

'Yes, he's been hiding with me,' Grey Quinn said, tipping a glass of scotch at them as he led them into a dilapidated sitting room, a fire roaring in the hearth. He was in a shabby hotel at the edge of town, a run of converted townhouses that had probably been grand once, but were now cracked and mouldering.

His top button was undone, and he was wearing—

'ARE THOSE JOGGING BOTTOMS?' Diana pointed at his legs and his sock-clad feet, aghast.

'The socks are cashmere,' he said, as though by way of explanation. 'I suspect you're not here to judge me. Is that a clock I hear ticking?'

Mallory was barely paying attention to any of this, and was instead staring at a murder board behind Grey. It was unmistakable: it had *TW: MURDER* written in the centre, with various borderline illegible squiggles around it that were not Theodore's writing.

'Are you trying to solve Theodore's murder?' She tried and failed to keep the incredulity out of her voice.

'We had an arrangement, yes.'

'Which was?'

'No, no. I must insist, you go first,' Grey said. 'Why are you bothering me at home?'

'This is home?'

'In a manner of speaking.'

'Theodore sent us to you. It was the last thing he said before he—' Diana stopped, looking to Mallory and Cornelia.

'We think he's headed into trouble,' Mallory said.

'Why?'

'Why what?'

'Would I help you?'

'If you help us, you probably won't die tonight the way we think everyone in this town is otherwise going to. We just need to know why he'd waste his last breath – figuratively,' she added, as Grey raised an eyebrow, 'on sending us to you.'

Grey considered her. 'Is he really in trouble?' he asked quietly.

Softly, she thought. Like Theodore was something to be gentle with.

He gestured for them to take seats, and Mallory perched on a wing-back with an iron blanket over it.

A chair for Theodore. In the 'home' of his once-greatest enemy.

She had no idea what it meant.

Diana and Cornelia bickered until they found a comfortable way to share the second wing-back, and Mallory filled Grey in as far as she felt safe to, which was not very far or safe at all.

It felt strange to treat him as an ally – even if he had been all along, in his own way – but Mallory pushed down feelings around it and spilled what she knew. The time for being coy was over. If Theodore trusted him – and really trusted him, enough to make it potentially his last ever message to them – she had to, too.

'So in summary,' Grey said after Mallory finished, with countless breathless interjections from Diana and Cornelia. 'The Ghoul Council is an abject failure of an organisation—'

'That's what I said!' Diana smiled happily.

'—Jacob Gabbott is back after he was imprisoned in a giant centipede for two years, and has been talking to Theodore inside Theodore's head, which would explain many – but not all – of his strange mannerisms of late, and why his default reaction to any difficult conversation was to bolt out of here like Morrigan herself had told him to. And now you, for some misguided reason, think you need *me* to help you find Hexana's memento mori before Jacob does, or there will be untold danger of potentially apocalyptic scale.'

'That's about it, yeah.'

'I would like to offer a "goddess, you're fucked" in these

trying times, but I don't think even that can save you,' Grey said, pouring another scotch. 'Sorry, where are my manners? I'm so used to Theodore waving an arm through my glasses in an attempt to achieve contact intoxication, I've forgotten humans like to drink.'

'Pass the bottle,' Cornelia said, and he did. They unstoppered it with their teeth and took a sip. 'Do you have any mixer?'

'That's twelve-year-old scotch. You want to *desecrate* it with *mixer*?'

'I'll take that incredulity as a compliment.' Cornelia passed the bottle to Mallory, who took a tentative sip herself. Burning warmth flooded her chest and she felt briefly lightheaded as her veins dilated, soothing some of the pain.

She passed it back as Grey rummaged and produced a different bottle, clearly having decided that caring was too much effort.

'So, memento mori. Fascinating. My friend Hollis Hadley—'

'We met,' Diana reminded him, and Grey squinted at her.

'I'll just have to trust you on that one. But he had a lot to say about Occulture, for an Apparent. I think he was circling the concept of memento mori from the outside, so to speak. I digress, though – I'm assuming if Theodore has one, and the Ternion have them, then Jacob must have one too.'

Mallory froze, shame settling on her like an unwanted blanket. Of course he did. *Of course he did.*

'Yes,' Cornelia said, a bit too loudly. 'We had obviously thought of that already. We had definitely considered that there is, *obviously*, a physical way to stop Jacob. Assuming Theodore's theory that destruction of memento mori equals death of the Samhain ghost.'

'You really did need me,' Grey said silkily. 'Have you any idea what his might be?'

Mallory had no idea where to begin. 'I don't know anything about him. I don't know what he likes.'

'He likes his mother,' Diana offered.

'You think his mother is his memento mori?' Cornelia asked.

'And more to the point, are we going to have to kill Delilah Gabbott for the greater good?' Mallory asked.

'Surely not. She suffered enough having to deal with Van Doren,' Cornelia said.

'It's probably not a person,' Mallory said. 'He was in an orchestra. Maybe he has a favourite... flute?'

This was a monstrously funny statement to everyone else in the room, and Mallory felt her cheeks burning in confusion.

'Sorry, Mal,' Cornelia said. 'We've no idea what it could be.'

'Great. And you're Wrackton's best PIs, did you say?' Grey asked. 'Any idea what Hexana's memento mori might be, then?'

'We were thinking – *I* was thinking,' Diana started, 'that Hexana's might be in Oakpass.'

'Pray tell?'

'Because Blair's ring was there once,' Mallory said, a sudden memory of a scrapbook full of newspaper cuttings hitting her. 'We saw a photo of it in Oakpass Manor, the day you let us in to investigate. Lady Larkin wore it on a chain, and it went missing.'

'I really have done you so many favours over the years, haven't I?'

'Not the point, *Grey*. Is that short for anything, by the way?' Cornelia asked, taking another swig from the bottle.

'No.' He drummed his fingers on the table in front of him.

'Blair had a ring, Elisabella had a knife… The myth is that Hexana had a star, isn't it? What could that have transmuted from, over the years?' He set his glass down. 'I keep trying to think of things to say about the Ternion and I find myself floating away. Strange, I'd never noticed that before.'

'Welcome to the club,' Cornelia said sullenly.

'We haven't found a way around it yet,' Diana said. 'And now we never will.'

'We don't know that,' Mallory said suddenly, making a decision. 'Has anyone seen my phone?'

Kingston arrived within minutes of summoning, Felix at his heels.

'Are we having a party?' Grey asked Mallory, but moved aside to let them in.

Kingston bowed to Mallory. 'At your service. What do you need?'

'I need you to tell me what Hexana's star is,' Mallory said urgently. 'Nothing else, just what her star is.'

'It's a symbolic representation of her manifestation of power, her omniscient abilities,' Kingston said, frowning at the room. 'You're lucky I just dosed, I had to dig deep for that one. Where are we?'

'At the mercy of my hospitality,' Grey said.

'Are you wearing *jogging bottoms*?' Felix asked, scandalised.

'Goddess forbid a man experience comfort in the privacy of his own home,' Grey snapped.

'You *live* here? Whoa, how the mighty have fallen,' Kingston said, touching the peeling wallpaper. 'The mess with Oakpass Manor really fucked you up, didn't it?'

'What is he doing?' Grey said sharply to Mallory. 'Why does he know… anything about me?'

Kingston grinned lazily, his pupils enlarged, eyes unfocused. 'I drink blood and I know things.'

Grey fixed him with a look over the rim of his glass. If Mallory didn't know any better, she might say he was impressed.

'What does what you said about Hexana's star mean in practice?' she asked, trying to redirect Kingston's attention before he wandered off completely. 'Blair's ring was an object that was important to her. Elisabella built the death blade to help end the Vampire Wars, and it was clearly so important to her before death that it became her magic special object. Hexana is associated with… the *concept* of stars? That can't be it. A star has to mean something.' Mallory gestured at the star tattoo on her hand that had appeared when they'd been Besieged. 'It has to have something to do with ghosts, and the Besiegement. It has to be linked, but I can't focus on it long enough to work it out.'

'Something small, and tangible. Something to do with stars…' Kingston sank to the floor, crossing his legs. 'What are stars?'

'Luminous balls of plasma,' Felix said.

'No, my beloved. I mean in Occulture.'

'Luminous balls of plasma,' Felix said again.

'Luminous balls,' Cornelia repeated, sniggering.

'Connection to the goddesses,' Mallory offered as Kingston looked around helplessly for serious input. 'Look up at the sky, see a star, speak to a goddess.'

'So maybe it's a communication method,' Kingston said. 'Something unorthodox. Something that would let you speak to ghosts, perhaps.'

'Like a planchette,' Diana said slowly, the colour draining from her face. She set her glass down and stood. 'Does anyone have a witchlight?'

Felix, Kingston and Cornelia rummaged in their pockets, and three were produced in a rapid quick-draw. Diana was back in seconds, her face still ashen, but she had a black stone object clutched in her fingers that Mallory had completely forgotten about. An object Mallory hadn't seen in over a year.

'Do I want to know what that is?' Grey asked.

'It's a planchette. We stole it from Oakpass Manor,' Diana said. 'What are you going to do about it?'

'If it's the memento mori of a goddess of Occulture? Probably nothing, actually.'

'We showed this to Theodore and he freaked out,' Mallory said. 'But either he's completely forgotten about it, or he knows we have it and is… pretending we don't?'

Grey raised an eyebrow. 'I haven't known Theodore as long as you, but I believe he's capable of that level of deception. He had a monster talking to him in his head for years and said nothing.'

'Wait, what?' Felix held up a hand and folded their palm, orange stiletto nails glittering in the firelight. 'Back up. I thought Theodore hated you?'

'I suppose you're also going to tell me you didn't know they were going to die tonight.' Grey laughed over the rim of his glass.

'What the fuck is he on about, Mallory?' Felix asked.

Grey lowered his glass. 'Oh, come on. Surely they…?'

'Thanks, Grey. You pillock,' Diana snapped. 'Yes, we've been Besieged, we die tonight. Et cetera et cetera.'

'And you said that when I say "et cetera" it wasn't very emotionally intelligent of me,' Cornelia said, at which Diana actually growled.

'No. Back it up. Rewind,' Felix said to Mallory, and Mallory did. They looked on the verge of tears after Mallory's succinct explanation, while Kingston's whole face had dropped.

'It's very sad, we know,' Cornelia said. 'We're sorry we didn't tell you. I'm even more sorry that we don't have time for this right now. We need to figure out our next move – If the planchette is Hexana's star, we're already ahead of where Jacob expects us to be.'

'Now we just need his memento mori, quick brainstorm to solve Theodore's murder, and we should be golden,' Diana said.

Mallory held the planchette, turning it in her fingers.

She thought back to when they'd shown it to Theodore, after Diana had found it in Oakpass Manor, a lifetime ago. His jaw slackening.

'Evil… It's evil. It's evil. Take this back to where it came from… And never bring it back again. This evil.'

And then he'd acted like nothing had happened.

'I don't think he remembers,' Mallory said. 'Which puts us a step ahead. Jacob… he doesn't realise how much has changed since we first met. How much *we've* changed. We're different, but he's not. He's fundamentally the same person. We know he likes puzzles, and we know he has a tendency to over-prepare. He's trying to get us to gather up the memento mori for him. We have to make sure he thinks we're still searching.'

'He's playing checkers,' Kingston offered, standing over Grey's chessboard with his fingers on the king.

'And he's pretending it's chess.' Mallory pulled herself to her feet with difficulty. 'This time, we know his playbook. We can beat him at his own game.'

TWENTY-NINE

Theodore was, to put it very mildly, in a bad mood.

He was devastated that Jacob had destroyed Mallory's trust in him again. He was disgusted that he'd had to watch a giant centipede blow up. And he was completely and utterly furious that Jacob was now also a Samhain ghost.

'Isn't this *fun*?' Jacob asked playfully, keeping easy pace with Theodore as they moved from the centipede-entrailed bunker (Red, as he'd suspected – he was starting to get the hang of the different underground locations, largely by process of elimination) on to the Memorial Garden bunker.

A labyrinth beneath Wrackton, untouched for centuries, waiting for them. Waiting for this.

'I really couldn't have done any of this without you, you know,' Jacob continued.

Theodore side-eyed him, strong revulsion sinking to where his guts should be, but he kept walking. Jacob was terrifyingly powerful, more so now that he could move as Theodore moved (Theodore's memento mori aside).

'You're not shy, are you? Not like you at all.'

'Just focused,' Theodore said.

Jacob smiled, and Theodore didn't return it. Jacob's face fell a little, but there was a bounce in his step as he followed.

It felt like a role reversal – like Jacob was following him – but Theodore couldn't change course if he wanted. Even now there was the thread of connection pulling him towards the Memorial Garden, demanding he finish what he started.

'Theodore,' Jacob said, touching his arm lightly. The air crackled, and Theodore stopped walking.

The dirt and stone tunnel around him felt like it was closing in.

'I know you're nervous, but the reward is coming. I promised then, I promise now. If it works for me, it'll work for you. And then you'll be the free man I said you'd be. The proof is—'

'You've said this already. The Besiegement Curse proves it's possible. I get it.'

I need to get it. I need to remember that I get it. Theodore be nice, Theodore be contrite, Theodore resist proving yourself right!

Jacob looked at him from under his eyelashes, a painful crackle building between them. The anthesis to sexual tension, and a growing, tangible sense of unease.

Though perhaps Theodore was the only one who could see it for what it was.

Jacob continued, 'I don't think you *do* get it. You're so brilliant, Theodore. You're smart, and you're clued in, and you're determined. You like working through problems, finding fast solutions. Me, I think things through. I work through problems until they reach a satisfactory conclusion.

Everyone vastly underestimated me two years ago, when I was the Whistler. My father, Occulture, myself. What I haven't shared with you yet is that all of this, now?' He gestured with the death blade. 'This is what the Ternion were trying to do. This is their original plan, and the reason they didn't want me to join them is because they were afraid I'd succeed where they'd failed.

'I was meant to make this happen. I don't believe in destiny, but I do believe in bloodlines.'

'Wait, what?'

'And I believe that I see things others don't,' Jacob continued, as if Theodore hadn't spoken.

Van Doren was his father, a woman called Delilah Gabbott was his mother. Aside from that, Theodore had no idea about his lineage, and had never cared to. This Jacob – the one not exercising persistent control over him, but instead seeking his company – was so annoying that Theodore had a hard time reminding himself of the hold Jacob had over him.

'I have the ability to take ordinary occurrences and turn them on their heads. To envision a possibility that others can't, to imagine a world better than the one we inhabit. Better for me, I mean.'

'Well as long as *you're* happy, that's all that matters. Sure, I will have spent my one precious unlife doing things to further your cause, but all that matters is that my great and definitely benevolent captor is satisfied.'

'I don't mean to insult. I really do think you are a particularly excellent ally. And that is why I will reward you. It has to be me. Don't you see that?'

'Hard to see anything when you keep putting your proverbial, staticky little hands over my eyes.'

'Theodore, listen. You looked at the Besiegement Curse and you saw terror. Ending. Death. Destruction. Right?'

Theodore didn't dignify him with a response.

'I saw birth. Life. The blossoming expanse of Occulture and all it has to offer. And now we're in the final phase. The apocalypse beckons!'

Theodore faltered, and Jacob kept walking, either because he was unbothered or because he simply hadn't noticed.

'What do you mean, *apocalypse*?'

Jacob waved a hand. 'Nothing to worry about.'

Theodore could feel the ghost of his stomach clenching, the walls of his lungs crushing against each other. He could be caught in a panic loop for days if he wasn't careful, so he focused on reminding his brain he was already dead.

'Jacob, seriously. What are you doing? What is all of this?'

'All in good time, Theodore.'

'No. You told me... You told me you were fixing things. Making Wrackton safe again. Correcting the mistakes of the past. You didn't say *anything* about an apocalypse.'

Jacob smiled disbelievingly. 'Surely you read the note I left for your little friends?'

'Of course I read the note. It had a bad pun in it.'

'Surely you turned the note over?'

Theodore goggled at him. 'Of course I didn't turn the note over. Who puts extra bits on the *back* of a crime scene note? That's deeply unintuitive.'

'Mallory intuited it. So sorry to hear you lack basic instincts.

What were you doing in that investigation agency? Although we all remember your last efforts at "solving a mystery"... Anyway, so sorry to not have said it plainly before now. I assumed you knew.'

Theodore was sure, if being sick was possible, he would be sick. But no, he was like a giraffe, or a rabbit, or a horse. Doomed to continue the cycle of nausea until it... it couldn't end him.

He was just doomed.

'I didn't know,' he said in a small voice.

'My dear Theodore, you didn't *need* to know to do anything! I called, you answered! I prepared for all of this. I keep telling you – nobody sees things the way I do.' Jacob took his hand and Theodore fought the urge to wrench it free, static crackling dangerously between them. 'I unfold the world like a map and I examine the pathways. I think of every outcome possible with the information I have, and I prod and push and prepare. It's a science – I throw up roadblocks until I am sure that I know that if *x* and *y* happen, I can bring things back around. Easy as A, B, C, but it goes all the way to Z. I was *wasted* as a flautist, and even more so as a Mayor's aide. But no matter! All that changes tonight. On you go,' Jacob said, ushering Theodore down the tunnel.

'What?' Theodore stumbled, confused, as Jacob placed a hand on the tunnel wall and pushed. The stone wall slid back, revealing a narrow passageway Theodore had never seen before, despite him spending a disgusting amount of time crawling around in the tunnels like some sort of cryptid. Like a worm desperate for sunlight.

Like an accidental villain with a pathetic desire to *live.*

'You will always be my greatest work,' Jacob continued. 'A true sacrifice of the heart. A debt you may never be able to repay. But it'll be so worth it, to be alive again. You still want that, don't you?'

He was right. Theodore hated how right he was. By tonight, Theodore would be human. He would flex his hands, stretch his muscles. He would know tiredness and hunger. He would know rest and peace. He would fix everything.

'I'm grateful you're giving me that chance,' Theodore said, making sure his tone was as sycophantic as possible.

Jacob beamed in response and Theodore fought off the revulsion. He wished Grey was here. That Mallory would come bursting in and save him from himself.

'You've just got a few more things to do and the world is yours again.'

'I thought I was to find Hexana's star?'

'Change of plans. We'll both need to be flexible for the next few hours. Anticipation prevents mistakes. Ah, I wish I had a watch. So much to do, so little time to do it!'

'Would you like me to shine your shoes for you while I'm at it?' Theodore asked bitterly, all efforts at sycophancy evaporating.

Jacob moved closer, his warm hand touching Theodore's shoulder. It felt— it felt like he was alive. Like they were both living. *She'd* felt like that too, the one time he saw her as a ghost. This electric sense of belonging.

But he hadn't hated *Her.* Not at the beginning. He could recall that much.

Not the way he hated Jacob.

'Laws of thermodynamics, my friend. I know you're

impatient. You've waited so long for this. It's ending soon. I promised you so long ago.'

Theodore gritted his teeth, a thread in his head prompting him to look away, to grind out, 'Thank you. For remembering your promise.'

'I remember everything,' Jacob said. 'And I am benevolent.'

This was, of course, a lie, but Theodore swallowed down a retort. He reached into his own mind, into the safe place Grey had made for him.

Remember the plan, Teddy.

'So, find Hexana's star. Be done in a jiffy! What else am I to do to aid the apocalypse? Round up the villagers?'

'No… but you raise a good point.' Jacob smiled. 'No, for you – my most loyal soldier – your task is to find my memento mori. You know what it is.'

'And then meet you on Mount Hallow. Got it.'

'Ah – no. You've sadly lost the privilege of my trust there. I worry Mallory is still able to manipulate you, so we'll keep you in Wrackton for now. Meet me in the Memorial Garden, topside. I'll outsource the other job.'

Theodore did not at all like the sound of this.

'Okay,' he said, hating how cowardly he was being, hating how easy it was to simply agree and go along with Jacob. He could probably take him. Jacob was taller, but Theodore was scrappy—

Jacob released his hold on Theodore and gestured to the tunnel.

As soon as Jacob was out of sight, Theodore ran and ran, stopping only to rest his head on the dirt wall beside him. Had he been able to cry, he would've.

'And one more thing. But you know what it is, and you know the consequences if you don't,' Jacob whispered in his head.

Theodore closed his eyes.

He'd been afraid he'd say that.

THIRTY

It was just like the best of times, back when they'd started the agency up, which were a lot like the worst of times, in that the Undetectables collectively felt like they were desperately trying to be taken seriously again.

Mallory opened the door and admitted a flood of people into her parents' house. A crowd huddled around her sofa and spilled into her kitchen where they opened cupboards and rummaged in the fridge and murmured approval, as though it was a particularly disorganised house showing and not an attempt to assemble every ally they had ever had.

Some of whom might be unwitting murderers.

Dr Ray, Sully, Kingston, Felix, Langdon, Taylor, Grey Quinn, the four Broadwicks and more were crammed into the sitting room, and Mallory felt a sudden pang at the obvious absence of Observer Johnson. He'd have been deeply displeased and heavily bemused at the summons, but would nonetheless have been there.

Mrs Blackburn had burst through the door at the last

second, Maisie the dog under her arm (though Mallory privately thought that either the dog was ageing backwards, or she was a replacement).

'I knew you were up to something,' she snapped at Diana when she tried to redirect her to anywhere but Mallory's house. 'Saw the lot of you heading this way, acting too casual. I still haven't forgiven the three of you for not solving what happened to my Paul's body.'

Given that the Undetectables had not, in fact, been able to recover Mr Blackburn's body after Theodore dug it up, there was no reasonable way to explain this, and so Mrs Blackburn joined everyone else in the living room.

Cornelia was deeply displeased to see their parents and siblings, especially when the twins tried to pull them into a hug.

'It's the last one I'm going to get to give you,' Agatha said crossly. 'You're being such a *beast* about this!'

Cornelia looked at Mallory for help, who leaned against the front door for strength.

Their guests swivelled to look at her, eyes wide.

'They're looking for you,' Dr Ray said, by way of unnecessary explanation. 'In connection with the murders. You're meant to be under arrest.'

'And you're not going to say anything,' Diana said fiercely. 'Mallory is only *sort of* on the run.'

'Broke out of prison, did you?' Mrs Blackburn asked, eyes gleaming. 'Nice when police go rogue.'

'We're *not* fucking—' Cornelia started, but Diana silenced them, nodding to Mallory to start.

'I don't expect you to know why we've gathered you here today, or to understand the nuances of whether I'm a fugitive, but we need your help.' The room quietened completely as Mallory spoke. 'I don't wish to alarm anyone, but if we don't solve our current case by midnight tonight – if we don't stop what is about to unfold – we won't be able to fix this. Earlier this year, we were cursed.'

'Mallory,' Ezra Broadwick admonished. Once a leader of the Ghoul Council, always someone who expected their authority to be unquestionably respected.

'We kept it secret for five months out of respect to the others affected,' Mallory said, omitting the part where they'd also kept it secret out of denial. 'But it's called the Besiegement Curse. Come midnight tonight, our bodies will be taken over by ghosts, and we will, effectively, die.'

Mallory half-hoped that everyone would take this news neutrally, so she didn't have to bear the brunt of their feelings on the matter.

This, of course, did not happen, because the people they'd gathered for assistance were not monsters. There were exclamations of horror, and hands reaching to hold her and Cornelia and Diana, a unified voice of protest, of denial, of refusal.

Her attempts to re-command the attention of the room failed until Grey Quinn placed two fingers into his mouth and whistled sharply. The sound made a chill run down Mallory's spine.

She explained in a stilted manner what was to come. They only seemed to fully believe her when she, Diana and Cornelia (and after much cajoling, the Broadwicks) raised their hands to show the star tattoos inked there between finger and thumb, a constant reminder and now, finally, proof. There was, apparently, nothing less likely than the idea of Imogen Broadwick willingly branding herself, especially on such a visible part of her body.

'Is this why you stepped back from the Ghoul Council, Imogen?' Dr Ray asked.

'Is this a professional enquiry?' Imogen asked stiffly, to which Dr Ray raised an eyebrow, but did not respond.

'We were searching for a cure,' Ezra said. 'We created a sub-committee, and handed over the running of the Council to Khan and Reid.'

'There isn't a cure coming,' Mallory said. 'What's happening in Wrackton – what will happen across Occulture, and maybe the whole world – will cease to affect us after tonight. We will, to our understanding, still be here, but we won't be *us* anymore. Our jobs, our lives, everything will end. But *you'll* be here. You'll be living in the middle of it. We don't want that for you. You let us take your cases. You charged us with the responsibility of keeping you safe. We don't want to leave you with nothing.'

'Very valiant,' Mrs Blackburn said, and Mallory had no idea if she was being sarcastic.

'What is happening with the latest murders?' Langdon asked. 'Apart from you being a wanted witch.'

'Our friend Hayley was murdered, the community has lost Julian Johnson, and I am getting the strangest sense of déjà vu,' Dr Ray murmured.

'The murders feel familiar because they *are* familiar,'

Mallory said. 'Each one has been designed to exactly replicate the Whistler murders, which I'm sure you all recall.'

They nodded.

'Are you going to tell us who's behind it, or do we have to guess?' Dr Ray asked.

Mallory took a deep, fortifying breath. There was no going back from this.

'Jacob Gabbott.'

Agatha and Ethel gasped.

'Fuck off,' Mrs Blackburn said, and the whole room turned to look at her.

'Has Nova been informed of this?' Ezra asked. 'Surely *someone* would've informed us, *if*—'

'He is back,' Mallory said firmly.

'He crucially also never really left,' Cornelia said. 'And the mechanics by which he is back are... confusing.'

'Mildly inexplicable,' Diana added. 'But all you need to know is that he's a Samhain ghost now.'

Imogen paled.

'There's also a possibility that several people in this room are unwittingly behind the murders, but we'll come back to that,' Diana continued.

'Sorry, one of *us*?' Taylor said, wrenching her hand free to turn on Felix. 'Surely not.'

'I'm much too pretty to commit murder,' Felix said, aghast.

'And it can't be us, we've just arrived,' Agatha said.

'In any case,' Mallory continued, 'He's back and wants to destroy the Ternion, largely because they rejected him last time.'

'Despite him trying very hard to make sure they rejected

him if they weren't absolutely sold on him joining their little witch trio,' Cornelia added.

'And we only *think* he said this, because only one of us speaks giant centipede,' Diana said.

'We believe he wants to become the only goddess of Occulture, and he wants to make sure he's the only one in charge. We need to stop him. We need your help. We need all the resources available to us.'

'Has Theodore been helping him?' Dr Ray asked.

The elephant in the room.

'Yes, but I believe against his will,' Mallory said quickly. 'There is a physical connection between them—'

'But not sexual. Or consensual. Or really romantic, or anything positive,' Grey said casually. 'A connection of minds, I think he'd say.'

'Has he told you that?' Cornelia turned to him with interest.

'Goddess, no. We don't have that kind of relationship. I don't think he knew he could tell me, or was even able to tell me anything to begin with. There were times when he was pulling away from me. Pulling away from the room, lost inside his own head.'

'"*Times*"? How long have you been harbouring a fugitive, Grey?' Dr Ray fixed him with a look halfway between betrayed and impressed.

'We don't have time to list all of my crimes, and I don't care to share. I had reason to think he was innocent.'

'What reason was that?' Sully asked.

'You're barely even a police officer anymore,' Grey admonished. 'Why the sudden focus on me?'

'I'm not *not* a police officer,' Sully said. 'For what it's worth.'

'Not very much. Mallory, what is it you need from us?' Grey asked. 'Give us a clue.'

Mallory blinked, forgetting for a moment that she'd asked the room for help.

Clue.

Theodore told her he'd tried to leave clues.

A second time someone broke in.

She started looking at what was out of place when they'd arrived back at the house. Cornelia was the first to realise what Mallory was up to and followed her around, gathering up the files and dropping them beside Diana's Wrackton diorama, slapping Agatha and Ethel's hands away as they tried to reach in to touch the Mayoral Offices.

'Erm, sorry. Yes, we need to figure out a way to stop him – that one, Cornelia – and I have some ideas. We need to find Jacob's memento mori, first and foremost. That's like—'

'An object important to him when he died,' Cornelia said. 'The rat bastard.'

'That's the key to ending this,' Mallory added. 'And we need— Diana, can you tell me what's out of place here?'

'The Mayoral Offices and the Observatory switched places. There are lights over the Redwoods and Broadwick Mansion…'

'Oh, is this a mystery?' Ethel asked eagerly. 'Can we help?'

'Talk amongst yourselves,' Diana said. 'Grey will make you tea in the kitchen.'

'I will the fuck not.'

Diana shot him a sweet smile and turned her back on him,

scanning her diorama.

'Here are the case files that were disturbed,' Cornelia said. Mallory tugged them out of their hands as Diana continued scrutinising the diorama. The Ternion's names were ringed in red pen, and she now noticed letters scrawled in Theodore's unmistakable handwriting.

'It says *ALIAS*.'

'Unless he's lamenting Apparent TV shows he used to like again, this is meant to be a clue.'

'Was there anything else?'

'He's just underlined the shit out of the word "VANE" on this old case file,' Cornelia said, waving it at Mallory.

Mallory buried her face in her hands. 'I really don't have time for Theodore's whimsy right now. Tell me what's changed with the mini witchlights.'

'One over Broadwick Mansion, one over the Redwoods,' Diana said. 'I had one witchlight over the Larix, and two over the Observatory.'

'Five witchlights,' Mallory murmured. 'Vane. Alias. What else?'

'He's written *Halloween* on the side of the diorama. Actually *written* it on it. Permanently! But *een* is crossed out.'

'What on earth is a Halloween?' Langdon asked, at the same time as Taylor said, 'Finally, something I know about! That's what the Apparents call Samhain.'

'Haven't you noticed the town has been overrun by Apparent tourists who keep calling it that?' Agatha asked, biting into a biscuit. 'Mother and Father would've never allowed this to happen if they were still in charge of the Ghoul Council.'

'Yes, thank you, Agatha. We put our efforts into not letting us all *die*, darling,' Imogen said.

'And we're going to, because you didn't move fast enough!' Ethel said.

'We tried! We were following leads, we had you two picking through the findings from the Lake—'

'I thought we said talk amongst yourselves!' Cornelia snapped, but Mallory waved a hand.

'If you've got useful input, come over here. Otherwise please be quiet,' she instructed. 'What could he *possibly* have meant by that? Why would he cross out— *Hallow.* Why does that sound familiar? Hallow. Hallow...'

'Mount Hallow,' Kingston said softly. 'North of here. Sacred vampire hills. Where the... You-Know-What began.'

Even as Mallory thought the words *Vampire Wars*, they drifted from her mind like cobwebs on the wind.

The Undetectables looked at each other, cogs turning.

'What does this mean?' Dr Ray said.

'This might not even end in Wrackton,' Mallory said after a moment. 'Maybe he's taking things to Mount Hallow. Maybe there's something there. We can't be in two places at once.'

'The Ghoul Council went to Mount Hallow earlier today,' Ezra said. 'I could give them a call.'

'Wonderful – I'd like to personally break the news to Khan and Reid that a serial killer has returned on their watch,' Grey said.

'We'll take a small group of volunteers,' Ezra said, straightening. 'Everyone else, retire to Broadwick Mansion and await further instruction.'

Mallory could've sworn she saw Grey wince, but she was too busy feeling complex amounts of gratitude to really question it.

'We're coming too,' Agatha and Ethel said.

'No you're not,' Imogen said firmly. 'Wait here. Take care of Mrs Blackburn.'

Mrs Blackburn cackled and the twins looked forlorn.

'We'll go too,' Felix said. 'We're at your service.'

Like an out-of-body realisation, Mallory saw the room for what it was: full of people. Normal people, who would be deeply affected by Jacob after she was gone. Unless a miracle happened, she would never stand in a room with these people again. She'd slip away. Her face would become a fuzzy, hazy memory. Her legacy would be a handful of murders solved and a to-do list that wouldn't shrink.

'No. Felix, Langdon, Kingston, Taylor – I want you to track down Blair. I can explain further in private,' Mallory said, avoiding the curious-to-horrified stares from the Broadwicks. 'The rest of you, go to Mount Hallow. Appeal to the Ghoul Council, maybe see if they can get a curfew in place? We need to keep everyone safe. We don't know if he's planning to kill again.'

'And we need to figure out what his memento mori is, before we do *anything* else,' Cornelia pressed. 'It's an object important to him, something significant. This can't be hard, we have all the greatest minds in Wrackton in one room.'

'And then some,' Dr Ray said, not quietly enough, as Agatha and Ethel preened.

'Did he have anything on him that he wore, like a watch?' Taylor asked, resting her head on Diana's. 'Or like a pen or something?'

'The only person who would've paid that much attention to him was Theodore,' Mallory said softly.

He had been infatuated at the time; she'd thought it was mutual.

The room fell into silent contemplation, punctuated only by Mrs Blackburn rummaging through a packet of biscuits.

Grey stood, stretching. 'Let's go, then. Unless you want to be the one to say let's go, Ezra? This is pointless. I knew I didn't like Baby Van Doren the first time I set eyes on him and his stupid little beanie. I don't trust *anyone* who mixes formal wear with *unnatural fibres*. Could've strangled him right there and then and we wouldn't be in this mess.'

'BEANIE,' Mallory, Cornelia, and Diana chorused.

Grey raised an eyebrow. 'Couldn't be that simple. Could it?'

'But it could be.' Kingston nodded, his gaze far away. 'It feels right.'

It was good enough for Mallory. 'He wasn't wearing it when we saw him. Dr Ray, are you still—?'

'His personal effects were returned to Delilah Gabbott – his mother,' she explained to Mrs Blackburn, who had opened her mouth with a profanity locked and loaded.

'Do you have an address?' Mallory asked. 'We need to make a visit.'

She knocked thrice and waited, heart hammering. Delilah Gabbott lived in a ground floor flat right on the edge of Wrackton.

'Do you think she knows?' Cornelia whispered. 'About all of this.'

'I don't know. He practically deified her the first time round, but this time… He's angry, and I'm not sure he cares about anything other than himself.'

'What are you saying?' Diana hissed on Mallory's other side, and Mallory repeated it.

'In that case, do you think he'd kill Theodore?' Diana asked, voicing something Mallory hadn't wanted to contemplate.

'I don't know. I would like to think not. Surely even Jacob understands the need for allies.'

'He killed him once before,' Cornelia pointed out. 'But didn't destroy his lightbulb. Are we sure this is enough?'

'I don't think he *did* kill him that time. I think he just stole his soul. Something *like* death, that wasn't, but that meant when Theodore came back, he was indebted to him.'

'Which suggests he was indebted to someone else fir—' Diana started, but was cut off by the door swinging open.

Delilah Gabbott leaned on her cane and took the Undetectables in with surprise.

'Can we come in?' Mallory asked. 'We have some questions.'

'I had his hat,' Delilah said, as Cornelia and Diana poured tea into cups. Delilah had aged dramatically in the last five minutes as Mallory had gently explained that her son was back from the dead and that she was in terrible danger, but she was holding onto composure. 'I had all of his belongings. I was so disappointed in him, I couldn't bear to hold onto the hat. I knitted it for him one year, when I was very ill. Took me a week to do each line. He said it was his favourite thing anyone had ever given him. And you need this why, exactly?'

'It's complicated,' Mallory said. 'But the object would have to mean a great deal to him.'

She wanted to say something comforting, like *he must've really loved you*, or *he's still your son deep down*, but there was nothing she could say that wouldn't sound hollow. She just wanted the hat. She wanted, so badly, to end this quickly.

'I threw it in his grave,' Delilah said. 'I couldn't look at it, didn't want him to be parted from it. But when that was… exhumed, I was called to collect his personal effects from the Mayoral Offices. And I just… didn't.'

'Oh,' Diana said. 'I mean, that's fine. Do you know where in the Mayoral Offices?'

'I don't like the idea of digging up things that should stay buried. He's dead. I mourned him. He was meant to be the best thing that happened to me, the most precious result of putting up with Vinny for as long as I did. An ending to a rotten family line. I need to be allowed to move on.'

She stood. 'I need to lie down. Let yourselves out, please.'

'Dr Ray has no idea where his personal effects would be, because that was Theodore's job,' Diana said, reading a text as they swerved around groups of Apparent tourists clogging up the main thoroughfare. Mallory pulled her hood tighter, keeping her head down, aware she was tall and conspicuous and on the run.

'He used to bring things down to the bowels of the Offices, but of course we can't get in there because of the creatures. Then again, that was bricked up before Jacob was buried, or indeed exhumed. So a moot point.' Diana scrolled. 'She also says they're on their way to Mount Hallow. The twins are in Broadwick Mansion and are "eagerly awaiting your return", Cornelia. It's practically a demand.'

'Great. That's how I want to spend my dying hours – responding to the demands of my sisters.'

Mallory had stopped listening, had stopped moving, had stopped everything. Crowds milled past her and she was frozen in place, the cogs turning in her head, understanding blooming. She pulled her phone out of her pocket and read a text, the words barely registering.

ALIAS. Vane. And distantly, a memory that felt so far, far away, '*Have you news of my sister?*'

'I know what he was trying to tell us,' Mallory said breathlessly. 'Diana, where were the witchlights? On the diorama.'

'Mayoral Offices – though swapped with the Observatory – Larix, Redwoods, Broadwick Mansion. Why?'

Another memory, this time of Tate confronting her with the fact Van Doren's heart was carved out, left on a plate. A different sort of murder. A sacrifice, almost.

'Bunkers,' Mallory whispered. 'Theodore would never tell me what he knew about her. Would never admit he knew her. But if Jacob brought him back – did a sacrifice of the heart spell, a real one, and brought him back with control over him – then *surely* that was taken from someone else. But she insisted he was meant to *help* her. Every time we saw her she said something about the "cat man" and I just assumed— but what if…?'

'Are you going to finish a sentence anytime soon? People are dying, Mallory!'

Mallory turned on her heel.

'This way. Quickly,' she said. 'Felix just texted and said they're about ready to go into the tunnels to look for Blair, and I was just thinking it was a pity we haven't met Hexana. And then—'

'What? Mallory!' Cornelia caught up to her, falling into step beside her. 'What are you talking about?'

'I know who can help us. And if I'm right about this… it will change the way we look at Occulture forever.'

THIRTY-ONE

'I'm very sorry about this,' Theodore said as Blair screamed and screamed and screamed at him. 'If it helps at all, I actually had a *different* plan and really didn't think I'd be grubbing around in the labyrinth beneath Wrackton. There was a point where I was meant to be commanding a giant bug army, if you can believe it! But alas, I think the army has been scrapped. My friend – well they're not my friend anymore, I don't think. Entirely my fault, of course, but friend at the time – used to call them *Chilopoda titanica* – that was the centipede kind, but I have come to the conclusion that all giant insects could be *titanica* if we so desired – and honestly, when you see them first you're like, "wow, they're so magical" which, as a goddess, you probably aren't that amazed by. But now that I've been in caverns with one and have witnessed its… *undulating*, crawling body, witchlights bouncing off its thorax and tarsi, my other friend – though probably also not my friend anymore, it's a very complicated story, you understand – said they were *horrible*, and I rather think she's right, you know. Could you stop screaming, please?'

Blair thrashed and screamed angrily as Theodore bound her tighter in the iron-reinforced ropes Jacob had left him with.

Is this even worth it?

Theodore checked a few times to be sure that was his own thought, but didn't know how to tell. He had not, at any point in his quest to be human again, thought he would be restraining a goddess of the Ternion. Blair, with her heart cut out – a reminder of how Theodore had come to be, how Jacob had a hold over him – and her face contorted with rage. Completely understandable rage. That he was causing. For reasons.

'You know I used to actually *work* with these giant creatures. It was my job to find out what they were. We had no idea, really.'

'The vampires,' Blair snarled. 'They belonged to the vampires.'

'You would know,' Theodore said cheerfully.

'*Did you do it?*' Jacob asked.

'Yeppers,' Theodore said. 'Absolutely have done everything you asked.'

'*Don't be glib.*'

'Okie-dokie!' Theodore said, and returned his attention to the very angry goddess he was trying to frog-march down a tunnel. 'It would help if you had any giant bugs to help me out. A mantis, maybe. A bumble bee. A— oh!' he exclaimed, as something very large and round rattled down the tunnel towards him, wide-set eyes close to the ground, armoured back rising in a hump behind it, covered in magically-wrought spikes.

'My woodlouse!' Theodore said. 'The least horrifying of all the *titanica*! I was wondering when I'd get to see what I'd made.'

He tried not to think of the implications – of the fact two people had died to form this woodlouse, that they were somewhere inside this creature, or the fact he had no idea if they were as sentient as centipede-Jacob, nor had he enough time to figure it out, or indeed of the fact he had done the whole thing entirely against his will.

'*You're welcome. Deliver the package*,' Jacob said, and then the connection between them crackled out.

'Who were you talking to?' Blair asked quietly.

'Ah, that was... You'll meet him soon.'

'Where are you taking me?'

'I can't tell you,' Theodore said, and it was true – there was something preventing him from giving her the information she desired, the information that he wanted to divulge. 'But I'm going to need you to climb aboard.' He gestured to the woodlouse – a sweet, gormless-looking little-big thing, really, that did not appear to have a human consciousness – and Blair shot him a look that reminded him so much of Diana he almost needed a little sit-down.

'I do not understand why you're doing this,' Blair said. 'I just want to find my sister. Can you bring me to her? Please?'

If there wasn't so much at stake, Theodore would do just that. He knew better than literally everyone what it felt like to be a ghost, to have things he wanted that he could not achieve. What would it matter, if she was to be with her sister? What would it matter in the grand scheme of things if Blair had a moment of happiness?

'I don't call the shots,' Theodore said. 'I don't even know if this is...'

'If it is what?'

Worth it, he answered silently, making sure the thought

stayed in the place Jacob couldn't reach it. What did living *mean*, anyway?

He hadn't started living until he came to Wrackton. In the time since he'd died, he'd made real friends. He'd made *magical forensic advances*, for fucksake. Something he hadn't even *considered* until he was dead. Even being a fugitive with Grey Quinn hadn't been that bad. It had even – and he was glad nobody could hear this thought – been *nice* at times. Fun, even. Like they were two people who could spend a lot of time together. Like he was starting to break down an invisible wall between them. Sure he was irritable and constantly focused on the idea of getting his body back and being human again. But if he really stopped to think about it: was it terrible? Was any of it terrible? Was *he* terrible, for going along with this?

For the millionth time, he felt a flush of sorrow at the thought of his old friends. All the lies between them. All the ways he had tried to avoid hurting them, and had hurt them anyway. And he had tried! He had tried so, so hard. He'd been deliberately vague about his work in the Mayoral Offices, because he wasn't really doing a job, most of the time. He'd been running around at *Her* behest, piecing together tiny fragments of information to try to build a bigger picture.

He knew, reading between the lines, that the story Occulture believed about the Ternion was riddled with lies. That the so-called peace of Occulture post-Vampire Wars was built on a tower of cards that could come tumbling down at any moment. It would only take one person able to see beyond the veil.

He'd pieced together so much, despite knowing so little.

Multitudes and shades of truth contained in his little blonde head.

Theodore James Wyatt had been nobody, until She found him. He'd been Just Some Guy, generally dissatisfied with his life, until he stumbled into the wrong place at the wrong time. Offered a friendly hello. Scientist's curiosity overtaking him. She touched his hand and he saw what She wanted him to see – a mix of colours and feelings he couldn't comprehend. A wash of something bigger than him, something older than him, something tangled and complicated.

She had doomed him, he now realised. Someone had killed him, but She had cursed him first. Hexed him into an afterlife, quietly and without him knowing. He existed in fear of worse things than death, afraid to say no. He had been content with the suffering he was already enduring, thank you very much. To accept an unknown suffering sounded preposterous, and not in a cute way. He'd gone to work every day and looked for the creatures and filled in paperwork, and served Her as best he could. He could remember that much. He could know that much. He had tried, very hard, to please Her, asking nothing in return.

All he'd ever wanted was to know who killed him, but now he wanted to know why it had been him at all.

He wished it had never happened. That She'd found someone else.

'You have not spoken for a very long time,' Blair said, cutting across his reverie. She was seated atop the woodlouse – Roly, Theodore decided. A sweet giant baby – and staring at him with a look he did not think a goddess was capable of.

'Sorry. Erm. Greetings, subterranean dweller,' Theodore said to Roly, drawing himself up to his full, unimpressive height. 'Onward, to the destination.'

Blair rolled her eyes, still struggling with her bindings.

'Sorry,' Theodore said meekly.

'You know, you have all the power you need at your fingertips,' she snapped. 'So use it.'

'*This is the culmination of my very original plan*,' Jacob said, as though he'd rehearsed a speech.

Theodore fought the urge to point out the obvious: this was not his plan, and never had been. It was someone else's – stolen, over generations. Each bright spark believing it was theirs to carry out.

Centuries of attempts, Theodore suspected, though none as advanced as this.

'*Your handsome reward will be granted tonight. Are you excited?*'

Theodore gritted his teeth, a crackle of static blurring his vision, willing himself not to keep talking. If he kept talking, he'd see doubts, and if he saw doubts…

'*If I didn't know any better, I might think you weren't trying as hard as you could be.*'

'You promised,' Theodore said flatly. 'I do this, I get my body. We walk away from each other.'

'*I'm kidding! Trying out a fun little villain thing. Can't believe I ever thought I might want to date and, indeed, or do other things to and with your body. Aside from the obvious. You're no fun.*'

'Really takes the romance out of necromancy,' Theodore said, and Jacob laughed. A soft, curling laugh and Theodore heard it fill his head and he hated him he hated him he HATED HIM—

'And then you say things like that, and I remember what it was about you that I lov— liked so much, all that time ago.'

Roly roiled, as though he'd heard what Jacob said, until Theodore realised he had his own thing going on: Blair was trying to escape.

'Please don't,' Theodore said, catching her. He brought his mouth to her ear, whispering as quietly as he could, 'if you leave, I can't figure out how to help you.'

Blair stilled, hopefully believing him. Roly nudged her and she climbed back onto his back.

Theodore sank down against the tunnel wall and buried his head in his hands. He was running out of time. Here he was, Notorious Theodore Wyatt, Controller of the Titanic Army of One, ruler of the Undead Complex, a necromancer's wet dream come true. But he was also a coward. A loser. A failure.

'Here's the signal. Plan B commences.'

'Okay.'

'I do wish you'd come around to "yes master",' Jacob said regretfully. *'It would feel so much better. But I think you've earned the truth.'*

Theodore felt a wave of dread wash over him.

'Truth?'

His voice sounded distant.

'I know I said this would all be over tonight, but it's just the beginning.'

'The beginning of what?'

'Surely you've... no, I did a good job of hiding it, I mustn't

blame you for not realising, note turning over aside. The apocalypse is just the start. Did you think Occulture would accept me, no questions asked? No, we'll have to assert ourselves. Together. You'll get your body back as promised, but I'll need you to stick around.'

Theodore had a sense that he was unravelling, static thread by thread.

'Jacob, that wasn't what we agreed.'

'I know it's hard for you to accept what I'm doing – what we're *doing – but I promise it's for the greater good. Aren't you sick of the greed? Aren't you sick of the corruption? Of the ways the Apparent world rubs off on Occulture, of the way we Observe goddesses like they aren't incredibly powerful? Like we don't, collectively and culturally, fear what we can't control?'*

He was wrong. He was wrong he was wrong he was wrong—

'There is a grain of truth I can get behind in that, yes,' Theodore the Almighty Coward said.

'If one can believe, others will follow. It's never worked for me before, but I see it now. I've never been what one might call a "natural leader", but here we are. Now! Samhain's approaching, and you know what that means!'

'Break out the nice tea pot,' Theodore mumbled.

'Onward. Bring her to me.'

Theodore snapped his fingers and Roly rattled into action, carapace clicking, antennae twitching. He took the helm as they began the long, slow march towards the Memorial Garden, moving into the darkness, inch by terrible inch.

The final countdown was on.

THIRTY-TWO

It had come to this: they were gay, and they were doing crimes.

There was no more right or wrong, no more wrangling of Mallory's steadfast morality. There was only what could be done, and what could be done quickly.

And in this instance that meant 'break into the bricked-up section of the Mayoral Offices without anyone noticing'.

But it also meant 'wandering around in dirt tunnels found at the back of the bunker in Broadwick Mansion with no idea how far to walk'.

'Are you sure?' Diana asked for the fifth time. An intermittent *buzz* was emanating from her bag every five steps or so, and Mallory wished she'd put her phone on silent.

'Yes, I am sure this is the only way in,' Mallory said patiently, also for the fifth time. 'I think this is what Theodore was trying to tell us. I am certain there are several bunkers beneath Wrackton, all inter-connected. A labyrinth. The Redwoods, the Mayoral Offices, the Broadwicks' garden, maybe even the

Larix. I would bet the last few hours of my life that this network goes all the way out to Oakpass Manor. And that when we find the entrance to the Mayoral Offices in this tunnel, it won't be bricked off. A loophole the Council didn't consider.'

'What makes you so sure?' Diana asked. 'I don't want to find out I stole all this ghost catching equipment from the Ghoul Council for nothing.'

Mallory, who had not realised Diana's handbag contained contraband, did not know whether to feel relieved Diana was so prepared, or alarmed their list of crimes began hours ago.

'There's always a loophole,' Mallory and Cornelia said in unison.

'Who even built these? Why doesn't everyone know about them?' Diana continued.

'They probably did know about them at one point,' Cornelia said. 'Apparents are constantly re-discovering catacombs that were thousands of years old. Presumably at some point these tunnels were joined up on purpose. Or else some wild ancient warlock came down here and did it without saying anything. Shame we exploded the Mayoral Office archives that time. We'll never know who knew.'

Diana stopped walking, yanking her bag open. 'That buzzing is driving me— oh shit,' she said, as it buzzed again.

'Did I leave a Lyrespy in there?' Cornelia asked, trying to peer into the bag with Diana, resulting in them getting flicked on the nose.

'No.' Diana pulled out the planchette. '*This* is buzzing.'

As if on cue, it buzzed again.

Diana took a step back the way they'd gone and it buzzed

insistently, the buzzing fading as she returned to the path they were taking. She looked at Mallory.

'Ask me if I'm sure again,' Mallory said, a slow smile spreading across her face.

Before long they reached an arbitrary point in the tunnel and the planchette went wild, buzzing and jerking in Diana's hand. Mallory and Cornelia felt around the walls for some sort of give.

'It's here,' Mallory said, and the wall slid open. They stepped into a familiar green-tiled hallway lit with torches, and Mallory felt her stomach twist. This looked a lot like the corridor she and Diana had entered two years ago through a hatch in the back of a cupboard in the then-Night Mayor's office.

It was, in fact, that exact corridor. The hole Mallory had made to access it the year before – the last time a case had brought her to Katherine – was bricked up, Katherine and everything else with her sealed away from the rest of the Mayoral Offices. From the rest of Wrackton.

'They've sealed the whole corridor with glue and iron. Like, they've stuck bits of iron into the gaps and glued them in.' Diana scowled. 'Incredibly shoddy craftsmanship, but there goes our plan to exit through the Mayoral Offices. It would take all day to chip away at it – we'll just have to retrace our steps through tunnels. It's time we don't have, but I don't see any other option.'

'*We* can't get through it, but I have friends who can,' Cornelia said smugly, reaching under their jumper for a pouch.

'Please tell me that's not a fucking spider,' Diana said.

But it was.

'They can weaken the glue,' Cornelia said excitedly. 'With their poison silk. It contains an enzyme that—'

'For the second time, I don't want to know. I have *hours* left to live, I do not want to burden my mind with this information!'

Cornelia released the spider and brushed it lightly on the back, which seemed to prompt it to release some corrosive silk, scuttling over the glue. Their prompt exit secured, Mallory led the way, an invisible clock in her head counting the seconds down, down, down. This had to work. It *had* to.

Katherine Vane was exactly where Mallory had last seen her, standing in a corridor, a flickering shadow with shorn hair and a dress coat that matched Blair's attire.

'I know you,' Katherine said, swinging close when Mallory approached.

The others froze.

'I'm Mallory Hawthorne. We met recently. You wanted to know where your sister was.'

Cornelia and Diana separated, hands clutched around iron netting, until the three of them were surrounding her.

'You need to help me,' Katherine said desperately. 'You're my only chance. Samhain approaches once again and I—'

'Now,' Mallory said decisively.

They'd discussed this precisely once before going through the passageway, so it was surprising they managed to deploy the iron netting Diana had stashed successfully, catching Katherine in the centre of a web. She struggled, a small animal in a cage. It was unlikely to hold her for long, but it just needed to keep her present for long enough for Mallory to do what she came to do.

'I know what happened to Theodore,' Mallory said.

'Is that what we're starting with?' Diana asked, but Cornelia shushed her. They didn't even hex each other over it.

'Theodore... The cat man.'

'Yes. We know what happened to him.'

'I showed you the truth.' Katherine struggled harder. 'Showed you that it was them. The Broadwicks. They killed him. He was meant to help me.'

'No that's not the truth, Hexana,' Mallory said firmly.

Katherine froze. 'Who told you to call me that?'

The real truth had been staring them in the face for far too long. Blair – Rosemary Vane – was Katherine Vane's sister. They'd been told for the longest time that the Ternion – Elisabella, Blair and Hexana – were sisters, although Mallory was starting to doubt Elisabella was actually a relative. This was what Theodore had tried to tell her.

He had sent her to Katherine. Katherine, the third Ternion goddess, under their noses the whole time. She would have the answers. She could help them.

If she was suitably motivated.

Mallory didn't reply. A static charge built around Katherine that expelled a lightning flash as she, presumably, divined what Mallory was getting at.

'It is not what you think,' Katherine said. 'It is not like that at all. I won't say anything else, I refuse to allow my words to be twisted.'

'Someone is trying to find you. They're trying to find your star, and they want to kill you.'

'Who? Cat man?'

There was no use mincing words or worrying about semantics. 'Yes. At the behest of someone else.'

'Pointless. It has been lost to time. Out of my reach, away from my magic. I have suffered and suffered and *suffered*, waiting for Rosemary and Ruth to find me. To help me. It all went wrong. It all went *wrong*. The three of us. Me, Ruth— RUTH!' she screamed, closing her eyes. Her voice softened. 'And Rosemary. My sister.'

Mallory tried to keep control of the conversation, but details were slipping away even as she tried to commit them to memory. She kept making connections that weren't allowed, adding pieces to her puzzle that were forbidden by whatever force would not let her think about the Vampire Wars. *Remember their names remember their names RUTH ROSEMARY KATHERINE. ELISABELLA BLAIR HEXANA.*

'They want your star. They have Elisabella's knife—'

'NOT HER,' Katherine snapped. 'Not her not her not her not HER NOT HER—'

'He has the death blade. He got it from us. But we have the ring, and we think we have your star. It's not lost. We found it. We think we can get you out of here. But we need you to listen.'

Katherine stilled, briefly mollified. 'How?'

'It's a long story,' Mallory said. 'But we need your help. We have friends out searching for Blair – she's here somewhere, in Wrackton. And then we need to stop him. Together. All of us. We'll get you out.'

'We'll petition the Ghoul Council to not treat you like specimens,' Cornelia said.

'And you can maybe enjoy total freedom, if our understanding of the memento mori is correct,' Diana added.

'I care not for any of this. I am here as a punishment. I am part of the land,' Katherine said, lying down under the net. 'I cannot leave.'

'You can leave. If you had your star, you could leave. That's what you wanted Theodore to help you with, wasn't it?'

Katherine nodded stiffly. 'I wanted to be free.'

'Did Theodore know?'

She shook her head, obstinate as a child. 'I asked for help. I let him talk to me, and I talked to him, and I made him come visit. But it's so confusing here. I wanted a companion first, and freedom second. Then he vanished, and I had no star. What happens if… whoever, finds it?'

'If he gets his hands on it, he's going to kill you,' Mallory said. 'Jacob Gabbott, not Theodore. When this is over, he won't have use for you anymore. He's decided the Ternion are over. Blair, Hexana, and Elis—'

'NOT HER!' Katherine screamed again, but she'd stopped struggling completely as Mallory's words seemed to sink in. 'He can't. He wouldn't.'

'He will. He knows how.'

'He'll never find it,' Katherine said, her eyes staring into Mallory's as though she was feeling her way into her soul. 'We were going to sacrifice ourselves, you know. If it didn't work, we could say we tried. That was the plan. But Elisabella took matters into her own hands. She cut out her heart. Said it was for me – that it was her *sacrifice*, for me. I found my sister dead in the Observatory gardens and I screamed to the heavens to help me. Begged Hecate and Morrigan to undo this. We died anyway, on Samhain. All three of us, dead. And I woke up, convinced it was all a dream, but found myself trapped in the tunnels beneath the Observatory. Wrackton was burning. Everyone here was at war. Vampire fought vampire fought troll fought demon fought witch fought faerie. Our lie spiralled out, grew legs of its own, became fact.' Katherine's face cleaved in two, her mouth stretched in rage. 'She's not who you think she is. She's more. Pass through the oak to avoid the elder. But you can't avoid her any longer. She's been here the whole time.'

The story hissed and spun in Mallory's head, knotting and tangling like a fading memory as she tried to hold onto as much of it as she could, fistfuls of smoke dissipating.

'What does this mean?' Diana hissed.

'I think it means everything we've ever thought about the Vampire Wars – in so far as we've been able to think about the Vampire Wars – has been wrong. It has, in fact, been much worse,' Mallory said slowly.

'You'll forget all this. Our curse demands it. Leave me. They're all dead. You told me they were,' Katherine said, drifting to the end of the corridor.

'They're not,' Mallory said. 'We were wrong. They're like you. They're Samhain ghosts too.'

Katherine paused.

'Plus, we have your star,' Diana said, holding up the planchette. 'We need you to come with us. Non-negotiable, at this point.'

'Where did you get that?' Katherine drew closer, her brow furrowed.

'We found it at Oakpass Manor last year.' Diana's fingers were clenched tight around it, ready to hide it away if Katherine lunged.

But she didn't. She'd stilled, her expression clear.

'That's not my star. That belongs to *her*. To Morrigan.'

THIRTY-THREE

The only thing that could make Theodore's situation worse for him would be company. And the only thing worse than that would be *bad* company.

So naturally, Theodore got both.

'Oh, no,' Theodore said, emerging into the Redwoods bunker. He had been looking forward to taking the sharp right turn out of there and heading straight on to the Memorial Garden, if only to no longer have Blair sniping at him. The nightmare, close to ending. (Or *closer*, at least.)

And now, *this*.

Nathan Tate stood in the bunker, a serene smile on his face. He stared through Theodore, which was rude enough as it was, but Theodore was distracted by the movement beyond him.

Dozens of Wrackton's townsfolk and a not-insignificant number of tourists were gathered behind him, the bunker door open and a crowd pushing in, their eyes glazed and unseeing, drifting like they were waiting for something.

'Can I help you?' Theodore asked acidly, searching around in his head for Jacob, who was not responding.

'We're ready,' Tate said.

Theodore had seen this happen twice before, but there was still something deeply unnerving about full ghost possession. Tate's expression was shifting and sliding like he was asleep, his eyes shifting beneath his lids and darting back, forward, back, forward. If he remembered – if he survived long enough to remember – it would feel like a dream.

'Don't move,' Tate said lazily, waving a hand. The townsfolk stopped shifting, organising themselves into neat rows and accommodating more of the crowd pushing to get in. 'I'm the messenger. And the guardian of the sacrifices.'

'And I'm Theodore. Some might say this is a demotion for you, wouldn't they? Detective Inspector to *puppet*.'

The lack of correcting him on the 'Chief' part of his title was enough verification for Theodore that Tate really was being possessed by Jacob.

Shit.

'Can I see who you've got there? Hang on a minute, Roly – don't let her go,' he said. Roly's giant eyes flickered (Roly's innate sweetness made it difficult to remember he was two dead souls in a woodlouse coat; finally, Theodore understood Cornelia Broadwick's fascination with insects) and shifted his carapace against the wall, trapping Blair.

Theodore drifted among the townsfolk, finding four Broadwicks in quick succession – Ethel, Agatha, Imogen and Ezra all looked through him, focused on the wall beyond – as well as Dr Ray, a very rumpled Sully, Mrs Blackburn and her tiny rat dog, and a whole host of faces he recognised. He searched and searched for Mallory or Cornelia or Diana, but didn't see them in the faces he knew, until one gave him pause.

Grey, who still had some light in his eyes, who was clearly fighting, fighting, *fighting* against whatever Tate was doing to persuade him to stay in place. Theodore drifted closer. So close their lips were inches apart. Then an inch.

Grey's eyes flicked to his and Theodore jerked away.

'What do we mean, sacrifices?' Theodore shouted back across to Tate, who had not moved.

'The apocalypse is coming,' Tate said. 'We need to start again. Burn the town down. They are the ones who will burn.'

'Ah, of course. Can't burn down the town without angry villagers,' Theodore said.

'We will set them alight. We will start over. Burn the town. Burn the town,' Tate said.

The crowd rumbled in agreement, a congregation murmuring along, 'Burn the town. Burn the town. Burn the town.'

As they rumbled, Theodore heard a noise from the secret passageway behind him. There was scrabbling and swearing and a chorus of voices saying 'shut up!' and then a distinctly Irish voice said 'sketch!' and there were sounds of feet thumping away. Theodore frowned, but Tate did not appear to notice, though Roly did, one giant eye turned towards the source of the noise.

'Burn it down. Burn it down. Burn it down.'

'*You're not afraid of a little fire*,' Jacob whispered in his head, and Theodore fought the urge to… to…

Do nothing. Do nothing, because he was a coward.

No.

None of this mattered anymore. He had promised and promised Theodore, from the moment Theodore escaped that death blade two years ago and became conscious in the basement of Broadwick Mansion – had hugged Mallory, and heard a crackle like a radio tuning, and Jacob's voice spoke to him so quietly he thought he must be dead. He must be dreaming.

The second thing Jacob promised was that Theodore would get his body back. That he would be allowed to live again, if he just did one *tiny* thing for him.

There was a line that Theodore had probably crossed some time ago – a line that was unforgivable, that he would have to reckon with. There were so many times he should've stopped it, even if he didn't know how.

But he drew the line here. Now. With murdering swaths of villagers and tourists, even if he cared less about the tourists.

With murdering Grey.

The thought lanced him. Forced him into action.

He needed a plan. A good one.

Abscond with Blair. No, that would never work. She was much too furious at him for holding her captive. That couldn't be plan A. Plan A had to be fast. Watertight.

He needed *time.*

That was it. It was time for plan T.

'Onward,' Tate said.

'WAIT!' Theodore shouted. 'Erm. Avast! The sacrifices are getting away! Out there! I hear voices!' He pointed at the door of the bunker opposite to where he'd heard the voices, and Tate marched over to look.

Once he was outside, Theodore ran to Grey again.

'Sorry about this,' he whispered, and reached a hand into his head. Grey jerked.

'Sorry sorry sorry sorry,' Theodore said in his head. *'Open the door. Please open it.'*

Grey's eyes rolled back into his head and Theodore kept pushing, moving past the persuasive magic Tate had on him as the ornate door of Grey's innermost thoughts materialised. He had no desire to press too hard. Either Grey wanted him in there, or he didn't. Desperation aside, he would not use anyone for his own gain.

Then Grey unlocked the metaphorical door and Theodore slipped inside, closing it gently (also metaphorically).

'Hi,' Theodore said.

'Hi. What are you doing in here?' Grey replied, and Theodore felt a frisson of excitement.

He'd done it! He'd ethically possessed someone! Take *that*, Ghoul Council and their handbook of rules that did not mention anywhere that ethical possession was an offence (and Theodore should know because he'd read them cover to cover on many an occasion).

'Trying to save you. I can break his hold, I think. Hang on,' Theodore said, reaching for the threads of persuasion magic holding Grey in place.

If someone had asked him – which, to be fair, nobody had – he'd say brains looked a lot like spider-webs. Delicate threads of connection. Easily broken.

The threads holding Grey in place were blue, and Theodore carefully reached in and detached them one by one, leaving a few scant threads of shimmering violet-white.

Grey blinked and Theodore withdrew until he was standing close to Grey again, aware of the villagers and the Tate and the Roly and the Blair of it all.

'I can stay in your head, until you're safe. I need you to find Mallory. Help her. Go now. Quickly.'

Grey nodded once, and with Theodore's harried directions, slipped down the tunnel past Roly and Blair, who glared after him.

'Where is he going?' she asked, but thankfully nobody replied.

'Onward,' Tate said, coming back into the bunker. He flicked a hand and Imogen Broadwick peeled open the next door.

Sharp right, and straight on to the Memorial Garden.

The townsfolk poured down into the tunnel, an endless stream of blank face after blank face, until the bunker door clanged closed.

'Go,' Theodore said. Roly marched on ahead of him, Blair still seated – as helpless as any other witch would be in these circumstances, despite her goddess status and ghost stature – and Theodore bringing up the rear.

Every step sounded like a list of his crimes to date.

He had to hope he'd done enough.

He had to hope he'd been clever enough.

Oh, Mallory, I am so sorry, he thought.

THIRTY-FOUR

Wrackton was utterly deserted.

Barely an hour before it had been teeming with life, with revelry, with no idea of the threat looming on the horizon. Now it was empty. Front doors hung open, hallways deserted. Gates swinging in the breeze. The only signs of life were sirens blaring, signalling a lockdown, and an automated voice asking tourists to remain indoors and to report any sightings of creatures to the dedicated tip line.

It would've been nice for Mallory to believe that everyone had run for safety. That the emptiness was a sign of warnings heeded. That folk were so hell-bent on escaping, they'd left their doors open in their haste.

Her walk through Mayoral Square had forewarned her that this was not the case – both the utter emptiness, despite the tourist population, and the fact that there were untouched three foot high letters burning on the ground that read:

SHE DIDN'T START THE FIRE.

And in slightly smaller letters below it:

NOR DID SHE KILL ANYONE!!!
SINCERELY, NOTORIOUS T WYATT

'So *that's* how he broke you out of prison,' Cornelia said.

'Would you believe that breaking me out was plan B?'

Cornelia scoffed, but there was a fondness to it. Theodore had always been great at grand gestures and terrible at constructing plans.

The further into Wrackton they got, the more empty it felt.

'Look,' Diana said, and Mallory saw smoke rising into the darkened sky.

'That's over by the Observatory,' Cornelia said grimly.

'Samhain approaches,' Mallory said. 'We have Katherine, and Elisabella and… not a lot else. Not enough, anyway.'

'It's not our fault Morrigan's stupid planchette doesn't do requests.' Diana waved it in the air like it was a phone with no signal.

'It's not going to show you Jacob's beanie, Diana,' Cornelia said. 'It can't even show you Hexana's star.'

'It was worth another try!' Diana protested, as though they hadn't wasted over forty-five minutes wandering around the Mayoral Offices, Mallory with a hood up and a Ternion goddess in her pocket.

'This is hopeless,' Mallory said. 'I can't see how we can continue.'

'Is that you or the Curse speaking?' Cornelia asked.

'I have no idea.' Mallory was fading so badly. So exhausted.

So not ready to die, but so sure she was about to fall at the final hurdle.

No Hexana star. No memento mori beanie. No response from Team Locate Blair. No realistic way to stop Jacob. He was stronger than them, he had more time than them. This was the end.

Mallory wrapped her arms around her forensics kit and sank onto a sizeable sack of salt tossed at the corner of a side street, her head resting on a cold brick wall.

'In general, I don't think I can go on.' Mallory felt tears welling in her eyes. It was all too much; too bright, too loud, too painful.

Cornelia crouched beside her. They carefully moved a strand of Mallory's hair away from her face. 'Stay here. I want to look around, see if we can figure out where everyone's gone.' They handed over a packet of Mallory's emergency painkillers, crumpled from being in the inside pocket of their coat, some water and a set of earplugs, and Mallory's tears actually did fall. 'We'll be right back.'

'We?' Diana asked warily, but trotted after them.

Mallory spent a few minutes trying to collect herself, pressing her eyes closed and letting the muffled sounds from inside the earplugs dull out the sirens as she waited for the painkillers to take the edge off. She had barely two hours left to live, and this was how it was going to go.

She'd lived so many lives since all of this had started. If this was the end – really, truly the end – it would not be fair. It was not fair that anyone should have to live in so much pain. But at the same time, she could honestly say she hadn't wasted it. She had friends she loved, interests that got her up in the morning, and amidst it all she had created a job that fulfilled her (when it wasn't also trying to kill her). Had she only achieved a fraction of that, it was a life well lived. Fourteen-year-old Mallory would've been so proud of her, and that was all that mattered.

She sat reckoning with herself for what felt like hours until there was a gentle tap on her shoulder.

She pulled out an earplug, wincing as the sirens swelled around her.

'There is not a single soul around,' Cornelia said into her ear, making Mallory shiver. 'My guess is he's rounded everyone up somehow. Tourists and all.'

'We got you this,' Diana said, handing over a smooth black cane. 'It was in the doorway of Mrs Blackburn's place, I'm sure she'll mind terribly.'

Mallory smiled, a bitter ache in her heart at how little time she had left with her friends. She let them haul her to her feet, using the cane to keep herself steady. She didn't feel *better*, exactly, just no longer on a knife's edge of unbearable pain.

'I'm sorry that it's ending like this. We're basically handing ourselves over to him. I haven't solved Theodore's murder – not fully. There's something I still don't understand, something I can't quite *grasp*.'

'Diana, could you at least *listen* to Mallory when she's—'

Diana had frozen, hands on her phone.

'Grey texted.' Diana's voice was strange, and it made Mallory's stomach plummet.

'What?' Cornelia and Mallory asked in unison.

Diana turned the phone so Mallory could see. Written on the screen was one single, plaintive word.

Grey Quinn
Help

THIRTY-FIVE

The first thing they heard was people. At least a thousand whispering, shuffling, anxious, afraid Wrackton folk amid tourists in slogan T-shirts and novelty witch hats. The Memorial Gardens were heaving with a crowd packed with faces known and unknown to Mallory. Some visibly terrified, some unbothered, all shuffling and alive.

Mallory leaned on the cane as they skirted the edge of the crowd, simultaneously grateful for the support and annoyed at herself for not thinking of it before. Her life could've been so much easier if she had stopped listening to the voice in her head that told her she was *giving in* by listening to her body. By taking the support she needed, when she needed it.

'Are you here because you want to be?' Diana asked the nearest troll.

The troll shook her head fractionally, terror in her eyes that was soon smoothed over and replaced with blank serenity. The next person and the next person and the next all had the same non-response. A demon Diana tried questioning managed to dart their eyes away across the edge of the crowd, and then Mallory saw it: the giant woodlouse moving across the flowerbeds.

'Do we think it's magic or the giant roly-poly keeping them in place?' Diana asked.

Grey hadn't been exactly helpful when asked to elaborate on how the villagers had been abducted in the first place, but had taken pains to mention the elephantine woodlouse in the room.

'Both,' Cornelia and Mallory whispered in unison.

'Any sign of Grey yet?' Mallory added.

Diana shook her head, and Mallory's stomach twisted in fear. They had one chance to get this right. One chance to beat Jacob at his own game. One plan. A checkmate. So many moving parts.

'I don't mean to alarm you,' Cornelia said in Mallory's ear, but Mallory had already seen it, the crowd gathered around a central point, bodies pushing against bodies.

Next to the Ternion Memorial was the Larix stage, liberated from its usual home – velvet curtains and all.

On that spangled stage was, unmistakably, a murder board, featuring large photos of their former Copycat suspects blown up on it – Sully, Sam Bridewell, Remington Davis, Theodore. Under a heading of *DEMONS* was a photo of Nathan Tate, Grey Quinn, and, like a hideous blast from the past, Lyle Whitlock – the Dollhouse Murderer. Mallory hadn't considered his existence in years.

Next to this was a floating whiteboard with a column of five stars drawn down the left-hand side, and next to that, a huge mechanical timer, which, now that Mallory was taking things in and could properly process sounds, was ticking down the remaining time until midnight.

Until Samhain.

Until the end.

But that was not the strangest sight of all.

No, the strangest sight was Sandi Clementine at stage left, a microphone in her hand, initiating a countdown to 'THEE PERFORMANCE!' and trying to get the listless crowd warmed up.

'What fresh bullshit is this?' Cornelia whispered.

Mallory didn't know what to make of it. She thought back to Sandi sobbing in the basement of the Larix and considered the fact that Sandi was a beloved actor. The possibility she had been duped.

Until Sandi said, 'I am just as excited as all of you *fabulous* Occulticals to see who the main guy is in this thing. I've never been on such a secret set before, but the director assured me it's someone you all know really well. So exciting! Neecromancy IS real!'

'Director?' Cornelia mouthed at Mallory, who shook her head.

Sandi was many things, but a willing participant in the true purpose of whatever this was, was not one of them.

'Do you like my stage?' Sandi shouted. She had the same microphone she'd had in the Larix and she lovingly stroked the velvet curtains behind her. 'I asked the director if we could bring this here. Some of you helped, I hear! Make sure you put that on your acting CV, directors love versatility these days.'

The crowd ebbed and shifted as the Undetectables made their way to the stage. The townsfolk were whispering among themselves – words that Mallory couldn't hear, but that made Diana pull her hearing aid out in frustration.

'Fuck. Agatha! Ethel!' Cornelia said, reaching into the crowd to grab two arms and pull them close.

The crowd shifted around them, swallowing them, and Mallory pushed her way through, frantically searching for Cornelia. She caught sight of Ezra and Imogen and the twins, the former of whom were unreadable, the latter of whom were terrified-looking, but all had that same listless sense of obedience.

Grey had not been lying about everyone being under persuasion magic.

'Can you move? Can you fight it?' Cornelia demanded, but the Broadwicks didn't answer, the crowd moving them away despite Cornelia trying desperately to keep hold of them.

The crowd surged and Mallory's hands touched the stairs at stage left. As she stumbled up, away from the crowd, she could see a skeleton suspended from the hands of the Memorial. Its arms reached for the sky, body in a state of late decay. It was wearing a short purple robe that looked sickeningly like it belonged to Observer Johnson, stars patterned down the hem.

It was, however, too small and too rotten to be Observer Johnson. By the looks of it, the decedent was at least eight years gone, and shorter than Mallory. Somewhere between five foot four and five foot seven.

It also looked like a pair of cat ears wouldn't be out of place on their head.

Her stomach roiled. 'I don't like this at all.'

'And nor should you,' said a voice, and the air around her grew warm as Jacob Gabbott materialised in front of her, balanced on the stairs with an air of showmanship she was unfamiliar with.

Mallory took an involuntary step back, stumbling as she forgot to pull the cane back with her.

'I see you got my invite to the party of the year,' Jacob said, smiling. 'And by that I mean, you followed the trail of empty houses. Good, good! Just as well, because *you're* the entertainment. Sandi's been keeping the crowd warm for you. Don't worry, I'll give you a few minutes to set up. Sorry there's no green room, but we do what we can! I'll help her vamp with the audience, although they're all rather sedate, wouldn't you say?'

'Oh, shut up,' Cornelia said, pulling out a ghostlight.

They threw it at Jacob, and Jacob flicked it away with his fingers. It bounced in the grass and rolled off among the feet of the gathered townsfolk who had pressed even closer, pushing Diana onto the first step.

'Ouch,' Jacob said as an afterthought. 'Oh, no harm. I'll let that slide. Performance anxiety, I dare say. Although our mutual friend tells me you're usually one for dramatic denouements, so this should be no different.'

'What friend? We have plenty, I don't think you have any,' Diana said.

Jacob tilted his head, amused. It was still so hard to reconcile the soft, friendly man who had tried to 'help' them with their first case with this. The Whistler. The Copycat Murderer.

Just a person. But a dangerous person.

'I've changed my mind about the vamping, we've all waited long enough. Let's go!'

He bounded up onto the stage, crackling wildly. Sandi gestured excitedly and encouraged the audience to clap, which they did not do.

In a sonorous voice Jacob said, 'Friends, enemies, and those somewhere between. We've got an exciting game for you tonight, with some very special guests. Are you ready? Do you know it?'

He cast a glance back at the Undetectables. Mallory thought her heart might burst from her chest with fear.

'Let's play… SOLVE THAT MURDER!'

THIRTY-SIX

Mallory wanted, so very badly, to tell him to go fuck himself. But there was an hour and twenty minutes until midnight, and that didn't seem a wise use of her remaining time on earth.

To get ahead of him, she had to play the game. Just long enough for their plan to work.

The Undetectables climbed up onto the stage and Mallory lowered herself onto an ornate chair (also liberated from the Larix), staring out at the unblinking, bobbing crowd. Mallory wiped her sweaty hands on her trousers. She'd never been one for being centre of attention.

'The name of the game is the *aim* of the game,' Jacob said enthusiastically. 'So, my old friends. Are you ready to solve the mystery of who's been murdering in Wrackton this week?'

'We know for certain that it's you,' Cornelia said. 'Game over, surely?'

'Ah, my old friend. You know but half the story. The name of the game is the *aim* of the game, as I said! You solve that murder for the grand prize of sparing the lives of whoever you want! Up to a maximum of five people, of course.'

'AND WHAT A PRIZE,' Sandi cheered.

Jacob looked at her askance, but her smile did not move.

'We should introduce you to the audience,' Sandi said, not reacting as her microphone popped loudly in her hands. 'WELCOME, ONE AND ALL, TO—' she paused. 'Sorry, line?'

'Solve that murder?' Jacob said, brow furrowing. It was the most human thing Mallory had seen him do since he'd taken on a human form.

'Right. Director, keep rolling! WELCOME, ONE AND ALL, TO SOLVE THAT MURDER. Meet your gracious host tonight. He's someone you all know very well. He's a necromancer—'

'I'm not a necromancer,' Jacob said.

'Oh, but you ARE. Just like my character, Ruthless Monroe! Anyway, your host tonight is a man who needs no introduction from me. I'll let him do that. Who are you, and where are you from?'

Jacob smiled. 'I'm Jacob Gabbott, and I'm from your nightmares. Contestants, are you ready?'

Mallory's blood ran cold. A wordless conversation passed between the Undetectables, and Cornelia and Diana finally nodded.

'Okay. We'll play.'

'Fantastic! Wrackton, meet our three contestants for tonight's game – Mallory Hawthorne, Diana Cheung-Merriweather and Cornelia Broadwick!' He raised two fingers and the crowd burst into mechanical applause, out of sync and jarring.

'We'll take Mallory first. Welcome to the game, Mallory!'

'Clap for Mallory!' Sandi agreed.

Applause again, eerie against the sirens that continued to scream into the night. Mallory could hear an insistent buzzing coming from Diana's bag again. 'The game is perfectly simple – you will solve, using every bit of your skillset as private investigators, the puzzle of the hand that committed the murders of Hayley Eason and Julian Johnson. Pull out all the stops!'

'That's not really how it works—' Mallory protested.

'I want you to do a denouement. Tell everyone what you've so cleverly figured out. Show your process. Prove to everyone that you've put the work in over the last two years. That you're a worthy adversary. A worthy *person*.'

It should've been impossible for Jacob to know to press the buttons he was pressing, but Mallory felt a pang of panic.

'Erm. Well.'

'Oh, I almost forgot. Twenty minutes on the clock, you're allowed to gather up whatever materials you have already, but if you try to run or escape – we kill Diana!'

'I nominate Diana to go collect the materials,' Mallory said quietly.

Diana glared at him, but accepted the proffered witchlight he held out.

'And if *she* does not return, we kill Cornelia! Sixty seconds, Diana. Go!'

Diana was back in a flash with an armful of case notes and her diorama, which she assembled and organised with a wave of her hand, her expression furious.

'Okay, so—'

'Into the microphone, please,' Jacob prompted.

Diana whispered into her hand and held it up to Mallory's face.

'THREE— sorry. Three days ago, someone started killing in Wrackton again,' Mallory said, her voice echoing and loud in her own ears. 'At first these murders were baffling. They were almost identical to a case we'd seen before. A case that plagued the residents of Wrackton two years ago, when we faced down the Whistler.

'We believed the Whistler was gone. That he had perished in the Mayoral Offices when his original plan—'

'Not that original,' Cornelia interrupted.

'"Original" meaning "initial", not "not previously attempted", Mallory amended, 'went awry. His body was recovered, and he was buried earlier this year. Part of solving a mystery is trying to find the simplest explanation, as that is usually the one that is correct. The other part is accepting that if pieces don't fit together, there is something missing. We were operating under the assumption that Jacob was dead, and that was the flaw. We saw what we wanted to see, and believed what we wanted to believe, but the evidence didn't fit. Neither did our search for a motive. Despite the dawning of witchlights as a valid transportation method, we surmised that the killer had to be someone who had means and opportunity.'

'Use the murder board,' Jacob whispered.

Mallory did not like taking instruction, but did as she was told.

'On the murder board, you will see we had suspects based on evidence we collected at Hayley Eason's crime scene, that led us to assume the killer could be Alyssa O'Sullivan, Sam Bridewell,

Remington Davis or Theodore Wyatt. We determined, through forensic investigation, that Hayley was murdered by a witch with Apparent heritage.'

She stole a glance at Cornelia and Diana, who wore nothing but trust on their faces. Cornelia nodded encouragingly, so subtly only Mallory saw it.

Sandi stood with her hands clasped, enraptured.

'Tick, tock! Tick, tock!' Jacob called. 'The killer is on that board.'

Diana adjusted her microphone and Mallory took a deep breath, calculating the facts of the case. The limited evidence. Her gut instinct, for all that it was worth.

'I believe that these murders were opportunistic. Like all of you here tonight, guided by an unseen hand into standing here and listening to me, the murdered folk were people who happened to be available. I also believe the killers were unwitting pawns.' She shot a glance at Jacob. 'Actually, scratch that.'

'Are you about to earn a bonus point?' Jacob said, grinning widely.

Mallory hated him, oh she *hated* him, but she opened her mouth and said, 'They weren't opportunistic. Hayley Eason was killed because Jacob killing Van Doren two years ago didn't destroy her. It *made* her. She was not a victim of his attempts to burn the town down. She made a new life for herself. Found peace. We just couldn't see the motive, because we'd made a wrong assumption right at the start.'

'Very good, Mallory! Bonus point to you! If you get two more bonus points, you get to take a shot at the roulette board and could potentially go home with ONE! MORE! SOUL!'

'ONE MORE SOUL! ONE MORE SOUL!' Sandi chanted.

The townsfolk cheered and Mallory swallowed.

'Are you ready to tell us the name of the killer of Hayley Eason?'

'Yes. There were pieces missing from her story, that only now make sense if we understand that she was not acting of her own accord. If we understand that the holes were present because her memory had been altered.' Mallory searched for her face in the crowd. Finding it and seeing her eyes glazed, her expression unseeing. Her voice didn't waver as she said, 'The person who did your bidding to kill Hayley Eason, was Alyssa O'Sullivan.'

'Fuck, I was hoping that wasn't the case,' Cornelia whispered.

The gathered townsfolk booed. It was a quiet sound at first, like a distant horn or the braying of cattle, and then the sound swelled and rose into the air, shrill as the alarm that had sounded in the streets.

'CORRECT! Very good – one point to the Undetectables!' Jacob said, clapping. 'Who do you vote to save?'

It was hardly a question – Cornelia nudged Diana, who shouted 'TAYLOR ROSE O'GORMAN.'

Her name appeared on the first line on the whiteboard, scrawled by an invisible hand. Diana exhaled with relief and Mallory took a deep, steadying breath. The only thing between her and the ground was the cane, her fingers white-knuckled around the handle.

'Very good. And the fire?'

'The fire wasn't Sully, or you.'

'What has you so sure?'

'Because you wouldn't ask us if that was the case,' Mallory said calmly. 'Trick question aside, you don't know how or why the fires started. Or who started them.'

'Oh, I know who, and I've a good hypothesis as to why,' Jacob said as an aside. 'But let's keep going. Great work, Mallory! Our next contestant is…'

He made a show of wavering between Diana and Cornelia, and Mallory wanted to cleave him in two. Cornelia's jaw was clenched, their eyes resigned.

'…Diana!'

'Give it up for Diana, everyone,' Sandi implored. The crowd remained silent.

'Let's play SOLVE THAT MURDER! For a second life, please answer the following question: WHO MURDERED JULIAN JOHNSON?'

Diana enlarged her miniature Observatory diorama and was spinning it around in the air, examining it from all sides, muttering under her breath for a full ninety seconds while Jacob watched in silence.

Sandi did some *oohing* and *ahhing*, but she had lost focus on what was happening, peering out into the crowd like she wanted something.

'He doesn't have showmanship,' Cornelia whispered. 'How can you orchestrate this whole horrific thing and not have *any* charisma?'

Mallory hated this. She wanted to burn him with fire, with ice, cast him into Bonemarrow Lake and kill him, get him away from Cornelia, from herself, from Wrackton completely.

'Okay,' Diana said, her hand amplifying her voice. 'I've got it.'

Mallory had nothing but trust in her, but even still, she felt a frisson of terror at Diana's confidence. She had no idea who'd done the second murder, apart from them being a demon. She hadn't had enough time to think about it, or contemplate the suspects on the board. Tate was the obvious answer, but she felt it was almost *too* obvious.

'The second murder was, like, way harder than the first one. We initially wondered if Theodore Wyatt was behind it, because he was so notorious and stuff,' Diana said, batting her eyelashes at the audience. 'We got a clue from the scene – I put on a little outfit and went out there myself. Witches in STEM, are you with me?'

The audience remained silent, as it might have even if they weren't under the influence of persuasion magic via Samhain ghost.

'Anyway. We found out it was a demon, as per the murder board. Really cute pictures, by the way,' Diana said. 'There really can only be two demons in question. Nathan Tate and Grey Quinn. It's obviously not Lyle Whitlock, because as far as we know he's still in jail – he was likely the prelude. A pre-test.'

'I would love to tell you all about that sometime,' Jacob said. 'But not tonight. Tonight, Diana. In exchange for one more life. Who killed Julian Johnson?'

'It's so easy, anyone could've solved it,' Diana said, voice catching. 'It was—'

'Jacob,' a reproachful voice said. 'What do you call all this?'

THIRTY-SEVEN

Theodore arrived just before the Undetectables did and stashed Blair beneath the Ternion Memorial, as instructed. He released Roly to roam around scaring the townsfolk and hid himself, watching from afar as his former friends attempted to solve unfair mysteries in exchange for saving people they loved, as a clock ticked down and down and down behind them. He'd had no way of knowing this was how Jacob intended it to play out, and he hated and hated and hated him for it.

Jacob was grandstanding, soapboxing for an audience of controlled zombies who had no choice but to witness it. Sandi Clementine was also there for some reason, and did not appear to be under Jacob's control. (Yet another thing Jacob hadn't mentioned. First, Theodore's expected role in the apocalypse, then this *hack*tor.)

He clocked the skeleton and felt a burn of outrage. It was his! Hanging over Wrackton like… like a balloon!

Revulsion overtook him. He should've seen all of this coming. He should've known Jacob wouldn't just let his friends die – he would humiliate them first. That he would humiliate Theodore. Make him beg for his body. Theodore had been so *fucking* naive in believing things would be okay in the end, that he could take something bad and make it into something good.

Then Delilah Gabbott appeared.

Delilah Gabbott, clutching a piece of fabric in her gloved hand and shaking it in Jacob's direction. Her expression was not that of a woman who had recently lost her son, but of a woman who was supremely disappointed to learn that he was still, sort of, alive.

'Just tell me what's going on. What are you doing?' Delilah's voice was uncertain.

'What are you doing here?' Jacob's eyes were round and sad and a little bit awed, the grandstanding evaporating.

'I could ask you the same, seeing as you're supposed to be dead. Who are all these people?' She looked to the crowd, to the Undetectables, to Sandi with not a small amount of bemusement. 'Could you give me and my son some privacy, please? I'd like him to look me in the eye as he explains.'

'Director, CUT!' Sandi shouted, shielding her eyes. 'I can't even see where the cameras are. Should we roll back to Diana starting to solve her murder?'

'Now's not really the time.' Jacob gestured to his army of zombified villagers. 'I'm in the middle of something. I can explain later, but this is the culmination of my life's work—'

'Is this really what you've been doing all this time? Drugging villagers, murdering even more people? Is this how I raised you?' Delilah asked.

'That's… incredibly hurtful. Do you understand how *hurtful* that is to hear? You raised me to want more. To aim high. This is— I'm doing something for myself, first of all. But it's also for you. I want nothing more than to change your life for the better.'

'Change it?' Delilah scoffed, gloves squeaking as she curled her hands into fists. 'Jacob, you're *ruining* it. You ruined it when I had to stomach the fact that you were a murderer. When I had to come back here, face down these people in this town, and have them look at me with pity every day. The mother of a murderer. What kind of mother was I, that you turned out the way you did? And it's all about *this*, isn't it?'

She held up the piece of fabric again and Jacob lunged for it. Delilah pulled back, her eyebrows drawn.

'Don't make a fool out of me, Jacob. This is what you wanted, isn't it? I get given a plastic bag of your belongings after your death and you'd take even that from me.' She unfolded the fabric to reveal a beanie, which she jammed on her head. 'All of this, over a hat!'

Theodore drifted closer, the static blur of movement obscuring a flash of a witchlight as several someones who had not been in the crowd materialised and discretely dispersed among the townsfolk. Four someones, stumbling under the weight of the items they were carrying, unaffected by Jacob's control or Tate's persuasion.

'I need you to stop messing around and give me the hat, Mummy. It's so important. I wanted to have you here, I just thought it would be a bit— Tate, are you *ever* going to intervene?' Jacob squinted off into the distance, face a mask of confusion.

There was no response, and Jacob turned back to Delilah.

'You knitted that hat for me, remember? It's why it's so important. My connection to *you* keeps me here. And now you've brought it back to me. Because you care, right? You care! You love me! And you understand why I hate this town. Why I hate these people and want them all to suffer and die terribly. It's so we can start again!'

'I could destroy it,' Delilah said dangerously.

Jacob paused, appearing genuinely confused. 'I'd die. Immediately. And all of this would be for nothing. I would not lead Occulture out of rot and corruption. And you would have to live without my forgiveness.'

'I don't remember this part of the script,' Sandi said. 'Director?'

Jacob took another step towards Delilah. She didn't move, her gaze burning into his. Theodore continued drifting through the crowd, stopping when he reached Roly's side. He placed a hand on his flank (or whatever it was called; entomologist he was not) and waited, holding his breath for effect.

'I thought you wanted this,' Jacob finished pathetically.

'I didn't ask for this. I didn't want any of this,' Delilah said. 'You didn't ask *me* what I wanted.'

'You didn't know,' Jacob said. 'When you met Vincent, you didn't know. Did you? Tell me you didn't.'

'Know what?'

'Who he is. Who *we* are.'

Delilah looked at him blankly.

'WE HAVE AN EXCITING REVEAL,' Sandi said, tuning back in. 'Jacob, what's your secret?'

Jacob grinned, the showboating returning. He rolled

his shoulders and took another step towards her, his words directed at the audience, not at his mother.

'Do you know what happened, in the beginning? Perhaps none of you do. You could infer it, I suppose, but in my experience people do not take the time to figure things out for themselves. They don't spin thoughts around and look for new conclusions. Rosemary Vane had a baby with a man named Edwin Dorren. Her husband was so distraught after her untimely death that he gave the baby her name *and* his name. Thus, a line of Vane-Dorrens that passed through Occulture, holding important positions and doing important things. And over time, the barrel was lost, changing the name slightly. It became ubiquitous within Wrackton, and probably beyond. The Van Dorens have always held power here. I stand before you, a real child of Morrigan and Hecate, because *I* am the great-great grandchild of Rosemary Vane.'

'Don't be such an idiot,' Delilah snapped, though she was faltering, like Jacob had veered wildly off script. 'What does that matter? Vincent didn't want anything to do with you. I let you live your life the way you wanted. He came to you with some bullshit story about my house – which is paid off, I'll have you know – and you got sucked in again. I told you not to, and you didn't listen.'

'Because you were wrong! He said… He said…' Jacob trailed off.

'Wild how the steam goes out of the villain when his ma is there, telling him he's a gobshite,' Taylor whispered, and Theodore jumped violently. 'All done, by the way. Sit tight.' She winked and melted back into the crowd, and Theodore allowed himself to feel a momentary hope. Things would be okay. He could get out of this. Nobody else had to die.

He took another step towards the stage, and another, and another, drifting on a static cloud.

'Where's your cane?' Jacob asked suddenly, and Theodore stopped dead.

'What?' Delilah asked.

'Your cane.'

Delilah took a step back. 'I didn't need it today.'

'You always need it,' Jacob said, frowning at her. 'Always.'

'This is beside the point,' Delilah said, but Jacob lunged for her.

He was fast and, as a semi-corporeal being, he was strong, stronger than he had been in life. He grabbed at Delilah's hands and worked a glove off as she pushed at him, slamming the palm of her other hand into his head repeatedly, sparks flying.

'NOW!' Mallory shouted.

Cornelia threw a ghostlight that opened and radiated around Jacob for one glorious moment until he snapped his fingers and there was a *WHOMP* as the air around him moved, throwing the Undetectables across the stage like skittles. Mallory screamed and Diana swore as she tried to pull Cornelia back to their feet.

Jacob wrenched the glove from Delilah's hand, revealing a ring. An emerald green ring.

'What is this,' Jacob said. Not a question; a statement, his voice layered with anger and betrayal.

Delilah didn't answer, struggling to get away. Jacob pulled the ring free, her finger bleeding, her body twisting into someone taller, and stronger and more familiar. And wholly demonic.

'Oh, fuck you,' Grey Quinn said, kicking Jacob and wrenching his fingers back. The faerie glamour on the decoy beanie faded, revealing felt cat ears. He was grinning broadly, Blair's ring clenched in his bleeding fist.

This was working. The plan was *working*.

Theodore stepped forwards, a ghostlight in his own hand, ready to do what needed to be done. He looked to where Taylor, Langdon, Felix and Kingston were trying to funnel villagers over a newly-poured salt line that neither he, Jacob nor Roly could cross, trapping them within the circle of the Memorial Garden.

It was all going very well, until Sandi Clementine stumbled into the middle of things.

'*J'ACCUSE!*' she announced. 'I've just noticed my fiancé is on this murder suspect list. That's right – *my fiancé*! But I am forced to CONCLUDE he is perhaps not my fiancé anymore, because he told me thirteen hours ago that he was going to buy a magazine and hasn't returned. So either he's been mu*rdeered*, or he is…. A LIAR. But probably not a murderer, he wasn't very interested in detective stories, or violence.' Her robes billowed in the breeze.

The entire crowd of zombified villagers turned as one to look at Sandi, as though the way to break a ghost-demon hold was to offer them piping hot gossip.

'Does this seem like an appropriate time for grandstanding?' Jacob asked, his voice undone.

Sandi beamed beatifically at him and Theodore snapped his fingers.

'*Now!*' he said into Grey's head, and Grey closed his eyes, adjusting the hat as he rolled to his feet.

Taylor, Kingston, Langdon and Felix surrounded Jacob, a webbed net between them that was definitely detrimental to Theodore's wellbeing. He jumped back as they grabbed Jacob, restraining him. Sparks crackled and burned as they grunted, trying to keep him in place, straining to hold him down, but they were *doing* it. Theodore reached in and pushed, ghost magic fracturing and splintering between them.

'ANY SECOND NOW, MALLORY!' Theodore shouted, and Mallory held up her necklace. The one with the binding spell inside.

'BIND!' she shouted.

Jacob stuttered, frozen, and Cornelia scrambled around for the lost ghostlight, only to discover shattered pieces.

The scene blurred before him, everything happening so fast. Jacob tried to lift his arms and couldn't. He twisted his head, eyes meeting Theodore's.

'*Et tu*, Theodore?' Jacob said, and Theodore realised the villagers had looked away from Sandi, had looked away from everything, and were focused entirely on him, their faces contorted with rage that matched Jacob's.

'Et me, bitch,' Theodore said. 'Mallory, Diana, Cornelia – are you all okay?'

'No! NO! Stop this! Go get my real mother. She doesn't understand what I could do for her. I can take care of her. I can take care of all of us. I am a GOD!' Jacob screamed.

'I'm really tiring of villain monologues,' Mallory said, leaning heavily on her cane. She looked about ready to collapse.

'SAME. I am *literally* perimortem right now and it is my dying wish that I don't have to listen to bullshit reasons for wanting to ruin Occulture,' Diana said. 'It's all the same. You were mad at your dad and wanted to burn down the world.'

'Diana I am really surprised at you,' Jacob said finally. It was odd to see him affect dignity when he was burritoed on the ground. 'You're so close to putting the pieces together, and you just *haven't done it.* We didn't really get a chance to talk last time we met, but I've been watching you. You're better than this. Unhand me, the three of you. Grey, give me my memento mori.'

'I don't have it,' Grey said. 'You're done. Let everyone go.'

'*I still have control here*,' Jacob said in Theodore's head.

It went wrong, then. Theodore saw it flash in front of his eyes in the seconds before it happened.

Tate stumbled into the middle of the crowd and shouted, one long, wordless sound that mobilised the townsfolk, his hands duct taped (Felix's idea) and his expression vacant. The townsfolk swarmed, pulling Jacob's net free, hands pulling and reaching for Kingston and Taylor and Langdon and Felix, dragging them down as they screamed. Tate was shoved from behind and Theodore watched him go down, face not registering the feet slamming into his head and torso. Grey scrambled out of the way, trying to reach into the heads of those closest to him and only succeeding in stalling Sandi Clementine, who had decided to drift forwards to watch, as she kept loudly insisting, 'This take'.

Hands reached for the Undetectables on the stage, wrapping around Mallory's cane and dragging her down. Theodore was by her side in a flash, scooping her up and putting her back where she'd fallen from as though it hadn't happened.

Then Jacob broke free of the binding spell.

There was a second where time stood perfectly still. Theodore was too far away to do anything. No matter how fast he moved, he couldn't move fast enough.

Jacob reached for Grey. He wrapped his arms around his neck, their bodies intertwined as he lifted him up into the sky above the Memorial Garden, hands reaching for them, sirens silenced.

It was practically erotic, if not for the fact that Grey was turning a decidedly unsexy shade of purple.

'I don't like liars, I don't like cheats, and I don't like you,' Jacob said, squeezing. The townsfolk hissed as one. Jacob's face was angry, his composure lost.

Theodore had never seen Jacob kill. Had never seen what went into it. He just knew Jacob didn't enjoy it.

Or hadn't, until now.

'Let him go,' Theodore whispered.

The cat-eared beanie slipped as Grey struggled and writhed, whatever magic he had completely unusable against Jacob. Cornelia and Diana threw spells in his direction and Mallory shouted and shouted, but Jacob placed his fingers carefully on either side of Grey's face, and twisted.

It shouldn't have worked. It should've been a vaguely pathetic turning his head too quickly to one side.

But there was an audible crack.

And Grey fell from the sky.

THIRTY-EIGHT

Jacob bent over Grey's corpse, curled in on itself and lifeless. 'Yep, he's gone.' He twirled Blair's ring around and around between his fingers, delighted. 'And we've got two out of three! Theodore, I hope you've managed to find Hexana's star because you *really* need to redeem yourself.'

Mallory sank to the ground, a sense of defeat crashing over her.

She had been so sure this would work. That they had the power of everyone on their side. That he could be restrained. That this could be stopped.

'Tate,' Jacob snapped.

Mallory swivelled to see a deeply injured Tate crawl to his feet, face blank, body bruised and bloodied.

She wondered if he was even still alive.

Tate twisted his neck as Taylor, Langdon, Felix and Kingston climbed to their feet, movements unnatural, and joined the rest of the zombified crowd. No Grey to help keep them free. No demon on their side.

Her eye caught Theodore's and she saw him frazzled and anxious, his body producing sparks faster than usual. He and Grey had tried to help her. This had been his plan, fed through Grey.

And now Grey was gone, and Jacob still controlled Theodore.

Sandi tottered back up the steps of the stage and shook her head.

'That was a great take, really realistic effects,' she said effusively. 'Mr Director,' she addressed Tate. 'it would be great if we could get some close-ups of me looking horrified.'

'This is my show, Clementine,' Jacob said, and Sandi jumped, head twitching grotesquely, before she joined the rest of the townsfolk. 'Thank you, Tate.'

Tate didn't respond, his features still glazed.

'Now, you three.' Jacob rounded on Mallory, Diana and Cornelia. 'My old friends. I'll forgive your little transgression if you're willing to answer things in my FIREBALL ROUND. For one of your *own* lives, answer me this: who set fire to Hayley Eason's body?'

Mallory looked helplessly at her friends. Everything had gone wrong. She'd been so hopeful, so *sure* it would work.

'TICK TOCK, TICK TOCK!' Jacob shouted.

'Give a bitch a minute,' Diana snapped.

'WHO SET FIRE TO THE BODY?'

There was one glaring answer. One that only made sense if she trusted herself, her gut instinct that she had spent so long trying to tamp down. She understood what she'd failed to see at the time. Someone who was trying to help, even if he was going about it in completely the wrong way.

'Theodore Wyatt,' Mallory said. His name echoed out over the clearing.

The buzzing from the planchette was growing louder by the second, until even Diana, who was not wearing her hearing aid, was casting her bag suspicious glances.

Jacob clapped his hands. 'DING, DING, DING. CORRECT! And you know what that means, don't you?'

'No,' Cornelia ground out.

'It means, friends, it's time for… FIREBALL!'

Mallory ducked as a static ball flew over her head and hit the Ternion Memorial. The robes on the skeleton caught fire and lit the sky in brilliant white, sparks falling in a cascade like shooting stars.

The skeleton of Theodore Wyatt burned with it, and he fell to his knees, his one chance at being human again going up in flames before him.

'No,' Theodore sobbed. 'I did everything you asked. You promised me.'

'I really don't like lying, Theodore. Did you even *want* your body back?'

Theodore raised his head, locking eyes with Mallory. There was something beneath the surface of his gaze, something defiant. Something *Theodore*.

'It really depends what we consider "lying" in this context,' Theodore said. 'I mean, what is a lie, when we think of lying? Is omission a lie, or is it something else—'

'I should've paid closer attention to your demon boy toy. Did you think I didn't know how close you'd got? Was setting fires his idea? The fugitive and the failing businessman, working together to thwart the god?'

'I have absolutely no idea what you mean. Grey didn't set any fires. He didn't know anything. You kept threatening and choking me to prevent me saying anything!'

Jacob walked over to Grey's body and nudged it with his foot. 'It saddens me that in his final hours, he resorted to such blatant trickery. He could've been such a good ally. The hat, though. A lesser god may have fallen for it. But, in the end, 'twas just a cat.' He stopped, squinting into the audience.

The planchette buzzed louder still, and Mallory jerked her head at Diana, silently urging her to take her bag and follow the sound. Diana crept away, slipping behind the curtain, and ran full-tilt towards the Observatory.

Jacob didn't appear to notice.

'You know I love a bit of audience participation. Do you folks enjoy audience participation?'

That braying *boo* again.

'It's so close to Samhain, I thought we could really get the party started. One nice big performance that you can all get involved in. This is a celebration! My life, as some of you know, has been one big, lovely performance. It's been my birth right. Written in the stars!'

Mallory didn't know what to say, what to do with her hands, how to rescue any of this. The determination to save her friends leeched away from her second by second, the clock ticking closer to midnight with every breath.

'Okay. Nathan Tate. Over to you.'

Tate strode into the middle of the crowd, a knife in hand.

He staggered and swung his leg, bruising hollowing out his features, his nose crooked and bloody, a smile plastered in place.

Mallory tried to move. She didn't know if it was Jacob stopping her or her worst fears realised, but she couldn't move. Couldn't blink. She sat on her ornate chair and watched as Tate loomed over a tiny witch, tilting his face up towards him.

'Do you accept our future Lord of Occulture, Jacob Gabbott, as your saviour?' Tate asked.

The witch, momentarily freed, shook his head violently.

Without a second thought, Tate stabbed him in the neck.

Mallory gasped as the witch crumpled to the ground, gurgling as blood spurted from the wound. Tate wiped the knife on a crisp handkerchief and moved on to the next person, and the next, until the first bright spark decided to agree with him. To accept Lord Jacob of Occulture. (Whatever that meant.)

Tate pressed the knife tip against the throats of those who pledged allegiance, waiting for signs of doubt. Those who subsequently refused met a predictable stabby fate. Faerie after troll after vampire after witch fell, interspersed by the occasional demon willing to stand on principle.

Mallory tried to keep Tate in her line of sight as he moved through the audience, no signs of remorse as he killed and killed and killed. No sign of anything. Just blank delivery. Just stabbing. Just Jacob, delighting in every single kill. So different to the cowardly little man she'd met two years prior. So changed by his own rot.

Tate made his way across the crowd, until he came to the twins. Cornelia struggled, trying to stand, and Mallory wanted to reach out a hand to them. To reassure them that no matter what happened, it would be okay. Even though that was a false comfort. Mallory had no choice but to watch (and worry about Diana, who had still not returned) and wait.

Tate smiled at them. 'You were very helpful,' he said, stroking Agatha's cheek with his knife. To her credit, she did not move, her hand grasping Ethel's like it was enough to save her. 'Jacob's old pen pals. Via a proxy, of course.'

Jacob leaned across to Mallory to stage whisper, 'He's talking about Lyle Whitlock! He did a lot of good *convincing* via letter. So handy, to have such close proximity to the Ghoul Council.'

Mallory felt her stomach clench. After they'd rescued the twins from the Wickermere Reaper, she'd asked the twins what the letters from Whitlock were about, and they had not been able to answer. So many of the cases they'd taken on had been a tangled web, woven on purpose, and Mallory hadn't had enough of the big picture to put it together.

'Do you two accept our Lord Jacob Gabbott, ruler of Occulture, saviour of our people?' Tate continued.

'Yes,' Agatha choked out. Ethel hesitated, but nodded too.

'Good girls,' he said, and Mallory felt a jolt of spite working its way through her.

Spite, as it turns out, was temporarily stronger than pain, stronger than magic, and she managed to pull herself to her knees.

'Ezra and Imogen,' Tate said, pressing the tip of his knife against Ezra's cheek. 'Lord Jacob would like it to be known that he does not like either of you.'

Ezra didn't respond, eyes blazing.

'Do you, Ezra and Imogen Broadwick, accept Jacob Gabbott

as Lord of Occulture? Will you cherish him as you have your goddesses? Will you throw parties in his honour?'

Jacob's lips mouthed along in unison with Tate, a puppet on strings forced to say whatever bullshit Jacob wanted.

There was a beat. A moment where Mallory could see Imogen nodding, accepting the terms. Where she could see Ezra shaking Tate's hand, letting Jacob in to control him. Joining him. Merging the Ghoul Council with Jacob's reign. Enabling this, to save themselves.

'No,' Imogen said.

'Never,' Ezra said.

'Oh,' Jacob said. 'That's a pity.'

He flicked his fingers dismissively.

Tate lunged and Ezra tried to move, tried to fight, but the combination of Jacob's mind control and Tate's brute force overwhelmed him.

Cornelia screamed as Ezra went down, Imogen with him, and after two very long minutes Tate surfaced, wiping blood from his forehead.

Mallory thought that the world could end there and then and it wouldn't be too soon.

There was silence as Tate composed himself.

'You there!' Theodore called, moving into the centre of the clearing. He climbed up beside the charred, still smouldering remains of his skeleton and clapped his hands. 'Giant Woodlouse! Please ensure you are fulfilling your duties, or our future Lord Jacob will have something to say about it. That is all.'

Jacob drifted closer and Theodore clambered down, looking pleased.

All Mallory could do was watch.

'If I didn't know better, I'd say you were trying to impress me,' Jacob said quietly, as though the audience had ceased to exist.

Theodore lifted his head, his eyes softening. Their gaze met, and Mallory felt herself burning with the need to look away, but she couldn't.

Theodore had been alone in his struggles for so long – not entirely alone, with other ghosts in his head for years, but alone in his search for meaning for himself. Mallory couldn't blame him if he chose another Samhain ghost. If he chose power over what was right.

Not much, anyway.

Theodore gazed up at Jacob from under his lashes. 'But you *do* know better. So what am I doing?'

Jacob leaned in, his face so close to Theodore's that any slight movement would result in a kiss.

'Theodore. I think you're stalling,' he said, and the earth burst open.

THIRTY-NINE

Or that's what it felt like, at least.

There was a roar and a burst of bright light as the Ternion Monument erupted, the force of it bringing Theodore to his knees. Jacob stumbled, gripping his head, and Theodore made sure not to catch him. When the cacophony passed, the clearing was empty. Tate was spread-eagled on the ground, arms and legs bent at unnatural angles, his control over everyone lost. Everyone who wasn't dead had run away, with the exception of the Undetectables, their friends – Dr Ray, Sully, Langdon, Felix, Taylor and Kingston stood just outside the salt circle, faces set with worry – and Sandi, who clearly would not be deterred from the film set she seemed sure she was on. The gardens were littered with bodies. Bodies of people Jacob had killed.

And Roly was still there, unmoving in the way woodlice often are.

Jacob pushed at the salt line, his face twisted in annoyance.

'*Never mind*,' he said in Theodore's head. '*I'll have someone move it after midnight.*'

Theodore gave him what he hoped registered as a sarcastic thumbs up. He was done listening to Jacob. He was done betraying himself.

Mallory and Cornelia were on their feet. Diana had returned from whence she came, gripping a small stone object. Cornelia had two hands wrapped around the hilt of an oily knife, and Mallory's mouth had curled into a determined smile.

A figure stood in the midst of the carnage, crackling in the night air, her hair shorn, her dress coat in tatters. A glowing blue stone was balanced in the palm of her hand, the other curled into a fist.

He'd known where to find her – had almost gone to Her for help, before Mallory was arrested, but he had never really believed he would *see* Her again. A false summoning of bravery he'd been saved from having to act upon.

She'd existed in a faint swirl of memories. But here She was, crackling and as undead as he was, and those memories were brought into technicolour relief, like wiping a blurry eye, or cleaning dust off a mirror. Her name. Their meeting. Years of Her voice in his head, tormenting him, controlling him (gently. So gently) and now She was right in front of him. Real. Centuries-old. A secret out in the open. A secret he had both known in broad strokes, and that had been kept from him.

Katherine Vane.

Hexana.

Her.

She seemed smaller, somehow. She had been imposing and terrible when he'd met her. Frightening and impossible. And now he felt she could be someone Mallory was friends with.

Just another young adult. (If not for the being dead and the aforementioned tormenting, that was.)

There were thirty-six minutes to midnight, and nobody moved.

(Theodore considered simply leaving. Taking Grey's body and going somewhere else. Somewhere he could process the numb horror, somewhere he could ruminate on an endless loop if he'd killed him. If this was yet another thing that was his fault. But he couldn't break the salt circle, so he remained where he was, being thoroughly neutral on the subject of Katherine Vane.)

Jacob stared at Katherine. Mallory, Diana and Cornelia stared at Jacob staring at Katherine. Theodore stared between all of them. He would never admit it to anyone, but for a moment he was afraid nobody would do anything but stand there imagining a terrible scene where everyone was maimed and killed – or worse, that they'd just *talk* instead of taking action.

'Auntie Katherine,' Jacob said, falling to his knees. 'It is an honour to be in your presence. To meet a fellow god. Hello.'

Diana and Cornelia both let out an audible snort as Hexana stared him down. He straightened, like he was in the presence of a revered family member instead of an emotionally stunted twenty-something year old who had tried to overthrow the world in pursuit of a comfortable life.

'Do not *hello* me,' Hexana said.

She was very lucid, Theodore noted. Possibly the most lucid he'd ever seen her. He would never understand what went on in the Mayoral Offices – why they were Like That, for instance – but he had a sneaking suspicion the Offices themselves messed with one's mind. That there was magic at play, beyond his comprehension.

'You stole my servant,' she continued, and Theodore's positivity soured.

'I have a name,' Theodore said icily. Neither member of the extended Vane-Dorren family responded.

'Where is my sister?' Hexana asked. 'I want Rosemary.'

'I'm here,' Blair said, stepping out of the ruins of the Ternion Memorial. She was free of her binds, and she barely spared Theodore a glare before running to her sister. (He wanted very much to beg forgiveness for his part in pretending to capture her, but did not think it was the time for it.) 'You made a wicked miscalculation, Jacob. You thought they would not be able to solve the unsolvable. You thought they would pose no threat to you.'

Hexana and Blair hugged with the relief of two sisters who had searched for each other across decades. Centuries. Who had never given up hope that the other was out there somewhere. Katherine and Rosemary Vane, together again at last.

'Is this not very bad for the whole "Ternion shall not walk the earth lest the Vampire Wars start again" thing?' Felix shouted across the circle. Nobody acknowledged them.

Hexana handed over the glowing blue object, and Blair held it up to the sky. Her expression was unreadable, if 'unreadable' meant 'disproportionately murderous for Theodore's understanding of the situation, suggesting he was missing vital context'.

'Do you understand?' she asked Jacob. 'Do you understand what you have failed to do?'

'I mildly underestimated Theodore's ability to undermine me. Let her out,' Jacob said pleasantly, though with a tangible flicker of uncertainty. 'It will be nice to face the three of you before we finish this.'

'You don't want us to do that,' Hexana said.

'He doesn't understand,' Mallory said, her voice firm. 'But I think I do.'

'Understand what?' Jacob asked. 'Oh, you're stalling too! I'm not falling for that. Where's Tate?' he looked around to see Tate crumpled to the ground, unmistakably dead. 'Ah. No matter. I'll find another demon.'

'We call upon *Elisabella*,' Blair said, her mouth curling unpleasantly around her name.

Theodore watched, enraptured, as Elisabella emerged from the ghostlight.

Her face was impossible to focus on. Long dark hair cascaded down her back, her form flickering yet more imposing than Blair or Hexana's. Unlike the latter two, who reminded Theodore of Diana and Mallory – frightened, determined, smart, but human – Elisabella was someone with experience. An imposing ruler. A bona fide goddess.

'Rosemary? Katherine?' Elisabella took a step forwards.

Blair looked angry. Hexana's reaction was muted, as though she was looking upon someone who was not the person she'd thought they were. As though she was frightened.

'There is no point in calling you Ruth. You traitor,' Blair snapped.

'Rose,' Hexana said, placing a hand on her arm.

'Where are we?' Elisabella asked.

'We are in Wrackton again,' Hexana said quietly.

'Where it started. Where you betrayed us,' Blair said.

'Do you still believe it was a betrayal? That it was not the plan?'

'*We* had a plan; you had your own idea of how things would go,' Blair snarled, ignoring Hexana's obvious attempts to stop her.

Elisabella tossed her head. Even without her face, even with Theodore's less-than-stellar ability to 'read' the 'tone' of the 'room' (not quoting anyone in particular; in fact it was the chorused voices of an oft-repeated refrain) he could tell she was indignant.

'I did everything for us. To make the change happen *for us*. We were three witches – three *powerless* witches – who took matters into their own hands. Everything moved so fast. It was all slipping through our fingers. So forgive me, for wanting extra security. I went to Mother Morrigan. I asked her advice. She told me what to do. To call it *betrayal…*'

'You cut out Rose's heart.' Hexana pointed at the gaping wound in Blair's chest that would never heal.

'A sacrifice of the heart. It was a fail-safe,' Elisabella said.

(Scornfully, Theodore thought.)

'Are you happy? We did make the world different,' Blair said. 'The whole world knows our names. But we are once again trapped in Wrackton. And what we did, the things we did together, it was not enough. There will always be someone who wants more power than they should have. We created this. We created *him*.' She pointed accusingly at Jacob, who had the sense to look mildly chagrined.

'That is not our legacy,' Elisabella said.

'This *is* your legacy, Elisabella,' Jacob protested. 'I'm doing what you couldn't. You three tried to stop me before. I believed you deemed me unworthy, but I see now that *you* aren't worthy. This is what you decided, the day you shrouded Occulture in lies. *You* started the Wars. *I'm* ending it.'

'*She* is not ending anything,' Blair said. 'You still don't know who she is?'

'Elisabella?' Jacob said uncertainly.

Theodore made a big show of adjusting his cardigan, flapping it about. Jacob's eyes flicked to him, then back to Blair.

'Try again.'

'He does not deserve to know,' Hexana said, grabbing Blair by the arm. 'I have watched him for years. He is unworthy of the truth. We do not have to bare our shame for him.'

'I think it's more that he, perhaps, *can't* know the truth,' Mallory said.

'Not that she's a Jacob apologist,' Diana said.

'No,' Mallory agreed. 'But – and perhaps you don't know this – whenever anyone tries to talk about, or think about, or really do anything about the Vampire Wars, they…' She trailed off.

'They what?' Blair prompted.

'What was I saying?' Mallory asked Cornelia quietly, who shrugged.

'Oh, for the love of Morrigan,' Blair said scornfully. 'I know what this is.'

'Enlighten us, sister dear,' Hexana said.

'I really can't follow,' Diana said, scratching her head in annoyance.

'It is the curse,' Blair said.

'Ah,' Hexana said. 'And as we well know, all curses can be broken.'

Blair snorted, a lifetime of secrets and private jokes passing between them.

'What curse?'

'I should think you perfectly well know what curse,' Blair said. 'As it was your idea.'

The stone object in Diana's hand buzzed and she jumped.

'Follow that,' Hexana said, pointing to it. 'It will show you the way.'

'Or it will lead you to your death,' Blair cut in. 'She really is unpredictable.'

'I am not the villain you wish me to be,' Elisabella said.

'I've already followed it,' Diana protested. 'It brought me into the Observatory to look at the Ternion glass, made me feel sick to my stomach. And then you all appeared, so I thought I was better off over here, instead of lying down in a darkened room.'

Blair raised an eyebrow. 'So what's the issue? You already know the answer.'

'Cornelia,' Mallory said slowly, that look in her eyes she got whenever something suddenly made sense. 'Do you have your spiders on you?'

Cornelia did, in fact, have Lyrespies on them. With some coaxing in front of an audience of ghosts, the Lyrespies advanced upon the Observatory and took to the Ternion glass. It was, Theodore realised, even from the outside, an unfaithful representation of Elisabella, Hexana and Blair, lines and stars and circles behind their graceful, iridescent heads. A lie

Occulture had kept for too long. The – as Diana put it – 'hideous little beasts' spun webs that obscured the glass entirely.

'They can't break the bonds,' Cornelia said. 'They're not strong enough.'

Theodore surveyed the three alleged goddesses continuing to do nothing, and reached around in his head for a thread of connection. He saw Jacob form an idea and try to hide it, a silent plea for no one to do what Theodore was now, certainly, about to.

'Stand back,' Theodore said, seconds before Roly charged at the side of the Observatory.

The Ternion glass shattered into a thousand rainbow shards, bringing with it the full force of centuries of suppressed knowledge that made Theodore fall back in shock, ideas and connections and understanding overwhelming him. He felt a little pulse of excitement. Mallory had figured out what he'd tried to tell her months ago! How excellent!

'What is this?' Jacob demanded. 'Elisabella?'

'The gift of Morrigan,' Hexana said, and Theodore tried not to feel deflated.

'Not really fair to give all the credit to a goddess nobody thinks about,' he muttered, but nobody heard him.

'She made it so everyone would forget who started the Vampire Wars,' Hexana said to the Undetectables. 'Even *we* forgot most of the truth. Centuries passed and history was rewritten. Morrigan and Hecate were forgotten. The Ternion honoured in their place. All a lie. I couldn't say for certain what it was – flashes of memories, trapped in that tunnel. But I could remember I hated her. That I feared her. I held onto it. Blair. The baby.' She reached out to touch her sister, the air crackling around them. Blair smiled sadly at her. 'But tonight, we know the truth. Wrackton remembers what you wanted us to forget.'

'It is not like that,' Elisabella protested. 'We did not do— I mean, I did not do this—'

'Save it. I knew it before we made our move. I could sense it. The change in you. But you aren't you anymore, are you? I've been angry at Ruth Montrose—'

'Like my neeecromancer, Ruthless Monroe!' Sandi shouted across the clearing, and Theodore had a mind to put her in a bunker for a bit of peace and quiet.

'And I've been angry at Elisabella. I've feared her, but now I see her limitations. Now I see the lie of her. The myth that we helped create.'

Hexana drew herself upright, lifting her palms so her audience could see the cuts in them. 'Defensive wounds, they call them. I forgot why I had them. The cuts in my hands to prove a point. I just remembered you doing them. I remembered trusting you. And I wondered, for decades, for centuries, if I was wrong.'

'Wondered about what?' Jacob asked. 'What happened to your hands? Who is this?' he gestured at Elisabella. 'Is she the third Ternion goddess or what?'

'Mallory?' Hexana asked, eyeing the stage. 'Witch. Tell us the truth. Solve the unsolvable. Tell us who killed Theodore Wyatt. And tell us why.'

Theodore wanted her to do this. He wanted to hear her measured reasoning, her logic leaps. More than anything, he wanted her to see him. He wanted to be known. To be understood.

'Mallory still needs to prove herself,' Jacob agreed, as if anyone cared what he had to say. 'She was set a task and she didn't stop the apocalypse – though I did think she'd realise earlier on that there was something *off* about the note. Disappointing, even at the end. She can redeem herself now, though. I am benevolent in that way.'

It was almost painful to watch him affect godliness. To pretend he belonged on a stage among the Ternion. To pretend he had earned his place at the head of Occulture. (Almost painful, because Theodore was deriving petty pleasure from watching him flounder.)

'I think I understand now.' Mallory sat on the edge of the stage, legs dangling. 'In the beginning, I think the three of you – Rosemary and Katherine,' she gestured to Blair and Hexana in turn, 'and Ruth, was it?' she gestured uncertainty at Elisabella.

'Ruth Montrose,' Hexana said.

'The three of you started the Vampire Wars because you wanted the glory of ending it. That's why none of the stories can pinpoint the truth, curse aside. Historians and legends cannot agree if you were sisters, or what your role in the Wars was. If you ended it, or if you started it to end it. I think it's the latter – easiest to obfuscate in recounting. Easiest to blame on the vampires, on Occulture as a whole. The idea we were at each other's throats centuries ago, and you stepped in to save us all. You either had the idea yourselves and found a guide, or you found a guide who convinced you it was a good idea. Someone to advise you, to suggest to you how to go about achieving what you wanted. I think you went to Morrigan.'

'We found her beneath Oakpass Manor. Pass through the oak, avoid the elder,' Blair said, her eyes on a distant memory. 'We wanted to free her first. But we wanted to free ourselves.'

'And she took matters into her own hands,' Hexana said.

'What does any of this have to do with Theodore?' Jacob asked.

'*You have one more chance to do the right thing*,' he whispered in Theodore's head.

Theodore ignored him.

Elisabella raised her blurred face. 'The truth was always meant to be known eventually. Continue, witch.'

'The Ternion glass kept your secret in plain sight for centuries. Right here in Wrackton, the story of your lies could be shattered in an instant.'

'But only with the help of an Undead Complex creature,' Theodore added.

Mallory closed her eyes. 'And all the Undead Complex creatures were contained within the Mayoral Offices – the former site of the Observatory.' She cast a grateful glance out to Kingston, who gave her a thumbs up. Theodore had no idea what he'd said or done to give her that information, but was grateful to him nonetheless. Her voice rang out across the clearing, moonlight bathing the dead. 'Consequently, the glass was never in danger of being broken. The more time passed, the more the story got twisted and mangled to suit whatever narrative worked best. The Ternion were heroes. The Ternion's return would herald the start of the Wars again. The Ternion were goddesses. The Ternion were dead.'

'All of that aside, the answers were right in front of us, as they usually are. The Ternion glass told Occulture to associate the Ternion with circles, lines and stars. Over the years we've learned circles were for Blair's ring. Lines, for Elisabella's death blade. That left Hexana's stars. This mystery within a mystery within a mystery. Some core part of our understanding of magic out of reach, all because of this glass. This failsafe Morrigan had you put in place. All the stars in the sky, and none of them Hexana's. We thought it was a communication device. Some way of reaching beyond Occulture. It led us to a piece of the puzzle I could not put together. But it's occurred to me that Hexana's star is what it always comes back to for us. Theodore's murder. The Whistler. Last year, with the Wickermere Reaper. The same motif repeating time and time again. Hexana's star is not a planchette, or a metaphysical concept. It's a witchlight.'

FORTY

Jacob tilted his head, smiling uncertainly.

'Where is she going with this?' he asked.

'She's going to solve my murder,' Theodore said proudly. 'Watch her.'

Unbidden glee bubbled up Mallory's throat. She wanted to laugh. To cry. It all made sense now. It was not her *fault* she hadn't understood.

There were sixteen minutes to midnight, and she was finally making good on her promise to Theodore.

'It should've occurred to me earlier, but. Well.' She gestured at the glittering shards of broken Ternion glass. 'Eight years ago, we found an extinguished witchlight at Theodore's murder scene. We weren't the first ones to know about witchlight travel – someone clearly told Jacob, as he used it again in the Whistler case. But we were the first to stumble upon it *organically.* Or at least, the first to be required to inform the Ghoul Council. That witchlight wasn't just an escape hatch for the murderer – it was a calling card.'

'A warning,' Hexana corrected. 'Should Elisabella return to Wrackton. A warning that I was still powerful. That things went wrong, but could be righted.'

'It wasn't just things, was it? *Elisabella* went wrong. Guided wrongly, by Morrigan. Blair was killed, and returned as a Samhain ghost.' Mallory tapped her fingers together. 'Hexana died, and returned as a Samhain ghost days later, because Elisabella cut out Blair's heart. A sacrifice of the heart that brought her back. Someone took care of Elisabella and Blair – threw them both in ghostlights in Bonemarrow Lake, where they remained until we found them. That left Hexana on her own in Wrackton – stuck in the confines of the old Observatory.'

'Even with the glass, everyone had a sense something bad had happened here,' Hexana said softly. 'So they changed the town. Moved the Observatory to safe, sacred ground. "Buried" our remains here. Dispersed the objects they'd found with us to influential families who passed them down or sold them on.'

'Then they built the Mayoral Offices,' Mallory said.

'And the Vane-Dorrens were never far away,' Elisabella said. Sarcastically, almost.

Mallory was still working things out, trying to keep one step ahead of her own thoughts. The pieces were falling together, as though her mind understood she had minutes left to live. As though it wanted her to understand the Besiegement in full before it happened to her, too.

'Sweet Theodore,' Hexana said, turning to him. 'You know what happened to you now, don't you?'

Theodore straightened, meeting Mallory's gaze. 'Not fully,

but Mallory does. And that's good enough for me. Who did it, Mallory?'

'Hexana killed you,' Mallory said. 'I'm so sorry. I should've known, when you wouldn't – but it was *couldn't* – tell me who Katherine was. I should've guessed.'

Theodore closed his eyes, the tear tracks on his face shimmering.

'The puppet master, holding the strings,' Mallory said to Hexana. 'You met him in the Mayoral Offices and found a proxy to control to make sure Theodore Wyatt died that Samhain. Just like Jacob used a proxy to kill Hayley and Julian, you did the same to Theodore.'

Hexana licked her lips, but did not respond. Theodore, for once, appeared to have nothing to say. He was trembling, but his eyes had softened with acceptance.

'You told us it was the Broadwicks.' Mallory threw a hand towards the place where the Broadwicks lay, anger rushing through her. 'All because you were afraid we'd figure out the family connection. You didn't want us to look in the right place, or it would all unravel. The fact Jacob was entirely your fault would unravel.'

'I wouldn't say that's *entirely* accurate, Mallory,' Jacob said.

'Really?' Mallory rounded on him. 'Are you going to pretend that you came up with all of this yourself? That you just *happened* to understand how to summon the Ternion. How the memento mori worked. You just happened to have all this information within you?'

'I really did,' Jacob said, stunned. 'I don't know where else you think…'

'Did you not once read some letters I sent to your father?' Hexana countered. 'There must have been hundreds of them. He thought he was communicating with a long-lost great aunt with a fondness for telling stories.'

'I...' Jacob trailed off. 'I got it from a comic book.'

'What?' everyone said at the same time, briefly united in shock.

'There was a series. Very famous. About necromancers. I realised the story paralleled a number of things we believed about the Ternion, and necromancy, and wondered if it had some truth.'

'Are you seriously telling me *Undead Complex* by Hollis *fucking* Hadley is the reason the Whistler and the Copycat exist?' Diana exclaimed, and Theodore looked... troubled.

Mallory did not know what to think. She had been so sure Jacob was under the same control Theodore had been, that she didn't know what to do with this information.

'On the subject of letters,' Hexana said, clearly choosing to ignore Jacob. 'I'm part demon – very easy to write down a persuasive line or two. He appealed to the demon Quinn – poor fellow. May *Morrigan* hold him tightly.' Her eyes alighted on Elisabella again, who stalked away to the salt line. 'And then I was happy to pull anyone's strings to kill him. Opportunity over all else. The Broadwicks, Quinn, Van Doren... any of them. I just wanted to be free. I needed to find Elisabella. Get her voice out of my head. End her. And I needed Theodore Wyatt to do it.'

'Why not take any of the others? Van Doren, or Quinn, or the Broadwicks?' Cornelia asked. 'Why Theodore?'

'Because of us,' Mallory said simply, the answer so obvious it was painful. 'Don't you get it? Elisabella is not Ruth Montrose. She hasn't been Ruth Montrose for a very long time. She's been possessed. Besieged. She's Morrigan.'

Elisabella turned back to the group as her face – her true face – swam into view, like wiping away the blur on a lens, or eyes opening fully upon waking.

Her face did not belong to her body, a shadow of something… older. Something more magical.

Morrigan.

Hexana and Blair paused, cycling through a variety of surprisingly human emotions.

All at once, the fear two thirds of the Ternion had expressed towards Morrigan, about Morrigan, vanished. Hexana stormed across the gardens towards her, hands raised in fury. Blair made a half-hearted attempt to stop her.

'You changed Ruth. You took her for yourself. You wore her face like your own! I have lived lifetimes in fear of you, but I realise now, Morrigan, that you are as trapped in here as we are.' She pointed to the salt circle. 'Your attempts to manipulate us failed. You made her into something she wasn't!'

Elisabella raised her head. Her face flickered, changing into something Mallory thought she recognised. Softer.

Hexana stopped advancing. 'Ruth?'

'I'm still in here,' Elisabella said. Her voice was different, too, less imposing. Mallory could imagine her alive and human, parading around with coils of hair piled effortlessly on her head. She could imagine all three of them, trapped in Wrackton, desperate to change Occulture.

She had felt that way once, too.

Elisabella's head twitched and Morrigan's face reappeared. 'I encouraged Ruth, but she was the hungriest of the three of you. She wanted change more. She was not willing to back down. It was very easy to ask her if she wanted to share her body with me. A Besiegement without the curse, the way Hecate and I used to move through the world before we were forgotten. She understood the risks you were undertaking. How the three of you had so much more power than you realised. How you could make choices that would change Occulture for ever. I explained how much easier it would be if she allowed me to take over her body. I could ensure her plan would not fail.'

'But it did!' Hexana screamed, grabbing her by the shoulders. 'It failed! It was meant to be the three of us, changing the world like you said. Finding peace! Putting the world at our feet for a change! HEXANA! BLAIR! ELISABELLA! WITCHES THREE!'

Elisabella tilted her head almost pityingly. 'Elisabella, as you have understood her, never got to exist. By the time she accepted the moniker, the invention, she was already me. It was days before you noticed anything amiss. She gave me permission to Besiege her. To allow my soul inside her willing vessel. To live as she lived, to wear her face for as long as she continued to walk the green earth. To use her magic, and she mine. I can still hear Ruth Montrose,' she said, tilting Hexana's neck as though to whisper it in her ear. 'I can feel her wishes. She still loves you. She wants better than this for you. She made sure I tried to save you. But I could only save you by killing Blair. She has not forgiven me. We did not consider the power the child, the life she had outside the Ternion, would have. We did not think Blair would return. I am sorry for the sacrifice.'

'She has a conscience,' Blair snapped, passing a hand over her destroyed torso. 'How wonderful.'

Hexana relaxed her grip on Elisabella's shoulders.

'Did you really want this, Ruth?'

Elisabella nodded, her eyes shining. 'Ruth never asked me to leave. I never wanted to take over fully. Hecate and I were the Hallowed Ones. We wore the faces of witches for generations. This is not new to me.'

'I don't see what any of this has to do with me,' Theodore interjected. 'Not to be self-centred.'

'This is what Hexana wanted us for,' Mallory said, refocusing. 'She understood what had happened to Ruth, even if she couldn't grasp the extent of it. Right?'

Hexana nodded, her eyes still on Elisabella.

'Hexana spent so long down there, atoning for her actions on her own in the dark. When she met Theodore, she wanted to try to be the goddess in charge. To exert control over mere humans, in order to better understand what Elisabella did. I always felt as though the cases we've faced as an agency were happening *to* us. We weren't seeking them out – they were drawing us in. That was the point, wasn't it?'

Hexana smiled softly. 'I always liked you, even if I didn't always fully understand who you were. It was so hard to be down there. Circling memories. My star, so close and yet so far. I could not tell Theodore what it was, and he did not understand what I needed. I wanted him to take heed from me, but to guide you. I knew he would meet you at that party. It was not a coincidence that you walked in when you did. I hoped that if Theodore failed, you would succeed. That he could convince you to fix things, once and for all. That he would be the final turn of the cycle. That you three would break it, as we failed to. I could sense the hunger in you. Sense the desire to change things. Theodore could guide you.'

'And I refused,' Theodore said. 'I couldn't refuse anything else, but I could refuse that.'

'You refused.'

'I didn't want you anywhere near Mallory or Diana or Cornelia,' he continued, dragging his cardigan around himself the way he did when he was feeling particularly defiant.

'Evidently.'

'And I doubled down on that after I died again. After—'

'Careful, Theodore,' Jacob said. 'I'm still here.'

'The important thing to understand is that the Ternion are a lie. Were always a lie,' Elisabella said, turning back to Hexana. 'And I am sorry.'

She looked at her with such tenderness it made Mallory's heart ache. Two people – in as much as they were people, and in as much as Elisabella still contained the soul of Ruth Montrose, which was unmeasurable – obsessed with each other through time. Willing to do anything for the other, no matter the consequences.

Blair scoffed. 'I never should have trusted you.'

'Edwin worked it out, you know,' Elisabella said, and Blair stilled. 'After you were dead. After… never mind. He discovered I'd killed you. Locked me away and took me to Lake Wickermere. They put more souls like us in there – there weren't many, but many have tried. I tried to make more from the mavericks, but I'm afraid I only made monsters.'

'He discovered it because I told him,' Blair said. 'No matter. They used to revere the Hallowed Ones. That's what Morriga— What *you* told us. They should've worshipped you anyway.'

'They did not understand what I was.' Elisabella's mouth quirked into a knowing smile. She drifted towards Mallory, who resisted the urge to scramble away from her, both because she didn't want Elisabella to know how scared she was, and because she was solely constructed of adrenaline and did not think her legs worked anymore.

'Over time, the Hallowed Ones were relegated to mere ghosts. Shells. They changed our name, instead of considering us goddesses. Nuisances, instead of leaders. Unknowns, instead of feared. Although in the case of Mr Wyatt, it appears you've injected some much-needed fear back into Occulture. Perhaps in time they will treat the Samhain ghost as a goddess, as they deserve.'

'I'm sorry,' Theodore said, faltering. 'Not sorry at all, actually – what do you mean, "as a goddess"?'

'Surely you suspected,' Blair said, frowning.

'He could not,' Elisabella said. 'We made it so. All anyone had to do was smash the glass and this would've been over years ago.'

'I did try to tell everyone this months ago,' Theodore said primly. 'But as usual, nobody listens to old Theodore!'

'I do think if you'd said "The Ternion glass contains a curse that prevents us from understanding the Vampire Wars and therefore the truth of the modern state of Occulture", we'd have heard that,' Cornelia said.

Theodore folded his arms, but did not retort, and Mallory made a mental note to go back to it, should she ever get a chance.

'Semantics,' Blair said. 'Why are we still here? We can end all of this now.'

'We CANNOT,' Elisabella said.

'We can,' Hexana said.

'We've got about ten minutes before we all die,' Diana said, as the countdown timer on stage behind them began to click rapidly.

Mallory's heart hammered in time with the beat.

'Van Doren killed Theodore,' she said quickly. 'But he wouldn't remember it even if he was still alive.'

'I cannot believe that I was right about the Van Dorens *twice*,' Cornelia said, punching the air. 'I can die happy. FUCK YEAH.'

'I am afraid I pulled the trigger, and I used my grand-nephew to do it. Vincent Van Doren was a soft touch, but he could not be distracted. It was meant to be the demon Quinn. Hence your costume. He was distractible. I am sorry for your loss,' she added to Theodore, who quivered.

'There are eight minutes to midnight,' Jacob said, striding into the centre of the gardens. 'What do we do now? Do you accept that your reign of terror is over? That the Ternion are a disgrace? That Morrigan is a lie? That everyone knows, now, that you are frauds and that I should replace you? That I am a god, a true god, capable of bringing about the apocalypse that you were too disorganised to continue? Theodore!' He snapped his fingers and Theodore jerked, his arms and legs moving independent of his torso as his face scrunched with the strain of resisting.

'Why don't we ask Elisabella?' Blair suggested, folding her arms. 'I'm sure if she can find another way to rip my heart out, she'll take it.'

'I don't want to,' Theodore said.

'He doesn't want to,' Hexana repeated firmly. She raised a hand and Theodore's lurching march stopped.

'We don't have time for this,' Jacob said. 'I can thank you, Mallory, for this one. Ahem. BIND.'

He waited, expectantly it seemed, for Hexana to be contained somehow.

She stared back at him, deeply displeased.

Blair's mouth turned down, her beautiful soft features marred by disapproval. 'What did you hope to achieve with that?'

'That's not fair,' Jacob said. All his desire for revenge seemed to have leeched out of him, his deepest desires just out of reach.

'This is what you wanted,' Theodore said, and Mallory realised it was true.

All the bravado. All the planning. He just wanted to be witnessed by the Ternion. To be validated. To have someone more powerful than him acknowledge his existence. To believe he really was someone special, and not just some arsehole who decided to burn down the world for myriad poorly-defined reasons that tangled up into one big, poor justification.

The rest was window dressing.

'I wanted the world to burn so we could start over again. Just like Elisabella and Hexana and Blair. My ancestors. My family. This is my right.'

'Is that what you take from this?' Elisabella raised an eyebrow.

'You think we studied at the feet of our goddesses Morrigan and Hecate and did *no* assessment of trial and error?' Blair demanded, gesturing begrudgingly to Elisabella.

'You followed a formula. We *made* the formula. Morrigan and Hecate were our *life*. Our *religion*. And we established what needed to change. We planned to become gods, so that Apparents would consider us equals. They have their own gods, we have ours. We wanted to be something to believe in. Something tangible, to keep our magic, our world, our customs alive. You do not understand because you are a silly little man but back then, the *use* of magic was dying. We were pushed to the fringes of the world, forced to go underground. Magic was arcane. Specialist. Only vampires continued to use magic as freely as we all once did. Their means of obtaining it was mechanical. We no longer possessed that ability. Something had to change or magic was going to die,' Hexana said.

'We wanted to link Occulture together,' Blair added. 'We had this idea—'

'*I*...,' Hexana cut in.

'—*Hexana* realised we could recycle our magic. Take the power of Occulture's dead and channel it back into our magic system. Let it spread. If Occult folk married into Apparent families, the magic would remain undiluted.'

'Necromancy in its purest form,' Hexana said, with the recognisable air of a scientist. 'We did not think souls could leave the earth. Not really. And we needed the dead to test it. Seven souls. Seven powerful souls. But of course, you cannot kill a soul. It lingers as a god, if the conditions are correct. But it lingers no matter what. It is life force. It must remain.'

'Energy cannot be created or destroyed, merely converted from one form to another,' Jacob said, evidently uncomprehending how much the Ternion predated the work of Apparent scholars who would not exist for years to come. 'We call that thermodynamics.'

'We did not have that knowledge,' Hexana snapped. 'We only understood lives were souls. That magic was part of who we were. You could not change the fact of us. Occulture is within us. And in Wrackton then… we had candles, paraffin, firelight. So much of our lives in darkness. I wanted us to ascend with a gift. Proof we started the apocalypse for a reason. So I brought us into the light. I created something beautiful. All it took was a simple crystal. While I worked I remember thinking, "*If nothing else, the world will remember our witchlights*". And they did.'

Mallory felt her limbs shaking, and not just from pain. For her scientist's mind, this was one of the most amazing processes of early scientific discovery she'd ever heard. She could see Hexana at a bench, working and recording her findings, the way she herself had so many times in the lab in Broadwick Mansion. Her hands moving as Hexana's had. No idea of the future, but needing to know, to discover, to understand the world around her in the hopes of making it better.

'Fascinating,' Jacob said earnestly. 'So innovative. I can't believe I am an ancestor of the true philosophers of Occulture.' He was so preoccupied with the sound of his own voice, he didn't seem to notice the Ternion moving towards him.

The clock pinged three minutes to midnight, the ticking speeding up.

'It truly hadn't occurred to me that you were the *inventor* of witchlights. I should've known. They're ubiquitous. Yet another thing we should honour our family for.'

'Hush,' Blair commanded. 'You are a disgrace to our family name.'

Jacob pulled back as though he had been slapped. 'That's a bit harsh, wouldn't you say?'

'You used us,' Blair said. 'We are not harsh enough. I remember what you did two years ago.'

'I recall *you* stopped me joining you two years ago and allowed me to be murdered by the souls I'd collected. But no matter. I am, whether you like it or not, a god,' Jacob said.

'He was going to kill you,' Mallory said, raising her voice. 'He was going to kill all of you. He doesn't care about Occulture. He cares about himself. He wants… I don't actually know what he wants.'

Jacob sighed. 'What is it with you people? All the clues in your hands and you still can't put them together. Hello! I had Theodore dig up bodies because I am going to *reverse* the Besiegement. Repossess my own body. Cheat death. Cure it. World's first proper necromancer.'

'That's not happening,' Elisabella said, at the same time as Hexana said, 'World's *first*?'

Elisabella raised her face to the sky. 'Son of Rosemary. Son of Blair. We deny your birth right as insignificant. Family has always been about choice.'

'You are literally sisters,' Jacob said, pointing between Blair and Hexana.

'Half-sisters,' Hexana corrected. 'And Ruth was wholly a choice.'

'Still can be,' Elisabella said softly.

'We do not choose you,' Blair said to Jacob.

'You have no choice in the matter,' Jacob said, his composure returning. 'I did foresee a situation where you wouldn't understand what I was doing. There was a slim chance you would accept me as the maverick I am, but failing that, I was prepared. *Woodlouse!*' he sang, and the giant woodlouse bumbled towards the Ternion, body damaged from colliding with the glass window.

It stood on Cornelia and used its remaining front tarsi to rip the death blade from their belt as they shouted and fought against it. Diana tried to hex it, but it did not appear to notice.

Jacob snatched the blade from the woodlouse and, with his bare hands, snapped it.

Seven souls escaped into the air and surrounded Elisabella, pulsating colours that attempted to go up her nose, in through her eyes, her ears, until she was completely hidden from view, screaming in discomfort.

Hexana's eyes widened in shock, but neither she nor Blair moved.

'This is what you asked for,' Jacob said, strength returning. 'I am sorry to be the bearer of bad news, but you are all going to have to die this way. I can't risk it otherwise.'

'I fear we produced stupid ancestry,' Hexana said in a low voice to Blair, and Blair cracked an almost-grin.

Hexana snapped her fingers and the souls vanished.

Elisabella twisted her neck in annoyance where she stood, unchanged.

'A pathetic attempt,' Elisabella said.

'I—'

'She's fully Morrigan now, you dullard,' Blair snapped. 'You just killed whatever was left of Ruth Montrose.'

'I did tell you not to have a child with Edwin Dorren,' Hexana said, though her eyes were fixed on Elisabella and there was a desperate note in her voice. Pain unexpressed over centuries of mourning. Of suspicion.

'A fair assessment, given the evidence,' Blair said.

'It... Theodore! Come here!' Jacob said, desperation plain. 'Plan Q! Come on!'

'Forget it.' Hexana pulled something from the inside of her dress coat before Theodore had to move a single ghostly muscle.

She held it up so Mallory could see what it was.

Then she snapped her fingers, and set fire to Jacob's beanie.

FORTY-ONE

The thing about wool is that, if a goddess wants it to, it burns. It burns and it burns, hot blue flames curling the fibres, and the goddess holding it will not flinch.

It burns and it burns, and if it is someone's tether to the earth, if someone has attached their entire existence to this object, they will burn too.

They will crackle and they will light and they will scream.

They will die a second terrible violent death, and they will cease to exist. Energy neither created not destroyed, but expended into the atmosphere.

It will go on for a long time. The creature Roly will cower in fear but it will not break apart just because the master of its fate has died. It will watch too, with interest.

Because Jacob Gabbott was a bastard to all and friend to none.

And Jacob Gabbott was dead.

For good this time.

All the while, the clock struck twelve.

Mallory, Diana and Cornelia came together to grip each other's hands, wrapping each other up in a wordless goodbye as the timer reached zero, as the clock in Mayoral Square tolled the midnight hour and Samhain was upon them, quickly and all at once.

Time slowed as Mallory took in her reality for the final time.

They would miss the resolution of everything that had happened. They wouldn't know what happened to the Ternion, but Occulture would be different, if not better. Against all odds, they'd stopped Jacob. And now they would die.

Mallory would stop being Mallory. And if the ghosts were malevolent... Felix, Kingston and Taylor had agreed to be their killers, if it came down to it, though they refused to call it killing.

'Peace-making,' Felix had said firmly, as they'd scrambled to pull together a plan with Grey. And Mallory tended to agree.

The idea of peace felt blissfully close.

She watched Jacob's fire burn to nothing, her arms around Diana and Cornelia, the power of three pulsing through her like a heartbeat as the timer finished trilling.

Over Diana's shoulder, the Ternion had a wordless conversation that somehow lifted the mystique between them. It made them seem like the young women they had been before all of this started, all those years ago. Confronting the mistakes they'd made. The cost of their ambitions. The deaths they had caused.

Accepting the end, in tandem.

Mallory cast a glance over Cornelia's shoulder. Theodore, kneeling beside Grey Quinn's fallen body, was on the verge of tears, hands clutched to his face in despair. At the edge of the gardens, their friends watched. Taylor *was* crying, all-out sobbing, clawing her way towards Diana even as Felix and Kingston held her back, pressing their faces into her shoulders, trying to reach her in anguish. Langdon, Dr Ray and Sully watched in silence, throats moving, faces set.

They all kept their distance as agreed. Nobody was to touch the Undetectables when the Besiegement came, just in case.

'Do you miss Jacob? Did you care for him?' Blair asked in surprise, noticing their tears.

'No, we were Besieged,' Cornelia said, wiping their face fiercely. 'Five moons ago, in Wickermere.'

'Ah,' Elisabella said. 'I believe I may be responsible for this. Dorothy Early, was it not? She meddled where she was not wanted. Taunted me with promises of reunion. She wanted a goddess to do her dirty work, and I am afraid I did not respond well. Not my fault, obviously.'

She gestured at her crackling form as if that answered things.

'Obviously,' Diana echoed.

'A goddess does what a goddess is asked,' Elisabella offered. 'I am responsible for my part in it only. I did not Besiege you. The disposed souls of the lake... not many of them are like us, you understand. But some were older than the Ternion. Some as old as Hecate and M— and me. My time in the lake made me realise how futile an attempt it was, trying to get Elisabella, Blair and Hexana on side. How myopic I'd been in my ambitions. Ruth Montrose wanted to raise the dead, and I tried to give her the power to do it. I forgot the real goal. Forgot what I wanted.' She closed her eyes. 'There was a time when magic was absolute. Witch and vampire and faerie and troll and demon were one and the same. Things changed, as they do. The vampires of the Ternion's time were the last to believe we – Hecate and Morrigan – represented a different future of Occulture. Everyone else had forgotten, but drinking blood gave the vampires the knowledge that was to sustain Occulture for ever. Each vampire lived through multiple generations, their lifespan far longer than anyone else in Occulture.'

Mallory thought about how Kingston had resurrected after being stabbed during the Dollhouse murderer case, and figured there were endless questions about vampires that she could not seek answers for in her remaining seconds of life.

'Faerie honesty was meant to keep us safe,' Elisabella continued. 'Troll memory of faces was meant to give us clarity. The persuasion of demons was meant to grant us unity. The versatility of witches was meant to keep us well. All of that magic remains around us after we die. The ghosts of Occulture are what give us magic. Magic is, because death is.'

'And that's what powers witchlights,' Cornelia whispered in wonder. '*That's* why it hurts to go through a witchlight. You're being passed through hundreds, maybe thousands of souls.'

Another tiny mystery, solved. Mallory felt close to tears, terrified of what was to come.

'Yes,' Elisabella said, tone mildly impressed. 'When I met the Ternion – when I met Ruth and Katherine and Rosemary. I could sense hunger in them all. Ruth would lie awake at night imagining having power. Katherine had this wonderful idea of how to give magic to everyone in Occulture. A simple crystal that channelled ghosts. She wanted it to bring light, but I knew it could be more. Travel. Spellwork assistance. A reminder of our collective strength.

'Ruth wanted, ultimately, to be the first true necromancer, and that is why I asked to Besiege her, and not Hexana. If Hecate and I had not made a sport of wearing the faces of departed witches in the centuries prior, Ruth's single-minded ambition would have been admirable. If she had started small, perhaps the world would have changed piece by piece. Perhaps necromancy would have been accepted, made safe. But to disrupt the order of things in such a way, to unmake what has come to pass... Some things are not possible.'

Mallory felt this was a particularly surreal perimortem to experience, though she had little frame of reference that wasn't outright murder.

'But some things *are*,' Hexana said. 'Some things are wildly possible. You just have to want them. Occult magic is *wholly* literal.'

'That's my line,' Theodore protested.

'It is,' Hexana agreed.

'The Curse is going to take us any second now, we're all out of possibilities,' Cornelia said.

'Did I not explain myself well enough?' Elisabella arched an eyebrow.

Mallory stared at her, bewildered.

'You do have free will,' Blair said vaguely.

'Pardon?' Mallory whispered.

'YOU DO HAVE FREE WILL,' Blair repeated loudly. 'Hecate save me, is this what we have as our legacy? Three witches and a ghost in a cat costume?'

'You keep saying ghost, but I think you mean "goddess" by your own definition,' Theodore said smugly, though his heart was evidently not in it. He had Grey's head cradled in his lap, his fingers gently stroking his face.

Grey Quinn was very obviously dead, his limbs unmoving, Theodore's movements sparkling lightly.

This would be the last time Mallory would ever see Theodore.

She raised a hand in farewell. A pointless gesture he returned, his face tender.

The clock ticked over to three minutes past midnight, then four.

'Nothing's happen—'

Mallory felt a rush of energy pressing on her head, begging to be let in. Voices demanded access, reminding her she had promised, that she had agreed.

She remembered Theodore begging to be let in over a year ago, how desperately he'd clamoured, how his voice had come through her but she had not let him. She had refused.

She held firm, her hands gripping Diana and Cornelia's. She felt other, less corporeal hands touching her body and she fought the urge to shake them off even as some of them brushed painful joints and that part of her back that felt like she was being electrocuted if the nerves were touched the wrong way.

There was another, stronger power rushing through her as a flood of memories flickered behind her eyes. The power of all the lives she'd touched in her lifetime, all the lives she'd saved and friends she'd made and people she'd helped and murders she'd solved and bodies she'd helped lay to rest, a scaffolding supporting her. She'd always thought she had so far to fall, that there would come a time when everything would end.

Everything did have to end, one way or another.

But it could be born again into something new.

'I do not consent,' Mallory said aloud, her voice swallowed up in a rush of static.

She had not wrapped up the loose ends. She had not finished with her time on earth. Her story could not end here.

'I do not consent,' Diana said matter-of-factly, like she was ticking a cookies box on a website.

'Get out of my fucking head,' Cornelia said.

There was another push, this one of anger.

'YOU HAVE ACTIVATED THE BESIEGEMENT CURSE THE TIME HAS COME TO CLAIM THE SOULS OF MALLORY HAWTHORNE DIANA CHEUNG-MERRIWEATHER CORNELIA BROADWICK AGATHA BROADWICK AND ETHEL BROADWICK,' an angry chorus said.

'No,' Mallory said firmly.

'NO IS NOT AN OPTION.'

But it was.

'A wise ghost—'

'GODDESS,' Theodore corrected loudly.

'—once told me that magic is literal. The terms of the Besiegement Curse were that I had to tie up all my loose ends. I haven't managed to do that.'

Silence. The pushing stopped momentarily, then started with a vengeance that brought Mallory to her knees with the sheer force of it.

'DIANA CHEUNG-MERRIWEATHER. YOU ARE–'

'In possession of two names,' Diana said firmly. 'What's my other name?'

'WE ARE UNAWARE OF–'

'I have an English name, and a Chinese name. In your best Cantonese: what. Is. My. Other. Name?'

A pause.

'CORNELIA BROADWICK–'

Mallory looked to them in a panic, but a sense of calm had overtaken Cornelia in the last minute or so. Their glasses had slipped down their nose and they pushed them back up, looking up at the sky defiantly.

'When the terms of the Besiegement were placed on me, you referred to me as "she". Which is now incorrect. That person doesn't exist – never did, actually. Because I contain multitudes: I am not the Cornelia Broadwick you Besieged.'

'And before you start on us,' Agatha Broadwick said, her voice quivering. Mallory had not seen the twins approach, but they were there, clutching each other's hands, eyes shining with tears but faces set in familiar Broadwick defiance. 'Ethel and I had no part in any of this. We were not given an opportunity to even *know* the terms of the Besiegement, let alone accept the consequences.'

'Our family friend is a lawyer and I've watched at *least* three legal dramas in my life, and I think this is like... like an unsigned contract,' Ethel finished.

'And if you're looking for Imogen and Ezra Broadwick,' Cornelia said softly. 'They took the "get out of ghost jail free" card and passed, without letting you collect.'

Silence, so loud it echoed through the dark sky above the Observatory.

There was a loud, ominous hiss and Mallory felt something rain down on her head, forcing her and Diana and Cornelia into a huddle, arms around each other at the end of the world.

The sky turned a brilliantly blinding white. And then there was nothing at all.

FORTY-TWO

'Open your eyes,' Theodore whispered.

The Undetectables were on the ground, the Memorial Gardens torn up like a hurricane had hit it. There had been a brilliant white flash and everyone had hit the deck. Salt scattered on the wind and he felt like his body was cleaving in two, but there was nothing more important than his friends.

He leaned over Diana and Cornelia, brushing his hands over their hair, trying to shock them into waking, but they were still.

He turned back to Mallory. 'OPEN THEM,' he commanded.

Mallory's eyelids fluttered. Her lips parted. Her eyes snapped open.

'Mallory? Are you there?'

'Theo?'

Theodore fell to his knees, a bubble of joy rising up his throat at the feeling of cold radiating from his friends. The sense of their *living* overwhelmed him. 'Mallory!'

'Are we all still ourselves? What's happening?' She moved her fingers experimentally. Scientifically.

Cornelia and Diana twitched and groaned, eyes still closed.

The Ternion watched this play out dispassionately.

'How do you do, fellow goddesses?' Theodore said, addressing the Ternion. 'And could you please tell me what happened?'

'Free will,' Hexana repeated, as though nothing had happened since the last time she spoke. 'You have always had free will.'

A thought occurred to Theodore then, one that would bother him for the rest of his days if he didn't voice it. 'I would like further expanding on the hypothesis. If it pleases you, that is.'

'We are not a court,' Hexana said, frowning. 'I know of such things.'

'Very good, yes, sorry. What I mean to say is, *I* didn't have free will. You bound me to you first, then Jacob bound me to him.'

'And?'

'So are you saying I killed— Erm… Did… a number of unsavoury tasks because I *wanted* to, somehow?'

Hexana laughed, high and clear as a bell.

'I don't understand what's so funny,' Theodore protested. 'I am genuinely asking about my own culpability in this matter. I already feel guilty. I feel tremendously, awfully guilty and I don't think I'll ever stop feeling that guilt. I will never stop feeling awful about my part in this.'

Hexana wiped at her eyes, as though she was capable of producing tears. 'I don't remember the last time I laughed. Thank you, Theodore.'

'Can *anyone* explain what's so funny?'

Mallory, Diana and Cornelia were still unconscious, and their friends were still behind the salt line, so there was no one close enough to illuminate him.

'It's so human, to care about culpability,' Hexana said carefully. 'It's so representative of the world you live in. Of the rules you've followed under the Ghoul Council. You're a god, Theodore Wyatt. You can do whatever you want.'

'I think we should have rules— Sorry, did you say human?' He looked down at his body, which was still, sadly, of a semi-corporeal nature.

'Human in spirit,' Blair said.

Theodore bristled. 'I don't think it's time for a *spirit* joke, do you?'

Hexana laughed again and Theodore wondered if his entire approach had been wrong. If he'd had free will. How much he was responsible for. What ways he could atone.

Perhaps there was only one real ending for him.

'Oh, now we're laughing at the little guy who didn't know he was a god. I'd say it was insensitive, but—'

'We've been hidden away too long,' Hexana said, looking at Elisabella. She wore an expression of something akin to acceptance. 'I believed the powers keeping me in place were too great. I believed the voice in my head was stronger than me. But that voice was in a witchlight in Bonemarrow Lake, miles away. She never could hurt me.'

'Nor would I have wanted to,' Elisabella said. 'Ruth may be gone, but her wishes were my wishes.'

'We, as they say these days, fucked up,' Hexana said.

'We did fuck up,' Blair said, resting her beautiful face on her soft hands. 'I always hoped my child would become something great. That he would carry on our legacy. The obsession with legacy is what got us into this mess in the first place.'

Mallory sat up slowly, shaking Cornelia's shoulder. Cornelia's eyes opened and Theodore watched as Mallory looked into them for a long time, before whispering their name.

'Mal?' Cornelia said, sitting up fully. 'Are you still…?'

They grabbed Diana and shook her hard.

'OUCH! Stop that!' She sat up, batting their hands away, then looked down at her hands in surprise, like she was expecting them to be replaced with pincers, or knives. 'Am I…?'

'You're all still here,' Theodore said with wonder. Diana either ignored him or didn't hear him, and Theodore looked back to where Grey – his Grey – lay motionless on the ground.

It made his heart ache, the thought of losing him.

He had not wanted to admit it. Had *never* wanted to admit it. But there it was.

He had once thought his heart was only big enough to fit his friends in it. He had briefly thought Jacob could fit into that space (before Jacob had transpired to be, as Cornelia so eloquently put it, an arsebadger).

But Grey had wormed his way in. He had not judged Theodore, no matter how Theodore had felt about it at the time. He had pushed back at what he considered to be 'dramatics' – a ludicrous notion, Theodore was nothing but honest in his displays of emotion! – but Grey had only ever been there for him, when it came down to it, where it mattered, and the thought of existing without him was so agonising, he briefly thought about destroying the lightbulb himself. Going out like Jacob had. A penance for his involvement in the almost-apocalypse.

The Undetectables lived.

'All of you must remember you have free will. That is the spirit of Occulture. You can exist outside of the bounds of the world woven around us. We are free. Magic simply *is*. It exists as living and dying does. It is all around us. It is within us. We do with it what we please,' Elisabella said.

'I don't know whether this is the best thing I've ever heard, or the most clapped-out load of bollocks anyone has ever come up with,' Taylor said, pushing past Theodore to wrap her arms around Diana and shower her face with kisses. She was sobbing with relief, and Theodore wished he could join her.

He had been so close to being human again. He had risked everything for it.

'I think I understand,' Blair said slowly.

'I understand too,' Hexana said.

She was gazing at Elisabella like she was seeing her for the first time. Which, given that she'd been blurry until a few minutes ago, was not impossible.

'Do you want to tell us what you mean?' Cornelia asked, though their attention was on the twins, who had crept across the Memorial Gardens unseen. They were huddled next to Imogen and Ezra's bodies, their expressions numb.

'We want to be destroyed,' Blair said plainly.

'You have it, I assume?' Hexana said, addressing Mallory.

Theodore eyed her quizzically, but Mallory smiled tiredly and pulled a witchlight from her pocket. She disappeared into it, and returned moments later with a second red witchlight clutched in her hands, doubled over with exhaustion, but triumphant. 'Here.'

'All that time, and my star was just... there,' Hexana said. 'I could have had any soul who ventured near me fetch it. I could have found my way to the tunnels at any time. To freedom.'

'What do you mean? What is that, Mallory?'

The witchlight flickered, a familiar annoyance to it that made Theodore feel incredibly, impossibly stupid for not realising it before.

It had only mocked him every single time he walked down the long corridor to the Night Mayor's office, winking above the door.

Design, not flaw.

'Hidden in plain sight, all this time,' he whispered to himself. 'How did you...'

'About the time I realised her star was a witchlight,' Mallory said. 'I just kept thinking how there were so many witchlights in the world, and how we would never find it, and filtered through all the unusual witchlights I'd ever seen and—'

'Remembered that one,' Theodore finished.

'And Diana, you have something for me,' Elisabella said.

Diana handed over the stone object Theodore now recognised as a planchette. He'd seen it once before, and the energy off it was both so strong and so terrifying he'd drastically over-reacted in an effort to stop Jacob knowing he'd seen it.

He checked for the Voice, just to be sure. His head was silent. Jacob Gabbott was *dead*, dead.

'Could *I* have known it was that witchlight?' Theodore asked Hexana. 'When you were bouncing around inside my head.'

'I did not know, and so I could not tell you. Theodore, I can only apologise to you for claiming your life the way I did. It is insufficient, I know. But I thank you for your service. All of you. Living and dead and in between. I spent so long trapped in there. Met several who wanted a goddess to do their bidding and did not know what they had found.' Hexana closed her eyes, tilting her face towards the moon. 'I want to go. Remember what we did. Remember that goddesses were mortals. Just remember.'

'We've spent our entire lives revering you,' Diana said. 'The idea of killing you feels wrong, when our whole culture is geared around pleasing you.'

'What better way to please us than to do what we ask?' Elisabella said.

'What kind of world wants arrogant goddesses?' Blair scoffed. 'We did not create Occulture. *Morrigan and Hecate* did not create Occulture. We were overly ambitious. And look where it got us.'

'I found this,' Mallory said, handing Blair's ring to her. It had been sitting on the grass where Jacob had dropped it.

'Do we agree?' Hexana asked.

Blair nodded immediately. Elisabella took longer to consider, her regal eyes unreadable. Unknowable.

Eventually, she nodded once.

'Perhaps Theodore can do the honours,' Hexana said. 'It is only fair.'

Theodore felt a frisson of excitement at being included, before remembering Grey was dead and he wanted to go out this way, too.

'Are you sure? Could we not, say, all put them on the ground and burn them and then nobody is responsible but—'

'Destroy,' Blair said firmly, tossing him the ring.

'Destroy,' Theodore repeated, fumbling to catch it.

Hexana handed over the witchlight, and Elisabella handed over the planchette. Theodore balanced them on his palms.

Three little objects. Centuries of chaos. Mysteries he would never get to examine again.

'This is the last time I'm doing your bidding,' Theodore said firmly. 'After this, I'm my own god with free will.'

He reached inside the objects as far as he could go and felt how horrible, how evil they were. They were cold, devoid of life. A symbol of their lies, instead of something that kept the Ternion on the earth.

He felt the fragile centre, the beating heart that let the Ternion live as ghosts.

He wound his metaphorical fingers around the metaphorical threads, and got ready to pull.

'Goodbye,' Blair, Elisabella and Hexana said together.

They sat in a careful triangle on the obliterated plinth of the Memorial Gardens, holding hands, heads bowed, as young and human as the young and human Undetectables.

Theodore pulled on the threads and the memento mori caught fire just as Jacob's had, pyrite-white mixing with the gases inside the witchlight. White and blood-red flames rose and rose, taking the Ternion over, swallowing them in an inferno.

They did not scream.

Theodore did not move.

The air cleared, the fire dying off.

It was over.

Grey was dead, but it was all over.

Mallory turned to him and Theodore felt himself shrink under her gaze.

'Did you personally make Sully kill?' she asked sharply. 'And Grey?' she added as an afterthought.

'How do you know who—' Diana started.

'To punish Theodore,' Mallory said, without waiting for her to finish. 'He didn't know Grey was an ally to us. We wouldn't care if it was Whitlock or Tate. The only reason to make us reveal the name of the second person on stage like that wasn't to test my abilities, it was to wound Theodore. Have us think that he was in on this. So I ask again. Am I right? Or were you involved?'

'No!' Theodore said quickly. 'I did have to set up the scenes for Jacob. Make sure he could get in and out unseen. But afterwards… I burned the bodies. He wanted to experiment on them. I couldn't bear the idea of watching him do it again. Playing with the dead felt… wrong. It *went* wrong, the first two times. I didn't want to see it again.'

'Did you kill anyone else?'

It was time for the whole, shameful truth. There was no going back. If he choked this time, it would only be on his own guilt.

Theodore took a deep, unnecessary breath.

'I *did* facilitate the deaths of Mr Blackburn and Freya Evans last year. But hear me out! We talked, Paul Blackburn and I. Well *he* talked, I couldn't get a word in edgeways. Turns out Mrs Blackburn does all the talking in that relationship so he was glad for a willing ear. He was ready to die – rather, he was interested in the idea of immortality, which I tried to explain was not all it was cracked up to be. Ultimately, he wanted to not suffer anymore. He was old, and sick, and being kept alive by machines. He wanted to go on his own terms. I helped him. When I found Freya Evans, it was the same. She was terminally ill, had been through so much. We talked over several days. Discussed every aspect. I chose so carefully. I didn't want to hurt anyone. Mallory, please believe me, I did not want to hurt anyone.'

'How did they die?'

'I provided them with high doses of Bellissima. It meant I fulfilled Jacob's demands – provided him with souls – but I did not kill anyone myself. I never lied about that.'

And then Jacob made him combine those souls into a giant woodlouse. He'd have to instruct Mallory on how to release them from Roly. How to let them pass on.

'I tried at every turn to do the right thing. I promise you that, for whatever it's worth.'

'He was going to give you back your body, wasn't he?' Mallory said quietly. 'You were going to get be human again. So even when you fought against him, he had a hold over you.'

Theodore felt the tear tracks on his cheeks burn. 'Jacob thought I wanted to be alive more than anything, and I did. Sort of. For a while. Being dead is *terrible,* Mallory. I'd give anything to live a normal life. But not this. I didn't want this.'

She was going to vote to destroy him too. He could feel it, and knew he deserved it.

It would be okay, because Grey was gone, and Theodore didn't think there was anyone else worth living for.

Mallory considered him, the cogs turning in her mind. Theodore waited in agony, ready to hand over the lightbulb. Ready to accept his fate. His involvement wasn't uncomplicated. Removing all the Samhain ghosts – all the gods – from Wrackton would give Occulture a clean slate. Room to start over completely.

'I believe you,' Mallory said finally.

Theodore blinked at her, his hand halfway to his pocket.

'I trust your judgement,' Cornelia said to her.

Diana looked at him, her eyes narrowed. 'I trust myself. I believe him, too.'

Theodore closed his eyes, a rush of gratitude sparking through him. He didn't say any of this; instead he peered at Diana's face. 'You look exhausted. Radiant as always, obviously! But exhausted.'

'There's still a lot of work to be done,' Diana said, stretching. 'Starting with explaining to Grey why he'll be sticking around for all eternity.'

'Oh, you spoiled the surprise,' Grey said, and Theodore felt his heart explode.

FORTY-THREE

Grey Quinn. His clothes were rumpled, his body crackled with the telltale sign of having come down with a recent dose of death, but his eyes, his *face*. Moving, almost-alive. Real.

His eyebrows raised in an unmitigated display of openness. His hands lifted, as if to say, 'What do you think?'

All that, and the beanie on his head, cat ears pointing upwards.

Theodore's mouth spread into a slow smile that he fought to push down.

'Oh, you're still here,' he said dismissively. 'That's nice.'

'For you, yes. For me, not so much.' He reached down to his pocket and pulled out his familiar pocket watch, twirling it. Theodore knew what it said on the back.

Love will rise again

A memento mori.

'We can thank Hollis for this particular piece of foreshadowing,' Grey said, and Theodore felt himself deflate somewhat.

Hollis Hadley would always haunt the narrative in some

way. If there even was a narrative to haunt. Theodore hadn't even *said* any of the things he was thinking about Grey, about them as a potential unit, but Grey seemed to be reading them on his face, as his expression softened.

'I don't know what this means for ownership of Oakpass or any of my businesses,' Grey continued. 'My debts are meant to evaporate with my death, but I don't know if there is a Samhain ghost – sorry, was that "*god*"? – clause. I shall have to consult a good lawyer. Not my cousin. There's much to consider, perhaps new precedents to be set. The Broadwicks will also have left quite a legacy, but hopefully not to their idiot elder children. Not wishing to be indelicate, of course,' he said, attempting to not smile and ending up somewhere in the vicinity of a smirk.

'I am so sorry for your loss,' Theodore said to Cornelia, meaning it.

'I don't know if I am yet, or how much, or how I'm meant to feel at all,' Cornelia said. 'But thanks. Both of you.'

'Do you think your sisters will be in charge now?' Grey asked, and Theodore fought the urge to elbow him, then realised with a thrill that if he *did* elbow him, it would feel more solid than before. More real.

'Time will tell,' Cornelia said. 'But I wouldn't hold your breath. Or do, seeing as you can do it infinitely.'

'You can let Theodore know when you know,' Grey said.

'I don't see what any of this has to do with me,' Theodore said hotly, but he admittedly enjoyed hearing Grey talk about him like he mattered.

He *did* matter, he knew that. He was a *god*, for fucksake. That mattered very much.

Grey levelled his gaze at him. It felt as though there wasn't anyone around them, not Diana who was hitting Taylor in the arm repeatedly in wordless glee, not Cornelia who seemed largely oblivious to the whole thing, what with the death of their parents and everything, and not Mallory, who wore an expression of dawning comprehension as she looked between them. Theodore wanted to ask her *what*, exactly, she was comprehending, because he wasn't sure.

It maybe felt too good to be true. Especially as he had yet to actually voice a thought.

'I think us gods have to stick together,' Grey said, after far too many seconds of saying nothing. 'And I believe your free time has just been returned to you.'

Theodore listened in his again head for signs of Jacob, but found none. Instead, he could feel the smallest push of the tendrils of a thought.

'*Fancy seeing you here*,' a soft voice said.

It wasn't Jacob, or Hexana.

Theodore couldn't fight the smile anymore. He tried something he hadn't dared to with any of the other people who'd had this kind of connection with him. '*How? Also, how much did you see?*'

'*You cried over me. It was quite sweet.*'

'*Doesn't answer my question, Grey, and I have so many of them.*'

'*I think I died just close enough to midnight for it to count. I learned to be invisible from the best. I just don't feel a pathological need to talk to myself aloud.*'

'*That doesn't mean we need to be in each other's heads, though.*'

Grey raised an eyebrow. *'We're already in each other's pockets, what's a little telepathy between friends?'*

Theodore waited a beat. He had never done this, had never been so forward, but if subverting the apocalypse had made him do anything, it was learn how to be brave. (And also, he was keenly aware Grey could probably read his more obvious thoughts anyway.)

'Is that what we are?'

Grey rolled his eyes and then, so quick Theodore almost missed it, he winked.

He felt as though he might explode.

Diana cleared her throat. 'We should be going. You continue having weird wordless conversations where you just make faces at each other, we have to go find the twins and reckon with the fact we're not dead and they're not dead.'

'And I'm sure Grey needs to reckon with the fact of his being undead,' Mallory added. She seemed tired. Pale. Like she'd almost died.

She smiled at Theodore, but it felt final. Like she was saying goodbye. Like she was letting him go. Like believing him wasn't enough to bring things back the way they were.

He looked to Grey.

'*Go*,' Grey said. '*I'll figure out the being dead thing in my own time.*'

'MALLORY! Erm, Mallory,' Theodore said, trying to regulate his volume as he caught up with her on the steps of the Observatory. These kinds of conversations usually went better when he'd had a chance to rehearse them. He'd been planning what he'd say to Mallory for months – years, really, if he was fully honest with himself – but he had never given himself a chance to properly rehearse it.

'I need to go with Cornelia,' Mallory said – fairly, Theodore thought – but Diana waved her on.

'I've got this,' Diana said – ominously, Theodore thought – but Diana had her arm around Cornelia and seemed to be doing a good job of holding them upright.

'I'll be right with you, text me,' Mallory said, and the rest of the Undetectables left Theodore and Mallory alone.

Mallory sank down onto the steps and Theodore hovered before hunkering down beside her. He pulled his cardigan around himself, a protective bubble between him and whatever Mallory was about to say.

He didn't trust himself to speak, and so the seconds stretched out.

'It's okay if you—' he started, just as Mallory said, 'I think we owe you—'

They both stopped.

'What?' they said together.

'Can I go first? I need to go first,' Theodore said, the words rushing out. 'You three have been my home for the last eight years. You gave me your friendship and I got the pleasure of seeing you grow into yourselves. Everything that's happened to you has, in part, been my fault, and for that I am so, *so* sorry. I didn't know— I didn't know a lot of it, when it was happening, and then I *did* know a lot of it, but was magically prevented from saying anything. I tried to steer you in the right direction.

That's not to take away from your achievements! You achieved so much on your own! Everything you've figured out, your machines, your science, that was all us. Well, you. Me a little bit also, but mostly you.

'What I'm trying to say is, I am sorry. I wanted to tell you everything, but Hexana had a hold on me, and then Jacob did, and it was impossible to say. Literally impossible – he choked me if I tried. Often, I had no idea of his real plan. I tried to get ahead of him. I tried to help you – burning the bodies was supposed to stop him raising the undead army, smashing the glass in the Broadwick basement was meant to be a clue about the Ternion glass. The hold it had on us. In hindsight, I accept that one was a little obtuse. I also tried to tell you about the Vane-Dorren to Van Doren pipeline. I don't take any credit for anything you solved,' he added hurriedly. 'I don't know if anything I did actually helped in the end. I even tried to tell you, inside your own head. I know I've tried to possess you and I've betrayed you and I've done the worst things I can possibly imagine. I will never, ever forgive myself for any of them. And I understand if you never want to see me again. If you decide I should be destroyed, I understand that too. As long as someone takes care of Grey – I'm sure being a new ghost will be very hard on him, even if he's putting on a great show of being very calm about the whole thing – there is no reason to keep me around. I accept my fate. Do it quickly, though.'

He squeezed his eyes shut and held out the lightbulb, waiting for the feeling of Mallory taking it from him.

She didn't.

He kept his eyes closed, certain she was gearing up to it,

but when he opened them Mallory was trying very, very hard not to laugh.

'What?'

'Theodore. I can't blame you for half the things you did. I can blame you for some of them, but it could be years before anyone figures out the extent of your culpability on a moral basis, let alone a legal one. I also trust you're going to beat yourself up about it for eternity, and that might be punishment enough, honestly. I believe you when you say you weren't fully in control of yourself.' She composed herself with difficulty. 'You promise you did everything you could to tell me the truth?'

Theodore nodded uncertainly. 'He was going to give me my body back. There will always be a chance I was too selfish to see another way out. But I think I tried my hardest, even if it feels as though I didn't. Even now I can't think what I could've done differently.'

'Then how could I blame you? You were in an untenable position. I won't lie, it'll probably take some time for us to... you know, go back to normal. If there is such a thing as normal.'

Theodore nodded, more vigorously. A seed of hope had been planted in his heart and he was witnessing it unfurl in a tentative bloom.

'I can give you all the space you need. In fact, I can move away right now, should my proximity be an issue to you! How's that?' Theodore scooted away and Mallory reached out and caught his arm, sending a shower of sparks up between them.

'That's not necessary. In a literal sense, anyway. I think Cornelia is going to need all the physical and emotional support we can give them, and that's where I'll need to put my energy. But I'll make time for… for us.'

'They've been left in charge of the twins,' Theodore said solemnly. 'I can't imagine a worse fate for anyone.'

'I don't think they know how they feel yet. It'll take a while for the Broadwicks' deaths to sink in. But I'll check in on you in a day or two. And we can see where we go from there? I think someone's waiting for you,' Mallory said.

Grey had been casually leaning against the Observatory. He had the smoking remains of his phone in his hand and was staring at it in careful dismay.

'*Don't. Say. Anything,*' Grey warned.

'I'll see you in a few days.' Theodore smiled, feeling the burn of his tear tracks against his skin. 'Thank you. Just… thank you.'

'I'm also sorry,' Mallory said.

'For what?'

'Van Doren killing you by proxy means you never got to do The Speech.'

Theodore's heart leapt at the idea she'd remember how badly he wanted to face down his murderer. For years he'd had grand plans to perform it at the official denouement, once Mallory solved it for him.

'Don't worry,' Theodore said, smiling. 'Even if Van Doren had no awareness of his part, he heard me rehearse it enough in the Mayoral Offices I as good as delivered it to him. Hexana had access to my head the whole time – less invasively than Jacob, of course. She wasn't entirely lucid, but I daresay she heard The Speech one or two dozen times over the years as well.'

Mallory stood and Theodore moved to join Grey, reaching for him with his mind, his heart lighter than it had been since the day he'd first died.

'And Theodore?' Mallory said.

He turned back to her. 'Yes?'

Mallory's mouth quirked into a sad, relieved smile. 'I love you.'

FORTY-FOUR

Seven weeks (and two days) later

The party in Broadwick Mansion was in full swing and the lights had just gone out.

Mallory excused herself from the tangle of Occult folk who kept stopping her to talk to her and present her with elevator pitches for potential cases, faces lit by witchlights as an over-eager volunteer scuttled to the basement to find the fuse box. She headed for the garden in search of Cornelia, who had abruptly left the festivities thirty minutes in. The band kept playing – an Apparent quartet who were startled but largely unbothered by the abrupt darkness.

Agatha and Ethel spun around the ballroom, accepting both solemn condolences, and compliments on their catering choices. Diana and Taylor had commandeered the buffet and were both many, many flutes of champagne deep. Sandi Clementine had planted herself in the middle of the ballroom, wearing custom-made necromancer robes in bright red. All the most important witches, trolls, demons, vampires and faeries in Wrackton and beyond were there, including the remaining members of the Ghoul Council. They'd arrived earlier in the day to meet the Broadwick siblings, to discuss the fate of Rowan House and their operations going forward. Cornelia had not wanted any part of it, but Mallory had convinced them that Agatha and Ethel were a compelling enough reason for them to at least attend.

The party itself was a step too far, Mallory felt, though it was fitting. It was also what Agatha and Ethel wanted, and what Imogen and Ezra Broadwick would've insisted on. Next year, the ball would return to Samhain, and it would be about remembering everyone who had died in the community. It would be a celebration of life, and remembering the warnings of the Ternion, the dangers of manufactured war among Occulture. Tonight was about Imogen and Ezra Broadwick, Hayley Eason, Julian Johnson and every other poor soul who had died at the hands of Jacob Gabbott. (Including Grey Quinn, who was not strictly dead, and Nathan Tate, who had died before anyone could ascertain if he was a willing participant, but who was generally disliked enough to warrant a few polite 'very sad's from Wrackton's elite.)

The cool night air hit Mallory as she picked her way across the lawn, and she shivered.

'Hey,' she said, finding Cornelia sitting on the garden swing beneath the willow tree.

The moon was full and Cornelia was wearing a tuxedo Diana had forced them into – a sharply tailored jacket with a bowtie that Cornelia had immediately loosened so it hung open around their neck.

They were staring into the distance, and startled as Mallory approached. 'Hey, sorry, it just got too much for me in there. I told Diana where I was going, but she and Taylor were trying to convince Dr Ray to do shots so I assume that message was lost.'

Sully was back in charge of the Wrackton police station, and Dr Ray had resumed full duties. Both were planning an extended leave of absence beginning in the new year, once a new way of doing things was in place, and Mallory suspected they were going to conduct their own research into Samhain ghost possession. The guilt Sully felt over Hayley's death, despite it being clear she had no memory of her involvement, was too much for her to bear.

'They're currently making a Sandi Clementine drinking game and playing it with whoever will listen, so you left at a good time. Agatha and Ethel have everything in hand. They were made to host parties.'

Cornelia shifted over on the swing and Mallory sat down carefully. Diana had convinced her to wear a deep purple dress with a high leg slit, and the winter air on her skin was unpleasant. She shivered, and Cornelia shouldered off their jacket before Mallory could protest.

'Do you want to talk about it?' Mallory asked, as Cornelia carefully draped their jacket around her shoulders.

'No,' Cornelia said. 'Yes, but no. I want to talk, but I don't know what to say. They didn't have to die, you know? They gave up. I didn't think Imogen and Ezra were capable of giving up, but they did. They let Tate kill them because they were too afraid to fail. I'm torn between twisted admiration, anger, and something else. Relief, maybe? It's complicated.'

'There is nothing more complex than grief. There is no logic to it, and no right way to feel,' Mallory said. 'We just can't come back from the dead. No matter what Sandi would like us to believe.'

'I was just thinking about Sandi, actually,' Cornelia said, and Mallory let them abruptly change the subject. 'But actually, what I was thinking was how right Hollis Hadley had been about *so much* Occult lore, and probably had no idea about it. I wish I could tell him.'

They looked down at the ground, and Mallory tentatively reached over to take their hand.

'I think remembering him is the best thing we can do. That, or you could write about it. Point out the Occult roots of his work.'

Cornelia's fingers closed around Mallory's and they sat in silence for a few minutes. Every breath still felt like a miracle to Mallory.

'On the subject of Sandi – it feels like a lifetime ago we were running around suspecting Sully and Remington Davis and Sam Bridewell of being murderers.'

'I've been thinking about that,' Mallory said, staring at their joined hands.

'Of course you have.'

It indeed all felt like another life, but Mallory had let the cogs turn in the back of her head in the weeks since everything had settled down and she'd had a chance to evaluate things. There were big plans in the works for the future of Wrackton, and the bones of an inquest into the whole ordeal – the murders, the Ternion, Morrigan, Theodore, the Undetectables – had been suggested, though Mallory expected she'd be in her forties before the UML and the Ghoul Council – if the Ghoul Council even existed, in an absence of ghouls – made a decision on what had happened. Whether anything would change in the interim remained to be seen, but something seismic had shifted in the world.

More importantly, something seismic had shifted in Mallory.

'I think Nathan Tate was under Jacob's control long before he started murdering villagers. To the point that I think he was, partially, Besieged himself. Maybe since as far back as the Dollhouse Murderers case.'

'That Jacob tested out his theory on folk he thought would be useful?'

'Theodore probably wasn't sufficient for him to carry out his plan in full. I don't really think he ever intended to give Theodore his body back – or at the very least, was only planning on it being a by-product. Jacob was too scared to kill us himself – he had no idea who'd Besieged us or what the rules were – but it never sat right with me that he was okay with us running around, risking his plan. So I think Besieged-Tate persuaded Sam Bridewell to show up at the Observatory, to make sure there were photos of us arriving on the scene. He *wanted* me to be arrested – Jacob, through Tate, set it up that I would be. Tate already disliked us, already had suspicions about us before Jacob got to him, so it wasn't hard to tip the scales. What Hexana said, about Ruth's ambition... I think Tate had that ambition too. But then Theodore was so determined to break me out of prison that Jacob pivoted and used Theodore to get me to bring him Elisabella's death blade. I think Sam Bridewell was simply an unwitting participant. He didn't even seem convinced when he said he was interested in crime scenes.'

'Wrong place, wrong time,' Cornelia said thoughtfully. 'What about Remington?'

'That's very simple – Remington Davis does not like women,' Mallory said, and Cornelia burst out laughing. 'He was using Sandi for her contacts. He hired Sam Bridewell to come to Wrackton and photograph them. The day after Samhain, there was a massive exposé on Remington and Sandi's relationship, full of Sam's photos of them being a loving couple doing all sorts of cute touristy things. And it just so happened to coincide with the "rumour" that Remington had booked a mega role – something he'd wanted for years, that is being helmed by a very good friend, possibly an ex-husband of Sandi's. It was all an obvious farce, and the only one who didn't know about it was Sandi. When the whole pretend-fiancé thing became unbearable, he left Wrackton completely, ostensibly to prepare for his next role. Sandi doesn't seem that bothered, though. She still thinks he stepped out to buy a magazine and is on the hunt for fiancé number nine.'

'How do you know all this?'

Mallory blushed. 'When we were very unemployed, I spent a lot of time watching press junkets and reading gossip sites. Just for fun, I started paying attention to what actor was being signed to what agency and who was directing what film starring what people, and so on. I realised it was all a network, a web, and that half the things we were hearing about celebrities were engineered. I knew that already, obviously, but when I really paid attention, I found out just how rampant it was. Remington and Sandi met on a film set, where the director rumoured to be directing Remington's big project was working. In the exposé I saw, a "source" – read, Remington in a trench coat – said that Remington was "so in love with Sandi" before he'd even met her, so he visited the set in hopes of meeting her. Of course, there've been rumours for years that he and the other male lead from the West End show that made him semi-famous have been a thing. Anyway, that's all it was. Remington was in all the places we were because he was trying very hard to be seen in a variety of locations with Sandi, and Sam was there too. I knew there had to be an answer that made sense.'

Cornelia grinned. 'Once a PI, always a PI.'

'We can add that to our motivational quote book.'

'Is Sandi ever going to leave Wrackton?'

'I suspect we'll have to put up with her and the resulting drinking games for the rest of our lives. She told Diana she wanted to buy Oakpass from Grey and become a "real British princess", but "an Occultical one", so make of that what you will.'

'Your genius never ceases to amaze me.' Cornelia nudged her shoulder.

A stillness came over both of them, and Mallory felt a rising urgency, like she needed to speak now or she never would.

'I need to tell you something,' Mallory said quickly. 'Or ask you something, I guess.'

'I'm all ears,' Cornelia said.

'Earlier in the year, when you... made me tea,' Mallory fumbled. 'We said some things... or rather, I felt some... things...'

'Things similar to the things you felt the night after all of this happened?' Cornelia asked, and Mallory could've sworn her whole body blushed in response.

The night the Broadwicks died and Jacob was defeated. Diana and Taylor had gone to bed, Kingston, Felix and Langdon had been sent off home, and Mallory's phone had finally stopped ringing. It was just her and Cornelia sitting on the sofa, staring off into nothing, the embers of a fire Diana had lit fading out.

Mallory had said she was going to bed, and Cornelia asked, very simply, if Mallory wouldn't mind sleeping in with them. There was no reason not to. They fell asleep side by side to the sounds of each other's gentle breathing.

Then Mallory remembered waking in the darkness. She turned over and knew without asking that Cornelia was awake too. Their lips inches from hers, breath soft and sweet on her pillow.

She remembered closing the distance. The sheets rustling as she planted a gentle, feather-light kiss on the corner of Cornelia's mouth, a silent question enthusiastically answered by the feel of Cornelia's lips on her jaw, and then a frenzy of movement that seemed utterly impossible and everything she'd ever wanted. She remembered hands and mouths and Cornelia breathing in her ear. Fingers tracing skin, feeling somewhere half between awake and asleep. An alternate timeline, where she forgot to be self-conscious, or anxious or afraid. She'd had a sense of falling and falling and falling as she lost herself in what had seemed like a dream, like wishful thinking.

She woke up the next morning, locked around Cornelia's sleeping frame, their heartbeat steady and their legs tangled in hers, neither of them wearing the clothes they'd gone to sleep in, and was forced to consider the facts.

She'd quietly disengaged, dressed, and hadn't mentioned it again.

If it had been real, it had come from a place of grief.

But it probably hadn't meant what she thought.

'I... yes. Kind of,' Mallory hedged. 'And I feel I didn't... make it clear, how continuously I feel that way. About you. I was so sure the lake was a dream, and when it wasn't, it made sense you wouldn't want to be with me in these circumstances. Dying.'

Cornelia stilled.

'Want to know what I remember from the lake?' Cornelia asked quietly.

Mallory nodded, her eyes glued to their linked hands.

'I remember realising I'd been in love with you for as long as I could remember. That I can't remember the exact point it happened, but that you are the star I orbit. That when I want to know if the world is going to be okay, I just look to you and I know I can do anything. This last month would've been impossible without you. Diana has been doing her best, but you've been the life saver. The reason I keep getting out of bed. Even on the days I don't, you're the reason I wake up at all.'

Mallory blinked, thrown. It had felt so important to be the one to say it first, but she realised it didn't matter. Cornelia understood her.

'I thought *you* didn't want to be with me on these terms. I was waiting for it to happen, because I'd been so *sure* it was a dream. You didn't drink the first cup of tea I made and it took me weeks to work up the courage to try again. And when I did, I thought you were saying it was pointless. I said I didn't want to watch you die because I was so determined for us to live. I thought I was telling you that I wanted you, that I wanted *us,* and that I was expressing my lifelong regret for not having figured it out, and my cowardice for not addressing it immediately after kissing you in the lake.'

'And I thought you meant you couldn't bear it, so it couldn't happen.'

Cornelia laughed, pressing their fingers into their eyes. 'Great. Amazing. I like to think of myself as a highly intelligent individual, but *goddess* that might be the stupidest thing I've ever done. I thought I was being perfectly clear, when all I really had to do was say, "Hey, Mallory, what do you want?"'

'I want you,' Mallory said simply, squeezing their hand.

'I know you probably wanted to be the first to say it. But you did, that day in the lake. You've been saying it every day, in every single thing you've done for me and with me. And while it hasn't sunk in yet that we're not going to die – now, I mean. We *will* probably die someday. But, given that we aren't going to die unnaturally early, do you think we could—'

'Yes,' Mallory said, smiling. She stood and Cornelia's free hand wrapped around her waist, pulling her close to them. Mallory had to bend slightly, but she placed her fingers gently on Cornelia's face, staring into their eyes. She gently traced their lower lip. 'I think we can make a go of it.'

Cornelia lifted their face and Mallory's lips met theirs. Warmth spread down her arms and her chest, her body tingling where Cornelia's touched hers. It would never get old.

She would never get bored of how alive she felt, how *wanted* she felt like this. Cornelia stood, pulling Mallory closer, their hands slipping down Mallory's lower back, their lips on her neck, whispering in her ear until Mallory broke away.

'We should get back to the party,' Mallory said, trying to compose herself.

'Fuck the party,' Cornelia said, taking Mallory's hand again.

They led her inside and to the stairs. The lights were back on and everyone appeared to be accounted for, but Mallory had eyes only for Cornelia.

Until, that is, she met Diana's gaze over the banister.

Diana stared at her, at Cornelia, at their joined hands.

She passed her drink to Taylor and held out her empty hand. 'YES! I win,' she announced, the words unmistakable even over the music.

Mallory laughed, half in horror, half in delight, as Taylor, Felix, Langdon and Kingston all reached into their pockets and bags and produced bank notes, which they slapped into Diana's palm.

Her laughter turned slightly more horror-stricken as Dr Ray paced over and dropped a fifty on top of the pile.

'How long have they all been waiting for us to—' Mallory started, but Cornelia just grinned and pulled her closer.

'Doesn't matter. None of it matters anymore.'

And in front of every single person they knew, Cornelia kissed her.

FORTY-FIVE

Eight years later

Once upon a time, three young witches vowed to cheat death and have since lived to tell the tale. (This is similar to an old story, and it won't be the last time it's told.)

'Remember that your results must be *replicable*,' Mallory said, shifting behind the podium. 'Recording every step is paramount. I am, as I say every time we meet, *extremely* open to innovation and I am willing to hear any ideas you have, particularly if you're looking for support for your PhD applications. I have space to take two of you on, but I can refer you on to others.'

Twelve heads bobbed in unison. Mallory checked the time.

'I'm available during office hours, and our guest workshop host should be landing any minute – there're a handful of places left if any of you haven't taken it before. It'll be a full afternoon of non-stop crime scene reconstruction fun.'

Her students bolted out of the room. Mallory stood slowly and gathered her things, loosening the stiffness of two hours of sitting and talking.

She'd just shrugged on her coat when there was a knock at her door.

She looked up to see Cornelia standing with a bag of pastries and two teas branded with the *ETHEL&AGATHA'S WICKED BAKES & BREWS* logo, having clearly let their students go a few minutes early, too. Mallory kissed them softly and together they strolled out towards the pier, breathing in the fresh autumn air.

'Were we ever that young?' Cornelia asked, nodding over at where Mallory's students were crowded around the *ETHEL&AGATHA'S* coffee cart, which stood at the far bank of the distinctly-less-haunted Bonemarrow Lake. Rowan House rose above them, majestic as ever, fulfilling a much better purpose now than it ever had for the Ghoul Council.

'We're literally thirty,' Mallory said. 'We've never been younger. Have you heard from Diana yet?'

'She said their flight landed at ten. Taylor's with her, she's back in Larkin Studios again for the rest of the year. Diana said she might join her. I think she's bonkers, personally, but they've put so much effort into the reopening. And they've offered Taylor head of department, so there's that, too. Speaking of, they should be here imminently.'

Mallory sat at the edge of the pier, letting her legs dangle over the edge. The tips of her boots just grazed the calm surface of the water, crystal-clear.

'I hope they're not late again, Diana's workshop starts at one.' She peered at her phone screen, which stuttered.

The air warmed around her and she grinned.

'You're early,' Theodore said reproachfully. 'We were hiding for effect!'

'Students wanted time out,' Mallory said, pointing back up towards Rowan House, where all her post-grads were mingling with Cornelia's.

'I suppose that's okay,' Theodore said, settling down beside Mallory, who gave him a hug.

'Hi Grey,' Mallory called to where he stood a little distance away.

His cat-eared hat waved in the breeze as he jotted things into a notebook, holding up a finger until he slammed it closed.

'Mallory, hello. Good to see you again. Theo, I can *hear* you thinking I need a new assistant, but it is not my fault that I have yet to find a competent being that even does a halfway good job of taking my thoughts and communicating them electronically!'

'I said nothing! You can't police my thoughts! Is it a crime, to have a thought? A succulent, terrible thought?'

Mallory laughed. 'How have things been?'

'Oh you know. I get to study the intersections of ghosts and goddesses and try to figure out a way to ethically separate the souls in giant insects across the countries under the UML's purview. I continue to cooperate in the ongoing treasure-trove inquest, metaphorically speaking, into the Wrackton Incidents. I continue to feel enormous guilt at my part in it all, and enormous gratitude for a second chance at existing. Grey gets to run his empire as long as he's available for questioning. We continue to be mildly, infuriatingly telepathic. I get to call him my boyfriend. Same as it ever was.' Theodore beamed, squinting up at Rowan House. 'Two years in, how are you feeling? Your students came back, that's a wonderful sign! They must've been deeply enchanted by my para-anthropology lectures. I have an *excellent* topic for this year's lecture, provided I can wrangle enough hours—'

'Do you think it's working?' Mallory asked.

'Opening a school for magical forensic science? No I think it is possibly the worst thing anyone's ever come up with,' Cornelia said.

Mallory swatted their arm. 'Shut up. I mean do you think the *timetable* is working! *Obviously* the magic school is working. People fucking love magic schools.'

Cornelia pretended to be wounded, then checked their phone, yelped, and tossed a witchlight onto the pier behind them just as Diana and Taylor emerged from it, laden with suitcases.

'Fucking Hecate, that was a *horrible* flight,' Diana said, fluffing her hair.

'So dreadful to fly first class from Hong Kong,' Taylor said. 'However will we cope?' She stooped to hug Mallory and Cornelia in turn, accepting a hug from Theodore as he babbled about his lecture plans.

'I'm fulfilling my lifelong dream of storing every hideous insect imaginable in Diana's room,' Cornelia said.

'She's gotten braver since last time. And she's got me to defend her, so you'd better watch it,' Taylor said playfully.

'Show them,' Diana said, ignoring all of this.

'Show us what?' Cornelia asked.

Taylor held up her hand, a shy smile on her lips, and Mallory and Cornelia shrieked in response at the sea-green stone on her engagement ring.

'I brought her to meet my grandmother while we were in Hong Kong. There was simply no reason not to make it official.'

'You very admirably waited a long time before giving in to society's expectations around marriage,' Cornelia said approvingly. 'Well done on not being a pair of queer stereotypes.'

Taylor kicked them gently in the kidneys and Cornelia rolled to avoid falling into the lake before scrambling to their feet, a happy, relaxed grin on their face as they dusted off their jumper and enveloped Diana and Taylor in hugs.

'You'd want to watch it – Mallory loves societal expectations,' Taylor said over their shoulder, and Mallory grinned.

'Are my students here yet?' Diana asked anxiously, checking the time. 'I'm still debating cancelling the whole thing.'

'*Our* students, and yes, the first stragglers arrived, and no, you can't cancel, they're too excited about it. It's a bit weird to mix them all together, it feels like… I don't know.'

'The meeting of alternative music fans, a vape convention and some anthropomorphic costume enthusiasts?' Theodore suggested.

'What an oddly specific metaphor,' Taylor said.

'Nonetheless, that's what it feels like!'

'He's, weirdly, right. Turns out all kinds of people love learning about crime, and even more enjoy learning about magical crimes. We've got our first Apparents this year!' Cornelia said.

Between entomologists fascinated by Cornelia's discoveries, Mallory's general specialisation in magical forensics and innovative methods of investigation, and Diana's crime scene reconstruction and specialist model making workshops, the available boarding rooms in Rowan House were filling up fast. Mallory's initial five-year plan had gone from feeling wildly ambitious to terrifyingly achievable in just two short years.

'I want to see the village,' Taylor announced. 'I need *Ethel&Agatha* cake, and I need it yesterday.'

'Then cake you shall have, fiancée mine,' Diana said, and the former-investigators-turned-consultants-and-lecturers-once-known-as the Undetectables and their ghost-slash-god friends walked into a wholly rejuvenated Wickermere village.

It was busy, and lively and crawling with Lake District tourists – Occult and Apparent alike – and had been put back on the map in the last few years, metaphorically and literally, as though it had never vanished. It helped that all funds intended to promote Wrackton tourism were diverted five years ago, revitalising a VISIT WICKERMERE campaign that had been long abandoned by the Ghoul Council.

Sully had gone on trial and been acquitted for her part in the death of Hayley Eason. Things were moving slowly – Mallory hadn't expected anything less. Dr Ray was now the head of the Ghoul Council, with Nova Khan as her second in command. Olivia Reid had left to start her own research lab on magical forensics – Mallory had referred two of her students on to her in the last few years. Sully had created a number of social outreach programmes that had been adopted across all the UML jurisdictions, focusing especially on fostering positive vampire relations in a post-Do No Harm Charter world, and on Occult folk in Apparent communities, ensuring that distance from a magical town did not lead to disadvantage (or murder). It was still effectively a type of policing (and so Cornelia was still effectively critical of it), but it was one that seemed to be having a positive impact across communities. It had done wonders for Sully, too.

Wrackton would always be home, in a way. It was where

Mallory's parents had returned to, it was where she and Cornelia stayed in Broadwick Mansion whenever they had reason to return. It was where she'd started, and probably where she'd end. But for now, Wickermere was where the former Undetectables had settled, and it was where she saw herself remaining for a long, long time.

After cake – Agatha was very good at lemon poppyseed, while Ethel had perfected red velvet, and it was imperative to eat both – they all walked Diana back to Rowan House where she launched into her workshop, and Mallory headed back for office hours.

Even though Cornelia teased her for it, she loved office hours. She loved meeting with bright-eyed twenty-something students. Loved it even more when she could find a way to accommodate students who had chronic health conditions. It was so easy, she had no idea why other institutions made it look so difficult.

Most of all, she delighted in an excuse to turn off her inbox notifications. No matter how long it had been, or how uncontactable the Undetectables had made themselves, magical cases kept finding their way to her on a daily basis, begging them to take a look.

Some were interesting, but they were no longer Mallory's primary concern. There would always be murders to solve. There would always be crime. There would always be police to distrust and incarcerations to object to. There would always be a grey area in the world, and there would always be people who looked an awful lot like monsters.

But Mallory had learned to follow her heart. She had cheated death, and she had learned to ask for what she wanted. She had learned not to beat herself up for being in pain. She had, ultimately, learned to live.

The door opened and a young vampire walked in, her dark hair pulled back, her green eyes shining with excitement.

'Dr Hawthorne, have you ever looked into the formation of the tunnels in Wrackton?' she asked, without any preamble. 'They end in bunkers, but the bunkers form a shape – a sigil.'

She was Mallory's most promising PhD applicant of this batch.

'Just Mallory, please. And no, I've never even thought to. Tell me why it interests you.'

Her student pulled out a file – if one can imagine what a file looks like, that is what she showed her – and flipped to a survey map of Wrackton and Oughteron. She'd marked the locations of the bunkers in the grounds of Oakpass, Broadwick Mansion, the Redwoods, the Larix and the Mayoral Offices, with a line drawn out from the top that read MOUNT HALLOW in flowing script. In careful red pen, she'd connected the bunkers and tunnels to form a very obvious pentagram.

'And further to that – don't you think it's strange that Hecate has just vanished? They excavated Morrigan's remains from beneath Oakpass Manor like, a decade ago. And the Inquest findings say that Morrigan is officially dead. But Hecate is just… gone. Nobody knows where she is.'

Mallory sat back to listen as her student spoke of old gods and old magic and of vampire-specific lore, her mind already turning over what her student was saying, but also thinking about dinner, and Cornelia and the endless sprawl of her future.

Mallory Hawthorne could do anything she liked with that life. And she was only getting started.

ACKNOWLEDGEMENTS

And so, the story finally ends.

I started *The Undetectables* in 2019, and I never imagined how quickly the finale would roll around. Time flies when you're murdering fictional people. This book was written while I was busy tearing up roots and relocating to my forever home – 0/10 do not recommend as a simultaneous activity – and it feels symbolic that I should leave the place I got my first book deal mere weeks after I had completed a draft of the last in the series.

At Titan: thank you to my editor George Sandison for taking a chance on the Undetectables series and for letting me galaxy brain my way to the ending. I will cherish the fact I made you react with a genuine 'blimey' for life. Thank you to Elora Hartway for your harmonica – I mean, *harmonising* – editorial eye. Thank you to Kabriya Coghlan (and Charlotte Kelly, who has since departed for a new adventure) whose presence makes every event I do 100x more fun. (I still laugh when I think of the slippers.) Thank you to Julia Lloyd for rounding off the series with yet another banger of a cover – this one blew me away. Thank you to the sales team, the proof readers and copyeditors and typesetters and everyone who has laid a hand on the Undetectables series behind the scenes. Thank you also to the fabulous people at Gill Hess, especially Jacq Murphy, who has shoved the series into the unsuspecting hands of many a bookseller and industry professional.

At The Bent Agency: to Zoë Plant, my agent and Theodore Wyatt's forever co-parent: thank you for your patience, for understanding how my brain works, and for not being afraid to tell me that a perfectly tied up book is not necessarily the best one. A huge thanks also to Victoria Cappello for taking such incredible care of me this year.

A very special thanks to Sean Matthew Leary for sending me the Undetectables trivia questions. You taught me both that I would fail a quiz on my own work, and that I'd forgotten a very important detail for the beginning of book 4. And also thank you for the care package!

To Jacq Murphy, Amy Clarkin, Deirdre Sullivan and Meg Grehan: THANK.

To Nik, for being wonderful, and to every single bookseller who has sold, recommended and enjoyed the Undetectables series. Thank you all especially for responding so kindly to my yearly terrified requests to deface my books in shops. (I can't promise I'll get better at it.)

To Michael: my home, my soulmate, timesharer of the last brain cell we have between us. None of this is possible without you.

To Dr Niles and Dr Spencer, for various cat crimes and attempts to assist with typing. I'm glad you were here to be so deeply unhelpful to me. I love your stupid furry faces.

To iDKHOW, Mallory Knox, Fall Out Boy, Bring Me the Horizon and My Chemical Romance, for being the soundtrack to these past few years (both for my books and for life in general).

Last but not least, to you, my wonderful readers. Thank you for coming on this journey with me. I am so glad Mallory, Diana, Cornelia and Theodore are your friends now, and I hope you visit Wrackton again someday. It'll always be home for me.

ABOUT THE AUTHOR

Courtney Smyth is a caffeine fiend, one web search away from their newest fixation, and, most relevantly, a writer of stories. Their work has also appeared in anthologies *Into Chaos* and *The Last Five Minutes of a Storm*, and in *Paper Lanterns Literary Journal*. They have been writing about ghosts, demons and murders since they were ten and have no plans to stop. They are from Dublin, currently living and writing in Ireland with their partner and their pet corn snake, Steve.

@cswritesbooks
courtneysmythwrites.com